LOVING HARRY

The Scottish novelist Joan Fallon, currently lives and works in the south of Spain. She writes both contemporary and historical fiction, and almost all her books have a strong female protagonist. **She is the author of the following books:**

Fiction:
The Thread That Binds Us
Love is All
The House on the Beach
Santiago Tales
Spanish Lavender
The Only Blue Door
Palette of Secrets
The al-Andalus trilogy:
The Shining City
The Eye of the Falcon
Ring of Flames
The City of Dreams trilogy:
The Apothecary
The Pirate
The Prisoner

Non-fiction:
Daughters of Spain

Connect with Joan Fallon online at:

http://www.joanfallon.co.uk/index.html

https://www.facebook.com/joanfallonbooks

Joan Fallon

LOVING HARRY

Scott Publishing

ISBN 978 0 9570696 3 3
First published in 2012
Second edition 2020
Scott Publishing

LOVING HARRY

2010

CARLA

Carla knew something was wrong the minute she pulled into the drive; she could feel it. It was more than the usual dread that she always had when she got home. What had he done now? Would he be in a good mood, a good mood that didn't depend on having drunk half a bottle of scotch. Only the week before he had fallen and cut his head, so drunk that he didn't even notice the blood dripping into his eyes. Today it was different. The house was silent, no music blaring, no interminable golf commentary on the television. She called his name softly, in case he was sleeping. The lounge was just as she had left it, except that now the patio doors stood wide open, the muslin curtains billowing into the room. It was another blisteringly hot day, and at first she could see nothing untoward as she walked outside, the bright sun blinding her as it bounced off the swimming pool. 'Harry?' she called again. 'Harry, I'm back.' Then she saw him.

BARBARA

Barbara was preparing Sunday lunch when the telephone rang. It was one of those family rituals that she liked to hang on to, and a chance to get all the family together. Sylvia, Richard and Linda always came over, and Tom with his current girlfriend.

'Barbara, it's Tom. He sounds upset,' Ian said, handing her the handset.

She wiped her hands on her apron and took the telephone. 'Tom? Everything all right?' she asked. 'You're still coming over for lunch, I hope.'

'Hi Mum. Yes, I'll be there, don't worry.'

'Good, because I've bought this lovely piece of topside.'

'Mum, Carla telephoned me this morning,' he said interrupting her.

'Carla?' For a moment she didn't know whom he meant, then she realised there was only one Carla that they both knew. She felt her stomach turn over in trepidation. 'Yes?'

'Dad's dead,' he said.

'Your father's dead?' she repeated. 'Harry, you mean?'

'Yes Mum. Dad. He's dead. Heart attack or something. Not sure exactly.'

'When did it happen?'

'Yesterday. He was cremated this morning.'

'So soon?'

She sat down, her legs felt weak. She'd hardly given her ex-husband a thought for years but now the image that came to mind was not of the man who had left her that dismal Sunday morning, desperate to get away from her tears of rage, but rather the handsome teenager, walking her home from school, holding her hand and smiling lovingly at her.

'What is it?' Ian asked, sitting on the settle beside her.

'Harry's dead,' she said.

He took the telephone carefully from her hand. 'Tom, it's Ian. Do you have any details about what happened?'

'Not really. He died yesterday and he was cremated this morning. Carla wanted me to let the family know.'

'Did she say anything else? Is there to be a funeral?'

'I don't think so, she didn't say.'

'Okay, Tom, thanks for ringing. Will you let Sylvia know?'

'Yes, I'll ring her this evening. Bye Ian.' The telephone went dead.

'He sounds very upset,' Ian told Barbara.

'He's the only one who has tried to keep in touch with Harry, so I suppose it's natural.'

'Are you all right?'

She wiped her eyes. 'Yes, I'm fine. It's just a bit of a shock. Do you think we should ring his mother?' she asked.

'I'll do it for you.'

'Maybe we should go over there.'

'Whatever you want.'

'Teddy'll have to be told.'

'Don't worry, Tom's going to ring everyone. Let me make you a cup of tea.'

'No, something stronger, I think.'

ONE YEAR LATER

CHAPTER 1

Carla stared through the window of the aircraft at the sodden land below her; Britain had experienced weeks and weeks of unremitting rain and it showed in the waterlogged fields, the overflowing streams and rivers and the scattering of glistening ponds where none had been before. She heard the heavy clunk of the plane's wheels drop down; they were about to land. In no time at all she would be walking across the concourse, collecting a single suitcase from the baggage hall, picking up the hire car she'd arranged, and then there would be no going back. The one question that was beginning to haunt her was how she was going to explain to Harry's family why it had taken so long to bring him home. His son, Tom, had written a few days after she'd told them about Harry's death, saying that they wanted to bury him in the family plot. And here she was, almost a year later, finally doing what was requested. What on earth was she going to say to them?

She closed her eyes and braced herself for the landing. Already expected, it still came as a shock when the wheels touched down and the plane started to coast gently along the runway. She looked at the rain falling steadily from a steel grey sky, and longed to be back in Spain, somewhere that was more her home now than this alien country.

The funeral was tomorrow. At first she hadn't replied to Tom's letter, but as the months passed and she began to feel stronger, she wrote to say she would do it, she would bring his ashes back to Frieth, if Tom arranged everything with the vicar. He didn't ask why there had been a delay; he simply said he would email her with the date and let everyone else know. He made it sound as though a lot of people would be attending and she'd instantly regretted phoning him. How would she survive it? She didn't know these people. Harry never spoke about his family; she imagined it was more from guilt than dislike of them, but he never admitted to it. She went through each of them in her mind, ticking them off, like a shopping list: Harry's first wife, Barbara, abandoned with two young children, Tom and Sylvia, both grown-up now, and Phoebe his mother. And Teddy of course, his brother. He and Harry had been very close once, but something had happened to destroy that relationship. A few years before he died, Harry had finally persuaded Teddy to visit them in Spain; his brother had promised to stay for a month or maybe two, but instead he left rather suddenly. Neither of them told her the reason, and all Harry would say was that he never wanted to see any of his family again, and as he downed a large glass of scotch, he vowed never to return to the UK. She hadn't fully appreciated the depth of his anger until he removed the wedding photograph of Sylvia walking happily up the aisle on Teddy's arm, from its prominent place in the lounge. Whatever had transpired between the two brothers, it had a profound effect on Harry, and from then on he withdrew more and more into himself, finding solace in drinking alone.

Well, whether he wanted it or not, now he was returning to the place of his birth. She bent down and picked up the casket from the floor and placed it on her lap. His family had been waiting long enough for his ashes. There was such emptiness within her, an ache that would not go away, and it was for this too that she had come; she needed to find some closure, some peace, some forgiveness. Bringing Harry back to his family might give her that. Carla took a deep breath and blinked away the tears of self pity; she would get through this. She had got through worse. All she had to do was to take it one step at a time.

She closed her iPad and slipped it into her handbag. Tucked in there, between her passport and her boarding pass was another letter. This one was from Routledge and Routh, solicitors, inviting her to discuss Harry's will. She had been stunned to receive it; Harry had never mentioned making a will. Not really; he had said he'd like to leave something to the children, but not that he'd actually written a will. She had always imagined, that under Spanish law, what few possessions they had would pass directly to her, as his legal wife, so she hadn't done anything about it. That was the system. So what was this all about? What did it mean? The more she thought about it, the more she realised it wasn't just Harry's family she didn't know; she didn't know the man who had been her husband for twenty years.

*

It was almost three months after they met when he told her that he was married. They were having breakfast in the B and B in Norwich, where they had spent the night.

'More coffee?' she asked him.

'Yes, please.' He hesitated then looked straight at her. His eyes seemed bluer than ever in the bright morning light. 'Carla, I've got something to tell you,' he said.

She felt her stomach turn over; the tone of his voice was ominous. Was he going to end it so soon? 'Why so serious?' she asked, smiling bravely.

'Carla, I'm married,' he blurted out. 'Look, I meant to tell you before, but well, the time never seemed quite right.' She felt a chill creep over her body. What was he saying? He was married? She couldn't believe it. He'd been lying to her. For a moment she thought she was going to be sick and pressed her napkin to her lips. 'Are you all right?' he asked.

'What do you think?' Now she was angry with him. She was not this kind of woman. If she'd known he was married she would have walked away right at the start.

He reached across to take her hand but she snatched it away. 'Carla, I love you, you know that. I'll get a divorce and we can get married.'

'What about your wife, do you love her too?'

'No, of course not. I love you. My marriage is over. It has been for some time. I've only been staying there for the sake of the kids.'

Children, he had children as well, a wife and children. 'I don't believe you,' she said. 'You don't love me. If you loved me then you wouldn't have deceived me. You wouldn't have lied to me.'

'Don't say that. I do love you. I've never felt this way about anyone before; I promise you.' He looked distraught.

'Does your wife know about us?' He shook his head. 'Do you still sleep with her?' she asked. The enormity of what he'd told her was beginning to seep in, with all its intimate details and unanswered questions.

'No, we haven't had a proper sex-life for years, not since Tom was born,' he replied, his eyes pleading for her understanding.

'This changes everything, you know' she said. 'You've got a wife and family. They're your responsibility.'

'Don't do this Carla, please,' he was begging her now.

'But how can we go back to how we were, when you have another life?'

'You're my life now, Carla. It's you I want.'

'But I don't want to be the other woman, only seeing you when you can fit me in, sneaking around in case anyone sees us together. I don't want that.'

'It won't be like that. I'm going to get a divorce. I've been thinking about it for ages. It's just the kids...'

'I'm not going to be the one to break up your family; I couldn't live with that.'

'You wouldn't be the one to break it up. My marriage was over long before I met you.' She couldn't find the words to reply; she just wanted to wake up from this nightmare. 'Don't you love me, Carla?' he asked, dropping his voice to a whisper. She looked at him. Naked pain was written all over his face. She nodded her head. 'Please say something, Carla.'

'What do you want me to say?'

'Anything. Tell me you don't hate me, for a start.'

'Why would I hate you? I hardly know you.' She could see that her words stung him and was pleased to think that he could be hurt too.

'I had to tell you, Carla. I'm in love with you and I don't want there to be any secrets between us. I had to tell you. You understand that, don't you?'

'So where does your wife think you are today?' she asked, barely keeping the bitterness from her voice.

'She knows I'm in Norwich; she's used to my trips away.' He looked at her, his face solemn, his blue eyes, open and beseeching. She poured out some more tea. 'I need a life for myself,' he continued. 'I need someone to love. I need you, Carla. I can't continue living this lie.'

'But your children?'

'When they're older they'll understand.'

'Harry I don't want to get involved with a married man. I've seen it happen to too many of my friends, and they have always been the ones to get hurt. It's not going to happen to me.'

'Darling, I'd never hurt you, I promise. Just give me a chance.'

She spread the butter on her toast, but with no intention of eating it. 'Let's just see how it goes, shall we?' she said, pushing her plate away from her. She was no longer hungry.

He reached across the table and took her hand. 'That's all I ask, that we give it a chance.'

CHAPTER 2

Barbara had been surprised when Tom rang to tell her that Carla was bringing Harry's ashes back to England. She'd imagined that they had been buried, or scattered or whatever she'd decided to do with them, long ago. Barbara had ceased to think about Harry. She'd loved him once, but now she could barely recall the man she'd married more than forty years ago. The lies he'd told her and the secrets he'd kept from her had done that; their whole life together had been an enormous lie. She wondered if he'd been any more honest with Carla.

'I'm taking the dog for a walk,' Ian called through to the bedroom. 'Do you want me to bring you a cup of tea, before I go?'

'No. I'm fine. I'll get up in a minute,' she replied.

Barbara had married Ian one frosty, day at the end of 2000. They had kept the ceremony simple, inviting only their respective family members and a handful of close friends. After much discussion they decided to sell Barbara's house and buy a flat between them. There didn't seem to be much difference in her life; she realised she had become used to Ian's presence and the only big change was that now, instead of kissing her affectionately goodnight and driving back to Maidenhead, he was there beside her in their new, king-sized bed. Whether because of his long, enforced celibacy, or because they were so comfortable with each other in every other way, the sex when it eventually happened was everything she could have wanted. Ian turned out to be a passionate and thoughtful lover and more than once Barbara wondered why she had held him at arm's-length for so many years.

There had only ever been three men in her life, and each one very different. She'd married two of them; she'd lusted after the third, but there was only one that she'd truly loved. Now he was dead and today she was going to his funeral. Her mind drifted back to the days when she thought she knew him, when she thought they were happy.

*

Wimbledon was due to start next week and the weather seemed set for the usual rain and thunderstorms. They had been promised a dry summer, but there had been no sign of it so far. Barbara could hear Tom and Sylvia arguing down in the kitchen. She groaned quietly and rolled over, the bed always felt so empty without him. How she wished he didn't have to work at weekends. It had been years now since Harry had spent a Sunday at home; even when he was working locally, he was up early and out before anyone else was awake. She looked at the photo she had of him by the bed; how handsome he was. And still is, she reminded herself. She felt a rush of affection for him. They had met at

17

school when they were both in the Sixth Form; he was captain of the school cricket team and probably the handsomest and most popular boy in the school. All her friends had been in love with him, and so had she. At first she had been very much in awe of him, tongued tied and shy whenever she passed him in the corridor or sat in the same classroom. Then she had joined the 6th Form Photography Club and found that they had something they could both talk about with ease. A friendship soon began to develop between them and then, about halfway through the school year, one wonderful evening while walking her home from the club, he asked her if she would go out with him. She had loved him ever since.

'Mum, Sylvia won't let me have any yoghurt.' Her irate son was standing at the bottom of the bed, still wearing his Superman pyjamas and brandishing a teaspoon in one hand and a pot of yogurt in the other.

'He's eaten two already Mum,' his sister informed her. 'Little piggy,' she added, trying to wrest the yogurt from his hand.

'I'm hungry,' he shouted.

'Piggy,' the girl repeated.

'I'm not. You're a piggy. Miss Piggy. Miss Piggy.'

'That's enough. Tom take that yogurt back downstairs. You can wait until I get up then we'll all have breakfast together.'

'But Mum he's already eaten the strawberry yogurt. I wanted that,' wailed the older child.

'Well if he's eaten it there's not a lot you can do about it, is there. I'll buy some more tomorrow.'

The boy stuck his tongue out at his sister. 'And that's enough of that Tom. Go and get dressed the pair of you. Remember we're going to lunch with Uncle Teddy today.'

Harry's elder brother Edward, or Teddy as everyone called him, lived in Nottingham. It was a bit of a trek to go for lunch, Harry said, but she wanted to go and Harry had promised to get away early and join them there. She was very fond of Teddy, but he rarely came to visit them these days because he was always so busy.

Her bedroom window looked out over the River Thames; she could see a pair of swans gliding past, oblivious of the fine rain that was sheeting down on them. She loved it here and never tired of this view. It was a beautiful house, everything she had ever wanted. It was not grand but fairly spacious and comfortable. They had bought it not long after they were married, before there was road access to it and in those days they parked their car on the opposite bank and crossed over in a small row-boat. She sighed as she remembered it. They had spent years stripping woodwork, plastering, painting, laying paths, digging out flower beds and she had loved every minute of it. When at long last she had found herself pregnant, she had instantly given up her job at the local library and devoted herself to being a full time wife and mother. It was what she was born for; her career-minded friends affectionately referred to her as an earth-mother and she didn't contradict them. She liked to make jam and grow her own vegetables, she enjoyed cooking and baking, she was always there when her children came home from school to help with homework or ferry them to football matches, ballet classes, gymnastics, chess tournaments, whatever activity they had arranged. She was not bitter when she explained to her friends that because Harry's work kept him away from home so much, one of them had to be there for the children; she saw this as her role in their marriage. That was why she was about to drive two hundred miles so that the children could spend some time with their only uncle.

Her own childhood had been that of an only child; she had no brothers and sisters. For the first fifteen years of her life she had been happy, never having had any siblings she didn't miss them. Then her mother died, and her father, after a year of trying to cope alone, had remarried. That was when things changed for Barbara. Her step-mother was a cold woman, unused to children and teenagers in particular. She found it difficult to cope with the pubescent Barbara, who felt betrayed by her father and deserted by her mother. Until Barbara met Harry she had nobody to turn to, he became her brother, her friend, later her lover, and finally her husband. He was the corner-stone of her life.

'Mum, what shall I wear?' Sylvia said, opening the bedroom door.

'What about that nice green dress that Daddy bought you when he was in Edinburgh? You look lovely in that.'

'This one?' The child held the dress up in front of her. It was same shade as her eyes and complemented perfectly the mop of red curls that struggled to escape the restraints of two large hair-clips.

'Yes, that'll be fine.'

'What about Tom? He's just sitting playing with his soldiers.'

'Don't worry Darling, I'll see to him.' She went to her son's room. He was sitting on the floor, oblivious to everything but the two Action men he held in his hands. Tom was only five but he was tall for his age; his dark hair was cut neatly around his ears and curled down over the collar of his pyjamas.

'Tom,' she said rather sharply. He turned and looked up at her with pale blue eyes. 'Time to get dressed. We're going to see Uncle Teddy,' she reminded him.

'Is it far?' he asked, but still not moving.

'Yes, you know it is. Now get a move on.'

'Further than going to school?'

'Yes.' She took a clean T-shirt out of the chest-of-drawers.

'Further than London?'

'Yes. Have you washed?'

'I had a bath last night,' he reminded her. She placed his clean underwear and some shorts on the bed. 'Is it further than the moon?'

'Put those soldiers down for now.'

'They're not soldiers, they're Action men.'

'They look like soldiers to me,' she said as she started to dress him.

'They're in disguise. They're really spies.'

'Lift up your arms.'

'No, I can do it myself.'

'Well if you can do it, then get on with it. But I'm warning you, if you're not downstairs in five minutes there'll be no Frosties for you.'

'Is it Mum? Is it further than the moon.'

'No, of course it's not. Now hurry up.'

She went back to her own room and turned on the shower. It was like this every morning; unless she got Tom moving first he was never ready on time. Except when Harry was home, then it was different, her son was always the first out of bed. He would bounce into their room at some ridiculous hour, pull at his sleeping father and demand that he play football with him before breakfast.

She had just stepped out of the shower when the telephone rang; it was Harry. 'Morning Darling.'

'Harry, what a nice surprise.'

'I can't talk for long, the chaps are waiting. I just wanted to tell you that I won't be able to make it to Teddy's for lunch after all.'

'Oh Harry.' It was hard to keep the disappointment out of her voice.

'One of the guys is off sick, so I've got to stick around and help clear up. I don't think we'll be finished before four at the earliest. I'll see you at home.'

'Teddy will be disappointed,' she said. This would have been their first Sunday lunch together as a family for months.

'I know, sweetheart, I'm sorry. Give him my love and tell the kids I'll make it up to them.'

'All right, see you at home then. Bye.'

'Love you.'

'Love you too.' She heard the telephone click and he was gone.

By the time she got down to the kitchen both her children were sitting at the table in front of a collection of open cereal boxes. 'I told him not to open them all,' Sylvia declared.

'I was looking for the one with the toy animal in it,' he protested.

'Tom, you know you're not supposed to open a new box until the old one is finished,' Barbara said, taking up the freshly opened packets and re-securing them tightly. 'It makes the cereal go soft.'

'I told him Mummy,' Sylvia said triumphantly. Tom said nothing but jiggled the plastic animals along the side of his bowl.

'I couldn't find any clean socks,' her daughter continued. Sylvia was three years older than her brother and growing up quickly.

'Look in the airing cupboard. I'm sure there're some in there.'

She switched on the kettle, popped a tea-bag into a cup and sat down to wait for what was always to her, the best cup of tea of the day.

'Why isn't Daddy coming with us?' Tom asked.

'He's working.'

'But why? Jimmy's dad doesn't work on Sundays. He's taking them to the beach today,' he told them.

'That's because Jimmy's dad has a different job. Your Daddy has to work every weekend, that's when he's busiest. But Jimmy's dad isn't home on Mondays, is he?'

'No.'

'Daddy said he'd meet us at Uncle Teddy's,' Sylvia reminded them. 'He promised.'

'He can't now; he has to work.'

'Will he be home tonight?'

'Yes, of course.'

'Will he bring us a present?' asked Tom.

'I don't expect so; you can't have presents every time your father goes away. I don't suppose Jimmy's dad brings him a present every time he comes home from work, does he?' Barbara replied.

'Sometimes Daddy brings us presents,' said Sylvia.

'And that makes you very lucky children. Now get on with your breakfast and no more talk about presents.'

The boy ate some of his Frosties. 'Will Dad come and pick me up from school tomorrow?'

'I expect so.'

'Then we can go to the park and play football?'

'If it's not raining. Stop playing with your food and eat,' she told him.

'Will Alan be at Uncle Teddy's?'

'I expect so.' She sipped her tea and felt it begin to revive her; at last she could face the drive to Nottingham.

'Is Alan Uncle Teddy's friend?'

'Alan is his student.' She didn't want to go down the road of Alan and Teddy's relationship with her son.

'But why does he live with his teacher? I don't live with my teacher.'

'He's Uncle Teddy's lodger, as well,' she explained and before he could ask, continued, 'A lodger is someone who lives in your house and pays you rent.' She could see Tom thinking about this as he shovelled the last of his breakfast into his mouth.

'So we could have a lodger in our house?'

'In theory, but we don't have any spare rooms, do we?'

'I could move into Sylvia's room then the lodger could have my room and then we'd get lots of money and you could buy me a Game Boy,' he said, delighted to have found the solution to something that had been worrying him.

Barbara laughed. 'I don't think Daddy would like it if he came home to find a lodger in your bedroom, do you?'

'I'm ready, Mum,' said Sylvia.

'Good girl, let's just clear away the dishes and then we'll be off. Tom run upstairs and go to the toilet before we leave.'

'But ..'

'Now.'

*

The smell of meat roasting greeted them as they walked up the steps to the old Victorian house where Teddy lived. It was one of a row of imposing Victorian terraced houses that lined Oldfield Hill. Each had a patch of front garden, most of which, like Teddy's, was bereft of greenery and merely used as either access to the basement or as a storage area for bicycles, dustbins and anything else the occupants didn't want to lug up the steep steps. Teddy's house was situated halfway up the hill, which formed part of one of the main thoroughfares into the city. Once it had been a grand street, the homes of wealthy Nottingham families. Now all that was left of that grandeur were the plane trees that lined it and the red-brick houses themselves which, no matter what condition they were like inside, still retained their original elegance.

Barbara rang the brass bell that was set into the brickwork. Through the stained glass that decorated the upper part of the door, she could see the figure of someone approaching.

'There you are. Right on time as always,' said Teddy opening the door and welcoming them in. 'Where's Harry?'

'He couldn't get away.'

'That's a shame. Still it means I've got you all to myself now.' He laughed and gave Barbara a peck on the cheek then bent down and hugged his niece and nephew.

'All right kids?'

'Hi Uncle Teddy. Is Alan here?' Tom asked. He clutched a football to his chest.

'He is, Tom. But he won't be playing football today; he's hurt his leg.' The smile instantly disappeared from Tom's face.

'But you can kick the ball around the yard and I'll watch,' a cheerful voice said. A young man came limping out of the kitchen to greet them.

'Hi Alan.'

'Should you be walking around on that?' Teddy asked his friend. 'I thought the doctor said to keep your weight off it for at least a week.'

'Okay, don't nag. I'll go and sit down in a minute.'

'So how are you, young lady?' Teddy asked, turning his attention to Sylvia.

'I'm very well, Uncle Teddy.'

'And how are the ballet lessons?'

'Brilliant. We're going to learn how to do a pirouette next week.' She beamed at him and twirled around on the spot.

'She's stupid,' Tom interrupted. 'All she ever does is wander about the house pretending she's a ballerina. She can't even do the splits.'

'I can.'

'Can't.'

'Mummy, tell him I can do the splits.'

'If you two don't behave we're getting right back in the car and going home. I haven't driven all this way to listen to you quarrelling.'

'Why don't you come with me,' suggested Alan. 'You can write something on my plaster.'

'Yeah.'

Even Sylvia seemed interested in examining Alan's plaster so they followed him into the sitting room.

'He's a nice guy, Alan,' Barbara said.

Teddy smiled. 'I think so.'

'Something smells good,' she said, nodding in the direction of the kitchen.

'Roast beef and Yorkshire puddings.'

'Tom's favourite. Can I help with anything?'

'Yes, you can set the table for me, but first let me get you a drink.'

'A glass of wine?'

'I know, cold and dry.'

She smiled, the strain of driving up the M1 was gradually evaporating under the relaxing influence of Teddy's company. He was more than just a brother-in-law to her, he was a good friend and confidante. Five years older than Harry, he had his brother's pale blue eyes and aquiline nose, but there the resemblance stopped. He was tall, but more heavily built than Harry and his face was squarer, more pugnacious. He too had thick hair, but it was browner and he preferred to wear it very short, cropped almost, he always said that he took after their father and Harry was more like their mother. Beauty and the beast, Harry was the beauty and he was the beast.

'So where is he today?'

'Harry?'

'Who else.'

'He's in Leeds, that's why he suggested meeting us here. It's not far out of his way.'

'So why the change in plans?'

'One of his guys is off sick; he has to stay and dismantle the equipment. He rang early this morning.'

Teddy raised an eyebrow, and said, 'That's a pity; we haven't seen each other for ages. Are you sure he's not avoiding me? You haven't been telling him any of our little secrets, have you?'

'Of course not. You should come down one weekend. Bring Alan.'

'Maybe when term ends.'

'Yes, do that Teddy. It would be nice.'

'Okay, I'll ring you with the dates and you can see if we can arrange to coincide when that roaming brother of mine is actually at home.'

She took the place mats out of a drawer and set them out on the dining room table; she knew this house almost as well as her own. When Teddy had bought it he had asked her for help with the decorations. It had been a task that she'd loved. Her first instruction had been for him to employ someone to sand down all the old oak floorboards and seal them. Once that had been done she drove up to stay with him. It was before she became pregnant with Sylvia and she had spent a week there on her own before Harry had come up to join them. As she moved around the dining room, sorting through the cutlery and selecting which glasses to put out she was reminded of those two weeks; together she and Teddy had measured the windows and selected the material for the curtains, and they had sat poring over paint charts and drinking cheap white wine while they argued over which colours to choose. It was Barbara who had persuaded him to get the stained glass panels in the hall window repaired and have the original oak banister re-varnished. Together they restored the dilapidated Victorian house to something of its previous glory. She felt a sense of pride as she looked at the plaster cornices and ceiling roses, still intact and as fresh as the day they were carved.

'You've bought a new rug,' she said as Teddy came in carrying two glasses of wine.

'Yes, I saw it in a sale at Norton's last month and I just couldn't resist it.'

'It's lovely.'

Her brother-in-law perched on a chair and sipped his wine. 'So, how are things at home these days?'

'Great, couldn't be better. Tom has settled down really well at school; he's made lots of friends.' She laughed. 'It's chaos when he invites them for tea. Can you imagine it? Tom is bad enough on his own but when his friends are there, it's bedlam.'

'Harry still working long hours?'

'No, not really, well not as bad as before. His business has been going really well lately. He's got five men working for him now, so he's able to step back a bit from the hands-on stuff and devote himself to the creative aspects of the work.'

'Which is what he likes.'

'Exactly. Of course he's the one who has to find the clients in the first place but he quite enjoys that part of it as well.'

'Good, so you're seeing more of each other?'

'Yes, it's wonderful. He always manages to have a couple of days off in the week and now that the kids are at school we go out somewhere, have a nice pub lunch or take the dog for a long walk by the river. It's lovely having him all to myself for a bit.'

'Sounds romantic.'

She smiled. 'Yes, it is in a way. It's like when we were younger, only now we've got more money.'

'Ah, money does make a difference,' Teddy agreed.

'We're not rich,' she said, 'but it's nice to no longer wonder if there's enough money to buy new shoes for the kids.'

A high pitched beep from the kitchen alerted Teddy to the fact that the Yorkshire puddings were ready. 'Two minutes,' he said.

'Okay, I'll rustle up the others and get them to the table.'

She found Tom and Sylvia seated on the floor, one either side of Alan's leg, intent on covering every square centimetre of his once pristine plaster with their designs. 'Your children are very artistic,' Alan said, with a laugh.

'Oh my God, what have they done?'

'It's a landscape,' Sylvia said. Her side of the plaster was covered in trees, flowers and something that Barbara thought must be a rabbit by the size of its ears.

'And what's that?' she asked her son.

'It's a dinosaur,' he said, not looking up.

'Don't you mind?' she asked the smiling Alan.

'Not at all, it's much more fun than a boring white plaster.'

'I'm sorry but you're going to have to stop now, lunch is ready.'

'Oh, just another minute,' pleaded Tom.

'No, now. And go and wash your hands first,' Barbara said.

Alan stretched his legs. 'Sorry kids, we mustn't keep Teddy waiting or he'll shout at us,' he said.

Tom giggled. 'No, he won't. Uncle Teddy never shouts at anyone.'

'Today might be a first, my lad,' a deep voice called from the kitchen.

CHAPTER 3

The rain had stopped but the clouds hung over the Buckinghamshire countryside shrouding it in gloom. Carla slipped down the motorway to the next exit then cut across the high ground, through Lane End, across Moor Common and into the village of Frieth. Tall trees lined the narrow roads, water still dripping from their leaves and collecting in small pools amongst their roots. Autumn arrived later these days and Carla wound down the car window to let in that sweet, fresh smell that brought with it memories of mouldering leaves and smoky bonfires. It was good to feel the damp air against her face.

Apart from a new conurbation of housing at Lane End nothing much had changed in the area. She came to the crossroads and carried straight across and up the hill. The village shop was where it had always been, as was the Yew Tree pub and at first glance the narrow High Street seemed unaltered. She felt hidden watchers follow her progress from the leaded glass windows of the tiny brick and flint cottages that lined the road; she knew little went unnoticed in this village. The church was at the top of the hill but she decided to park the car in the pub car-park and walk the rest of the way.

'We're not open,' shouted a woman about to go into the pub.

'I won't be long,' said Carla.

The woman scowled at her.

Harry had brought her here once. It had been early in their relationship, a time when she could have made a different choice and then things would have turned out differently and maybe Harry would still be alive. Instead here she was, bringing him back to the church where he'd been christened, where his father and grandfather were buried.

*

Carla had met Harry at the charity fashion show. Baroness Zilinsky had invited her to take part in it to raise money to help deprived children, 'Young Sport' it was called. It had been a glittering affair, held in a hotel in Kensington and everyone who was anyone was there, ex-kings, Saudi princesses, pop-stars, Jewish bankers, Russian businessmen, actors and actresses; the Baroness had many contacts. Carla was thrilled to be included; she took some of her favourite creations: zippered jackets made of rough crocodile leather and studded with diamonds, full-length leather coats with embossed shoulders, blouses made of soft calf skin tied at the waist with chunky belts, suede trousers in soft shades of plum and aubergine. She fussed around the models, checking their make-up, adjusting their hair, she would have liked to have dressed them all herself but that was impractical, so she contented herself with making small modifications to the final look, a last tweak at a hemline or a gentle tug at a sleeve, before she let them out on the cat-walk.

She had been so involved in making sure that everything went well that she hadn't noticed him at first. It was only when she was sitting back, her heart in her mouth, hoping that nothing had been overlooked and that the girls would strut their usual stuff, that she saw him. He sat to one side of the catwalk, a fairly ordinary looking man, dressed in casual jeans and an open shirt, but there was something about him that commanded attention. Maybe it was his eyes, the palest blue eyes she'd ever seen. Or maybe his black hair, worn longer than the current fashion she noted, that flopped across his face like a teenager's. He seemed to be looking straight at her, and when he realised that she had seen him, he smiled and she felt a sudden jolt to her stomach. Perhaps it was because she was on a high from the show or just exhausted from all the preparations but the look he gave her made her feel weak. She felt her face grow hot and knew that she was blushing, so she hurriedly turned away to concentrate on the compère whose glowing introduction was making the Baroness smile with pleasure. The fashion parade began. She tried to concentrate on the models, resisting the temptation to turn and see if he was still there, but the girls strutting on the platform in front of her lacked their usual fascination and his face kept reappearing in her mind. He could be a poet, she thought, or an actor, definitely someone artistic.

The music stopped and the applause began. Carla stood, turned to face the audience and bowed in gratitude. It had been a great success and for a moment she felt like a celebrity. Now it was the turn of another designer. The compère reappeared and began to announce the next collection, so she gathered up her things and was about to slip away when a voice said, 'Hi, are you leaving already?' It was the man who had been looking at her. His voice was deep for such a slight man, and there was just a touch of some country accent, Somerset or Berkshire, she couldn't quite place it.

'Yes, I've got a lot to see to.'

'Time for a quick drink?' He smiled at her again, a wistful, lop-sided smile that turned her legs to jelly. 'My name's Harry, by the way, Harry Wilkinson,' he continued, holding out his hand.

She took it nervously. 'Carla Kane.'

'I know.' He nodded towards the banners with her name emblazoned on them.

She felt herself blushing again and was angry. This was not her, she was not a blushing teenager. 'As I said, I've got quite a lot to pack up.'

'Maybe later, when you've finished?' She hesitated. 'Come on, you should be celebrating; it was a great success.'

'You think so?'

'They loved it.'

'It is for charity you know,' she reminded him.

'I know, but it can't hurt your career, can it? There're some pretty important people here tonight.'

'I suppose not.'

'So, what about that drink then?'

'I'm supposed to stay for the party, afterwards. My agent says that's the most important part of the evening; it's when I could pick up some new clients.'

'So you'll still be working?' His eyes never left her face.

'I don't need to stay too long,' she found herself saying. What was she doing? Jenny would be furious; this was a big event. Milk it for all your worth, she'd told her, and here she was planning to leave early to have a drink with a man she'd only just met.

'Great. Do you know the Bull and Butcher? It's just around the corner; I'll wait for you there. Say around nine-thirty?'

'All right, nine-thirty.'

He smiled again and she felt the warmth of that smile reach out and touch her heart.

*

It hadn't been difficult to leave the party early. She ate a few canapés and drank a glass of champagne as she wandered about making polite conversation with the guests. Apart from the Baroness and a few of the models, she knew hardly anyone there; the guests had been invited not so much for their interest in fashion as for the size and generosity of their wallets. But the Baroness was delighted with the success of the event and at one point came up to Carla, squeezed her arm affectionately and said, 'I hope you are enjoying yourself, my dear. It has been such a success, I think we'll do it again next year. And you must come too, with your new collection.'

So it was with a feeling of euphoria that Carla eventually said her goodbyes and hurried round the corner to the Bull and Butcher. He was sitting at a small table in the corner, facing the door, a half-empty glass of bitter in front of him. When he saw her come in he was on his feet immediately.

'I thought you'd changed your mind,' he said.

'No,' she smiled. 'It just took longer to get away than I thought.'

'So, was it fun?'

'Well, if you like drinking champagne with the rich and beautiful, yes it was.'

'Sounds good.' His eyes were twinkling and he seemed unable to repress the smile that threatened to split his face in two. 'So what'll it be? More champagne?' he asked.

'No, I don't think so. A glass of white wine would be fine.' She brushed a stray curl off her face and deftly tucked it behind her ear. She wished she had delayed a bit longer and taken the time to check out her appearance; it was late and her make-up was tired, her hair unkempt and her dress creased. But after all, she reminded herself, I have been working and so has he. While he was at the bar she took out her compact and dabbed at her nose, then swiftly renewed her lipstick. That was better. There was not much she could with her hair; it was an unruly mop of tawny curls at the best of times and now, after the exertions of preparing for the show and the heat from the lights, it frizzed around her heart-shaped face like a bush.

Despite being a Sunday night, the pub was not too busy, and Harry was soon served. He gave her the glass of wine and tipped half of bitter into his original glass.

'So, have you always been in the fashion business?' he asked, after a short silence on both their parts.

'Yes, I suppose I have. It's all I've ever wanted to do, ever since I was a little girl. What about you? What do you do?'

'Me, I'm an electrician.'

For a moment she felt disappointed, an electrician, not particularly glamorous work after all. She would never have imagined that his job was so mundane. 'So why were you at the show?'

'Working.' He was watching her, waiting to see her reaction. Then he laughed. 'Actually, my company is responsible for all the lighting. We specialise in lighting unusual events, pop concerts, reviews, music festivals, plays, fashion shows, anything in fact that requires specialised lighting.'

'Don't the venues have their own lighting already set up?'

'The permanent ones do, but even then they may want some special effects that they don't already have.' She knew that light could be used to create certain moods or illusions but she had never really thought about how it was done. 'The lighting of an event is really important, it can make something quite ordinary look extraordinary.'

'Like flashing lights and changing the colours?'

'Yes. But of course it depends on the event. In this fashion show for example the aim is that the audience can see the designs as clearly as possible. You don't want to change the colours or blur the images. But in a pop concert we can be much more creative.'

'It sounds fascinating,' she said.

'Yeah, it is, especially when it's going well. I have to travel about quite a bit and most of the jobs are at weekends which can be a pain, but it's satisfying work.'

'And fun, I would imagine?'

'That too.'

'So, have you met anyone famous?'

'A few, Rod Stewart, Sting, Gary Lineker. We get to see lots of famous people but I don't actually meet many of them. Remember we're behind the scenes. My aim is that everything goes so smoothly that we're not noticed. Usually the only time that anyone notices us is when something goes wrong, and that costs me money.'

'Where's your next job?'

'In the North actually, Leeds. It's a small pop concert, nobody famous.'

'Yorkshire?'

'Yes, lovely part of the world. Want to come?'

She looked at him. Was he joking? For once he wasn't smiling, he was serious.

'I don't think that would be a good idea,' she replied.

'Why not? The concert's on the Saturday night; the lads'll go up the day before and start setting up and I'll drive up on Saturday morning to check everything's okay. You could come with me, watch the concert and then we could spend Sunday together. I'm not joking, it really is a beautiful place. As long as it doesn't rain that is.'

'But I'm pretty busy at the moment,' she replied.

'I'll take you for lunch in Haworth,' he said with a smile.

'Bronte country.'

'So you have heard of it?'

'Of course. Wuthering Heights is one of my favourite books.'

'So will you come?'

'I shouldn't.'

'Surely you give yourself weekends off?'

'Not really, I usually work until the job is finished.'

'Well it's time you did. What's the saying? All work and no play?'

'I suppose I could get it finished before Saturday.'

'Great, that's agreed then. I'll pick you up on Saturday morning. It'll have to be early, I'm afraid, say around seven?'

'Okay, why not.'

She couldn't believe she was saying this; she was agreeing to go away with a complete stranger for the weekend. She felt like laughing out loud. This was the craziest thing she had done in a long time. Maybe this man was right; maybe she had been spending too much time working and not enough time having fun.

'So where do you live? Address? So I can pick you up.'

'Oh, of course. West Ealing, Hammond Road, number 34.'

As he jotted it down on the back of the beer mat, she sipped some of the wine. Her pulse was racing. It was almost a year since she had broken up with Gary, a relationship of convenience on both sides that had been going nowhere. Since then she'd been too busy concentrating on building up her business to get into a serious relationship with anyone. Was that what she thought was going to happen here? Were they going to have a serious relationship?

CHAPTER 4

The smell of freshly cut flowers hit her as she entered the church. At first Carla thought she was alone then she saw a familiar shape sitting in the front pew, Teddy. She'd hoped he would be there; it had been so long since they'd seen him, almost five years. She thought back, it was just about the time that Harry started to drink heavily. Teddy had stayed in Spain with them for a week, but whether it was because of the row he had with Harry while he was there, or just that he couldn't bear to see the deterioration in his brother, he never repeated the visit.

'Teddy?' she asked quietly.

He turned and smiled at her. 'Carla, how lovely to see you, my dear. Come and give this old queen a hug. My, but you're as lovely as ever. No wonder Harry couldn't resist you.' He stood up, his long, black coat falling open to reveal a cream, silk shirt and loose fitting black trousers. The sombreness of this ensemble was relieved by a carelessly tied scarlet spotted cravat and a rakish fedora. When he held out his arms to her, she moved forward to embrace him; there was a strong smell of cologne and tobacco clinging to him.

'Teddy, this is nice. I didn't expect to see you, I have to admit.'

'Why ever not Darling? He was my brother after all. I just had to come and give him a decent send off.'

'But you left in such a hurry that time you came to visit us. I couldn't understand it and Harry wouldn't say what had happened. What did you argue about?'

'Oh, that? A brotherly disagreement. I'll tell you all the gory details one day, Darling. Not today.'

'Okay, that's a promise, then?' He smiled at her and nodded. 'Is Phoebe with you?'

'Mother? No, she's coming up with Sylvia and Richard.'

'What about Spring Cottage?'

'Oh it's still there, just round the corner. She wanted to sell it last year but I convinced her not to. Couldn't abandon the old place, not after all those years, so I took it over when I retired.'

Carla sat down in the pew beside her brother-in-law, and placed the bag with the urn inside it on the floor next to her.

'So that's him, is it?' Teddy asked, nodding towards the urn. 'Funny thing that. I'd never have thought I would have outlived a young chap like Harry, not with my wicked ways.'

'You never know when it's your turn, now do you?'

'Truly said, my dear. Best to make the most of life while you can.' He patted her hand and sighed. He was looking older than she remembered, but his grey hair was still thick and luxurious and his bearing was as erect as a man half his age. How old was he? She made a rapid calculation in her head and decided he must be about sixty-five.

'So how have you been, my dear?'

'Lonely. I think that's the best way to describe my life lately, lonely and frustrated.'

'Frustrated?' Teddy's eyes flashed with interest and Carla couldn't suppress a laugh.

'Not sexually frustrated, you fool, frustrated with my life, with growing old, with not having anything meaningful to do with myself.'

'Oh, yes, we all feel like that as we get older. You'll come to terms with it.'

'But I don't want to come to terms with it, Teddy. I want something more. These last few years I've spent so much time looking after Harry, there has been no time to have a life of my own, and now he's gone it's hard to adjust to living without him.'

The heavy wooden door of the church opened again, letting in a shaft of sunlight which danced its way along the aisle. An elderly woman, her white hair escaping from beneath a swathe of black chiffon, shuffled slowly towards them. She leant heavily on the arm of a young woman, Sylvia. Carla recognised her from her wedding photograph, Sylvia, with her unmistakable red hair and her statuesque beauty. The wedding photograph was as much as Sylvia would allow her father. He would never even have known that his only daughter was getting married if Teddy hadn't told him. Although deeply hurt by her actions, it didn't stop Harry placing the photograph in a prominent position in the lounge and pointing out his daughter's exceptional good looks to anyone who happened to enquire. The old woman must be Phoebe. Harry had only taken her to meet his mother once, not long before they left for Spain. It was a meeting that Carla preferred to forget. Phoebe had made it perfectly clear what she thought of her son leaving his wife and family for Carla.

'It's Mother,' whispered Teddy. 'I'd better go and sit next to her. See you later, my dear.   And don't worry, you've plenty of years left to enjoy life. Chin up.'

But did she? And did she deserve it?

*

One day Harry said he wanted to show her Spring Cottage and the village where he'd been born, and where his grandparents had lived. It was a dreadful day, the rain had not stopped since early morning. It fell steadily on the grey slate roofs, filling up the drainpipes and emptying out into the street, it trickled down the window panes, shut tight and closed to the outside world, it gathered on the sills and dripped into the cottage gardens, soaking the rows of dahlias and roses, it blew up the hill, past the village shop, with its red Victorian post box set deep into the wall, it lashed at a last minute shopper, flattening her hair into wet, lank streaks, pulling at her raincoat and running down her wet stockings onto her sodden shoes. It dripped down the glowing Virginia Creeper that screened Spring Cottage, where Harry had once lived, making its way leaf by ruddy leaf until it disappeared into the dark earth, newly turned and weeded. The doors to the Yew Tree pub were closed, but the rain battered against its porch, running down the flints embedded deep in the old walls. The rain fell on the gravestones in the church yard, it ran down the gables and washed the stained glass windows clean, it revived the wilting flowers in their plastic holders and seeped into the holy ground. It rained on the church of St. John the Evangelist and the graves of Harry's family.

Carla opened the car window slightly and a gust blew the rain onto her face; it was cool and fresh and smelled of wet fields and damp woods.

'Put the window up Carla,' he instructed her. 'You'll get wet.'

'But I can't see,' she complained, a hint of petulance in her tone.

He turned up the air-conditioning and a hot blast of air hit the windscreen, clearing the fog. 'Okay now?'

'I suppose so. Can we get out?' He didn't reply; she could sense his reluctance. An edgy silence had descended on the car since they arrived in the village. 'Well? Aren't we going to stop and look at the cottage?'

'Not a lot of point, Darling, not with all this rain. It will be shut up. We'll just drive through and go down into

Hambleden and see if we can get some lunch. Just thought you'd like to see the old place as I'm always talking about it. Another day, perhaps.'

She wiped the window with the back of her hand. He was driving quickly through the village and a scarcely audible sigh broke from his lips as he turned the bend and began the descent into Hambleden. She knew what it was; he was frightened some distant friend or long forgotten neighbour would recognise him.

After a while she felt him relax and the atmosphere lighten. She turned to him and smiled. 'What are we going to do Harry? We can't go on like this forever.'

'I know. I'll speak to her soon. I just need some time. It's not easy.'

'I understand that, but it's not easy for me either.'

They pulled into the car park of the White Horse and Carla got out, dashing for cover while Harry parked the car. The pub was empty except for an old man who, by the proprietary way he sat at the corner of the bar with a half empty glass of Guinness and an open newspaper, seemed to be a regular. She chose a table as far from the bar as possible and sat down to wait for Harry. She loved Harry, there was no denying it, but she was beginning to doubt that she was doing the right thing. She had friends who had fallen in love with married men and, seduced by their promises, had wasted too many years of their lives before realising that nothing was ever going to change. She was not going to let it happen to her.

'What will you have?' Harry stood before her, water running off the umbrella that he was trying, unsuccessfully, to close.

'If we're going to eat, I'll have a glass of Soave.'

The old man at the bar was talking to the barman, 'The water's up. I was down by the lock this morning and old Joe was saying it's the highest it's been this year.'

'Not surprising, what with all this rain.'

'Floods in the west country,' he continued, brandishing the paper at his companion. 'Says the River Stour has over-topped its banks again due to the high tides. It'll be doing the same here soon if they don't do something about it.'

'All this global warming, I expect,' the barman replied, his attention firmly on the pint of Theakston's bitter he was pulling for Harry. He handed him the menu. 'You're a bit early for food; it'll be about twenty minutes before the kitchen opens.'

'That's fine.' Harry took the drinks to the table and sat down next to Carla. 'Looks like they do a nice lasagne.'

'I'm not really hungry. Harry, we need to talk. I can't go on like this. It's affecting my work. I can't sleep. I'm on edge all the time. It's no good. I have to know what's happening. I'm no good at waiting. I told you I can't stand uncertainty.'

'Okay Darling, calm down.' He took her hand in his and stroked it gently.   'Of course we'll talk. I just don't want you pinning me down.'

'Pinning you down? How can you say that? It was you who said you were going to leave her. I never asked you to. I was ready to walk away three years ago but you persuaded me to stay. Now I want to know if you are going to leave her or not.'

'Of course I am. Just give me time.'

'How much time? What are you waiting for?'

'It's Sylvia's tenth birthday next week. I can't do anything before then. We're all going to the zoo to celebrate, you know, family outing. How would she feel if I wasn't there?'

Carla felt her frustration rising. She knew Harry loved his children but he was also aware of how guilty she felt about keeping him from them, and played on that guilt. Poor little souls, they were the innocent bystanders in this love triangle.

'Okay, so not next week. When then?' He didn't answer, but instead picked up the menu and studied it carefully as though what he said next depended on what he read amongst its pages. 'Harry,' she said, raising her voice slightly.

'Oh Carla, just leave it will you. I'll tell her. I promise. Now just let's enjoy our brief time together.'

Carla sipped her wine. It was cold but had a slightly oxidized taste as though it had been open a while. 'But you will tell her, won't you?'

'I said I would, didn't I. Now let's leave it.'

'Okay. By the way where are you supposed to be today?'

'Reading. There's a pop concert there next weekend and we need to suss the place out.'

'So?'

'I'll go this evening. It's not a big job, but I told Barbara that it would take all day. She's taken the kids across to my mother's for lunch.'

Carla knew the pattern by heart now, it had begun the week after they met and continued for nearly three years. She knew she couldn't go on like that but what was the option? She stifled a groan. It was as clear as day; she would have to accept that she shared him with his family or give him up. But was she prepared to do that?

CHAPTER 5

Barbara picked up the black suit she had laid out on the bed and hung it back in the wardrobe. The repeater by her bed reminded her that it was already nine o'clock. She sat down on the edge of her bed and put her head in her hands. What should she do? She couldn't face Harry's widow, a woman she had never met but who'd occupied her thoughts for years. But if she didn't go to the funeral, what would everyone say? She didn't want them thinking that she was still trapped in the past. She'd pulled her life together after Harry had left her and made a success of it. So why was she so nervous about attending his funeral? She went into the bathroom and rubbed some moisturiser into her face. Without her make-up she looked so old; she picked up the foundation and began to apply it skillfully, automatically, her fingers gliding across her face coaxing the creamy liquid into her skin, her thoughts still on Carla. What would she be like? She knew she was younger than her; Harry hadn't spared her that little hurtful detail. But now she too would be older. Had she aged better than Barbara? She opened the pot of eye-shadow and carefully applied it to her eye-lids. Well if she was going to go to the funeral she had better make herself look presentable; she didn't want people comparing her unfavourably to Carla.

'Barbara are you ready yet?' her husband shouted from the kitchen.

'Almost Ian. Ten more minutes.'

Just the mascara and a touch of lipstick and she would be ready to get dressed. The black suit would have to do; she could brighten it up with the pink blouse that Sylvia had given her for her birthday. Why look too severe? After all *she* was not the grieving widow.

Ian put his head round the bathroom door. 'There's some coffee for you in the kitchen.'

'Thanks Darling, I'll be down in a minute.'

'Don't be too long Babs, it's quite a drive to Frieth.'

'Okay, don't worry. I don't suppose they'll start without us.'

Their flat was spacious and well laid out; she had suggested that they buy it after Tom had left home. The house she and Harry had lived in for more years than she cared to remember had already begun to feel too large when Sylvia moved out to marry Richard, but without Tom and his friends crashing about the place, all lanky arms and long legs, loud music and half-eaten pizzas, it felt like a morgue. It had been a wrench to sell it but as she explained to her disappointed children this was going to be a new stage in her life; it was time to move on and at last she had the means to do so.

She rummaged in her chest of drawers until she found a new packet of black tights and hastily pulled them on. I wonder what Carla will be wearing she thought, pulling up the zip on her black skirt and straightening the blouse. She slipped on the jacket and buttoned it carefully then selected a matching silk scarf which she draped casually around her neck. One final look in the mirror told her that she looked fine, discrete and sober enough for a funeral but not too drab. In fact black suited her pale colouring quite well and set off the reddish tints in hair. She ran her hand over her skirt, it was a mixture of silk and wool and felt deliciously soft. It still gave her an enormous pleasure to know that she could afford to buy items of quality now and not have to worry about the price. The sale of her company had left her a rich woman. She wondered if Harry had ever known about her success. Or even cared. It was almost twenty years since he'd told her he was leaving them yet she remembered it as though it were yesterday. It had been the day after Sylvia's tenth birthday.

*

There was no problem getting Tom out of bed on the morning of his sister's birthday; Barbara heard him bounce into Sylvia's bed and her strangled shout of 'Go away.' Then there was the sound of laughter and their bedroom door burst open.

'Mum? Dad? Are you awake?' her son whispered.

'We are now,' Harry grumbled and pulled the covers over his head.

'What is it, Tom?'

'It's Sylvia's birthday.'

'I know it is.'

'We're going to the zoo.'

'I know we are but the zoo's not open yet.' Both children climbed onto the bed beside them. Reluctantly she opened her eyes and looked at the bedside clock. It was ten past six. 'Do you know what time it is?' she asked.

'Breakfast time,' said Tom.

Barbara sighed. 'Happy birthday Darling,' she said to her daughter. 'Come here.'

Sylvia clambered over the bed and snuggled down between her mother and father.

'Happy birthday,' mumbled Harry.

'Look why don't you go down and have some breakfast and Daddy and I will be down in a minute.'

'Okay,' said Tom and bounced off the bed. 'Come on Sylvia.'

'And close the door,' shouted Harry.

'Ten more minutes,' Barbara said and snuggled up to her husband.

He nibbled her ear and whispered, 'Do you think that will be long enough?'

She giggled. 'Not now, the children will hear us.' But his hands were already inside her nightdress, caressing her breasts.

'Not if you're very quiet,' he whispered.

*

Her friend, Mary had held a party for Sylvia the next day, but they had to leave early because Tom was violently sick. Sylvia claimed it was because he'd eaten three helpings of trifle and then gone straight outside to play on the Bouncy Castle. She was probably right.

'I don't see why I have to go home. It was my party.' she complained.

'It was almost over, anyway,' Barbara replied. 'And Tom needs to be in his own bed.' Her son was lying on the back seat, his face two shades paler than normal, being unusually quiet.

'But why have I got to go home too? It's not fair,' her daughter whined.

Barbara sighed. She turned off the lane and drove into their drive. Harry's car was parked outside the garage. 'Look, Daddy's home. That's a nice surprise; I thought he wasn't coming home until much later. Now aren't you pleased you didn't stay at the party?'

'No.' Sylvia got out of the car, slammed the door and went straight inside.

'Come on Tom,' Barbara said.

'Do I have to go to bed, Mummy?'

'Not if you don't want to, but I think you should sit quietly for a bit. Put the telly on if you like. And don't eat anything; give your stomach a rest too.' She followed her children into the house. 'Hello. Harry? We're home,' she called. She heard the television being switched on and the sound of Tom's favourite programme. 'Not too loud, Tom.'

There was no sign of her husband downstairs so she went up to their bedroom. One of their larger suitcases was on the bed and Harry was busily packing it with his clothes. 'Hi Darling? What are you doing? Oh, you're not going on another trip so soon, are you?' she said, sitting on the opposite side of the bed and kicking off her shoes. 'God, kids' parties are so exhausting. I'm absolutely shattered,' she continued, laying back and looking up at him. 'Tom was sick. Sylvia's in a bad mood. It's been a great afternoon.' Harry continued to fold his shirts and lay them neatly in the suitcase. 'You're home early,' she said. 'Was the Reading gig any good? It was The Skinks, wasn't it? Tom likes them. Be nice if you could take him along one day; he'd love it.'

He looked at her, his face taut. It was almost as if he were annoyed to see her. 'I need to talk to you,' he said in a strangled voice. It was the sound of his voice that told her something was wrong, but even then she was not expecting what came next. 'I've met someone else.'

She sat up, thinking that perhaps she'd misheard him. 'What did you say?'

'I'm leaving you,' he continued. 'I'm sorry Barbara.'

'I don't understand.' But understanding was dawning on her bit by bit.

'I'm so sorry Barbara. I've met someone else and I'm in love. I just can't go on living this lie anymore.'

'Lie?' Still she couldn't take it in.

'I didn't mean it to happen, please believe me. The last thing I would ever want is to hurt you and the children.'

She was not listening to his words; she was caught up in some nightmare and she couldn't escape. 'Who is she?' she managed to whisper.

He looked away and picked up another shirt to fold. 'Her name's Carla; you don't know her.'

'How long?'

'Does it matter how long? I love her.'

'How long has it been going on?' She had to know the extent of his deceit.

'Three years.'

'Three years,' she screamed. 'Three years and you never gave a sign.' Yesterday morning they'd made love as if nothing was wrong and today he was leaving her? It had to be a mistake.

'I didn't want it to happen. Believe me, I didn't want to hurt you.' He placed the last shirt in the case and took his socks from the sock drawer. 'I'm so sorry Barbara, it just happened. I wasn't ready for it; it just bowled me over and I couldn't do anything about it. I love her, you see.'

She felt the scream forming in her stomach and rising slowly through her body until it released itself in a cry of anguish. Realisation had taken hold; he was leaving her and the children for someone else. 'Believe you? How could I ever have believed you, you lying bastard?' She lashed out and knocked the socks from his hand. They scattered across the floor. She saw a look of shock on his face as he moved towards her, trying to hold her still, to stop her cries but she fought against him, hitting him with her fists until she collapsed exhausted, at his feet. He was talking to her but she couldn't take in what he was saying.

'Barbara I'm so sorry. I didn't want you to find out like this; I've written you a letter explaining everything.'

She looked at him through her tear-filled eyes. He was holding an envelope in his hand. Suddenly she realised the full calumny of this man, the man she loved, the man she had lived with for twenty years; he had hoped to leave before she returned home. He did not even have the guts to tell her to her face that he was abandoning her and the children. He had written her a letter. A cowardly letter. She snatched the envelope from his hand and tore it in two. 'How can you explain this to your children? Tell me that. How can you explain it to them? Have you written them a letter too?'

'Barbara, don't be like this; you know how fond I am of you and the kids. I love Tom and Sylvia .' She couldn't say anything; her tears were choking her and she felt unable to breathe. 'I'm really sorry. I hope one day you can forgive me.' He closed the case and swung it off the bed.

Forgiveness? Why did he talk about forgiveness? How could she ever forgive him? In the space of a few thoughtless moments he'd destroyed her entire world. So many years together and now what? He stood there looking at her, his face racked with guilt. For an instant she thought he was about to change his mind, but no, he picked up the case, looked at the socks scattered across the floor, decided against recovering them and made for the door. He paused, his hand on the door handle and turned to her as though he would speak. 'Get out,' she shouted, her rage making her voice harsh and ugly. The door closed behind him and with that click of finality she felt the bottom fall out of her world.

Slowly she dragged herself to a chair by the window. Her legs were heavy, reluctant to move, reluctant to see him actually leave her. She watched him throw his case into the boot of the car and drive away. How long she sat there watching the rain run down the windowpanes, she didn't know but eventually she heard Sylvia's voice outside the door, calling her.

She sighed, better that he'd died than left her for another woman, then they could all grieve for him and she could look back at their life with love and affection. Now all she had left was anger and resentment. The children wouldn't understand why he'd gone; they'd feel abandoned. She felt the bitterness growing inside her, and she knew it would devour her unless she took control. Well, she wasn't going to let him destroy her and her children in this way.

*

Ian was sitting in the car, with the window open and she could hear the strains of Berlioz's 'Harold in Italy' coming from the radio.

'Oh there you are. At last. Well I suppose it was worth the wait; you look lovely.'

'Thank you Darling.'

'Nervous?'

'Why do you ask? Do I look nervous?'

'No of course not; I just wondered. It's going to seem a bit strange, after all.'

'Yes, you're right. Actually I am a bit nervous. It's all a bit surreal isn't it. After all what role do I play? Ex-wife? Mother of his children?'

'Yes both of those. There's nothing to be concerned about. Remember, it will be you who will know everyone, not her. I take it all the family will be there?'

'Yes, they said they would be coming.'

'So there you are then, nothing to worry about.'

She saw him check his watch again. He hated to be late; she knew he had carefully calculated how long the journey would take, choosing the route with the least traffic and least chance of delay. He was such a meticulous man, kind, generous, affectionate but extremely pedantic. Perhaps it was his passion for detail that had led him into the law. She looked at her second husband with fondness; he was every inch the solicitor, with his charcoal grey suit, his highly polished shoes and his carefully laundered shirts that were delivered once a week from the local laundry despite her protests that she could easily do them herself. The Windsor knot in his tie was a work of art, folded and tied with precision, his hair was immaculately cut and combed to one side, the parting perfectly straight. Nothing was ever out of place. She smiled; he could not have been more different from Harry with his open-neck shirts and his chinos, and his thick, dark hair, always in need of a haircut. In his own way Harry had perfected the art of casualness. Sometimes she wondered if it was because of these differences that she had at last agreed to marry Ian. She loved him of course, as she reminded herself many times, but not with the passion of her youthful love for Harry, or sadly, with the lustful, middle-aged passion she'd had for Doug. This was a more comfortable love, unlikely to bring broken hearts or provoke sleepless nights. Yes, she reassured herself, she'd made the right choice. Ian was a good man and a loving husband. He had been a staunch friend when Harry left her, and he'd waited patiently until she had allowed their relationship to move to the next stage. Now he was a good husband. A solid man, her father would have said, dependable; her father would have approved of him she was sure. Her father valued dependability; he had not approved of Harry.

'Hurry up then; we don't want to be late Darling.'

She hesitated then got into the car beside him. 'I don't want to arrive too early, Ian. Let's see if we can slip in at the end,' she suggested.

'All right we can always wait in the car if we're early, but somehow I don't think we will be.' He pulled back his cuff to check his watch again then replaced it carefully, smoothing it into place. 'We really should be off, you know. It's already a quarter to ten'

She buckled her seatbelt and leaned across to kiss him on the cheek. 'Okay let's get it over with.' For the first time she was going to meet the woman who had ripped her life apart. What on earth was she going to say to her?

CHAPTER 6

'Telephone, Sylvia,' said her husband. 'It's Tom.'

'Hi, what's up?'

'Nothing. I just thought I'd ring you before you went to get Gran. I was wondering if we needed to get in touch with Carla about anything?'

She could hear the anxiety in his voice. She knew him so well, even now he was more like a son to her than a brother, always asking for reassurance, always concerned that he might inadvertently upset someone and looking to Sylvia for guidance. 'I can't see why. Ian's looking after everything.'

'It's going to be really difficult.'

'Difficult?'

'Well awkward, you know. At the funeral. What will we say?'

'We don't have to say anything. She can't expect to turn up after all these years, and be treated as if she'd never done anything wrong just because Dad's dead now.'

'Yes but don't you think it's a bit harsh. I mean she must be unhappy too.'

'Oh Tom, do you think I care what she feels after all that we've been through?'

'But Sylvia it was a long time ago.'

'Try telling that to Mum.'

'But Mum's happy now; she's got Ian.'

'That's not the point. Dad made her suffer. He abandoned her and us, his children, and all because of that woman.'

'He was in love. He told me. He said he never wanted to hurt us but he couldn't help it.'

'I know, you've told me all that before. It makes no difference. You say that he didn't want to hurt us but the point is that he did hurt us. That's what counts, not his maudlin excuses. Look Tom let's just get the next few days over then we can all go back to living our lies. I know it's sad that he's dead but it's not as though we have had much to do with him over the years. I'd like to cry and say that I'll miss him, but the truth is that I won't.'

'I will.'

'Well good for you.'

'If you feel like that, why are you going to the funeral?'

'I'm going for Gran's sake. Speaking of which I must get ready. I'll see you at the church, and don't worry.'

*

Sylvia hated Carla with a passion that was touched with madness. She'd never forgiven her father for what he'd done to them, and with the reasoning of a young girl, had blamed it all on Carla. Unlike Tom she'd been old enough to understand what was happening. Her mother had been angry when she learned about Carla but not broken; she had shouted and cried, long, hard, angry cries of rage and impotence but she had not collapsed, weeping and helpless the way she did after the divorce. It was Sylvia who had to help her then; it was Sylvia who took her cups of tea and forced her to eat a little toast, Sylvia who wiped her face with the wet face flannel and put her little arms around her.

'Please don't cry Mummy. Daddy will be back soon,' she'd promised. But her father didn't return and her mother continued to weep.

Now when she looked back on those years from the perspective of a mature woman, a wife and mother, she couldn't understand how his feelings for her and Tom had changed so quickly. She knew that nobody and nothing would ever come between her and her daughter. Unlike Tom, she'd known that her father hadn't contested the custody case; she'd overheard her mother telling her uncle Teddy, and although she hadn't fully understood all that was said, she was intelligent enough to realise that her father no longer wanted them. It was as her mother said, he'd made a choice between them and this new woman. At first she cried herself to sleep every night, but then she became angry, and that anger had never really left her. It had been refuelled when she got married and there was no father to give her away; Teddy had stood in as father of the bride and her mother, looking lovely in her pale blue wool suit had posed for the photographs holding his arm. It had been refuelled when her daughter was born and Richard's parents had sat in the hospital with her mother, waiting for the first glimpse of their new grandchild. It had been refuelled when that same child had come home from school one day asking why she had two grandmas and only one grandpa.

*

It was the month of the Eleven Plus exams and with the self-centredness of a normal eleven year old Sylvia was angry that her father hadn't waited until they were over before he had left them. The teachers never told you which day you had to take the exam; they didn't want the children to worry they said, but the rumours were flying around thick and fast. Everyone knew it would be sometime soon, then Ruth, whose mother was a dinner lady, said it was definitely that week.

They were all packing away their books ready to go home, when their teacher, a kind young woman with a Scottish accent, said, 'Right children, I want you all to make sure that you have an early night tonight and get here bright and fresh tomorrow morning.'

They knew she was telling them that tomorrow was their exam day, and a buzz of excitement swept across the class until she rapped on her desk with her ruler and said, 'That's enough noise. Quieten down children. Now have you got all your things? Right, class dismissed.'

They tumbled out of the classroom, chattering excitedly; the moment they had all been waiting for had finally come. All their studying and hours spent working through practice papers would be put to the test the next day.

*

It was difficult to sleep. Her mother made her a hot drink and told her to go to bed early so she would be fresh the next morning and do well in the exam. Her mother knew how desperately she wanted to go to Wycombe High School. Her best friend, Susan was already there; she was six months older than Sylvia and had passed the exam the year before. She hated the fact that Susan was at another school, because it meant that they only saw each other at weekends and in the holidays.

'You wait until you get here,' Susan told her. 'You'll really have to work hard. They give you loads of homework. But don't worry I'll help you. We can do our homework together.'

That was why it was so important to do well and then they would be together again. They would take the school bus together each morning and even if they were in different classes it didn't matter because they would see each other at playtime. Yes she had to do well.

She rolled over and looked at the bedside clock; it was eleven thirty. She was very thirsty. As quietly as she could, she got out of bed and crept down the stairs. There was a light on in the living room and her mother was sitting in front of the television. She was crying. Sylvia didn't know what to do; her mother did a lot of crying. She went into the kitchen and took a bottle of water from the fridge then crept back to bed.

*

Sylvia so desperately wanted to do well but, when she sat down with the others, in the serried ranks of Formica desks that had been set out in the Assembly Hall especially for the examination, she could think of nothing else but her mother crying quietly before the television, oblivious to her daughter's presence. She picked up her pencil and started to work methodically through the papers, but all the time it was as though her head was full of cotton wool and she couldn't think clearly. By the time the invigilator had told them to stop writing and put down their pens she was barely finished. She longed to answer just one more question but the woman's eyes were on her, and before she knew it her paper had been collected along with all the others. The children filed out, blinking in the autumn sunshine.

'How did you do?' asked Amy, her new best friend since Susan had left.

'All right,' she replied, but she didn't feel confident.

'I was dreadful,' Amy wailed. 'I'm sure I won't pass and we've got the Maths paper tomorrow I'm hopeless at Maths.'

'You'll be all right,' Sylvia consoled her.

'I won't. I'm not as brainy as you. You'll pass easily.'

Everyone was bemoaning their performances, playing down their interest in being one of the selected few. Sylvia was no different.

*

She missed being selected by two marks; it was nothing really. Two marks. Not selected, but what they really meant was that she had failed.

'We don't use words like "pass" and "fail," it's more a question of finding the right school for each individual child,' the teacher had told her mother at one of the parents' evenings. Call it what you liked, she had failed. She would not be going to Wycombe High School with Susan. Sylvia, who had excellent marks in every practice paper they had done, was not going to go to the Grammar School. She would have to go to the local comprehensive school in the town instead.

She tried to hide her disappointment but when her mother began to console her it all became too much and she could no longer contain her tears of rage and frustration.

'Darling don't cry, please. It's a lovely school and you'll know lots of children there. Amy will be there as well. You'll still be able to see Susan, just like before and you'll make new friends as well. Come on Darling, it's not as bad as that.'

'It's not fair,' Sylvia blubbered, unable to give voice to the feelings raging within her.

Her mother started to cry as well and they sat together hugging each other and crying until Tom came in wanting to know when he could have something to eat.

CHAPTER 7

The church door opened again. This time there was quite a procession of people: Sylvia's husband, Richard, dressed casually, but all in black, then Tom, looking young and fragile came in holding the hand of an anorexic-looking girl with dark hair. They were followed by a tall man in a charcoal grey suit who was supporting Harry's ex-wife, Barbara on his arm. All, except Barbara, nodded politely in her direction and positioned themselves in the pew behind Phoebe and Sylvia.

So here was Barbara; despite her years she was instantly recognisable as the woman Carla had seen in an old photograph she'd found amongst Harry's possessions. She stood there, her head slightly bowed, her face partially covered by a black and white scarf, surrounded by her family, by Harry's family. Carla began to feel exposed and uncomfortable, like the usurper they probably thought she was. She was amazed at the feelings seeing his ex-wife brought back; the old jealousy had flared up once more. This was the woman who had shared his life for twenty years and borne him two children. He had never talked about her and although he occasionally spoke about his children, the silence in which he had cloaked that part of his life excluded Carla and because of that exclusion she had become jealous of the woman whose place she'd taken. She tried not to stare at her but her eyes were drawn back again and again to the tall figure, the straight back and the designer suit; Valentino she was sure. This was a woman saddened by the occasion but not bowed by it. No, Barbara was nothing like she had imagined.

The organist had arrived by now and the church began to fill with music. Carla realised that a number of wreaths had been laid on the floor in front of the altar and that the urn had been placed on a small table among them. She focused her attention on the urn and tried not to think about the people sitting across the aisle from her. A small movement caused her to look up from her meditation; Jenny had slipped in beside her.

'Room for me?' she whispered with a smile. Carla squeezed her arm but didn't reply. 'Chris and Geraldine are outside, they'll be in in a minute. Gerry's just finishing her fag.'

Chris Kingdom had been Harry's best friend. He was one of the few people they had kept in touch with over the years. He and Harry had gone to school together, played football for the local team, and he had been the best man at Harry's wedding. Then he'd agreed to perform the honour a second time and officiated at Carla and Harry's wedding in Spain. He marched into the church now, with Geraldine trailing behind him, and sat down next to Carla.

'Hi there,' he whispered. 'Sad day.'

'Hello Chris, Geraldine. Thanks for coming.'

They were spared any further conversation by the arrival of the Reverend Fairmount, who glided down the aisle in black robes and a face that was prepared to brave all the sorrows of the world.

Carla looked across to where Harry's family had seated themselves in the right hand pew. Just like a wedding she thought; they're on the groom's side while I'm on the bride's. Only they had not attended her wedding; none of Harry's family had attended, only Teddy had sent them an extravagant wedding present and a note of apology. He hadn't needed to give his reasons; they already knew them. How long ago it now seemed.

*

Like she'd told Harry not long after they'd met, Carla had always been interested in fashion. When she was at school if you had asked her what she wanted to be, she probably would not have said a fashion designer, her aspirations were not so high, but she knew it had to be something to do with clothes. Neither of her parents was artistic, but her mother had been a very able needlewoman, she worked from home, making curtains and loose covers for the local drapers. Carla would sometimes go with her to collect the orders, helping her load the bundles of material into the back of the old family Ford Capri. Even when she was quite small she liked to touch the fabric and hold it up to the light to study the colours in the weave. Her mother made all their clothes and had a talent for recycling anything they had grown out of or discarded. As Carla's father was out of work more often than not, this talent was the only thing that kept the family respectably dressed. At first Carla copied her mother by making clothes for her dolls; she would sit at the end of the table where her mother worked, watching her carefully and trying to emulate what she did. Her mother began to teach her how to hem and back stitch, to sew on tiny buttons; she cut out squares of old material so that Carla could make skirts and coats for her dolls, and she always saved any scraps for her to practice. This was Carla's favourite pastime as a child, rummaging through the 'rag bag' as her mother called it, pulling out strips of pink satin, the remnants of an old nightdress or a piece of heather coloured tweed that once had been the pocket of an old skirt. Sometimes she would question her mother on the origins of a particular scrap and her mother would take the material in her hand and smile, remembering who had worn it and when.

As Carla grew older she progressed to sewing things for herself; she commandeered her mother's machine to put flares in her old jeans, she cut the hems off her dresses to make mini-skirts, she took her Dad's old overcoat and reshaped it for herself. A dress she had created to go to the disco one night would be unpicked and remodelled for the following week. She was the envy of all her friends. So when she'd taken her A Levels it seemed a logical step to apply for a place at the Chelsea College of Art and Design and train to be a fashion designer. Her mother was delighted with her decision. She knew that this was what Carla should do with her life.

Carla fitted in straight away. She was a good student, imaginative and adept; she could hand stitch so finely that it was almost invisible, her French seams were flawless and her skill at pattern making was rewarded with top marks. When she was not attending classes she continued working on her own designs, filling notebook after notebook with her sketches. But like many of her friends she never had enough money, so in order to eke out her paltry student grant, she began to make leather jewellery. She bought off-cuts in the market and fashioned them into bracelets and chokers which she and her friend Pam sold each weekend in the Portobello Road market. The jewellery was very popular, and by the time she graduated, three years later, she had built up a reasonable clientele and had begun to make and sell long leather skirts and matching waistcoats as well. That's how it began. She combed the flea markets for bargain pieces of leather, strips of vintage lace, ostrich feathers, useful items of discarded clothing; she tracked down a supplier of good quality leather in a tiny shop near Smithfield's and visited the markets looking for suppliers to bag makers, saddlers and shoemakers; she bought zips by the bundle, needles by the gross and bags of assorted buckles. Very soon she had a number of boutiques wanting to buy her garments and decided it was time to get herself an agent so that she could devote herself to the cutting and sewing. That was when she met Jenny.

*

Jenny was a young woman, no older than herself, who was a Londoner through and through. For someone so young, Jenny had a wide range of contacts; she introduced Carla to market stall holders, pop stars, musicians, actors. She knew who was opening a new boutique, who needed something special for that all important presentation, who had been invited to the opening of an exhibition. She had her finger on the pulse of who was who, what they were doing and more importantly, what they wanted to wear. Carla soon found she couldn't do without her. She produced two or three high quality leather garments a week, began to find herself in high demand and moved from her trendy Earl's Court bed-sit to a small flat in West Ealing with a garage that she could use as a studio.

'So who exactly is this actress we're going to see?' Carla asked.

'Melissa Stanford. She's been in a few TV things: a bit part in The Professionals, played the wife of the victim in an episode of Minder and now she has landed a part in Heaven is Made for Two.'

'Sounds awful.'

'No, she's actually very nice.'

'I meant the film.'

'Anyway she saw someone wearing one of your designs when she was at a party of Elton John's last month and liked it. She needs something special for the premiere of this new film.'

'But she knows I work mainly in leather?'

'Yes. She wants something different. I think she's talking about white leather and lots of sequins.'

'Oh we can do sequins. No problem.'

'Did you bring some ideas with you?'

Carla tapped her head. 'All in here.'

'Is that all?' Jenny asked, horrified.

'Of course not. I've got loads of sketches to show her and some swatches of leather. Don't worry. You just do the introduction and I'll do the rest.'

'Fine, I knew you'd be organised.'

'When am I not?'

'Well before you met Harry I would have said never, but now I'm not so sure. How is he by the way?'

'Just the same. Gorgeous.'

'Any nearer to leaving his wife?'

'Oh Jen, I don't know. He keeps saying he will speak to her but nothing happens. It's been three years now. I don't know if I can carry on like this.'

'Well tell him his time is up. Give him an ultimatum. That's what I would do.'

Carla looked across at Jenny. Was that what she had done? Given some man an ultimatum and he'd left her? She never spoke of any lovers or past boyfriends; it was a subject she shied away from whenever Carla tried to question her. What if she did give Harry an ultimatum and lost him? Then surely that would only mean that he had never intended to leave his wife in the first place. But could she take the chance? Just the thought of returning to a life without Harry made her stomach contract with fear.

'Here we are. It's a bit of a walk to her apartment, I'm afraid, but this is the nearest parking,' Jenny explained, pulling up beside a meter and skilfully manoeuvring the car into a space.

*

Melissa was a very pleasant young woman, with her sights set firmly on stardom. She listened carefully to all that Carla said, looking at the samples and the designs with interest.   Then she stood up, twirled around a couple of times and stopped, her hands resting on her slim hips.

'Okay Carla. I'll leave it up to you. I want something that will make me stand out from the others, something that will get me on the front page of the newspapers, but something with class. Fashionable but classy, that's the image I'm after.'

Carla swallowed hard; it was exciting to be given such freedom of design but she didn't always like the responsibility that went with it. She'd been there before, designed a special creation for someone only to have them turn round and berate her for it.

'Excellent idea. Carla has so many exciting designs. She will come up with just the outfit you're looking for,' Jenny replied before she could say anything. 'But I suggest that she does some drawings first to give you an idea what she's thinking of.'

'Okay, that sounds a good plan.'

'Carla?'

'Yes, that's fine. Let me take some measurements and I'd like a photograph or two if you don't mind.'

She measured her bosom, her waist, the length of her arms, across her shoulders, the length of her back, the drop to the floor, then she took a couple of snaps of the actress.

'This may sound a little strange but I wonder if I could look at some of your favourite clothes.'

'I suppose so, but I don't want anything like them. I want something different, something special.'

'Yes I know. It's just to give me a flavour of your taste.' Carla knew that even if she said she wanted something different, this young woman didn't mean radical, she probably meant a variation on a theme. Most people she knew kept more or less to the same styles despite the changes in fashion. If she wanted this to be a success she had to understand her client's taste and design something that flattered her. The dress had to be stunning, but it should never outshine the wearer. She wanted people to say 'You look wonderful' not 'that's a wonderful dress.'

She sat making a few notes in her pad while Jenny made arrangements for them to meet again in a couple of weeks.

'I must have it by the beginning of May, the premiere is on the 21st,' she informed them.

'That's no problem. You'll have it in plenty of time, I assure you.'

Measurements taken and pleasantries exchanged Carla and Jenny left and were soon sitting in a traffic jam heading west.

'Drop me off at the nearest tube station would you Jen. I want to see if Eddie has any white leather in stock.'

'Sure. What about the Elephant and Castle?'

'A bit further in would be better. Can you go past Waterloo?'

'No problem. Now what about tomorrow? Do you want me to make an appointment to see Mrs Goldberg again?'

'No, leave it until next week. I need time to get this job started before I start thinking about her wedding outfit.'

'Don't forget you've got that red jacket to finish,' Jenny reminded her.

'I won't. I'll give you a call when it's ready.'

'Okay then Carla, see you later in the week. And tell that boyfriend of yours to make up his mind who he really wants to be with.'

*

Carla heard the key turn in the door to her flat and hurried to greet him. When he opened the door and stood there, an enormous smile on his face, a bunch of roses in one hand and a bottle of Dom Perignon in the other, she knew that he'd made a decision.

'Marry me, Carla,' Harry said by way of a greeting.

She just looked at him and smiled. What could she say? Her heart was bursting with happiness. 'Why not,' she managed at last.

'This weekend. We'll drive to Gretna Green and get married there.'

'Don't you have to get divorced first?'

'Small detail.'

'Not sure I want to marry a bigamist,' she said, putting her arms around him and kissing him.

'Oh, all right, divorce first then.'

'Does that mean you've spoken to Barbara?'

'Yes, well her solicitor. She's agreed to divorce me on grounds of adultery.' For a moment he looked concerned. 'You'll be named, I'm afraid.'

'We always knew that would happen,' she said, trying to keep her voice light, although the thought of being the guilty party upset her.

'Anyway, cause for celebration, wouldn't you say? Where're the glasses?'

He handed her the roses and proceeded to open the champagne.

*

Later that night, over dinner, he said, 'I have something else I want to talk to you about.'

'What, something more important than a proposal of marriage?' She beamed at him. No matter what it was, it couldn't alter the way she was feeling right then. It was though the bubbles from the champagne were spreading through her blood and exploding one by one.

'Look Darling, we need to talk about money.'

'Money? We've got enough money; I'm working and so are you. I know you'll have to pay for the children, but we can manage.' She lifted her glass to him and said rather dramatically, 'What matters money when we have each other?'

'Yes, I know, but the problem is that all my money is in the business. I don't have a lot of cash, and of course I can hardly throw Barbara and the kids out of the house, can I? Anyway I know these bastard solicitors; they'll screw me for as much as they can get.'

'Of course you'll have to support your children, I understand that.'

'But it's not just that; I don't want us to start off our lives together, scrimping and saving like a couple of twenty-year olds.'

'So what are you saying?'

'I've been giving it some thought and it seems to me that the best way out, is for me to sell the business, and we use the money to move to Spain.'

'Move to Spain? Where did that idea come from? You've never mentioned living abroad before.'

'I know, but houses are cheaper there; our money will go much further than here in England.' He leaned across and poured some more champagne into her glass.

'But what about my work?'

'Darling just think of it, away from all these grey skies and the constant rain. Once we're settled we'll find some work; you can go back to your sewing and I'll find something to do. I reckon I can get a good price for the business; the equipment is worth quite a bit and my good-will list is worth even more. There's a guy who has been after it for some time; I'll give him a ring and see if he's still interested. More importantly if I sell it, I can hide the true value of my assets from the bastards a lot easier.'

For a moment Carla felt cheated. Yes she loved Harry, and yes she would like to marry him, but now he was asking her to give up her career. She'd worked hard to get the reputation she had, and each year her label was becoming better known. How could she just give it up? Sewing. Was that all he thought it was? Sewing. 'Hey hang on a minute Harry, this is all moving a bit fast for me.'

He paused, a look of surprise on his face. 'I don't understand. I thought that this was what you wanted.'

'To be with you, yes but we never talked about moving to Spain.'

'Oh I know. It's something I've just thought of, but it could be the answer to our financial problems. To be honest, it was Arnie's idea actually. He's got a lot of property in Marbella, says it's a wonderful place to live, much cheaper than the UK.'

'But it's a big step Harry. We don't know anybody in Spain.'

'That's not a problem; Arnie'll introduce us to his friends and we'll soon make some of our own. It's not as though you have many friends here,' he continued.

'I did have. It's only since I met you that I've neglected them. They're still my friends,' she said, indignant at the suggestion.

'Well, if that's the case, they can come and visit us. According to Arnie, his wife has a continuous stream of people staying with them. He says he comes back to the UK for a bit of peace and quiet.'

'What about my parents and my sister? My father is getting on now, you know.'

'Look Carla, one of the reasons for going to Spain is so that we will have a better standard of living. There will be enough money for you to go and visit your parents whenever you want. You can even fly to Florida and visit your sister.' The euphoria she had felt a few minutes before was quickly evaporating. 'Besides which Arnie said he'd fix us up with somewhere to stay until we could find our own place.'

'I thought you told me that Arnie was a crook?'

'Did I say that? Well not so much a crook, really. He does sail pretty close to the wind, I admit, but I'm pretty sure he's not involved in anything nasty.'

'Nasty? What does that mean? Drugs? Prostitution? Murder?'

'Now come on Carla, you're just being silly. There's nothing wrong with Arnie; I've known him since I left school, and to be quite honest he's been really helpful about this. It's going to make the move so much easier if we accept his help. We'll have somewhere to stay, and he may even be able to put some work my way. Don't put a damper on it, Darling. I know you'll love it when you're there.'

'I'm not sure, Harry. I need to think about it.'

'What's there to think about, Carla? We'll be starting a new life together. It's the perfect solution: new country, new home, new friends, new life.'

'What about my business? I can't run it from Spain; it depends on a one-to-one relationship with my clients. I need to be in London.'   She could hear the whine creep into her voice.

'You've got an agent haven't you? Let her get you the clients. You can always pop back once a month to see them. It's not as though I'm suggesting we move to Australia, is it?' A slight hardening of his tone told her that he was disappointed with her reaction.

She began to feel that she was being too negative; maybe it could work after all. 'I suppose I could talk to Jenny about it,' she said, reluctantly.

'That's the girl. Anyway I thought you wanted us to have a family? You'd have to give up work then.'

'I hadn't thought that far ahead actually, but maybe you're right.'

The truth was that her complete absorption with Harry had clouded her mind to any practical issues; she had imagined that she would be able to have him and continue with her existing life. Now she was being presented with a choice, and she wasn't happy.

He pulled her towards him and kissed her. 'Don't keep looking for objections, Darling. I promise you it will be all right. You see, in a few years you will wonder why you ever hesitated.'

Somehow she didn't think this was true. She'd worked hard to get where she was, and now he was asking her to give it all up. What would Jenny say?

CHAPTER 8

Carla had spoken to the Swiss-Italian owner of the pub the night before and arranged for him to prepare a light buffet for them after the funeral. Harry had always liked this pub, it had been one of his local drinking haunts before he met Carla. For obvious reasons they had never gone there together, so Carla looked around her now with particular interest. They were led through a small, public bar with a low, whitewashed ceiling and an uneven flagged floor; weak rays of sunlight struggled through the leaded lights in the windows and here and there cast their reflection on the horse brasses nailed above the bar, but did little to brighten the gloomy room. In the back room, the landlord had laid out a table with plates of cold meats, salads and patés. There was crusty wholemeal bread, tiny squares of hot pizzas and bottles of Italian wine. She sighed with relief when she saw that they were not to be seated formally around a table; there was no room anyway. People could mingle freely, plate and glass in hand, avoiding and greeting people as they wished.

Courtesy would not permit her guests to ignore her any longer, and one by one they approached her to offer their condolences. Sylvia was the first, and the briefest.

'Did you have a good flight?' she asked politely.

'Usual sort of thing, a bit cramped and no food, but otherwise, yes it was okay.'

'Hotel all right?'

'Yes, thank you for booking it for me.'

'Tom did it.'

'How's Linda?' she asked, looking round for Harry's only grandchild.

'She's at school. I didn't see much point in taking her out for the day. It's not as though she knew her grandfather, after all.'

'Yes, I understand. That was a pity, though. Harry loved children. He was so excited when Teddy told him you were pregnant; he would have loved to have seen his only grandchild.'

Before Sylvia could reply, her husband, Richard, appeared, brandishing his glass at Carla and saying, 'Excellent Brunello. Best I've tasted since we were in Sienna last year.' He offered the glass to his wife. 'Here, have a taste, Sylvia. What do you think?'

'No thanks. I need to speak to Mum.' She moved away before she was obliged to say anything else.

Her husband turned back to Carla. 'She's never been much of a wine buff, not like her Dad. He knew his wine all right, from what I hear.'

'Yes, Harry was very fond of wine, especially Italian wine, although after so many years in Spain he got to be quite an expert on Spanish wine too.' And grew too fond of it, she thought as she smiled politely.

'You must be Carla. I've heard a lot about you,' he said, with what Carla thought was almost a wink. 'Pleased to meet you. I'm Sylvia's husband.'

'Yes I rather guessed that.'

'God, is it that obvious?' He laughed and held out his hand. Carla had already heard from Teddy that Sylvia's husband worked for the Environmental Agency and was stationed at Wallingford. He looked the outdoor type she thought, with his unkempt beard and ruddy complexion.

'Your work must keep you pretty busy these days,' she said glad to have someone other than Sylvia to talk to.

'You wouldn't believe it. I'm actually on stand-by today. If this rain doesn't ease up we'll be on Red Alert again and I'll have to go in.' As though to emphasise the point he pulled his mobile out of his pocket and checked the screen. Satisfied that all was well he continued, 'We've been saying for years that allowing people to build houses on the flood plain was ridiculous. Okay, it's nice to have a big house with lawns running down to the river and your own personal jetty, but the insurance companies aren't keen to insure them anymore; there've been too many floods, especially along the Thames. We've spent a fortune shoring up banks and draining flooded areas, but in the end it's no good, the water still comes back. And we get the blame.' He popped a square of pizza in his mouth.

'Hello Rich.'

It was Tom; she recognised him from the photo Harry used to have by his bed. The young man's face was pale and drawn as though he hadn't slept well, and she fancied he might have been crying.

Richard gave him a friendly clap on the back. 'All right, lad? Come to speak to the delightful Carla?' He grinned and went off in search of some more wine for his empty glass.

'Hello Tom, how nice to meet you.' She reached forward and kissed him on the cheek, but felt him draw away very slightly. He seemed embarrassed. 'How are you?'

Tom fidgeted with the glass in his hand before replying, 'I'm fine. What about you?'

'You know, so so. It's lonely without your Dad.'

'Why now?'

'Sorry?'

'Why now? Why have you brought him back now? He died last year. I wrote to you. I told you we wanted him home.'

It was a question that Carla had hoped no-one would ask her, and she could hear the hurt in his voice.

'I don't really know Tom. You know that your dad wasn't very religious. We'd talked about it once, and he always said that when it was his turn he didn't want any fuss, so I just kept his ashes at home until I could make up my mind what to do with them.'

'But you received my letter?' he asked. She nodded. 'So what made you decide to bring him home now?' he insisted. 'Why now?'

'Just that, this was his home. I began to realise that we had no-one in Spain—all his family were here—so it seemed the natural thing to do to bring him home for you.'

Tom took a sip of his wine then, when he looked at her next there were tears in his eyes. 'Thanks,' he said softly.

'Really?' said a voice behind her. It was Sylvia. 'Seems a bit strange to me that it took you a year to remember that he had a family in England. Guilty conscience was it?'

Before Carla could reply, there was Teddy, all smiles and bonhomie 'This is looking all far too intense to me. What you need, my girl, is a glass of this excellent wine and something to eat. Come with me.' Before Sylvia could say anything else, he took Carla's arm and steered her towards the buffet table, leaving his niece and nephew staring after them.

She hadn't realized before quite how much it had hurt Harry's children when he left them to live in Spain with her. Their pain was still visible and it hurt her to see it.

*

Barbara was just settling down to spend an hour on her computer course before it was time to round up the children for bed, when the telephone rang.

'Hello, Mrs Wilkinson? This is Jane Phillips, Tom's teacher.'

'Miss Phillips, this is a surprise. What can I do for you?'

'I'm sorry to telephone you at home, but as you didn't manage to make our appointment yesterday, I thought it best to ring and see if there was a problem.'

'I'm sorry, what was that?'

'Our appointment, yesterday, after school. I sent a letter with Tom last Friday.'

'I'm sorry, I didn't know anything about an appointment. Are you sure you gave the letter to Tom?'

'Most definitely. And what's more, I asked him on Monday if he'd delivered it.'

'What did he say?'

'He said he had.'

'Just a moment Miss Phillips, can you hold on?' She put down the receiver and went into the hall, where Tom's coat and satchel lay on the floor, exactly where he'd dropped them when he came in from school. She opened the satchel and peered inside. What a mess. She tipped the contents out onto the carpet. Besides his rather battered reading book, a couple of exercise books and a well decorated pencil case, there was an empty coke can, an apple core, a pair of laces for his trainers, his black plimsolls, one football sock, his school cap, an assortment of chocolate wrappers, his empty lunch box, a dirty pair of blue shorts, two conkers, a piece of string, a stone with a hole in it, various football stickers and a grubby, white envelope. The envelope had the school crest on it and was addressed to Mr and Mrs Wilkinson. 'Hello, Miss Phillips?'

'Yes.'

'I've found the envelope. Look I'm very sorry, I'll have a word with him right now.'

'I still think we need to talk. Could you make it tomorrow after school? Say around four thirty?'

'Yes, of course. I'll be there.'

'I'm sorry to have had to bother you at home.'

'No, please don't apologise. I'll be there tomorrow.'

'Goodnight then.'

Barbara went back into the kitchen and sat down at the table. She opened the letter and read its contents. What did it mean? What was wrong with Tom's behaviour in class? And what was this reference to bullying? Surely her sweet, quiet Tom was not a bully.

'Tom,' she called. 'Tom, come in here for a moment.'

Her son appeared in the doorway. 'Mum, I'm watching something,' he complained.

'Sit down, will you Tom.'

'It's "Kali the Lion", you said I could watch it.' She held up the letter. 'Oh yeah, I've got a letter for you from the teacher,' he said.

'So why didn't you give it to me?' she asked.

'Sorry Mum, I forgot.'

'Miss Phillips has just telephoned me.' He started to play with Barbara's study notes. 'Leave those alone,' she snapped. He looked up, startled. 'I'm going to see her tomorrow to talk about your behaviour in class,' she said. The boy said nothing. 'Have you any idea why I've been summoned to see your teacher, Tom?' He shook his head. 'Are you sure?'

'No, Mum. Can I go now?'

'Yes, go on, but clear up that mess I found in your satchel, first. And put those dirty shorts in the wash.'

She went to the fridge, poured herself a glass of wine and sat down again at the table. There was no point saying anything more to Tom until she knew exactly what had been happening. She sighed and opened her course book again.

*

She could see that Mr Bates was not happy when she explained that she had to leave work half an hour early in order to get to the school by four thirty, so she promised to make up the time the next day. It was not much of a job, serving cakes every day, but it was convenient and fitted in, more or less, with the school hours. Neither was the pay very good but at least it was a job and she didn't want to lose it.

The school was unusually quiet. Apart from a group of the older girls playing netball in the playground, there was nobody around. She made straight for Tom's classroom and found Miss Phillips, sitting at her desk, marking a pile of exercise books.

'Hello Mrs Wilkinson. Thank you for coming.' Tom's teacher was a young woman, probably in her mid twenties. She had a pretty, pleasant face and a gentle way of speaking. Tom had always said how much he liked her. 'Please sit down. Mr Wilkinson couldn't make it then?'

'No,' Barbara said. 'So, what is this all about, Miss Phillips?'

'I think something is bothering Tom. He was always such a nice little boy, a bit quiet, but he worked well and he had plenty of friends. Just lately things have changed and I can't seem to get through to him.'

'Changed? In what way?'

'Well he has become very disruptive in class, for one. He can't, or won't, settle down to read in our quiet time. When we have a story he is constantly interrupting to ask silly questions. And of course he loves it when the other children laugh at his antics; it makes him worse. I don't like to keep punishing him, but sometimes there's no alternative but to send him out of the classroom. Otherwise it's not fair on the others.' Barbara didn't know what to say. 'I wondered if you'd noticed a change in his behaviour at home?' she asked.

'No, not really,' Barbara replied. 'I suppose if anything, he has become a bit more clingy since his father left.'

'His father has left home?'

'Yes, I suppose I should have come and explained it to you, but to be quite honest, I have had so much to think about that I never got round to it. The children seemed to be coping all right so I wasn't worried.'

'When did your husband leave?'

'He left last year. I filed for divorce about three months ago. It's due to be finalised next week.'

'Well that coincides more or less with the start of Tom's behaviour problems. Now I understand. I thought it was attention seeking, but I couldn't see any reason for it to happen so suddenly.'

'What else has he been doing?' asked Barbara.

'Well, and this is the reason I felt that I had to speak to you before it got any worse, he has started bullying one of the other children.'

'That doesn't sound like Tom. My son would never bully anyone.'

'I've seen it with my own eyes, otherwise I would never have known. I agree with you; Tom is not naturally a bully.'

'What happened?'

'There's a boy in the class who is much smaller than the others. He's only been here a couple of months and still hasn't made any friends. I thought, at first, that Tom had decided to befriend him, but then I realised that he was bullying this child into giving him his sweets each day. One of the girls came to me and told me, so I waited until playtime and then I saw it for myself. Of course I spoke to him right away, and I hope that that's finished now. But I thought it was necessary to speak to you about it.'

'Yes, of course.'

'Then there is the business with his scarf. We have a strict policy about school uniform, so wearing his Chelsea scarf in class is against the rules. Tom knows this, but he still insists that he wears it. I don't know what to do with him. I spoke to the headmaster about it and it was he who suggested that we just ignore it, he reckoned that if we stopped giving Tom so much attention he would soon give up. But now he's getting worse.'

Barbara felt sick. How had she never realised what Tom was going through? 'I have to apologise for my son's behaviour. I can only assume that it is a reaction against his father leaving. He wears that scarf all the time, you know, even in bed.'

'How often does he see his father?'

'Never. His father has left the country.'

'Does he phone him or write?'

'No, we have no contact with him.'

'So it's possible he is feeling abandoned?'

'It's possible, but he still has me and his sister.'

'Are you happy to talk to him about his behaviour? Or would you prefer to have the school psychologist have a word with him?'

'Oh no, he's far too young for that. I'll talk to him. I'm sorry, like I said he's been fine at home. I had no idea what was happening at school.'

'Maybe now we can work together and get Tom back on track.' She smiled and stood up. 'Thank you so much for coming in Mrs Wilkinson. I'm sure that things are not very easy for you right now.'

'Thank you for letting me know about Tom. I'll have a word with him this evening.'

*

When she arrived at Mary's house to collect her children, her friend was in the kitchen preparing their evening meal. Her sister Muriel and her three children were there as well. Barbara would have liked to have had a few minutes to talk to her friend about this new problem, but she could see it was impossible. She dragged her protesting children away from their game and drove home in silence.

'I don't know why you have to be so mean. We were having a great game with Sam and Jamie and their cousins,' complained Sylvia.

'Yeah. Why are you so mean, Mum?' echoed Tom.

'Just be quiet, the pair of you,' she snapped. How was she going to tackle this? She had to let Tom know that his behaviour was not acceptable but, at the same time, she didn't want him to think that she was turning against him as well.

'Did you see Tom's teacher, Mum?' asked Sylvia. 'What did she say? Has he been a bad boy?' Barbara didn't respond. She could see Tom's face in her rear view mirror.

He looked worried. 'Bet you're in trouble now, Tom,' his sister continued.

'Sylvia, how many more times do I have to tell you to be quiet?' her mother said.   She could see Sylvia poke Tom in the side and laugh. Tears were forming in his eyes. Any minute now he would be crying. 'Just stop that Sylvia. Leave Tom alone.'

Maybe she should get Teddy to speak to Tom, he got on very well with his uncle. No, that would mean leaving it until the weekend. This was something she would have to do herself.

*

She waited until Sylvia had gone upstairs for her bath before she spoke to Tom. He had eaten his supper, bathed and was sitting in front of the television in his pyjamas. He looked the picture of innocence with his scrubbed face and neatly combed hair. She sat down beside him and switched off the television.

'I was watching that Mum.'

'Tom, I need to speak to you. You know I went to see Miss Phillips this afternoon.' He nodded, his face suddenly serious. 'She told me some things that have made me very sad, very sad indeed.' She waited a moment then continued, 'What I would like you to do is tell me why you have started being so naughty at school? I thought you liked your school.' Tom looked at the empty television screen. 'Don't you like school anymore?' He nodded. 'So why are you being so naughty?' She could see the tears begin to trickle down his face. She would try a different tack. 'What do you think Miss Phillips feels like when you keep interrupting her stories?'

'Cross.'

'Yes, I expect she does feel cross. And what do you think she feels like when you won't read your book and you make jokes so that the other children laugh?'

'Cross.'

'I'm sure she is cross, but she also feels sad because she can't do her job. And what is Miss Phillips' job, Tom?'

'She has to teach us.'

'Exactly. And she can't teach the children if one silly little boy is interrupting her all the time, can she?'

'No.'

'So what are you going to do about it?'

There was a pause then her son said, 'Stop being silly.'

'Yes, I think that's a good idea, don't you.' He nodded again. 'But that's not all she told me, Tom. And this is something that I find hard to believe. She says you have been very nasty to one of the boys in your class. Is that true?' Tom wouldn't look at her, but he nodded. 'That's not a very kind thing to do, is it?'

'No, Mummy.'

'What have I told you? We must be kind to our friends or they won't be our friends anymore.'

'He's not my friend.'

'He's in your class and he's a new boy. You should be nice to him. He probably feels very lonely.'

'He's got no friends.'

'Now wouldn't it be nice if you asked him to play with you and your friends sometimes.'

'He's weird.'

'Maybe he thinks you and your friends are weird.' Silence. She could see him pouting. 'What if nobody wanted to play with you, you'd be sad wouldn't you? 'Again he nodded. 'Tom, I know you're not a bad boy. I want you to promise me, that when you go to school tomorrow, you will apologise to Miss Phillips and start to behave better. Okay?'

'Okay, Mum.'

'You don't have to be friends with someone you don't like, but that's no excuse for making their life a misery, is it?'

'No, Mum.'

'Now wipe your eyes and give me a kiss.' She leant down and hugged her son.

'Can I have the telly on now, Mum?'

She smiled. 'All right, but just until half-past, then bed.'

Her heart was aching as she thought of her children, did they really understand what was happening? Did they think they were in some way to blame for their father abandoning them? What on earth was she going to do to help them all through this?

CHAPTER 9

Teddy couldn't remember ever being in such an awkward position before; it was like walking a tightrope between his brother's family and Carla and her friends. If only Alan had agreed to come to the funeral with him, but he was too shrewd; he knew exactly what it would be like, and anyway he hadn't wanted a confrontation with Teddy's mother, who continued to treat him like her son's lodger.

Teddy followed his niece down the hill to The Yew Tree, where Carla had arranged the wake.

'Who on earth is that man talking to Carla?' Sylvia asked her uncle.

'Can't say Darling. Never seen him before but he doesn't seem to be Carla's type.'

'Maybe he's her solicitor.'

'Now why would she need a solicitor?'

'You've heard that we're going to sell the house?'

'Harry's house?'

'Actually it's our house now, Tom's and mine.'

'How do you know? I thought Ian still had to talk to Carla about the will?'

'Well, yes in a way, but as we were the only beneficiaries, Ian told us.

'I suppose it makes sense that Harry would want to leave you something,' said Teddy.

'Because he never did anything for us while he was alive, you mean?' snapped Sylvia.

Teddy decided to sidestep that comment, and asked instead, 'Didn't he leave anything to his wife?'

'No,' she replied, smiling smugly. 'There was only the house and he's left that to us.'

'But why sell it now?'

'Because I need the money,' his niece replied, helping herself to another glass of wine.

'Richard hasn't lost his job, has he?'

'Of course not, but the pay isn't very good, never has been. No it's because of Linda. Didn't Mum tell you? She's just been tested and they've discovered she's severely dyslexic. She can continue at her local school but the help they can give her is limited, so we want to send her to a private school that specialises in helping children with learning difficulties. It's not cheap and we just can't afford it on Richard's salary. The money from the sale would make all the difference.'

'Oh my poor Darling, can't your grandmother help you?'

'Gran? No she needs all her money in case she has to go into a nursing home. She's told me that she'll leave us both some money when she dies, but that could be quite a few years on yet. Linda needs help now.'

'What about re-mortgaging the house then?'

'Impossible, we're mortgaged to the maximum.'

'Of course, borrowing has been very difficult lately, I know.' Teddy had lost a lot of investments in the global financial crisis of the previous year. His professorship paid quite well and his outgoings were modest, but he still didn't have enough spare cash to help Sylvia.

'There's always your mother. Why don't you ask her?'

'No. I don't want to. She's had to struggle to get where she is today. I want her to enjoy it. Anyway, knowing Ian, he's probably persuaded her to invest it all in long term stocks and shares that can't be touched for years. The only solution is to sell the house in Spain. I know we can get a good price for it; people are moving out there all the time. I'd go too, if Richard would agree, but he loves England too much to leave.'

'So what about Carla? What did she say when you told her?'

'I haven't spoken to her. Ian is handling it all.'

'Where will she live if you sell?'

'How do I know? Do you think I really care about where Carla will live? She'll probably find someone else and shack up with them anyway.'

'Sylvia, that's a little harsh.' She'd been such a sweet child before Harry left.

'Maybe but she didn't care about us did she? Anyway I'm sure she has money of her own; she can buy another place, something smaller.'

'I'm not sure they had much money by the time your father died. Remember he sold his company twenty years ago; I doubt if there's much left by now.'

'That's her problem. She can go back to work, like the rest of us.'

It pained him to see her still so bitter about her father, but he could understand. She had worshipped Harry, but once he came under Carla's spell he didn't seem able to find time for his children. He hadn't made it easy for them, or for Barbara.

*

That Sunday it was all too much for Barbara; she'd tried to be strong for the children's sake but already the tears were welling in her eyes. She pushed her unfinished plate away and stood up, hating the thought that Phoebe would see her like this. 'Please excuse me,' she said, hurrying into the kitchen and closing the door behind her.

She had come here to tell Harry's mother what had happened between them but it was proving impossible. Instead of offering her sympathy she knew her mother-in-law would gloat. If only her parents were still alive; just lately she had felt their loss more keenly than ever. She splashed some water on her face and took a few deep breaths, then pulled out a tissue and dabbed at her make-up. The face that looked back at her from the mirror was beginning to look lined and tired; she was moving into middle age and the telltale signs were already starting to show; what Harry used to call her laughter lines were now crows' feet, etched into her skin. Her jaw line had thickened, and the skin under her chin had the faintest suggestion of a droop. Her reddish blond hair was sprinkled with grey, and the distress of the previous week had left her green eyes dull and lacklustre, all portents of what she had to look forward to in a lonely old age. She held back the desire to cry again and turned to her son who was watching her anxiously from the doorway.

'Mummy, Gran says we can go out to play. Is that all right?'

'Of course it is sweetheart. You run along.'

She watched as her children rushed through the yard and into the garden. The wind had come up and a sudden gust caught hold of the dead leaves that Phoebe had recently swept and piled next to the dustbin, blowing them along the path. Her neighbour's tortoiseshell cat leapt out of the hedge and gave chase, bounding along the path after the spiralling leaves, leaping and trying to catch them. The children laughed and ran after it; they were happy to be outside, free from the restraints of the dining table. Their laughter ate at her heart; how frail and vulnerable they were. What would happen to them now, with no father to look after them?

'So what's this all about, Barbara? It's not like you to have a bout of hysterics at the meal table.' Her mother-in-law came into the kitchen carrying a pile of dirty plates.

'Come and sit down Phoebe, I have something to tell you.' She led her mother-in-law into the lounge and sat down beside her.

'This is about Harry I suppose? What's he been up to now? And where is he today? Couldn't find time to come to lunch with his mother?'

'He's working.'

'Hmmn. Never seems to have time for his family these days.'

'That's his job, he always works weekends, and anyway he's been rather busy lately.'

'He hasn't been to see me since Christmas and I don't know when he last telephoned. You'd think he could find the time to pick up the telephone and ring his mother wouldn't you. It's a good job I've got Teddy. I don't know what I'd do without Teddy. He's such a considerate boy.'

'Have you heard from Teddy lately? Is he enjoying his new job?' Barbara asked.

'Oh yes. He's doing very well. He's Doctor Wilkinson now you know, PhD. He's doing extremely well.' Barbara already knew about his doctorate as Phoebe had been straight on the telephone to tell everyone the minute she had heard. 'He's still in that rambling old house near the university. I've told him it's far too big for him but he won't listen. He's got a lodger, you know. Sounds a nice young man, works in the chemistry laboratory. He probably sees my Teddy as a sort of mentor figure.'

'Oh you must mean Alan?' Barbara knew instantly that she'd said the wrong thing.

'Alan. Yes that's his name. How do you know him?'

'Oh it's just that Teddy and he popped in one day to see us. They were on their way somewhere and we were on route I guess.' She didn't know how much Teddy had told his mother about Alan so she decided to keep her comments vague. When her mother-in-law didn't reply she continued, 'Yes he's a very nice man. They stayed and had some lunch with us.'

'Teddy never told me.'

'I expect he forgot. It wasn't anything important, just lunch.'

'So what's this all about? I'm sure you didn't just want to talk about Teddy?'

'You're right. I want to talk to you about Harry. Harry and me.' She paused then continued, 'Harry and I have agreed to divorce.'

'That doesn't surprise me,' Phoebe snapped, without even a blink of surprise. 'When did this happen then?'

Barbara swallowed hard before answering, 'Last week.' The look of something almost akin to pleasure that appeared on her mother-in-law's face made it hard for her to continue; it was as though she were thinking 'I knew it would never last.'

'Just like that? What he got up one morning and asked for a divorce?' asked Phoebe.

'Not exactly, he's found someone else. He's not been living at home for almost six months.'

'But you never said anything.'

'No, I didn't want to worry you. Anyway I thought it was probably a mid-life crisis. I thought he'd come back and we'd work something out, but apparently not. He's in love,' she said bitterly. 'He's not coming back.'

'In love? What rot. That boy's never loved anyone but himself. He could never make a success of anything, not even his marriage. I could have told you from the start it would end like this.'

'That's not fair,' Barbara protested weakly. 'We've been married over twenty years and he's always been a good husband and an excellent father.' She was keenly aware of the irony in defending her unfaithful husband against his mother.

'But that hasn't stopped him going off with some floozy has it. Oh what will Teddy say about it?'

'Teddy? This hasn't anything to do with Teddy. It's us we're talking about, Harry and me.'

'I know, but Teddy has always looked out for his little brother. How's he going to feel now? Disappointed I can tell you. Let down.'

Barbara could feel the tears starting again, but whether they were from self-pity or sheer frustration she was not sure. They had been married twenty years, five months and thirteen days, happily married she would have said if anyone had asked. She still couldn't believe that this was happening to her. She had been so sure that they were happy; they had a good sex life, or so she thought, and best of all they were such close friends. It was this friendship that had bound them together for so many years. She couldn't bear it. She couldn't bear to lose him.

'Now there's no good crying over spilt milk,' her mother-in-law said briskly. 'What you have to do now is think of the children.'

'I know, but I can't focus on anything beyond the fact that he's gone.'

'What about this woman? What do you know about her?'

Barbara blew her nose loudly before replying, 'Not much. I think she's younger than me. She's something to do with fashion. Harry met her at a fashion show when he was working.'

'I knew that job of his would lead to trouble, all those weird people, pop stars and models. It's no wonder he's gone off. All that glamour's gone to his head. He was always like that, easily influenced. Just an overpaid electrician who thought he was something he wasn't.'

'He says he loves her.'

'What does he know about love? Love is feeding your family, putting the bread on the table, not prancing about with fashion models.'

'She's not a model,' Barbara insisted. She felt even more plain and dowdy. Already she was asking herself if it was her own fault. Had she let her appearance go? Had she become too narrow, letting her world shrink to the size of her home and family? In the early days of their marriage they had talked and argued about all sorts of things, politics, art, theatre. But once the children were born, slowly but surely, their conversations centred more and more on domestic details, and world issues had dimmed to insignificance. Maybe she should have returned to work once Tom had started school. Well that was exactly what would have to happen now; they would never be able to manage on what she knew Harry could give them. She stood up. 'Look I think we'll go. Thanks for the lunch. I'm sorry to bring you such bad news, but you had to know.'

'Never thinks of anyone but himself, Harry this, Harry that. What about the pain he's causing his poor mother, never mind his wife and children. I suppose he might find the time to tell me himself one day. Or is that too much to ask? If he's not too busy with his glamorous fashion model, that is.'

'I expect he'll ring you.' She left her mother-in-law still talking to herself and went to call the children.

*

As they drove home she could hear the children arguing quietly in the back seat; they were playing some game that involved spotting number plates but Tom couldn't really

113

grasp the complicated rules that Sylvia had devised. She switched on the radio and flicked through the channels; someone was playing Elgar's violin concerto, a favourite of hers but far too sad in her present mood, a man from the Environment Agency was talking about the need to spend more on flood defence, and a woman was giving recipes for home baking. Eventually she found something light and relaxing and was humming along to 'An Englishman in New York' when the broadcast was interrupted to give a severe weather warning, 'Strong winds and heavy rain are forecast for many parts of southern England and the Midlands today. You are strongly advised to stay at home unless your journey is absolutely necessary.'

She automatically slowed her speed and pulled back into the centre lane. It had been raining steadily since she had left Phoebe's, and now she could feel the car being buffeted by the wind. Although it was still afternoon the October sky was already dark, and visibility was poor. Perhaps she should have waited for an improvement in the weather before leaving, but she had not given it a thought in her anxiety to be out of earshot of her mother-in-law. The rhythmical clacking of the windscreen wipers grated on her already frayed nerves and she longed to switch them off, but the rain was too heavy. She slowed her speed to forty miles an hour and pulled into the slow lane, but this made it worse as cars continued to speed past, showering her car with a muddy spray that all but obliterated her view.

'I'm going to pull off the motorway, kids. I think we'll take the back road home, okay?'

Her children said nothing; they were too engrossed in what they were doing. She felt a surge of love for them, poor things; how would they cope when they realised that Harry was never coming back? A sharp pain ran through her chest; she didn't want to admit to herself that her marriage was about to be over; at least for a little while longer, she needed to cling to the hope that it had all been a mistake and all would return to normality.

She'd been thirty-five when Sylvia was born, almost at the point of resigning herself to a childless marriage. She and Harry had always wanted children; they both agreed that it would make their marriage complete, but try as they might she couldn't become pregnant. The doctor had sent her for dozens of examinations and tests, but they could find nothing wrong, no reason not to conceive. The doctor wanted to examine Harry as well but he refused. It was one of the few times that they had really quarrelled, but no matter what she said, no matter how much she pleaded he wouldn't go. 'If it's going to happen, it will happen,' he said. 'It doesn't affect how much I love you.' So she had left it and waited.

Quite a few cars were also pulling off the motorway and she found she was now in a slow moving queue of traffic leading down to the slip road. There were two routes home; the more direct one led through the town, the other, a mile or so longer, took the back lane down to the river. Their house was three hundred metres from the riverbank on the lower slopes of Town Marsh. She hoped the river was not rising too quickly; some years the bottom part of their garden flooded, but the water had never risen as far as the house.

Now what was her role to be? Mother and father? She suddenly felt angry with her husband. Well if he didn't want them, then they didn't want him. She would cope on her own. After all she was used to doing things without him; he had always been away so much anyway. With mind-clearing clarity it suddenly dawned on her that his trips had become more frequent over the past few years, and that even when he was working locally he had been coming home later and later. Now she understood why. She felt sick at how easily she had been deceived.

She arrived at the roundabout and turned out of the traffic and down the back lane. At first the track was clear but by the time she noticed that the water pooling on the road surface was rising, it was too late to turn back. She slowed down to a crawl, frightened of getting water into the engine compartment; it was already halfway up the wheels, and try as she might she couldn't stop the water from spraying up around her. She rounded a bend and braked hard; someone had stopped a van in the lane in front of her. She pressed hard on the horn but there was no response, so she tried to put the car into reverse, thinking that it would be better if she backed up after all and returned to the main road.

'Mummy, the water's getting deeper,' Sylvia complained. 'Let's go back, Mummy.'

In her haste Barbara let her foot slip off the clutch and felt the car stall. 'Oh God, please let it start again,' she said aloud. She could see the pale scared faces of her children watching her; tears were trickling down Tom's cheeks. She switched off the ignition then turned it on again. The engine gave a tired whirring sound but nothing happened. She tried again and then a third time.

'I think I'd better wait a bit in case I flatten the battery,' she explained to the children and switched the engine off. By now the water was coming under the car door and seeping across the floor. 'Tuck your feet up on the back seat kids. It's only a little water but there's no need to get your feet wet, is there. Good job you're not very big.'

'Good job Molly's not here. She doesn't like the water,' Tom managed to say as cheerfully as he could.

'That's true Darling. Cats hate water. She's probably curled up nice and dry on your bed right now.'

She swung her own feet across onto the passenger seat. There was at least six inches of water in the car by now and it was still rising. What should she do? She couldn't risk getting out and walking home, the water was sure to be deeper the nearer they got to the river. If she'd been on her own she might have tried it, but Tom was only eight years old, and although Sylvia was almost five feet in height and fairly well built for an eleven-year-old she was still a child. The lane was unlit and already the night was pitch black with both moon and stars hidden behind the dark rain clouds; she couldn't imagine either one of them wading through this deluge safely.

'Mummy, I'm frightened. Can't we put the light on?'

'No, Tom. I'm sorry but nothing is working now. We just have to be patient and wait a bit longer. Just think what an adventure this has become. You'll be able to tell all your friends about it at school tomorrow.' She reached down with her hand to feel the water; it was almost up to the seat now. What on earth should she do? At the moment the children were dry and sheltered but what if the water continued to rise? She needed to get to a telephone and quickly. There was a box on the corner, just before the turning into the lane. If she hurried it would only take her five minutes to get there. She looked at the children; Sylvia had her arm around Tom and was hugging him to her. 'Look, I'm going to phone for help. I won't be long. Stay where you are and don't move. Sylvia, lock the car doors when I get out. Okay?' She smiled at them. 'Don't worry, I'll be back before you can count to a thousand.'

Tom tried a brave smile then began, 'One, two.'

'Slower than that, silly,' Sylvia told him. 'Like this: one O'Reilly, two O'Reilly.'

Barbara heard the click as her daughter locked the door behind her. The water was cold and almost came up to her knees. She struggled back up the dark lane, slipping and stumbling in her haste. It took her only a few minutes to reach the main road; the telephone box was a hundred yards down on the right. The water here barely covered her shoes, and she ran, splashing through the stream until she reached it.

'Please let it be working,' she said as she dialled 999. The number seemed to ring interminably, at last an operator asked, 'Which service do you want? Police, ambulance service, fire service or coastguard?'

'Police,' she gasped. It took only a few minutes to explain to the policewoman who asked what had happened and where she was.

'I'm sorry Madam you will have to just sit tight for a while; we are inundated with emergency calls. We will get someone out to you as soon as we can.'

'But I have two young children here and the water is rising all the time.'

'I understand but please be patient. Stay in your car and keep the doors locked. We will get someone to you as soon as we can,' the woman repeated.

'Thank you,' she said, putting down the telephone. Barbara ran back to the car as quickly as she could; by now the rain was coming down heavier than ever and water was gushing along the lane in a torrent. She could just make out

Tom's face at the window, straining to see her. 'Let me in,' she shouted, banging on the door.

'Is someone coming for us Mummy?' Tom asked.

'Yes, Darling. The police will be along soon. Just curl up close to Sylvia and don't let your feet get wet.'

'We counted to nine hundred and ninety two, Mummy,' he said.

'So I only just made it then,' she said with a smile.

'Yes, but I was counting very slowly,' he admitted.

'Will they be long Mummy?' asked Sylvia.

'No, they'll soon be here, Darling.'

How could she have been so blind? He had known this woman for three years he told her. Three years and during all that time she'd never guessed that anything was wrong between them, until that day when he said he was going to leave them. They had even started to talk about how they would celebrate their twenty-fifth wedding anniversary. It was Harry who had suggested taking her to Florence for a week and leaving the children with his mother. That was to be a special trip, just the two of them together, a second honeymoon he'd said. It had all been a lie, designed to close her eyes to what was going on. Tears of disappointment and an unspeakable sadness overwhelmed her as she thought about it. She knew now that she had not only lost her future but also her past; she could never look back on their time together without a feeling of bitterness. It was as though all those wonderful years were lost forever; a scrapbook of memories cast on the flames of betrayal. In that moment, sitting there in the darkness with the water creeping up the side of the car, she decided that she would give him his divorce, put it all behind her and remake her life.

'Will the policeman be much longer, Mummy?' asked Tom.

How long had been since she'd telephoned? It felt like hours, but she calculated that it was probably no more than twenty minutes. 'Why don't we sing a song?' she said.

'Okay,' Tom replied a little reluctantly. Normally Tom loved singing in the car.

'How about Ten Green Bottles?'

'No, Old MacDonald.'

'Okay, you too Sylvia.'

Barbara began, 'Old MacDonald had a farm.'

'Eyai eyai oh,' sang Tom.

'And on this farm he had a cow.' Both children started to sing lustily and soon the car was filled with the sounds of mooing cows, clucking hens and sundry sounds from the farmyard.

They were into verse six when she noticed a light in the lane behind them. 'Keep singing kids. I think there's someone coming.' A large breakdown truck pulled up behind them and two men got out. Barbara wound down the window and stuck her head out. 'Over here. Can you help us, we're stranded.' By the light of the truck's headlights she could make out the men wading towards them. One wore a fluorescent yellow jacket and some sort of cap. 'Oh thank God. Am I glad to see you. My car stalled and now I can't get it to start. We've just been sitting here; I didn't know what else to do.'

'That's okay lady, you did the right thing to sit it out. The police gave us your location.' He flashed his torch into the car. 'Hello you two. Hang on there and we'll get you out of this in a tick.' He pulled the back door of the car open and lifting Tom clear, carried him back to his truck.

The second man put his head in the car. 'Hello Mrs Wilkinson. I thought I recognised the car.'

It was Dickie Reynolds, the lock keeper. 'Hello Dickie. I didn't realise that was your van. Thank goodness you came back; I just didn't know what to do. The water keeps rising and rising.'

'Now don't you worry. It's beginning to go down now. They've opened the sluice gates further downstream and the water's starting to flow more quickly. It'll soon be back to normal.'

Barbara reached down with her hand; he was right, the water level was dropping at last. She pushed open the car door and lowered her feet into the icy water and felt her calf muscles tense against the cold. She could hear the wind howling in the trees, an eerie, desperate sound that chilled her more than the water, and she was glad that these men had come to their rescue.

Dickie reached into the car and pulled Sylvia across his shoulder. 'There we go my girl, a fireman's lift for you,' he said. He made his way towards the truck and Barbara followed him, her shoes slipping on the uneven surface as she waded against the current.

She could see the water, black and shiny in the headlights, swirling its way down towards the river. Thank God it is almost over, she thought.

'You wait here in the cab while I hitch up your car. Won't take long then I'll run you all back to the town,' said the man in the yellow jacket.

'Yes I don't think it's a good idea for you to go home tonight. Better to wait until daylight when you can see what's what,' Dickie suggested. 'Where's Mr Wilkinson? Is he at home?'

'No, he's away on business,' she lied. One day she was going to have to admit it aloud, tell people that he had left her, but right now the humiliation was too great. No matter how blameless she was, people would always think that she had contributed to the break-up of their marriage. And maybe she had, by no longer being the woman he'd married.

'I'll take you to Spean's Field,' he said. 'They're using the school as a refuge. All the people from Towpath Lane have been flooded out of their homes. There's quite a party going on there.' He smiled at her. How kind he was, and her anger against Harry returned, refuelled by his absence in their moment of need.

'That's okay. Just give me a lift to the village and I'll telephone my friend. I'm sure we can stay with her tonight.' She turned to the children, who were beginning to tremble with the cold. 'You'd like that wouldn't you Tom, Sylvia? If we go and have a sleep-over at Mary's?'

Tom began to giggle. 'Mums don't go on sleep-overs,' he said.

'Maybe just this once sweetheart. Okay?'

The children nodded. She could see the exhaustion in their faces and again felt a surge of love for them; they had been so brave and uncomplaining. If only Harry had been there to see them.

CHAPTER 10

Carla had been surprised to see the church so full. A lot of people had made the effort to come to Harry's funeral. According to Teddy, many of them were friends from the old days: from his schooldays, from work and from the cricket club. Most of them, not unsurprisingly, looked a similar age to Harry. She watched Teddy smiling and nodding at them as they came into the pub; he was in deep conversation now with a man wearing a well-worn and rather faded cricket blazer. None of them spoke to her or even acknowledged her presence, although they surely knew who she was. Barbara too, knew these people. They were from her past, her life with Harry, not Carla's.

The man wearing the cricket blazer had got up in the church and paid a tribute to Harry, saying how much he was liked and respected by his friends, and reminding them of the time he scored a hundred runs and saved an important needle match against Maidenhead Cricket Club. He was talking about a man she barely knew and had long since vanished.

*

Carla crossed Waterloo Bridge and began to stroll along the Victoria Embankment. It was almost lunchtime and people were emerging from their offices to enjoy the weak, spring sunshine. She walked slowly, stopping from time to time to stand and gaze across the river at the Festival Hall. The terrace was filling up with people, mostly couples who sat at tables drinking café latte or sipping from large goblets of white wine. She felt alone, not lonely but alone. She needed someone in her life. Until she had met Harry she had been too busy for a steady relationship; there had been a few dates but nothing serious. She had been so focussed on building her career that her work had taken up all of her time. Now she realised that it was not enough. She wanted someone to share her life with. She would be thirty-six in a few weeks and she was beginning to realise that if she wanted to have any children she had better think about it soon.

She sat on a bench and began her mental checklist. She would begin with the 'cons.' The first and most important objection was that he was married, then there was the fact that he had two young children. At this she stopped. Why *young* children? Would it make it better if they were older? Probably not. They would be hurt by their father's betrayal whatever age they were. As far as she was concerned it was the children she felt guilty about; how could she contemplate having children of her own when she had deprived his children of their father? It seemed so unfair on them.

Then there were the economic considerations. It would be expensive to divorce his wife and Carla realised she didn't know anything about Harry's financial situation. She was not a mercenary woman but she was practical and she knew that lack of money could lead to acrimony. Who did the house belong to? Was the wife likely to be awarded the house because she had two children to care for? The children again. Naturally Harry would want access to his children. That would mean their precious time together would be eaten into by paternal visits, trips to the zoo, football matches, children's cinema. Would she be included? Would the children accept her? Then there was the risk that Harry might not want to have any more children as he had two already. Could she cope with that?

She began to feel depressed and turned to the 'pros.' Head and shoulders above everything else was the fact that she loved him and he loved her. But was that a good enough reason for breaking up someone's marriage, a small voice inside her head asked? Well she argued, he and his wife had fallen out of love a long time ago, so he would be getting out of a loveless marriage. It cannot have been good for the children living in a home where their parents constantly argued and slept in separate rooms. It would probably be good for everyone if he made a clean break.

So what else was so special about Harry? Well he made her laugh. He made her feel loved and when she was not with him she couldn't stop thinking about him. All very selfish considerations but, as she reasoned, if she stopped being selfish then she would walk away right now. She knew she couldn't do that, but at the same time she couldn't share him. He was going to have to make up his mind; either he wanted her or he wanted his wife, he couldn't have both.

Her mobile began to hum. It was Harry. 'Hi sweetheart. Where are you?'

At the sound of his voice she felt her resolve weaken and a wave of desire took hold of her so that when she spoke her voice trembled. 'Working,' she whispered.

'Oh. Look sorry to interrupt but I just wanted to hear your voice. You seemed a bit down yesterday so I thought I'd check that everything was okay.'

'Yes, it's fine.'

'Can I see you tonight?'

'Tonight? Don't you have to be at home tonight?'

'Yes but I can see you for a short while. If you would like to, that is?' he added, dropping his voice intimately. This was the point to say no, to refuse, to make up some excuse about being busy. But she wasn't busy and right now the 'pros' and 'cons' of their relationship didn't matter; she just wanted to be with him. When she didn't reply he continued, 'I could come round to the flat, say about seven?'

'Yes, I'd like that,' she replied, throwing away her mental checklist because she knew that she was never going to give him up, no matter what.

*

He was working in Bristol the following weekend, but she had decided not to go with him because she had some leather skirts to finish for a new boutique that had opened in Covent Garden. She was just hemming the lining of the last one when the telephone rang. It was Harry to say that he had something important to tell her and would be round in half an hour. She could hear the excitement in his voice but he refused to say any more.

'I want to see your face when I tell you,' he explained.

She tried to concentrate on her sewing but her head was buzzing with questions. It was now six months since he had told his wife that he was leaving her. He had packed a bag and moved in with Carla the same day. At first she'd been pleased that he had at last made the choice between them, but as the weeks went by and he never mentioned the subject of divorce, she began to wonder if he was really serious about it. True it was wonderful to wake up each morning and see him lying by her side, and to be able to go out openly without always having to worry who they would bump into, but gradually she began to feel that something was missing. They were in a steady relationship it was true but, no matter what he told her, the fact was that he was still married to someone else. Now when he worked late she began to worry that he was going to see his family without telling her. She had asked him once, saying that she wouldn't mind, that it was natural that he would want to see his children, but she would just like to know. He'd got angry and said no, he was not visiting Barbara or the children; for a start he didn't want to disrupt his children's lives any more than he already had, by coming and going. He'd made his choice and that was that. She had to accept it, but it didn't stop her wondering where he was.

*

She'd arranged to meet Jenny at Starbucks in Covent Garden; she was taking her to meet a new client, the wife of a well-known playwright. As usual Carla was early, or as she reminded herself as she looked at her watch, she was on time and Jenny was tardy as always. She ordered herself an espresso and positioned herself at a table in the corner where she had a view of all the comings and goings in that busy street. When she had a few minutes to spare this is what she liked to do, people watch. It was her way of keeping abreast of what was currently in fashion, not the fashion that she viewed in the glossy magazines or on the television but the fashion of the streets. It was almost the same as when she was at art college; then she gleaned her ideas from the styles of her peers now she looked to the youngsters for inspiration, with their eclectic and uninhibited style of dressing. Some of her wealthy clients, especially the older ones would probably be horrified if she told them that creations she had made for them had been inspired by a young girl in full Goth regalia or another dressed in a man's trench-coat obviously picked up at an Oxfam shop. She could see Jenny on the other side of the street, her head was down, pushing her way through a crowd of people. What would she say when Carla told her the news? It was all right for Harry to say that her business could go on as usual but it would not be that simple. How could she just pop over to London any time Jenny wanted her to meet someone? With a pang she suddenly realised how much she was going to miss living in London.

'Hi, been waiting long?' a breathless Jenny gasped, slumping into the seat opposite her. She pulled out a packet of cigarettes and lit one.

'Not really, I just got here. The usual?'

'Please. Make it a large one; I'm suffering from caffeine deficiency.'

Carla wandered back to the counter and ordered a double latte and another espresso for herself.

'Right, tell me about this playwright,' she said, putting the coffees down on the table between them.

'Joe Rushton? He's brilliant. His play, Summer Lies, has been in the West End now for almost a year. Have you seen it?'

Carla shook her head. 'No. When do I ever get time to go to the theatre?'

'You should. You'd love it.'

'Harry's not keen on live theatre.'

'What does that mean? He likes the actors to be dead?' Jenny giggled and stubbed her half-smoked cigarette into the ashtray.

'You know what I mean, he likes film and TV. He says the actors always seem to be projecting themselves in the theatre. He thinks it sounds false.'

'That's what acting's all about; it's not reality TV.'

'Anyway, tell me about Mrs Rushton.'

'Sandra. She's in her fifties, rather overweight and ordinary, but now that her husband has become famous she wants to improve her image.'

'So how did you get to know her?'

'She went to one of those colour consultants and was talking to a friend of mine about how difficult it was to find clothes that were flattering to her shape. My friend suggested that she get in touch with me.'

'So here we are.'

'Yes, it's quite a project for me, not only is she after some leather outfits but it sounds as though she wants a whole new wardrobe. I'm going to be busy for a few months with this one.'

'That's good, isn't it?'

'Any work is good, Carla.'

'You'll be her personal shopper?'

'Something like that.'

'Great, all that shopping and not having to spend your own money; I'd love it.'

'Anyway, like I said she's after a couple of leather outfits, some tight trousers and a long coat. Naturally I thought of you.'

'Naturally.'

Carla wondered whom Jenny would think of contacting when she was in Spain; it was not guaranteed that it would be her.

'What time did you say we'd be there?'

'Eleven-thirty, plenty of time yet. I thought we'd just take the Tube; I've parked my car miles away.'

'Fine by me. Tight trousers you said?'

Jenny grimaced. 'Yes, well you decide when you see her.'

Carla sipped her coffee and looked at Jenny, she was skimming through her engagement diary. 'Jenny, I've got something to tell you.' Her friend looked at her over the top of her glasses. 'Harry's asked his wife for a divorce.'

'Wow, he's done it at last. I never thought he would.'

'He wants to marry me.'

'That's wonderful Carla. God, you must be so pleased.'

'Yes, I suppose so.'

'What do you mean suppose so? This is what you've been on about for ages. Don't tell me that you've changed your mind?'

'No, it's not that. Of course I want to marry him.'

'So what is it?'

'He wants us to live in Spain.'

'What permanently?' Carla nodded.   'But what about your business?'

'My sewing, as he calls it? Harry seems to think I can sew anywhere; he doesn't see it as an obstacle.'

'Well I'm gob-smacked, just when your label is getting known.'

'He seems to think you and I can carry on working together as before. It will just mean a lot more travelling to and fro.'

'I suppose we can but it will need some thought,' Jenny replied.

Carla could see that the news had come as a complete shock to her friend. 'So I don't know if it's worth going to see Mrs Rushton, in the circumstances,' she added.

'Of course it is. When are you planning to leave this wet, cold country for sunshine and sangria?'

'The end of March. Harry's got to sell his company first.'

'So, at least six months then?' Carla nodded. 'Plenty of time to hook the overweight Mrs Rushton as a favoured client. Once she's bought one of your creations she won't care if you're in Spain or Timbuktu.'

'You think so?'

'Of course. It may even give your designs a certain cachet.'

'Jenny, you're fantastic. How can you always be so positive?'

'Look Carla, Harry's right in a way, when you've got a good product you can market it from anywhere. It'll be a bit more complicated at first, but Spain's not that far away and anyway it will give me a good reason for trotting off to the sunshine every so often, and I can claim it on expenses too.'

Carla drained the last of her espresso. Jenny's enthusiasm was catching; she would go to Spain with Harry and she'd continue with her career. She could do both.

CHAPTER 11

Carla leaned against the wall, surveying the room. These people couldn't wait to be rid of her. It was as though Harry's death had released them from any obligation towards her. Only dear old Teddy, vainly trying to tempt his mother with some triangles of pizza, was genuinely fond of her, but even he would never break the habit of a lifetime and speak out against the family. Jenny was happily engaged in conversation with Chris and Geraldine, but the rest of her guests looked as though they were waiting for the right excuse to leave. She felt an unbearable loneliness and wished that Harry, despite his failings, was there beside her. A howl was forming in her belly and working its way up to her throat; she swallowed hard and forced it down again, where it sat, a tight, twisted knot under her rib cage, refusing to go away.

'So Carla I suppose we'll be seeing a lot more of you now.' It was Richard, refilling his glass and leering at her in a slightly lop-sided way. She presumed the wine was starting to affect him by the way he was swaying slightly.

'Why's that, Richard?'

'Now that you're moving back here I'm sure that we can keep in touch. Family and all that.'

'I'm not sure I understand you. I've no plans for moving back to England. Whatever gave you that idea?'

'Oh, sorry, I just assumed that once the house was sold you'd come back here. Going to find yourself a pad in Spain, eh? Can't blame you, all that sun and sea.'

'Richard, you're not making yourself very clear. Which house is being sold?' The embarrassed look on his face made her go cold, and before he spoke she knew his answer.

'Why Harry's house of course. Don't tell me you don't know that it's on the market? Hasn't Sylvia's solicitor been in touch with you yet?'

Carla just stared at him, unable to keep her look of horror and astonishment hidden. They hadn't even discussed Harry's will with her yet, and already they were thinking of selling her home.

'Oh God. Look Carla, I'm so sorry. I thought you knew. I'd never have brought it up otherwise, especially today of all days. I'm so sorry,' he repeated, looking round the room in desperation.

The man in the charcoal grey suit who had accompanied Barbara into the church, came hurrying across. 'Hello Carla, may I introduce myself? I'm Ian Routh, the family's solicitor.' He offered her a rather curt handshake. 'I'm very sorry about your husband's death. I expect you got my letter?' He didn't wait for her to reply but continued, 'Barbara told me you were having this internment, but I didn't want to disturb you today. I thought we could discuss it when you come to the office and I'll go over Harry's will with you. But I see that Richard has already mentioned that the house is on the market.' He frowned at Richard, disapprovingly.

'Sorry-o. Didn't realise you hadn't told her, Ian,' he said.

They both looked at Carla expectantly, but she couldn't respond; her heart was beating too wildly and all she could hear was its frantic thudding in her chest.

'Today's not a good day; I can see that. We'll discuss it in my office. Would next Thursday at ten o'clock suit you?' said Ian.

Carla felt the blood drain from her head and for a moment she swayed, letting the room spin away from her.

'Are you all right, Carla? Here let me help you. Carla?' Richard took her arm firmly and someone pushed a chair towards her. She sat down gratefully, trying hard to regain her composure. She was aware that the rest of the mourners were watching her, and for a second felt more concerned about this slip of demeanour than the news she'd just received. 'Here, have a sip of this.' Richard, sobered by his gaff and smiling apologetically, offered her a glass of wine.

Carla took the wine and drank from it in silence, aware of a lull in the conversation. 'I'm fine. Please don't fuss. It's just been rather an emotional day.' So Harry hadn't finished ruining her life, reaching out from the grave to deal her one more blow.

'Of course,' murmured the solicitor.

She put down the empty glass and looked at him, her resolve strengthened by the alcohol and her anger at her dead husband. 'Thursday at ten o'clock, you said? And where exactly?' Her tone was hard and matter of fact.

'Here's my card. The office is in Maidenhead, Castle Hill. It's very easy to find and we have our own car park,' he added, smugly.

'Fine, I'll see you next week then.'

Carla's mind was racing with the news of the house sale but she didn't feel able to talk to anyone about it. She would have liked to grab Jenny's arm and run outside there and then so they could speak in private but she couldn't be the first to leave. As she turned to go back to the bar someone touched her arm lightly.

'Arnie. What on earth are you doing here?' she asked unable to keep the surprise from her voice.

'Not a nice way to greet an old friend, Carla. I've come to say goodbye to my old mate 'Arry, of course. Sorry I missed the funeral, but then 'Arry was never very big on funerals was 'e.'

'Sorry Arnie. It was just such a shock to see you here. I didn't realise that you knew I was bringing his ashes back.'

'Can't keep much secret in El Paraíso I'm afraid. Actually Maisie told me. I was coming over 'ere anyway. Got a few property deals to see to, so thought I'd come along and pay my respects.'

'That's very kind of you.' She could feel people watching them, probably wondering who this thuggish looking man was, and she squirmed with embarrassment. The truth was, she barely recognised him; he'd put on weight and was now completely bald, having shaved off what remaining hair he had. 'Help yourself to something to eat, Arnie,' she said, hoping to get away from him.

'No thanks, but I'll have a drink though. What more fitting way to say goodbye to my boozy, old chum.' He picked up a glass of wine and raised it in a mock toast. She felt her old dislike for the man returning. She hadn't seen him since well before Harry died; he too had dropped Harry when he became a social embarrassment. She hoped he wasn't going to talk to anyone about Harry's death; so far she had managed to keep her husband's drinking a secret from the family.

What was Arnie up to? Had he really just come to pay his respects, or did he have a wider agenda? He wasn't the sort of man who did anything without a reason. He had set his sights on Harry from day one. She thought back to how he had wormed his way into their lives.

*

Carla and Harry arrived at Málaga airport with four, overweight suitcases, their E111 insurance cards, passports, chequebooks and very little else. She couldn't believe it had all happened so quickly. Harry's friend had been as good as his word and loaned them a large villa with a swimming pool on the outskirts of Marbella. It was like living on a film set; she wandered from one marble-floored room to the next, the bathroom was tiled from floor to ceiling, with a bath that was big enough for three people and had gold plated taps. The kitchen was fitted with every labour-saving device imaginable, while the sunken lounge with its white leather sofas led onto a spacious terrace with views that stretched out across the bay. Palm trees lined a garden of immaculate lawns and carefully cultivated hibiscus, and alongside the kidney shaped pool were garden chairs and tables neatly set out under a large white canopy. He had even arranged for a maid to bring them fresh towels each day and clean up after them.

This was a level of luxury she was unused to and, after the initial delight of living there, began to feel increasingly uncomfortable with. 'Harry I think we should do something about finding ourselves a place of our own, don't you?' she suggested one morning after they had been living there for two months.

'I thought you liked it here.'

'I do, in a way.'

'So what's the problem?'

'It's like being in a hotel; nothing is ours.'

'I don't see anything wrong with that.'

'It's not a proper home. I'd like us to get our own place. That's what we talked about wasn't it?'

'What's the hurry? There's plenty of time to settle down. Just chill out and enjoy yourself.'

'But we can't stay here forever. We'd be taking advantage of your friend's generosity. Why don't we go into town and look around the estate agents?'

'If you want, but not today.'

'No, of course not. But we could go into town next week and just see what there is.'

'Just as you wish, Darling. Now come over here and give me a kiss.'

*

'The Harringtons are coming over to play tennis and then we're going to the club for lunch. Had you forgotten?' Harry told her over breakfast.

She hadn't forgotten but she had hoped that he had. Maisie and Fred Harrington had taken to coming over most days, and frankly she was bored with their company. Their conversation did not extend beyond tennis, the tennis club, their fellow members and where the best place was to eat that day. They were a couple in their early sixties who once upon a time must have had a normal life but now spent every waking moment trying to recapture their youth. He jogged before breakfast, swam, played the inevitable tennis and worked out at the gym once a week. She went to Pilates classes twice a week, did yoga each morning, played tennis slightly worse than her husband and spent a small fortune on creams and injections to restore her fading complexion.

'Can't we ring and put them off?'

'Whatever for? Don't you want to play?'

'It's not that I don't want to play tennis, it's just that I don't want to play every damn day. I want us to find a house of our own.'

'Don't you like it here? I thought you'd be happy in this house.'

Harry looked so dejected that she softened her voice before replying, 'No it's not that. Of course I'm happy here but it's like being on a permanent holiday. I want my own house and my own garden. I'm bored,' she finally admitted.

'Bored? I can't believe it. How can you be bored living in this beautiful house?'

'But it's not mine,' she almost screamed at him. 'I want us to look for our own place. I said that right from the start. You promised we'd look for one and that was ages ago. I want to get back to working again. I'm fed up spending all my time lying by the pool waiting for you to make a decision.'

'Okay. Okay. I've got the message. Tomorrow we'll go into Marbella and start looking. All right?'

'All right. And a job?'

'Don't worry about that. Arnie says he may have something for me, looking after his properties.'

Carla didn't bother to reply; this had become his standard answer. If only they could move away from here and get out of Arnie's sphere of influence then maybe they could get their lives organised.

*

Later that week Harry came home with a beaming smile on his face. 'Guess what, I've found us the perfect house,' he said.

'Wonderful. Is it that one we saw in Fuengirola?'

'No, that was far too expensive for what it was. No this is much better. It's just outside Marbella, on the road to Ronda, four bedrooms, swimming pool, great views, the lot.'

'How much?'

'Well within budget, in fact a damn good price. It's a repossession or something; Arnie arranged it for us.'

'What do you mean Arnie arranged it? What's Arnie got to do with it?'

'It used to be one of his properties. The guy living there hadn't been paying any rent, so he had to go. Arnie said it was a shame, but business is business and he needs the cash.'

She couldn't conceal her annoyance; once again they were tied to Arnie by yet another favour.

'God there's no pleasing you these days Carla. You said you wanted us to buy a house, well I've found one.'

'But why here? And why from Arnie? That one in Fuengirola that would have done us just fine.'

'Yes but at almost twice the price. Arnie's done us a good deal on this place and he's sending his guys over to repaint the whole house before we move in. What are you complaining about?' He poured himself a large gin and tonic and went outside.

'I would like to have been consulted,' she shouted after him. 'You've agreed to buy a house which I haven't even seen yet.'

Harry was clearly baffled at her lack of enthusiasm but how could she explain to him that she wanted to be free of Arnie and his friends? She wanted it to be just the two of them again, regardless of which house they bought.

Arnie had not been back to England since they arrived, and at the moment seemed to be happy to spend all his time in Spain. He came to the house most days and he and Harry would shut themselves in Harry's office to discuss business, but exactly what sort of business it was, Harry wouldn't say. She felt excluded.

Arnie made her feel uncomfortable. He was a Londoner in his mid-forties, overweight and with thick, greasy black hair. His attitude to women was pure pre-1960s and he vacillated in his approach to her between an oily lewdness and complete dismissal. His wife, whom Carla had met on a few brief occasions, was a timid, well dressed woman who wore enormous diamonds on her fingers, dangling earrings, and who followed blindly wherever her husband led. Harry's sequacity in all matters concerning Arnie was beginning to irritate Carla, but whenever she tried to mention her concerns it turned into an argument.

'I'm going back to the UK on Monday,' Harry said, coming back into the kitchen and refilling his glass. 'The date has been set for the divorce and the solicitor wants to go over the settlement with me.'

'Do you want me to come?'

'No need. I'll only be a couple of days. You can be getting things sorted out in the new house. I'll sign the papers tomorrow, before I leave. While I'm away it'll be a chance for you to do some sewing, curtains and things. Arnie says his wife will take you over if you want to measure up or anything.'

'Right. Okay. Do you want me to run you to the airport?'

'No need, Arnie's picking me up.'

She actually had a couple of orders to start, a jacket for Sandra Rushton, who had been so delighted with what Carla had made for her that she had told all her friends about her and an evening skirt for Melissa who had become a regular customer. She would be glad of some time on her own to get her work organized, despite feeling that she was being distinctly sidelined by the ever present Arnie.

CHAPTER 12

Carla was speaking to someone that Barbara didn't recognise, probably a friend of Harry's from Spain.

'Are you going to talk to her about the house?' Barbara asked her husband.

'Yes I've arranged all that and she's got my card, so don't worry.' Ian squeezed Barbara's hand affectionately.

'She doesn't look like I imagined,' she said softly.

'Have you never met her then?'

'You seem surprised. Why should I have met her? They moved to Spain not long after Harry left, and she didn't come to the divorce hearing. I wasn't actually going to bump into her, was I?'

'I suppose not. I thought that maybe you'd seen a photograph of her.'

'No, Harry was too careful to leave anything incriminating lying about. I had an idea of what she looked like from Phoebe and Teddy, but I never realised she was so lovely.'

'Yes, she's a good-looking woman, but she's not a patch on you,' he said, giving her hand another squeeze. 'You're not letting yourself get upset are you?'

'No of course not. It's twenty years now; I'm over all that.'

'Good. How about some more wine?'

'Okay.'

She continued to watch Carla while Ian went off to replenish their glasses. Was it true? Was she over it? Was the bitterness still lurking in her soul? Now that she saw her she wasn't so sure. True she'd pulled her life together and found a new man to love, but the sight of Carla after all these years had stirred up some painful memories. She didn't know how to react. At first she'd been surprised to hear from Sylvia that Carla was bringing Harry back to bury him, then she'd been angry that all the old wounds would be reopened, but now all she could feel was a general sadness, the lowering of spirits that always accompanies funerals. Despite being surrounded by her family she felt the odd one out; he was no longer her husband and she was not his widow, Carla was. She hadn't wanted to attend the funeral but in the end she felt it was the correct thing to do. Now how did she feel about Harry? What did one normally feel at funerals, sadness for an untimely death, the loss of a loved one, emptiness at the lonely life that stretched ahead? These didn't apply to her anymore; she was not the bereaved. She was not even the same woman that Harry had left all those years ago. That was the big difference; she had changed.

'Here you are sweetheart.' She took the proffered glass from Ian and smiled. 'Do you think I ought to speak to her? You know, offer my condolences?' she asked.

'It's up to you, Babs. Do you feel up to it?'

'I don't know. I'm not sure what I would say.'

'Why not wait until we leave then you can say something on the way out. That way it won't be too awkward for you.'

'Or for her. Yes, I'll do that.'

'Did you find out any more about how Harry died?' Ian asked, looking at his wife.

'Not sure, heart attack I think. Nobody has actually said what happened.'

'Did anyone try to resuscitate him? Did he go into hospital? Do we know anything?' Ian continued.

'To tell the truth Ian, I really don't know. The first thing I knew was when Tom rang me last year to say that his father had died, but by then he'd already been cremated.'

'That's what they do in Spain,' Teddy offered. 'Hot country you see. Can't have the bodies lying around for too long. All done and dusted in twenty-four hours.'

'So nobody really knows for sure how Harry died?' Ian persisted.

'Carla does of course.'

'But she hasn't told anyone?'

'Not in any detail. Look I don't know, Ian; you'd have to ask Tom. He's the only one who has had anything much to do with her,' Barbara replied. She didn't like the direction this conversation was going; it was making her feel uncomfortable so she decided to change the subject. 'Who's the man who was talking to Carla just now, Teddy?'

'Never seen him before. Looks a bit like a member of the Mafioso to me. No, wait. I heard someone call him Arnie. By the look of that tan, he's probably one of Harry's Spanish mates.'

'Mum, have you never wondered exactly how Dad died?' Sylvia asked, joining them and holding out her empty wine glass for Ian to fill it.

'Not you as well. All I know is what Tom told me, a heart attack.'

'I was just wondering the same thing, Sylvia,' Ian said. 'So, if it was a heart attack, do we know any of the details?'

'He had a heart attack and fell into the pool and drowned,' said Tom.

'And his body? Was there a post mortem?'

'I don't think so. You know they always bury them pretty quick in Spain. There's nothing sinister about that.'

'Yes, but he wasn't buried, was he. He was cremated.'

'Mmmn. Most people are cremated these days.'

'And why wait so long before bringing him home to be buried?' asked Sylvia. 'Even you found that a bit strange, Tom.'

'I suppose she just couldn't face it,' her brother replied.

'Couldn't face the questions more like. I think it's ridiculous that we're just going along with this charade and we have no idea how he died,' said Sylvia, her voice getting louder.

'Do you think it was foul play then?' Ian asked, looking relieved that he wasn't the only one with suspicions about Harry's death.

'It could be. Something's not right. I'm sure that woman's not telling us everything,' said Sylvia.

'Don't be ridiculous. Carla wouldn't do anything to hurt Dad. Why would she? What's she got to gain? He left most of his stuff to us.'

'Maybe she didn't know that. Maybe things were going on that we don't know about. After all, neither of us ever visited Dad and he never came to see us, except that one time when he came to sign the divorce papers.'

'This is getting stupid. If you really want all the gory details, ask her. I'm sure she'll tell you,' said Tom.

'Look Tom, you remember what a good swimmer Dad was. Why would he drown in his own swimming pool? It doesn't make sense.'

'I told you. He had a heart attack and fell in. The police were there. They'd have said something if they had thought it wasn't an accident.'

'How can you be so sure? It's Spain you're talking about, not London. They probably couldn't care less.'

'Sylvia, we need to go. Your grandmother is getting anxious,' said her husband.

'Yes, I know. Just a minute and I'll be with you.'

She watched Richard walk away in Phoebe's direction then resumed her conversation with her brother. 'I think we should ask Ian to make some enquiries.' She looked at Ian as she said it.

'Sylvia, don't you think it's a bit late for that?' her brother replied.

'No, I don't.' Her voice was raised and Ian noticed Barbara look at her in concern.

'Keep it down; everyone will hear you,' Tom hissed at her.

'So what? What do you say Ian? Do you think you could find out a bit more?'

'I suppose I could try.' He looked at Barbara. 'What do you think?'

'I think we should leave it. Harry's dead. There's nothing we can do about it.'

'But Mum, what if Dad's death wasn't an accident?' Barbara drew back and stared at her daughter. 'I just think we deserve to know the exact circumstances of his death, that's all. For example where was Carla when it happened? How could a strong swimmer like Dad drown in his own pool? Was there an inquest? Did he really have a heart attack?'

'Yes, do we know if he had problems with his heart before that?' asked Ian.

'Look Darling, let's discuss this later, when we're alone.'

'Yes,' Tom supported his mother emphatically. 'This is not the place to talk about it. This is Dad's funeral. Show some respect Sylvia.' He took the empty glass from his mother's trembling hand. 'Let me get you another drink, Mum. I think you've spilled most of that one. Another glass of red wine?'

Barbara nodded.

'Okay but I don't want this being swept under the carpet again. We need to know. I need to know,' Sylvia insisted.

Barbara hugged her daughter. She felt so sorry for her; Sylvia was eaten up with bitterness and desperate for someone to blame, and of course her anger was turned against Carla. The woman had ruined her childhood and left her broken and scarred. Her father hadn't just left them for another woman, he'd made it a permanent split by insisting on a divorce and then moving to a completely different country. And the worst part was that he never contacted Tom and Sylvia again. Her children had felt completely abandoned by him.

'Mum, we're going to take Gran home now, she's tired,' Sylvia said, putting her empty wine glass down beside them.

'Okay love. We'll be going soon as well.' She looked inquiringly at Ian. She longed to get away from this oppressive place, to leave the memories, the unanswered questions and the lies behind. Let them all go to the grave with him.

*

By the time her brother-in-law arrived carrying a large bunch of chrysanthemums and a bottle of champagne, the trauma of being caught in the floods had begun to ease. That morning Barbara had picked up her car from the garage and collected her children from Mary's house.

'So what's this I hear about you and Harry?' Teddy asked, pouring out the champagne.

'Your mother told you then.'

'Yes, so sorry old love. You've been together a long time now. It must be hard.'

'That's an understatement Teddy. It's bloody awful. I just can't believe he would do this to me, to us.'

'Here, try a spot of this. It's a new one I found in a little wine shop outside Nottingham. It'll perk you up a bit.' He handed her a glass of cold champagne. 'Cheers.'

'Why champagne, Teddy?'

'To toast your new life of course. Have to look to the future my girl. No point dwelling on the past. What's past is past. What's done is done. Here's to you and the future.'

She wouldn't have put it quite like that herself, but despite everything she felt cheered by Teddy's optimism and raised her glass. The champagne was dry and very cold, just the way she preferred. When had Harry last bought champagne? Probably last Christmas.

'It's just been such a shock Teddy. I really wasn't expecting this. I thought we were so happy together.' She sniffed and swallowed hard.

'So he wants a divorce. What will you do?'

'Give him one of course. I'm going to take your advice and look to the future while I'm still young enough to have one,' she added, holding her glass out for a refill.

'Mummy is that Uncle Teddy's car?' Sylvia called from the bedroom.

'Yes, come down and say hello.'

Both children rushed down the stairs, whooping and shouting with delight, 'Uncle Teddy. Do you know what happened to us last night?'

'We've been on a sleep-over and Mum came too.'

'It was really scary, Uncle Teddy.'

'The water was up to the top of my wellies but I didn't get wet. And a man gave Sylvia a fireman's lift.'

If Barbara had been expecting her children to be traumatised by their ordeal she was disappointed; their recovery seemed complete and the scare of the night before was now being retold as a great adventure. Once again she felt grateful for Mary's friendship; her support had helped them all. The champagne was beginning to go to her head and she lay back on the sofa and began to relax. Teddy was always so good with the children, and as usual he'd brought them presents and was watching as they opened them, ripping off the coloured paper in their haste.

'Great, a Transformer. Well good, uncle, just what I needed.' Tom began to pull at the stiff plastic.

'You don't need a Transformer, silly,' retorted his sister. 'Nobody needs toys. They want them but they don't need them.'

'I need it,' he insisted.

'Okay, don't argue you two,' Barbara interceded.

'Thanks Uncle. It's lovely. I wanted a new pencil case; I'll take it to school with me,' Sylvia said, going over and giving her uncle a kiss on the cheek.

'What's this, young man?' Teddy asked pulling at the long scarf Tom had wound around his neck.

'Chelsea,' Tom muttered, pulling away from his uncle.

'Why don't you both go and play upstairs for a while so I can talk to Uncle Teddy,' Barbara suggested.

The children climbed down from the wide expanse of Teddy's lap and collected up their things. 'You're not going yet are you Uncle Teddy?'

'No, not for a bit.'

'Uncle Teddy's staying for dinner I hope.' Barbara looked at her brother-in-law.

'Yes of course. Can't miss a chance to sample your delicious cooking, my dear.'

'Good. See you later then Uncle Teddy.'

'See you later alligator,' Tom echoed.

The children disappeared in the direction of the playroom. Barbara could still hear them bickering, and suddenly the lounge felt bare and empty without them.

'They're great children, Babs. You've brought them up really well,' Teddy suddenly said. 'I'm so proud of you.'

Barbara felt herself blushing. She knew her brother-in-law had a soft spot for her, so before he got too maudlin, she asked, 'How's Alan?'

'He's fine, putting in some extra hours on his thesis today.' He paused, his wide face crumpling into concern then continued, 'Actually he's a bit put out over me going to see Mother so often. We had a bit of a row over it. He says I'm too much at her beck and call. I suppose he's got a point, but what else can I do? She gets herself into such a state if I say I'm too busy.'

'Maybe Alan's right, maybe you do run after her too much.'

'She is my mother.'

'Have you told her about you and Alan yet?'

'I've tried to but she doesn't seem to understand.'

'Won't understand, more like.'

'Of course that's another thing that gets up Alan's nose; I never take him over there. How can I? As far as she is concerned he's a student of mine.'

Barbara laughed. 'A pretty poor student if you ask me; you've been using that old excuse for years. Shouldn't he have graduated by now? Teddy shrugged. 'Did you ever tell your father about him?'

'Yes, ages ago.'

'What did he say?'

'Oh he just smiled and said "your mother won't like that." I bet if I'd told him I was a mass murderer I would have got the same response.'

'I suppose they're both from a generation that doesn't talk about homosexuality. Unless it's "shock, horror, Oscar Wilde" they give it a wide berth.'

'I was thinking about inviting her over for lunch next week. She's not been to the house since Alan moved in. Maybe if she sees him in his own home she might realise.'

'Just tell her straight out.'

'What? Hi Mother, this is Alan; he's my partner and I love him. She'd probably collapse and have a heart attack.'

'What about Harry? Couldn't he tell her for you?'

'Not a good idea. She'd just think he was trying to screw things up for me, trying to get me disinherited.'

'Yes, you're probably right.'

Teddy poured them some more champagne and lay back in the chair. He looked very much at home. He'd removed his brown corduroy jacket and hung it over the back; underneath he wore a cream, open-neck check shirt with a deep red cravat that covered the loose folds of his neck. He crossed his long, elegant legs and took another sip from his glass.

'Good stuff this, eh.' She nodded. Teddy was always so immaculately turned out he sometimes made her feel dowdy in comparison, but he was a big man, tall and with the early stages of corpulence about him. Too much good living, he'd always been a bit of a *bon viveur*. 'Tell me, why's Tom so touchy about his scarf?' he continued.

'Don't know. It seems to have started when Harry left. He wears it all the time, even in bed. His teacher spoke to me about it; they tried to stop him wearing it in class but he got so upset that they left it. I think he might be using it like a security blanket because of Harry going. You know, the way some babies like to have a cloth or a blanket to hold on to. Anyway we've all decided to just ignore it for the moment and see if he gets over it.'

'Poor little chap. I expect it's hard on him. What about Sylvia? Is she coping all right?'

'Yes, I think so. To be honest Teddy I haven't said very much to them. I don't know what to say. I suppose I'll have to tell them about the divorce eventually, but I'm not looking forward to it. It's so hard. How can I make them understand that it's nothing to do with them? It would be easier if Harry kept in touch more but he doesn't come round and he doesn't ring. They must feel he has abandoned them.'

'Well he has, hasn't he? Are you sure it's nothing to do with the children?'

'How could it be?' She sipped her champagne in silence. 'Has Harry been in touch with you lately?' she asked. What she really wanted to know was if her brother-in-law knew anything about Harry's new woman.

'He rings from time to time, usually when he's bored or hanging around waiting for a show to finish.'

'Oh yes, his dead time he calls it, when everything is set up and there is nothing more he can do except pray it all works. He usually phones me then.' She stopped and added, 'Or rather, he used to.' She'd always enjoyed those brief but rather sweet telephone calls. He never had much to say; it was more a way of touching base, making sure she and the children were all right. Again she realised that there had been less of them over the last few years. When she'd asked once why he hadn't telephoned he said they were a man short these days and consequently he was too busy. She hadn't doubted his word for a moment. 'Teddy can I ask you something?' She thought her brother-in-law looked uncomfortable for a second but he nodded. 'Did you know about Harry and this woman?'

'Carla? Yes I did but I never thought it was serious. There didn't seem any point saying anything to you at the time. I thought it would all blow over.'

Barbara felt more hurt at this revelation than she would allow him to see. She realised he was Harry's brother, but she had always felt that she and Teddy had a particularly close relationship and for him to keep this from her seemed an enormous betrayal. 'So how long have you known?' Now she wanted all the details no matter how painful.

'I suppose he first mentioned her about a year ago.'

'A year? Before he left me? And you never thought to tell me? How many other people know? Am I the last to find out?' She stood up and walked across to the window. It was growing dark and the river below them was a mere black sash cutting through the gloomy fields. She pretended to study something in the distance but her eyes were not focussing; they were too full.

'I don't think he told anyone else. That's one of the reasons I didn't say anything. I was sure it was just a flash in the pan, mid-life crisis or something. Honestly Barbara I never thought it was serious. I thought he was just having a bit of a fling and when it was out of his system everything would be back to normal. You know, least said soonest mended,' Teddy continued.

She turned to face him, the empty champagne glass still in her hand. 'Well it isn't, is it,' she said bitterly. 'It isn't back to normal. When did you find out he was going to leave me?'

'I didn't. I didn't know anything about it until you telephoned me.'

'And still you didn't say anything?'

'What was the point? I still thought he'd get fed up with her and come back to you. After a few months living together I was sure he'd realise she wasn't the one for him.'

'But he didn't, did he? Now he wants a divorce.' Teddy didn't reply. Instead he refilled their glasses and waited for her to speak again. 'So do you know what he plans to do? Has he told you anything that I ought to know?'

'No he's not told me anything else. I think he wanted to but I stopped him. I said I didn't want to know. I told him how difficult it would be for me, if after all these years, he decided to make me his confidante. After all I am the children's godfather. I don't want to take sides in this. Look Barbara the best thing you can do is leave it all to your solicitor; he'll handle everything for you. You just said yourself that you'd give him a divorce.'

'I know and I suppose it makes sense but somehow it makes it all so final. I don't want to shut the door on him. I don't want a divorce. I want him back. Maybe you were right. Maybe this is only a mid-life crisis. Maybe he will come home if I just give him enough time.'

Teddy shuffled uncomfortably. He put down his glass and moved towards her. 'No Barbara, I don't think he's going to change his mind. I will tell you one thing he said to me; he's very much in love with this woman. He wants to marry her.'

*

After Teddy had left and the children had gone to bed Barbara remained sitting in the lounge for a while. The effects of the champagne and the half bottle of Burgundy she'd drunk with the meal were beginning to wear off and she no longer felt as confident as she had made out. She felt hurt and betrayed by the people she loved. Now the future stretched ahead of her, long and bleak. How was she going to manage to bring up the children without a husband? She had no money of her own and all Harry's money was tied up in his business. She would have to go back to work. Her mind whirled with self-doubt. Scraps of half-forgotten conversations floated through her mind, fragments of memories she'd thought forgotten. Barbara began to think of all the uncertainties and felt herself spiralling out of control again. She had to do something to stop it; she owed it to herself and the children. She couldn't let him destroy their lives. Barbara wiped away the tears and went to the bureau and took out some paper and a pen. What she needed was a plan of action. She picked up the pen and wrote phone solicitor, then underneath, go to job centre. She paused for a minute then added find child minder. She looked at the paltry list and her tears began to flow again, dropping onto the paper and smudging the carefully scripted words. Until then her to-do lists had been about inconsequential items, clean bathroom cupboards, pick up dry-cleaning, go to garden centre; they didn't contain these life changing events. Now that she'd started crying she couldn't stop; her body shook, wracked with sobs and she buried her face in the cushions, lost in a sea of self-pity, grief for her lost marriage and fear for the future.

CHAPTER 13

Barbara's eyes followed the progress of Carla round the room. How sophisticated she was, how elegant. She seemed quite at home among all these people she couldn't possibly know.

She could see Teddy approaching her and smiled; he was being his usual diplomatic self, dividing his time equally between the protagonists. 'Teddy, how are you? I haven't heard from you in ages,' she said as her ex-brother-in-law sauntered over to her, two glasses of wine in his hand. 'Thank you, I need that.' She took one of the glasses from him and tasted it. 'Mmn, nice.'

'I'm fine, my dear.'

'Here come and sit down beside me before you spill that wine.'

'Right'o my girl.' She could see from the flush on his already ruddy complexion that the wine was beginning to affect him. He had acquired a rose from somewhere, probably one of the flower arrangements and stuck it into his buttonhole. Teddy sat down heavily beside her and sighed audibly. 'Sad day, old girl. Going to miss the old devil you know.'

'It comes to us all,' she said awkwardly. She wasn't used to this side of Teddy's nature, he was always the jolly one, the strong and positive voice among all the dissenters.

'Younger than me you know. I should have gone before him. Older brother and all that. It's not fair. I should have looked out for him.' He pulled out a large red handkerchief from his pocket and blew his nose loudly. 'Well my lovely, what about you? This must feel very strange for you.'

'It does. I don't know whether to cry or just run out the door and go home. I'm beginning to wish I'd never come, but my pride insisted, so here I am,'she sighed. 'Too many memories.'

Teddy put his hand on her arm and whispered, 'I know. Just hang on to the good ones, old girl.'

'I would if I could, Teddy, but your brother destroyed even the good ones with his lies.'

'He wasn't the only one who told lies, remember,' he replied, rather pointedly.

Barbara stared at him. 'We never lied to him, Teddy.'

'No, we never told him a lie, but we let him think it. It amounts to the same thing.'

'You told him, didn't you? That's why you fell out?'

Teddy put the glass of wine to his lips and tasted it. 'Really nice little Bordeaux this,' he said.

'Teddy?'

'Well yes. I didn't mean to tell him, but it was when I went over to visit him in Spain. We'd been drinking heavily and it just slipped out. I didn't think he'd be so upset; after all it had been years ago. For some reason my befuddled brain thought he wouldn't mind, now that he had a new wife.'

'Oh, Teddy, how could you? What if he'd told the children?' She looked across at Tom, who was talking to his girlfriend. 'It wasn't just my life he destroyed; it was theirs too. If they knew what happened, it would devastate them.'

'But life is good for you, now, Barbara. You're happy, aren't you?'

'Yes, of course, I am.' She glanced across at Ian. 'But Harry was the love of my life. My world fell apart when he left me.'

'Sylvia and Tom seem to have come through it well. And only you and I know our little secret, so nothing to worry about.'

*

Barbara dropped the children off at school and turned into the High Street, heading towards the bridge. Ian, their solicitor, had telephoned the evening before and asked her to come in and sign some papers to do with the divorce. Every time she thought about it she felt sick; there was a heavy lump in her chest that refused to go away. She considered not going at all. Why should she accommodate Harry, just so that he could leave them? As she approached the Causeway she slowed down, tempted to turn left into Station Road and take the back lane home. She hesitated just long enough for an impatient motorist behind her to start pressing on his horn, then pulled herself together and drove on over the bridge. This was her rubicon; there was no turning back now.

She had known Ian Routh a long time; he had been a close friend of Harry's. They had played cricket together for years. Barbara choked back a sob as she remembered those lazy summer evenings, sitting by the village green with the other wives, drinking Brakspeare's bitter and cheering their men on.

His office was on Castle Hill. She hadn't been there before; there never had been cause to do so. When she contacted him to say she wanted to divorce Harry, Ian had come round to her house immediately. She thought afterwards that he seemed almost as shocked as she was at Harry's betrayal. Maybe Teddy was right, maybe Harry had kept the affair a secret from his friends. Strangely enough, there was some consolation in that thought. She parked her car on the forecourt and climbed the scrubbed, stone steps.

His secretary looked up as she opened the door. 'Good morning, can I help you?'

'I've an appointment with Mr Routh,' she said.

'Mrs Wilkinson?' she asked. Barbara nodded. 'Go right in, he's expecting you.'

Ian got up the moment she entered the room. 'Come in Barbara.' He kissed her lightly on the cheek then retreated to the other side of his desk. She sat opposite him, fighting back the tears.

'I can't tell you how sorry I am that it's come to this. I really thought Harry would come to his senses and ask you to take him back,' he said.

She swallowed hard. 'I don't know that I could have done that anyway,' she said. 'It's hard to forgive something like that.' Her throat was dry and her voice came out as a whisper. She coughed.

'Would you like some water?' he asked.

'No, I'm fine, really.'

'I suppose we might as well get on with it,' he said, pulling a file of papers out of the desk drawer. 'I've spoken to Harry's solicitor.'

'Max Atherton?' Max was another close friend of the family; she wondered what he thought about Harry divorcing her. All their friends would know by now; that kind of news had a way of circulating along the grape vine at an accelerated speed. The thought of their pity was humiliating. She could hear them now. Poor Barbara and the children, how will she cope on her own after all those years? Never had a proper job. What will she do?

'That's right,' Ian continued. 'He says that Harry is quite happy for you to have the house in Marlow; he will put the deeds in your sole name.'

'Is that all?' she asked. 'What about the children?'

'He'll be obliged to pay for the children of course; I will work out the maintenance payments and let you know how much. As for anything else, his solicitor says Harry doesn't have any money; apparently he didn't get as much as he expected for his business and most of that has gone on buying a new house in Spain. I will try to look more closely at his assets but now that he has become a Spanish resident, it is much more difficult.'

'A Spanish resident? When did that happen?' she asked in astonishment.

'According to Max they moved just before Christmas.'

So Harry was totally removing himself from their lives. 'I don't believe that Harry has no money; he was always very careful with money. It's just an excuse so that he doesn't have to pay me.'

'As I said, I'll look into it but it won't be easy.'

'So apart from the house, half of which is already mine, I get nothing?'

'And the maintenance money for the children,' he added.

'But for me, nothing? Twenty years of my life worth nothing at all?'

'That's the offer.'

'But I gave up work to raise the family and support Harry,' she added. 'And for that, I get no compensation?'

'That's how the law stands, I'm afraid. But you will have the house.'

'It still has a mortgage; not much I admit, but it still has to be paid. And what if I have to sell it in order to live?'

'I would hope it doesn't come to that, although, of course a smaller house might be more suitable in the circumstances.' She didn't reply. This haggling about money was more hurtful than she'd imagined. 'I will talk to his solicitor about the mortgage; if it really is quite small then maybe we can persuade him to pay it off for you.'

'That would help.'

'Now, more importantly, about the children, your husband has agreed to give you sole custody of Tom and Sylvia,' he continued. 'The good news is that he has not asked for any visiting rights or access to them.'

'What? He doesn't want to see his children?' She couldn't believe it; he was wiping them out of his life. He didn't want to see Tom and Sylvia, both of whom thought the world of him.

'He says it's for the children's sake. As he's living abroad he won't be able to see them on a regular basis, so he thinks it would be better not to disrupt their lives at all. He emphasises that it is for their benefit and not because he doesn't love them,' the solicitor continued, reading from his notes.

'Fine.'

'It's for the best, Barbara. This is much better than wrangling over who has which child and when. I can tell you it is always the children who suffer most when people get divorced.'

'Tell that to his children.' How on earth was she going to explain to them that their father never wanted to see them again? What words could she use to soften his abandonment?

'If you could sign these documents, Barbara, I think we're finished for today,' he said, pushing a stack of papers and a pen across the table towards her.

She picked up the pen and signed each one where he'd indicated with a cross. She didn't bother to read them. What did it matter anyway? She knew what they meant. This was her life she was signing away. Now she would have to make a new one, for her and her children.

*

Barbara felt numb and empty. She'd accepted Mary's offer for the children to stay overnight and now, wandering around her empty house, she felt more alone than she cared to admit. A momentous day was probably how Teddy would describe it. Everything had gone well; the respective solicitors had handled it all very smoothly, dividing up the possessions of a lifetime with the minimum of acrimony.

When the judge awarded her the custody of Tom and Sylvia, and she heard Harry's solicitor say that his client had no objection to this, she began to cry. Anyone watching her would have thought they were tears of relief, but actually they were tears of rage. Did his children mean so little to him that he could dismiss them so easily? She would have gone across the court room and confronted him, but her solicitor put his hand on her arm and stopped her. She knew Harry had been away from home a lot but he had always tried to make it up to the children when he was there. He seemed to enjoy their company. She couldn't understand why his feelings had changed. Wouldn't he miss them?

She'd just poured herself a glass of wine when there was a knock at the door.

'Barbara, it's just me, it's Mary.'

'Oh hello Mary, come in. This is a surprise. Where are Tom and Sylvia?'

'I thought you might be feeling a bit low today so I thought I'd pop by. Bill's looking after the kids, so there's no need to worry. Actually it was his idea; he thought you could probably do with a bit of company.'

'He was right. Glass of wine?'

'Please. So how did it go?'

'I suppose you could say it went well but I'm not sure it did. In fact it feels like shit. I suppose I'll get used to it but right now it doesn't feel like it.' Barbara poured Mary a glass of wine and topped up her own. 'Have the children said anything?'

'No, not really. I caught Sylvia having a bit of a cry this afternoon when she got back from school but Tom has been fine. I tried to explain to her that this sometimes happens between mummies and daddies and that it has nothing to do with her. I told her that you both still love her as much as ever,' Mary replied.

'Thank you, you're such a good friend. The problem is whether she'll believe that when she learns that she won't be seeing her father again.'

'So he hasn't changed his mind?'

'I don't say she'll never see him again but he doesn't want any visiting rights, and he seems quite happy to go off and live in Spain with that woman, so it's highly unlikely that the children will see much of him.' She explained what had happened in court that day.

'Well maybe it's for the best. You'll all be able to make a fresh start. At least the kids won't be tugged back and forth between you. Perhaps he's done it for them.'

'I doubt it. Just can't be bothered more like. Doesn't want anything to interfere with his new life. Well he may not want them but he's going to have to pay for them.'

'Maybe they're planning to have a family of their own.'

'I doubt it.'

'How do you know? I thought you said she was only in her late thirties? That's still young enough to have a baby.'

'No, it won't happen.' Mary looked at her in surprise. 'Trust me, I know he won't have any more children. Don't ask me how. I just know,' Barbara continued.

'Okay, if you say so. Had the snip, has he?'

'Something like that.'

CHAPTER 14

Carla edged her way towards Chris and Gerry; they were perched on a banquette eating cold pizza and chatting to Jenny.

'Hi guys, everything okay?'

'Fine Carla. Good spread,' Chris replied, his mouth full.

'How are you? You look exhausted,' Gerry said, standing up. 'Here sit down with us for a bit.'

Carla slumped down against the wall. It was good to get the weight off her feet; they hurt in the new shoes she'd bought for the funeral, and her neck ached from the tension of smiling at everyone. She sipped her wine and said nothing.

'We were just telling Jenny about the problems with our house.'

'The one in Wokingham?'

'No, we haven't lived there for years. We bought an old mill house in Sindlesham a few years ago, when prices were really cheap. It was all my fault, I know, I just fell in love with it the moment I saw it, even though Chris warned me against it. I've always wanted to live by the river you see and the Mill House looked just perfect for us. I just never thought the river would come up so high.'

'So what happened?' Carla asked.

'We were flooded. They built up the embankment but then the next year we were flooded again, so they built it higher still.'

'Did that solve the problem?'

'Yes in a way; we haven't been flooded since but we've still got problems with the sewage and the smell is awful.'

'Didn't you just redecorate?' interrupted Jenny.

'Yes we did but the mould keeps coming back, and to make it worse I saw some rats the other day. But Chris won't let me put down any rat poison in case the dog eats it.'

'Why not sell it and move away?'

She laughed bitterly. 'No-one will buy it. We've had it on the market for months now and nobody is interested. It's mortgaged to the hilt, and now it's in negative equity. We just don't know what to do.'

'Maybe it's just a question of waiting and seeing what happens to the market,' Carla suggested.

'That's what I tell her,' said Chris. 'But she is as determined now to sell it, as she was to buy it in the first place.' He shrugged. 'Anyway Carla what about you? Bearing up and that?'

'Yes, I'm okay I suppose. I think I'm about to have a bit more bad news, though.' She told them about the conversation with Ian Routh.

'That's dreadful,' interrupted Gerry. 'They can't do that. Surely it's as much your house as Harry's?'

'Actually Gerry I think they probably can. We'd have to have a close look at the wording of the will to see exactly what Harry has stipulated. When did he write his will?' Chris asked.

'I've no idea, but it must have been years ago,' she paused then continued, 'Probably in the '90s. It was when the housing market was going through a bad stage and prices were plummeting; nobody could get mortgages and the banks were cutting back on lending.'

'Like now, you mean?' interrupted Gerry.

'Yes, I suppose so. I remember him saying that he thought his children might need a hand in the future and all he had to leave them was his house. I didn't mind, especially when he said he would leave me some money and stipulate that I could carry on living in the house as long as I wished. It didn't seem a big deal at the time. They were his children so I felt he could leave them what he wanted. But he never mentioned it again, and I forgot all about it. I can't believe he actually drew up an official will and didn't tell me.'

'Why don't you ask Max to look into it for you?' Chris asked.

'Yes I suppose I could. I'm supposed to go and see Sylvia's solicitor next Thursday; it would be nice to have someone to give me some advice first.'

'Is that her solicitor over there?'

'Yes, Ian Routh. He has an office in Maidenhead.'

'I know him, he used to play cricket with us in the old days. Look how long are you going to be here?'

'I don't have anything planned. I came on an open ticket. Why?'

'I'll ring Max and ask him to look into it. Maybe I could arrange a meeting for early in the week and that'd give him time to go over a few things first. Okay?'

'That's fine with me.' Max had represented Harry during his divorce and Harry had said that he was very competent, so she felt confident he would help her find a solution.

'Look we're taking the kids bowling at the weekend, why don't you come with us?'

'Oh, I don't know. I'm not really in the mood for going out.'

'Go on, it'll do you good.'

'Yes, good idea Gerry. You'll love it Carla; it'll take your mind off things.'

'Oh all right.'

'Great, we'll pick you up around ten. Holiday Inn you said?'

'Yes.'

Jenny had wandered away during the conversation and Carla could see her now in a typical pose, a wine glass in one hand and her mobile in the other. She owed Jenny a lot. If it hadn't been for her friend's faith in her, she could never have kept her business going. Harry certainly hadn't been much support.

*

Monday morning she dropped Harry at the airport and continued along the motorway until the turning for Antequera. It took her another half hour to reach the town, perched high on the edge of the *Sierra de Chimenea* and overlooking the wide, flat fields of the *meseta*. It was a fairly easy task to find the industrial estate to which she'd been directed and locate the warehouse, a wide, basic storage area, built out of breeze blocks and corrugated iron sheeting. She parked her car and went inside, pulling her jacket around her against the unaccustomed cold. Long racks of shelving stacked high with skins lined each aisle, and the air smelled of leather and tanning. She wandered slowly along each row, looking carefully at what was on display. She knew exactly what she was after and when she saw a large bale of black leather skins she stopped and pulled it down from the shelf. Then she went through them one by one, holding each one up to the light to match its colour. When she was satisfied that she had six skins of the same colour, with no faults and no discolouration, she put them to one side and returned the remainder to the shelf. Now she wanted something more flamboyant, a fine calf skin printed with a leopard design caught her eye. She added it to her pile and routed around until she found an identical one to match, unfortunately there was only enough to make a waistcoat not a jacket. Still she would have them anyway. She continued her search, turning skin after skin until her arms ached and her feet were frozen from the cold seeping up from the concrete floor. At last she saw some skins that would make Mrs Rushton's jacket, leather as soft as silk and dyed an iridescent blue. Perfect. As she was making her way to the cash desk she noticed a bin of leather scraps and went to explore. One of her hallmarks was the way she used appliqué on her garments, here there was an enormous selection of off-cuts and scraps that she could cut and shape into the designs she wanted.

'Inglish?' the warehouseman asked.

'Yes.'

'I spik a little Inglish. Can I help you?'

'I'm looking for some small pieces of leather,' she explained, thinking that it was probably self-evident as she had her arms buried up to her elbows in the bin. He looked puzzled. 'Small, *pequeño*, pieces of leather,' she repeated, straightening up and her voice raising in volume despite herself.

'Ah. *Si*. Here is lots of small pieces. Only a thousand pesetas a kilo,' he explained pointing to the bin.

She smiled at him and returned to the task of sorting and selecting pieces until she had about a kilo of them which she added to her other pile. As she watched the attendant, a swarthy young man with brown, calloused hands and bitten fingernails, weigh and price her purchases she felt a particularly satisfying sense of achievement. If it was going to be so easy to find such excellent leather then maybe she would be able to continue with her work here after all. She thanked the young man, accepted one of their business cards, promised to return and set off for home.

The journey through the mountains had rejuvenated her and she felt her old creativity return. She drove back, the windows open, the cold, clean air blowing across her face and the radio playing a selection of Van Morrison hits while she thought about her new designs. For once her mind was not preoccupied with thoughts of Harry and by the time she arrived home she realised that she was actually looking forward to a few days without him. Maybe she would see about taking some Spanish lessons too.

*

She started working on the evening skirt first. Melissa as usual had a deadline to meet and Carla didn't want to let her down. By now she had all Melissa's measurements and unless the starlet had been dieting again or been on an eating binge it should fit her perfectly. She made the pattern first then before she committed her scissors to the leather took a break and made herself a cup of tea. It was important not to rush this part of the process. She sat on the terrace and looked at the Mediterranean; it was a fine day and the sea was completely calm, the light reflecting from it in pale swathes that dazzled the eye. A fishing boat was heading back to port and she could see a group of seagulls following the wash. As she sipped the hot tea she studied her designs; she had decided to emphasise Melissa's slim figure by designing a long, fitted skirt with slits up either side. Amongst the newly acquired scraps were some long pieces of snakeskin the colour of dull pewter, she would use them to make the design of a coiling dragon up one side. Yes, Melissa would like that.

She had set up her machine in the guest bedroom overlooking the terrace. Harry had moaned when she said she had to bring her machine to Spain with her.

'We're supposed to be travelling light,' he said. 'Not lugging bloody great sewing machines with us.'

'But Harry, you don't understand, this is a really good machine, designed especially for sewing leather. It may not be easy to find another one the same over there.'

'Don't be ridiculous. How do you think they sew all those leather coats and handbags? Of course you'll be able to buy another one.'

'Look Darling, I'm very fond of this machine. I've had it since I started work and well, to be frank, I'm used to it. I know all its little idiosyncrasies. I don't want to start with a new one now. Anyway I'm sure it won't cost that much to ship it over.'

'Oh I suppose not. Okay, but I think you're being ridiculous.'

And so the sewing machine had arrived. It was true she was very fond of the machine, it was associated with so many happy memories. Her career had not only given her a discreet but limited fame but had also made her many friends and acquaintances. There was Irma, a Jewish woman from the Czech Republic who had a leather shop near Smithfields. Carla always arranged her visits so that they could slip down to her favourite bistro in Covent Garden and have lunch together. Irma was a large lady with an equally large appetite for steak and red wine, and an even larger repertoire of stories. She had come to England in the early sixties with nothing, spent a few years living the hippy life, smoking pot and sleeping around then became a disciple of the Maharishi after listening to him one balmy Sunday evening in Hyde Park. Now she was a conventional businesswoman and had recently been tipped for the Businesswoman of the Year Award. Then there was Jethro who moved out from London's East End with his wife and two sons and bought a sixteenth century leather factory outside Guildford, where the river that they used to wash the skins ran right through the middle of the factory and a row of workers' cottages lined the opposite bank. There was Annette Lacroix, a Belgian designer who owned a string of boutiques and had once asked Carla to become her partner because she loved the uniqueness of her leatherwork designs. Her offer had been very tempting but in the end Carla had preferred to go it alone.

She sighed as she threaded up the machine. By the time she had agreed to Harry's plan to move to Spain she had six machinists working for her, all women she liked and trusted. It had been hard to say goodbye to them. How could Harry think she could continue to work from here? All her work had depended on having good relationships with people, clients, suppliers and employees. Again she thought about learning Spanish. If she wanted to grow her business in Spain she would have to speak the language.

*

Time passed quickly in Harry's absence. The Harringtons called round to see if she wanted to go out for lunch but she refused, telling them firmly but politely that she was busy. They looked a little put out at her refusal, so she explained that she had some orders to finish while Harry was away.

'Oh really, Harry said you liked to sew but I didn't realise that you were professional,' Fred said offhandedly.

His wife was much more interested. 'How lovely. perhaps you could make something for me?' she suggested.

'I'm not sure whether I'm going to continue with my work here or not, but come round one day by all means and I'll show you the sort of things I design.'

'Yes I will,' Maisie replied, beaming at her husband. 'It's time I had a new outfit.' She was wearing skin-tight jeans of a garish pink, which she called fuchsia, a white sleeveless blouse, tied at the waist in a large knot, pink sandals in the self-same shade as the jeans with three inch heels that caused her to totter rather than walk, and garlands of metal and bead chains around her neck. If she was trying to look younger, she had failed, thought Carla, she merely looked like a tired old woman wearing her daughter's clothes. Yes she did need a new outfit but Carla was not sure that she would be the one to design it.

'Yes okay,' Fred replied automatically to his wife, no doubt having heard it all before. 'Look, come on Maisie, if you want to go to that new fish bar in San Pedro we had better get a move on. Sorry you can't come with us, Carla. See you later.'

'Okay. Thanks for thinking of me anyway.'

'We told Harry we would keep an eye on you for him. You not knowing many people yet and all,' added Maisie. 'You know I could introduce you to the women in my yoga group.'

'Yes, possibly. Goodbye then,' Carla said, her body language indicating that the door was imminently about to close.

'Goodbye my dear.'

Once they had gone Carla returned to her work. They were a pleasant enough couple and Maisie seemed genuinely solicitous of her welfare, but she just found she had little to say to them, and the thought of spending an entire lunchtime with them on her own had horrified her. Harry was a great conversationalist and she often found that she could just sit back and let him talk for them both, but without him there as a catalyst the conversation would surely flag. As she cut and pressed and pinned she thought about what Maisie had said. Maisie knew lots of people: there was her yoga group, the women in her Pilates class, the gourmet dinner group they belonged to and of course the tennis club. Besides which there were her neighbours, all could be potential customers if she decided to continue with her business. It was just a question of building up a new network of contacts.

*

The next day was a Tuesday, the day of the weekly market in Fuengirola, so she decided to go along to see if it was a likely outlet for her clothes. She parked her car in a side street and walked in the general direction of everyone else until she could see the market in the distance. As she weaved her way past stalls stacked high with strawberries from Huelva, ripe red tomatoes, creamy yellow pumpkins sold by the slice, courgettes, broccoli, potatoes from the river valleys that bordered the town, sweet smelling oranges from Valencia, bananas from the Canary Islands, pink fleshed grapefruits sliced open to reveal their authenticity, it seemed on the surface that the market was the same as any other European street market. There were stalls selling every kind of spice imaginable, spices for cooking, to add to stews, to flavour chicken, to colour the rice, saffron, turmeric, chilli, ginger. Then there were the herbs: culinary herbs, herbs to make infusions, herbs to cure ailments, to make you sleep, to help your digestion, to relieve flatulence, there was something for everybody. She pushed on through the crowded aisles past stalls selling brightly glazed pottery, cut flowers and potted plants, past racks of cheap clothing, stalls with multicoloured cushions and polyester bedding, African traders selling designer sunglasses and fake handbags, and numerous craft stalls. Fuengirola market had a reputation for handicrafts and there were also people selling bead necklaces, hand painted scarves and jewellery made from semi-precious stones, one man had some presentable watercolours for sale and another carved wooden rocking horses, planing and smoothing his work while he waited for customers. The market was very busy. There were people pushing and shoving to get through the narrow aisles between the stalls, and the air rang not only with the cries of the Spanish stall holders offering *dos por uno, mejor calidad, ultima oferta,* but also the chatter of tourists, English, Danish, Russian, French and German voices all vying to be heard. Maybe this would be a good place to sell her leather work after all. She stopped to talk to some of the stallholders and soon ascertained that she would need a permit from the town hall before she could set up a stall. So she bought some strawberries and a kilo of oranges from an amply built gypsy woman then set off to talk to the town clerk. She knew it would not be the same as working in London but it would be a start. Right now she had to get her teeth into something, however small.

*

That evening she telephoned Jenny. 'Hi there, this is Jenny De Souta. Leave a message and I'll call you back,' said the answer machine.

'Hi Jen, it's Carla. I'm going to have Melissa's skirt finished by the end of the week. Do you want me to post it or do you want to collect it? Give me a ring when you get back.'

About an hour later the telephone rang, 'Hi Carla, how are you?' Jenny asked. 'I got your message.'

'Fine, I'm having a rush of creativity while Harry's away. Melissa's is finished and I've started on Mrs Rushton's jacket. She's going to love it.'

'Great. Look, don't post them. I'll come and get them. I could do with a break anyway.'

'Wonderful. I'd love to see you; it's been ages.'

'How about next week?'

'Perfect. Harry gets back in a couple of days and there's nothing planned for next week at all. I'll make up the guest room for you.'

'Great I'll email you when I've got my flight details, okay?'

'Yes and Harry or I will pick you up.'

'Fine. Look, sorry Carla, I'd love to chat but I've got to go out. I only popped home to change and saw there was a message.'

'No problem. Going somewhere nice?'

'Just dinner and then on clubbing afterwards.'

'New boyfriend?'

'Sort of, nothing serious. Look we'll catch up on all the gossip when I come over, all right.'

'Yes fine. Have a good time then.'

'Bye Carla. Be in touch.' As Carla hung up the telephone she felt a tinge of envy for her friend, but it didn't last. She'd had enough of the party scene, constantly meeting new people and having a succession of dates but never a serious relationship. Now she had Harry and that was what she wanted. She could imagine the scene in Jenny's small flat, the discarded work clothes strewn across the bed, the search for something sexy but discreet to wear, the fancy underwear just in case, the ring on the doorbell to say her taxi had arrived and a last minute dash to change the contents of her handbag. No not for her, what she wanted now was to get married and have a family.

*

Harry had been away almost a week and although she'd enjoyed the brief respite she was glad to have him back.

'Missed me Darling?' he asked when she met him at the airport.

'Very much. Did it all go well?'

'Yes, as well as could be expected, I suppose.' Was she imagining it or did he seem upset about the divorce? He certainly was not his usual ebullient self and there were dark rings under his eyes.

'Did you see the children?'

'No, I decided that it was probably best not to upset them. Max said that Barbara's solicitor had been in touch to say that all contact had to be through him. Stupid prick, used to be a friend. He was one of my best friends you know, now he contacts me through my solicitor, in writing.'

'Well that's what happens with divorces, friends have to take sides. They can't go on being friends with both, it doesn't work. They either take sides or they dump you both.'

'He's still a prick.'

'So has a date been set yet?'

'Sometime next month, he'll write to me when he knows. We have to wait six weeks for the decree nisi and then it will be all over and we'll be free.'

'Free?'

'Free to get married. I thought maybe an Autumn wedding or sooner if you like. What do you think?'

'Sounds lovely Harry, but let's keep it simple, shall we, just you and me and a couple of witnesses. And soon.'

'Whatever you want my Darling. By the way, I saw Chris and Gerry while I was there. Chris has agreed to be my best man.'

'That's great.' She beamed at him, at last it was going to happen.

'Well he seemed the best choice as he'd already done the job once before.' He laughed. 'You know, practice makes perfect.'

She knew Chris had been Harry's best man when he married Barbara, but it didn't bother her, she liked Chris and his girlfriend Gerry. He'd accepted Harry's decision to leave his family and not allowed it to affect their friendship. If he had an opinion on the wisdom of his friend's actions he kept it to himself.

She offered Harry the car keys. 'Do you want to drive?'

'No, you drive. I'm feeling pretty knackered. So what have you been up to while I've been away? Have you been to the new house?'

She pulled out into the traffic before answering him, 'No, I haven't had time. Actually I've been setting up my new business.'

'Already?'

'Yes. I've found some suppliers and I'm going to rent a stall in Fuengirola market.'

'A market stall? Is that really your style Carla?'

'It's just until I get going. I have to find customers somewhere. Anyway, that's where I started when I was still in art school. I'll be going there Tuesdays and Sundays.'

'Sundays? What about the tennis match?'

'Well you'll just have to play without me. Anyway it's only in the mornings, we don't usually play until five. I'll have plenty of time to do both.'

'Why don't you take your stuff to the Corté Ingles and see if they'd buy it?'

'No. Department stores are definitely not my style. For a start they'd want more than I could possibly make and they'd want a consistency of design that I couldn't promise. All my designs are one-offs. That's how I can charge so much. You'll never see another garment the same.'

'You won't be able to charge much on a market stall.' She glanced at him. Why was he being so negative? Surely he knew how much her work meant to her. She began to regret telling him about her plans. It would have been better to have waited until they were at home, relaxing by the pool with a glass of wine.

'As I said, it's somewhere to start. I'll soon find other clients.' She wished she felt as confident as she sounded. 'Oh by the way, Jenny's coming over in a couple of weeks.'

'Jenny? Again?'

'Yes, my agent. You don't mind do you?'

'Why should I mind?'

'No reason. It's just sometimes I get the impression that you don't like Jenny.'

'She's okay. Not really my cup of tea, but so what, she's your pal.'

'I thought maybe we'd take her to that new club in Mijas while she's here?'

'Good idea. I'll get Arnie and his wife to join us.'

She bit her lip. Arnie again. 'So how was Max?'

'He and Lara have split up. Lara decided she'd had enough of waiting for Max to propose so she's gone to the States to work.'

'Really. How does Max feel about that?'

'Not sure. You know Max, he doesn't say much about his personal life.'

Carla didn't really know Max. He was Harry's solicitor, and he and Lara had lived in a tiny flat above his offices in Oxford for about fifteen years, but she didn't know a lot more. No wonder Lara had got tired of waiting. Fifteen years. What did some men expect?

*

The next morning Rosita, her cleaning lady, arrived as usual, punctually at eight.

'Coffee Rosita?'

'*Por favor, Señora.*'

Carla poured her a large cup of strong coffee, topped it up with hot milk and two generous spoonfuls of sugar and took it into the bathroom where she had already started work. 'Rosita, do you know any women who can sew?'

'Sew?'

'*Coser.* Any women who like to sew clothes?'   S h e made sewing movements with her fingers.

'*Ah si. Muchas*. I know many woman that sew.'

'And use a sewing machine?'

'*Una maquina? Si. Porque*?'

'I would like to employ one or two women to do some sewing for me.'

'I will bring my sister here to talk to you. She sews very well and my cousin too.'

'Oh that would be wonderful Rosita. Next week perhaps?'

'*Si Señora*. I will telephone you.' She turned back to cleaning the sink.

Carla felt a glow of satisfaction. It was all starting to come together at last. She was going to make a success of it, she was sure, despite Harry's negativity.

CHAPTER 15

Barbara was in no mood for talking, but it seemed that Ian was. She closed her eyes and let the smooth movement of the car lull her into a sense of languor.

'What was that, Darling?' she asked. Ian had probably drunk more wine than he should, by the way he was rambling on. It was so unlike him. He was a man who didn't take risks and to be drinking and driving was something he never did.

'You're not listening to me, are you?' he said.

'I was dropping off,' she replied.

'My poor Barbara. It's been a stressful day for you, hasn't it?'

'Well it's over now.'

'Yes, once the house business is sorted out, we can forget about Harry and Carla, and get on with our lives.' Barbara looked across at her husband. It had been a stressful day for him too. 'Good to see old Jim, again though. Looking a bit old, I thought.'

'I expect we all look older, Ian.'

'We should give him and Jane a ring. Ask them to come round for dinner one evening. What do you think?'

'Ian, you haven't seen them in twenty years. Why do you want to start seeing them now? I didn't even know you were that friendly with them, back then.' Jim and Jane had been great friends of Harry. He and Jim had played cricket together every available weekend in the summer. She and Jane used to sit watching them and chatting, before making dozens of cucumber sandwiches for the cricketers' tea, while the children enjoyed running around and playing together. But that was in the past and that's where she intended to leave it. It brought back too many unhappy memories of those first few years after Harry left. 'No reason why you can't ring Jim and suggest a drink at the pub. But let's leave the idea of dinner for a bit, all right?'

'Yes, I might do that.'

She glanced across at him. She was very fond of her husband; they had a warm and loving relationship but Harry had been the love of her life.

*

Since the divorce Ian had been telephoning on an almost regular basis. He was the antithesis of Harry, sober and serious, a tall thin man with a bookish look about him. He wore immaculate suits that always looked freshly pressed, white shirts and discrete ties, his hair was perfectly cut and his soft brown eyes that peered through a pair of rimless spectacles suggested a kind heart. She had become quite fond of him and it was becoming obvious that he was hoping that their relationship would change from one of client friend to something more intimate. If asked she would have to admit she enjoyed his attentions, but something was holding her back. It was too soon to commit to another relationship she told herself, the wounds that Harry had inflicted still needed time to heal.

'Was that your solicitor?' Mary asked, when Barbara came back into the kitchen.

'Ian? Yes,' she replied pouring her friend a second cup of coffee.

'Everything all right with the divorce?'

'Oh yes, that's all done and dusted. The Decree Absolute came through last month.'

'So? Why's he still 'phoning you?'

'I've known Ian a long time. He and Harry were at school together.'

'That's not really answering my question. Does he fancy you?'

Barbara laughed. 'Don't be silly. We're just friends, that's all.'

'People our age don't suddenly become friends with someone of the opposite sex without there being an ulterior motive.'

'Well, maybe he'd like it to be more. I don't know. I'm happy just having him as a friend.'

'Is he married?'

'No. He's never been married. He worked overseas a lot when he finished university, voluntary work in Zambia I think. Then he came back and began studying for the Bar and somehow he never found time to get married.'

'Maybe he's gay?'

'No, I don't think so. He seems perfectly heterosexual to me.'

'I see. So has he asked you out?'

'Mary, behave yourself. You make me sound like a teenager.'

'Well has he?'

'We had lunch at Sloane's last week, to celebrate the divorce being finalised, that's all.'

'Wow, Sloane's. That's pretty pricey. I bet he does fancy you.'

Barbara stood up and began to clear away the coffee cups. 'Okay Mary, how about we change the subject?'

'Don't be such a spoilsport Babs. This is the best bit of gossip I've heard in a long time.'

'Now don't start telling everyone. It's nothing really; we're just friends.'

'Okay, okay, if you say so.'

'Don't start telling anyone what?' Sylvia asked, coming in and opening the refrigerator. 'Mum what's to eat? I'm starving.'

'Have a yogurt or there's some cheese on the top shelf,' Barbara replied, loading the cups into the dishwasher.

'Your Mum's got an admirer,' Mary whispered conspiratorially.

'Oh, you mean Uncle Ian?' Barbara looked up in surprise. 'Don't look like that Mum. We know he fancies you. It's obvious. Aren't there any strawberry yogurts? You know I don't like kiwi.'

'Tom finished the last one this morning.'

'See, I told you,' Mary said with a laugh.

'I don't want to talk about it anymore Mary. Anyway I must get on; I've got homework to do.'

'Oh your retraining course, how's it going?'

'Great, I'm really enjoying it and to be honest it's nowhere near as difficult as I thought it would be.'

'When do you finish?'

'I've got another six weeks then we have an exam. My big worry at the moment is where to find the money to buy a computer. I can't really do it properly without my own computer.'

'Ask the bank manager if he'll give you a loan. If you tell him it's for a computer so that you can work from home, I'm sure he'd agree.'

'I don't know. I've already got an overdraft. I'm frightened of getting into too much debt because I don't know how I'll get out of it. We just about manage as it is.'

'It's worth a try. Why don't you call in, on your way to work, tomorrow. Take him a bag of cakes.'

'I wish it were that easy.'

'Oh well I'll leave you to your studies, both of you,' Mary said, getting up and reaching for her coat. 'Thanks for the coffee. See you on Friday then.'

*

The journey to Phoebe's was fraught. Sylvia refused to speak to her mother, ignored Tom completely, and when they eventually arrived, she flounced into the house and sat down in front of the television, without saying a word to anyone.

'What's the matter with her?' Phoebe asked.

'Oh, just ignore her, she's annoyed because she can't have her own way, that's all. She wanted to go to the cinema with her friend. Where's Teddy?'

'He'll be along in a bit. He's had to pick up a colleague of his. Some chap from the university that's been staying with him. I said why not bring him along for lunch as well. One more won't make any difference to me.'

'That's nice. Anything I can do to help?'

The sound of a car pulling up, signalled her brother-in-law's arrival. 'That'll be him now,' Phoebe said, with a big smile on her face.

Barbara knew Teddy's partner, an attractive young man, with pale blond hair and even paler blue eyes that twinkled when he spoke. His round, smooth face always put her in mind of a public schoolboy, which he undoubtedly had been once. Teddy introduced him to his mother as a friend from the department, and Barbara was surprised to see

Phoebe preening and smiling at him in a rather coquettish way. It was a side of her ex-mother-in-law that she'd never seen before.

'Hello Uncle Teddy,' Tom said, looking up from his football magazine. 'Hi Alan.'

Barbara saw Phoebe look at Tom in surprise. 'We met Alan at Teddy's house once, he likes football too,' she explained.

'Hi Tom. Didn't you bring your football with you today?' asked Alan.

'No, Mum wouldn't let me.'

'Well, maybe we can look through these instead,' said Alan, handing him a box of football cards.

'Wow, thanks, Alan. They're brill.' He sat down next to him and they were soon deep in discussion about the various players.

'Teddy can you help me with the dishes,' Phoebe said.

'Right you are Mother.' Once she had him in the kitchen, Barbara heard her ask, 'So is this the same friend that has been your lodger all this time?'

'That's right, Alan.'

'I thought he was a student of yours?'

'He was, but I don't teach him anymore.'

Phoebe began to mash the potatoes, putting in a knob of butter and a dash of milk.

'Need any help?' Barbara asked. This had been Teddy's opportunity to tell his mother the truth about his relationship with Alan, but when she looked across at him he just shook his head and frowned.

'You can take this through,' Phoebe said. 'And get everyone to the table.'

'Right. Come on guys, lunch is ready,' she called.

'I bet this is a rare treat for you Alan, having a roast Sunday lunch,' Phoebe said, bringing the chicken to the table.

'Teddy usually cooks a roast most weekends but not often chicken,' he replied.

Phoebe looked at her son. 'Is that right Teddy? I never knew you could cook.'

'Bit of a hobby, Mother. Must take after you. Would you like me to carve?'

'Yes, please dear. Come on children, lunch is ready,' Barbara said.

'So you two see a lot of each other?' Phoebe asked when they were all seated at the table.

'We work in the same department, Mother.'

'Teddy's letting me rent a room in his house,' Alan said. 'Just until I can find a place of my own.'

'Yes, Teddy told me. So you're looking for a house then?'

'A flat more likely, something small and cheap. Can't afford much on a research assistant's salary.'

Despite the wine that Teddy had brought and his efforts to keep the conversation flowing, the atmosphere was far from relaxed. Only Tom seemed at ease and prattled away to Alan about various football teams and his favourite players.

'No Dad today then?' Teddy asked.

'No. You know your father, he's always out on a Sunday.'

'He's missing a wonderful lunch,' added Alan, his mouth full of roast potatoes.

'I'll warm something up for him tonight if he's hungry, but he usually doesn't want to eat. Waste of time cooking for him,' Phoebe added.

For the first time in a long time, Barbara found herself wondering where her father-in-law went every Sunday. When Harry had first taken her home to meet his parents she had met his father briefly, and they had spoken about his passion for football and the demands of scouting for new players. It had all seemed perfectly normal. But then, when he was always absent from family gatherings, even having to dash off to a meeting on Christmas Eve, she had asked Harry if there was something wrong between his parents. He had just laughed and said, no, that was how his parents liked to live their lives. Now the revelations about Harry's secret affair had left her suspicious about lots of things.

'So Harry's married that woman then?' Phoebe asked her son, as she dished some more green beans onto his plate.

'Yes, last month. They drove down to Gibraltar and were married in the registrar's office.'

'Hmph. Didn't bother to tell us.'

'I expect he found it a bit difficult Phoebe,' said Barbara, surprised that she was still apologising for her ex-husband. Something in Phoebe's attitude inevitably made her rise to Harry's defence. There had always seemed something intrinsically unfair in her constant criticism of her younger son.

'Rubbish, just can't be bothered with his family that's all. Self, self, self, just like his father.'

'What's for pudding Gran?' Tom interrupted.

'Bakewell tart.'

'Yummy.'

'Mum, I'm not hungry. Can I get down?' Sylvia spoke for the first time since they'd arrived.

'Oh yes, go on.'

'It's time you took that girl in hand,' Phoebe said. 'Sulking and flouncing about like that. What she needs is a firm hand.'

'She's all right Mother. She's just going through an awkward age, I expect,' said Teddy. 'It can't be easy for her, Harry leaving like that.'

'Takes after her father, that's the problem. Never thinks of other people,' Phoebe continued.

Barbara wanted to scream. The strain of being with her ex-mother-in-law, was giving her a headache. She would have to find an excuse for leaving early, before she said something she might regret.

CHAPTER 16

Carla went to settle her bill with Franco. She could see Jenny chatting to the by now well inebriated, Teddy.

'Thank you Franco, it was all delicious.'

'I'm glad Señora. I was very sorry to hear that Harry had died. I liked him; he was a nice man, always laughing and joking. Of course it's a long time since he was here but I remember him well.'

'Thank you Franco.'

'Come on Carla, we're going back to my place for a bit. I'll make you a nice strong espresso to sober you up before you go home.' Teddy was standing in the doorway supported by Jenny.

'Yes, come on Carla, just a quick coffee.'

'You two go on, I'll join you later. I have to go back over to the church before I go. I'd like to look at the flowers.'

At the mention of flowers Teddy and Jenny became serious. 'Of course. Just come over when you're ready, old girl,' he said.

They staggered out the door together and along the path, two people who'd always stood by her. Spring Cottage was only a few steps down the hill and Carla watched them until they disappeared out of sight then she walked across to the church. The churchyard was deserted, the gravestones glistening from the rain. Apart from a blackbird that sat in the hawthorn hedge singing for all he was worth, there was no sound. The verger had placed the flowers on the small grave and they added a flash of colour to the gloomy spot. She bent down to read the cards attached to them and began to relax. At last she could breathe and she felt the tension of the previous months slip away from her. She had done it. She had brought Harry home and now she could get on with her life. Moving to Spain with Harry had almost brought her career to a standstill, but she'd made the most of the situation, and until the last few years had built up a thriving business.

*

When Carla arrived at the market, people were already milling down the aisles, and queues were forming at the fruit and vegetable stands. Her new pitch was at the far end between a home-made jewellery stall and an Englishman selling second-hand books. As she pushed her way through the early morning shoppers something familiar caught her eye. There was a man's long, red and black leather coat hanging on a rack in the second-hand clothing stall. She stopped and took it down to check it was what she thought it was.

'Nice bit of leather that, love,' a rather buxom woman said in a north of England accent. 'Designer made.' She wore a canary yellow tee-shirt that strained at her rather ample bosom and a pair of tight jeans. The money bag slung across her shoulder marked her out as the stall holder.

'Yes, I know,' Carla replied. 'I made it.' She looked inside the neck for her familiar label, a rather fancy *M* and the legend Made in London. It was one of hers, she remembered this one well.

'Did you now? Well I never.'

'Where did you get it from?'

'Oh the wife of this old pop-star brought a whole load of things down last week.'

'Brian Red?'

'Yes love, that's him. He lives in a big house on the way to Mijas.' Carla turned the coat over. 'So you know them do you?' the woman continued.

'Not now. I made this coat for him a long, long time ago, when he had a big hit with Keep on Loving Me.'

'I remember that one. Lovely it was.' She began humming the tune to herself. 'So do you want to buy it?' she asked at last, eager to make her first sale of the day.

'How much?'

'Well I have to be honest, it's got quite a rip in it and the lining's not too good. How about five thousand pesetas?'

'Four?'

'Okay love, as it was you who made it in the first place you can have it for four.' She picked it up, carefully folded it and put it inside a plastic shopping bag. 'Changed a bit now he has. Bald as a coot and fat.'

Carla remembered him clearly, a tall youth with dyed black hair and a penchant for anything red. She had had quite a job getting enough red leather to make the coat but in the end it had worked out well by inserting long strips of black leather along the many seams. The vertical stripes made Brian seem even taller and thinner but he was pleased with it.

'He owns that restaurant down on the promenade, Krazy Kats. You can't miss it, everything's red.'

'Yes, I know the one but I've never been in there.' She counted out the money and picked up her package but the woman continued to talk.

'His wife is nice. She used to live near our old place in Whitby. Very down to earth she is, not a bit stuck up for all the money she has.'

Carla wondered if his wife was the painfully thin, pasty-faced girl-friend he had when she knew him. Crystal she was called. One day she'd rung Carla and asked her to make her a fur cape for a premiere she was going to in Norway. A rush job she said. Carla had sat up until midnight every night for the best part of a week designing, cutting and even stitching the cape herself so that she would have it in time. When Crystal neglected to pay for the garment Carla was not unduly worried until two weeks later when the girl brought it back saying that she couldn't possibly wear the fur of a dead animal, it was so anti-Karma. A few weeks later Carla was flicking through a magazine in her dentist's waiting room and there was Crystal, hanging on Brian's arm, wearing a beaming smile and the fur cape.

'Is her name Crystal by any chance?' she asked.

'No, I don't think so. It's Jean or Julie, I think, something very ordinary anyway, not Crystal. I told you, she's from Whitby. What about you love, here on holiday?'

'Me? No, I've just taken a stall here. Today's my first day.'

'Have you really, dear? Leather is it?'

'Yes, just a few bits and pieces to start with; I want to see how it goes.'

'Best of luck, love. You'll have quite a bit of competition, what with all those African traders we get here now.'

'Like I said, I'll just have to see how it goes. Anyway I'd better get going. Nice chatting to you.'

'All that table, a thousand pesetas,' the woman called across to two teenage girls who were rummaging through a motley collection of old skirts and tops. She gave Carla a nod and moved over to watch her new customers.

*

When Carla saw Jenny standing in the arrivals hall with her suitcase, she felt a rush of affection for her friend. She hadn't realised until then just how much she missed her old life.

'Hi, Jenny, over here.' She waved across at her. 'Good flight?'

'So so. Good to see you Carla. My, how you've changed.'

'Have I? Is that good or bad?'

'Good of course, browner, slimmer, blonder. You look great. And I like your hair short like that.'

'It's the only way I can control it; in this climate it just frizzes up.'

'It looks good.'

'You don't look so bad yourself.' She hugged her. 'I've missed you, you know.'

'What nobody nagging you these days?'

'Only Harry.'

'How is he?'

'Good.'

'Did he tell you we bumped into each other last week, at the airport?'

'No, he never said anything about it.'

'Yes, I was getting back from Dublin and he was on his way to his solicitor. He suggested we have a quick drink together.'

'How odd that he never mentioned it.'

'Well that's me, once seen instantly forgotten.' She laughed. 'So how's things?'

'Not bad, I'm starting to find my way around. There's some great places to buy leather here, and pretty cheap too.'

'Good, I've got a couple of new orders for you. Nobody you've met before but they could be good customers if we treat them right.'

'Great. Hey, do you know who lives around here? Brian Red.'

'What the pop star that you used to design things for, the one with the dotty girlfriend? Everything had to be red, that one?'

'Yes that's him; he has a bar on the beach.'

'Oh we'll have to go down and see him. Do you think he'll remember us?'

'I doubt it, he was always stoned in those days. I doubt if he remembers anything from back then.'

*

But she was wrong, Arthur Brian Sidebotham, as he used to be called back in his home town of Barnsley, remembered them very well. Just as the stall holder had said, he'd aged since Carla had last seen him, but he still had the style and panache of a pop star. There was no mistaking it. It was a style she'd seen adopted by other ageing musicians, people like Keith Richards, somewhere between grotesque and outrageous. Personally she preferred to see people grow old gracefully, more like Billy Joel and Sting, but she could appreciate the need to keep the pop star persona going. She also saw that Brian Red still had his penchant for all things red.

Krazy Kats was not the most sophisticated restaurant that she'd ever been in; it glowed like a small red button between the blocks of smart flats and canopied bars that lined the *Paseo Maritimo*. She wondered that he'd managed to get planning permission to paint it so vividly. Inside there was no respite from the colour, but she had to admit that otherwise the decor was pleasant; there were wide, glass windows that could be pulled aside in the summer, leaving the restaurant open to the cool breeze from the sea, the furniture was modern, lots of shiny chrome and ebony chairs and there was a gleaming white, marble floor.

'Seems a bit Japanese, don't you think?' whispered Jenny.

'Not according to the menu.' She pointed to a chalk board where the daily specials were listed:

Steak and Kidney pie

Fish, chips and mushy peas

Sausage and Mash

Lancashire hotpot.

Jenny laughed. 'Surely people don't order Lancashire hotpot on a day like today?'

'You'd be surprised,' a Yorkshire voice said behind them. 'People come here for a taste of home. Our traditional English food is what keeps this place going.'

The two women turned to look at him. He was essentially the same man he'd been twenty years before but fatter—he no longer looked as though he were in need of a square meal—cleaner, sleeker and happier. He obviously worked out on a regular basis and displayed his muscle tone by wearing close-fitting, sleeveless t-shirts. As the stall holder had said, he'd lost a lot of his hair and what remained was pulled back in a scraggy ponytail. His face was deeply lined and still betrayed the ravages of his youth, despite the Mediterranean suntan that he'd since acquired.

'I know you, don't I?' he said. 'Your face is very familiar.' He hesitated, staring at Carla. 'Got it, the designer. I knew it was you. Cathy, isn't it?'

'Nearly, Carla. How nice to see you after all these years.'

'That's it, Carla. I never forget a face, photographic memory I've got. Well, well.'

'Do you remember Jenny?'

He reached out and grabbed Jenny's hand. 'Of course. How are you doll?' He beamed at them. 'Sit down, here have this table, the best in the house. Well what a surprise. Let me get you a drink. What'll it be?'

'A couple of glasses of dry, white wine would be lovely.'

'Toni, *dos vinos blancos y uno para mi,' he called across to the barman.* 'So, you're here on holiday?' He sat down opposite them.

'Well, I am,' said Jenny. 'Just the weekend, sadly.'

'I moved out here just a few months ago. We've got a place on the way up to Ronda,' Carla added.

'Very nice. Well this is a surprise. Blast from the past.'

'I was in the market the other day and I bought an old coat of yours,' she said.

'My red leather one? I gave Julie hell about that. She wanted to clear out some space for visitors she said, then it turns out it's all my things that have to go. Bloody woman, threw out all my gear from the good ole days, high heeled boots, some fantastic shirts and that coat. I told her, You throw out any more of my gear and it's divorce, I said. Too small for me now, she reckoned I ask you.' He sat up straight as he said it, pulling in his stomach and moving his shoulders back.   'So you bought it did you?'

'Yes, mostly for old times' sake, but it was good leather and I thought I might be able to do something with it.'

'Still in business then?'

'I was until I came to Spain; things were going very well.'

'Yes, she has Melissa Stanford and Ron Potts amongst her customers,' Jenny said, accepting a glass of wine from the waiter.

'Melissa Stanford, she's gorgeous. Did you see her in Tender is the Night?' Carla shook her head. 'So ole Ron Potts has taken to wearing leather has he? Still playing the clubs I hear.'

'Yes, he's doing all right I think. He's got a tour of South Africa next month.'

'Has he, by God.'

Carla could detect a note of envy in Brian's voice. She knew how he felt. 'Don't you miss it Brian, the buzz, the applause, the fans?' she asked.

He sighed. 'Sometimes. But I don't miss the travelling, living out of a suitcase, hanging around airports, running my life around a timetable. And I don't miss the booze and the drugs. I've been clean for years now. Yes, I enjoy a drink with my friends,' he raised his glass as if in a toast. 'But that's all. Living my life on the edge is over for me now. Julie gave me an ultimatum, change my ways or she'd leave me and take the kids with her. I knew I'd no chance of keeping them with my record, so I checked into one of those fancy clinics and I've never looked back.'

'Do you still play?' Jenny asked.

'We jam around sometimes, the boys and me. Freddie Snow lives out at Estepona. You remember him? He was our drummer. And Bert Little has a holiday house in Benalmadena. The best guitarist on the Costa del Sol.'

'And ukulele,' added Jenny.

'That's right, doll.'

'Sounds good,' said Carla.

'Yeah, we sometimes put on a bit of a gig for the locals. Nothing serious you know.'

'Maybe you could make a comeback,' suggested Jenny.

'Naw, when Davie died, we said that was it.'

Carla remembered reading something about a guitarist being killed in a car crash on the M1, that was it, lead guitarist with Red Katz. Yes, now she remembered. 'Red Katz.'

'What?'

'Your group was called Red Katz.'

'That's right.'

'Hence, Krazy Kats.' She laughed. 'Business good?'

'Not bad. We're full most nights in the summer, then we have our winter regulars. You'd be surprised how much the Brits like their routine. We put on specials all through the winter, Monday is pie night, Friday is fish and chips and so on. I can tell you who will be here on a particular night. It gets so that, if someone doesn't turn up, the rest of the regulars get worried that he's died or something.' He laughed. 'Toni bring us the rest of that bottle, please. So you've given up the design business then?'

'No, not exactly. In fact that's one reason we've come here for lunch today.'

'And the other?'

'To taste your bangers and mash of course.'

He reached across the table and filled up their glasses. 'Would you like to order now?'

'Yes, all right. Well, as I said, sausages and mash for me.'

'Fish and chips for me,' said Jenny.

'Okay, so tell me what your plans are.'

'I'm sure you will recognise this when I tell you that I just can't spend all my time sitting in the sun, swimming and playing tennis, as though I were on an extended holiday. I have to have something to do, especially something creative.' Brian nodded sagely. 'Jenny has been great, keeping up the contacts with my old clients, but I realise that it won't last forever. I've got to find new clients here in Spain. I've taken a stall in the market to get going, but really I want to get my business back on to its former level.'

'So, how can I help?'

Carla hesitated. 'I need some recommendations.'

'You want an in with the rich and famous, is that it?'

'I suppose so.'

He lit a cigarette and looked at her, thoughtfully. 'I don't really wear that sort of gear anymore,' he said wistfully. 'I'm more the jeans and t-shirt guy these days. I suppose I could start by introducing you to Julie. She's the one who likes to spend money on clothes, and she's got lots of rich friends.'

'Does she work in the restaurant?' asked Jenny.

He threw his head back and laughed at the preposterousness of the suggestion. 'No, Julie doesn't work. Julie doesn't earn money. She just spends it.'

'If you could speak to her, I'd be very grateful. I have to admit I haven't had the time to meet many people yet, we've been busy getting the house and garden straight.'

'You should get out and meet them. There're plenty of wealthy people in your area. In fact I'm sure Julie's got some Swedish friend who lives up there, blonde girl with legs right up to her armpits. On the road to Ronda, you said?'

'Yes, about half a mile past the golf club.'

'Just leave it with me. I'll have a word with her tonight and give you a ring.'

The restaurant was beginning to fill up and she could see Brian was becoming restless to attend to his customers. She took a business card out of her handbag and gave it to him.

'Great. Ah, here's your lunch.' He stood up as the waiter arrived with their food. '*Que aproveche,*' he said. 'Enjoy your meal.'

'Thanks Brian. Nice to see you again.'

'You too Carla, Jenny. I'll be in touch.' Then he hurried over to a group of his regulars at the bar.

'That could be promising,' said Jenny. 'You handled it very well. I can see you don't need my services anymore.'

'I'll always need your help, Jen, even if it's only to keep me on the straight and narrow.'

'This is delicious,' her friend said, putting a forkful of flaky white fish into her mouth. 'Maybe we'll come here again. And he's not bad, either,' she added, nodding her head in the direction of Brian.

'Hey, I need his wife on my side, remember.'

'Okay, spoilsport.' She giggled.

*

Brian Red was as good as his word. He telephoned Carla a couple of days later and said that his wife would be happy to meet her and introduce her to some of her golfing friends. Now as Carla parked her Volvo in his drive, next to a white Mercedes, a red Porsche and a Mini Cooper S she realised she had made a wise decision speaking to him. It seemed that Brian's taste had not extended to the decoration of their home and there was, she was glad to see, a distinct lack of anything red.

Julie opened the door herself. She was a slim woman, with light brown hair brushed back from her face. She wore pink Bermuda shorts and a matching polo shirt. She looked very ordinary, not at all what Carla expected the wife of Brian Red to look like.

'Hello, you must be Carla. Brian has told me all about you. Do come through, we're sitting outside.' She ushered Carla through the house and into the garden, where a small group of women were sitting drinking wine. They were all wearing golf clothes.

'We've just been playing the Bennet Cup,' she explained. 'So I suggested they all come back here for a drink and then they could meet you at the same time.' She looked at Carla for approval. Her voice was soft, with just the hint of a north Yorkshire accent.

'That's great,' said Carla. 'I appreciate it.'

The women stopped talking as they approached and looked towards them. 'Right, let me introduce you to everyone. Listen up folks, this is Carla, she's a top designer that Brian knew from back in the old days.'

Carla smiled and nodded at the expectant faces. She felt uncomfortable. This was not really her style. She'd never been very good at selling herself, never had to be, she always had Jenny to do it for her. She wished that Jenny had come with her; she could have done with her there right then for moral support. 'Hello everyone.'

Julie launched into a round of introductions. 'This is Laura, she's a very old friend of mine and an excellent golfer,' she stressed the word old and grinned.

Laura, despite her golfing attire, was immaculately made-up and wore some discreet, but very expensive jewellery. Carla noticed a Cartier watch on her wrist. 'Pleased to meet you,' she said.

'And this is my four-some partner, Arabel. She's married to the most gorgeous Arab prince.'

Arabel smiled and held out her hand. 'You're the only one who thinks he's gorgeous. He's just a fat old bastard really,' she said and laughed.

'Muriel Spinks, she's our Ladies' Captain this year.' Muriel was older than the others, with carefully groomed grey hair and a square jaw. Carla could imagine her marching down the fairway with her clubs over her shoulder.

'How do you do,' she said, her accent one hundred percent Cheltenham Ladies' College.

'Nice to meet you,' Carla murmured.   Was she going to remember all these names?

'And this is Kirsten. Kirsten's from Sweden and I believe she's a neighbour of yours.'

'Hello Carla.' Her handshake was firm and positive. 'You too live on the way to Ronda?' she asked, her perfect English tinged with a slight Scandinavian accent.

'Yes, just after kilometre seven.'

'Ah yes, I know it. We are very close then. You must come and visit me one day. My house is the big wooden one you can see from the main road.'

'I'd love to, thank you.' Carla knew exactly which house she meant, it was more like a mansion than a house, if there were such things as Swedish mansions.

'This is another good golfer, Eve le Brun. She splits her time between here and Monte Carlo.' A dark haired, petite woman in her early thirties stood up and kissed Carla on both cheeks.

'Enchanté.'

'Hi.'

'Zoe, another golfer and her sister Dawn. Dawn doesn't play, well not yet anyway.' Dawn smiled awkwardly. Carla thought she looked slightly out of it amongst these rather confident, sophisticated women.

'There that's all the introductions done. Now, how about a glass of something?'

'White wine would be fine thanks.'

Laura, who seemed very much at home in the Red household, pulled up a chair for her and then poured her a glass of wine. Carla sat down, accepting the drink gratefully. She still felt rather awkward. 'You have a lovely home,' she said to Julie. 'The garden's beautiful.' It was, a gentle lawn sloped down to a copse of tall trees and beyond it was a panoramic view of Marbella and the Mediterranean. Just off to their left was a large swimming pool, surrounded by terraces and a pergola that was covered in sweet smelling jasmine, bignonia and dipladenia. A black dog, stretched out in the shade of a lemon tree, lifted its head and looked at her, but seeing she posed no threat, he let out a deep sigh and dropped his head onto his paws once again.

'Brian's very fond of the garden,' said Julie. 'Not that he gets a lot of time to do much.'

'That's what you've got a gardener for,' added Laura.

'So, Carla, what kind of designs do you do?' asked Arabel. 'Julie said something about leather.'

'Yes, I work entirely with leather. My label had become quite well known in London by the time I moved to Spain, and I'm still designing for my regular clients. However it's not quite so easy keeping up the close relationship I need with them when I'm living so far away. My agent helps me with the London end of the business, but that's not the same as personal contact.' The women nodded in agreement; they all believed in personal contact.

'What made you come to Spain?' asked Zoe.

'My husband, I suppose. He wanted to live here.' There was a murmur of understanding; this was something they could all recognise. She knew then she had these women on her side.

'So now you're looking for new clients?' asked Eve.

'Yes. I know that the life style out here is more casual than in other countries, but I still think that there are plenty of occasions when one wants something different, something just that bit special, something that no-one else has.'

'So all your designs are individual?' asked Arabel.

'Yes, I only design for the top end of the market. Each garment is tailor made to a design that is approved by the client. Sometimes, with my long standing clients, I will present them with the finished garment. I know their tastes so well.'

'Did you make that skirt you're wearing?' asked Muriel.

'Yes.' She had deliberately chosen to wear a mid-calf length skirt of fine, beige suede with a cascade of appliqué down the front panel, a white cotton t-shirt and sandals.

'I'd never have thought to wear a leather skirt with sandals,' said Julie.

'That's the beauty of leather, you can dress it up or go for a very casual look. Here in Spain, where people tend to be more relaxed about what they wear, it's nice to adopt the casual look, but with that extra bit of panache.'

She could see them looking at her appreciatively. Jenny would be proud of her; she would make a saleswoman yet.

'Do you have anything else you can show us?' asked Laura.

Carla took her portfolio out of her canvas bag. It contained glossy photographs of almost all her designs. She'd compiled it for herself, to keep an on-going record of her work, but now realised that it was a good way of showing these women exactly what sort of standard she was talking about.

'I've a few photos here of my designs, if you'd like to see them. Obviously you can't see all the details in a photograph but it will give you an idea.' She passed the book into Eve's eager hands.

'More wine?'

'Yes, please Julie.' She was relaxing now and sat back in her chair, looking at the group around her. Eve and Laura were leafing through her portfolio. Muriel was exchanging some golf club gossip with Kirsten, and Julie and Zoe seemed to be trying to cheer up Dawn. Dawn pulled a tissue out of her handbag and began blowing her nose noisily.

'I'm so sorry. I just can't help it,' she said.

Julie noticed Carla looking at them. 'Dawn has the most dreadful problem with her house,' she explained. 'They're threatening to pull it down.'

'My goodness, that's awful.'

'She's moved in with me, so she can get away from it all for a while,' Zoe added.

'Peter's staying on for now, in the caravan. He says he's not going to let them get away with it without a fight,' said Dawn, wiping her eyes.

'So what happened?' Carla asked.

Dawn accepted another glass of wine from her sister and seemed to regain some of her composure. 'I don't really know,' she said. 'We thought we'd done everything by the book, but now they tell us the house is illegal and it must come down.'

'It's ridiculous,' added her sister. 'Peter was meticulous in getting all the paperwork.'

'My husband used to be a civil servant,' Dawn began. 'He worked for Harrogate Town Council and we had a lovely house in the best part of Harrogate.' She sighed as if she wished those days were back again. 'Anyway when they offered him the chance of early retirement he jumped at it. We thought it was a chance to fulfil our dream and buy a house in the Spanish countryside. We came out on a few of those organised trips to look at property and eventually found exactly what we were looking for, our dream house. Except it wasn't a house exactly, it was a forty thousand square metre plot of land, overlooking a lake. The constructor had already built five other houses in the area and had planning permission for ours and three more.'

'It's a beautiful spot,' added Zoe. 'There're mountains all around and pretty little white villages. It's very picturesque.'

'We never expected any trouble,' added Dawn.

'So what happened? Did the constructor go bust?'

'No, nothing like that. We sold up in Harrogate, bought ourselves a caravan and moved onto the land, while the house was being built. It was exactly what we wanted. We didn't mind living in the caravan. In fact it was fun. The construction went ahead just as planned and everything seemed fine. We were really enjoying ourselves.

My husband is a very meticulous man, he went to a *gestor* and got him to tell him all the paperwork we needed. We had the architect's plans approved, permission from the town hall, approval for this and approval for that, the paperwork alone cost us a fortune, but we wanted to do it legally. We'd heard of people cutting corners and ending up losing everything. We didn't want that to happen to us.' She started to cry again.

Her sister put her arm around her shoulder. 'There, there, it'll sort itself out, you see. They just can't treat you like that.'

'It's so unfair,' she wailed.

'They put all their money into the house,' Zoe explained to Carla.

'So what happened?'

'Well when it was finished they tried to get the electricity connected but the company said they needed one final paper from the town hall, confirmation that the house was habitable. So they went to the town hall to get it and were told that the house was illegal. It should never have been built. They showed them all the paperwork they had, most of it issued by the same town hall that was now saying that it was illegal, but they just said that there must have been a misunderstanding,' continued Zoe.

'A misunderstanding, what rubbish. My husband went into it all thoroughly. He was a civil servant, he's used to bureaucracy. There's no way he made a mistake.'

'Anyway, they got themselves a solicitor, but nothing helped, the town hall wouldn't give them the papers they needed. So now it's stalemate; they can't get any electricity connected so they can't live in the house.'

'And now, on top of that, the *Junta de Andalucia* says that we have to pull it down. They say that the town hall had no right letting us build there in the first place. It's such a mess. We don't know what to do. Every penny we had is invested in that house. If they pull it down we'll have nothing.'

'Can't you go to the European Courts?' asked Kirsten.

'Our solicitor is looking into that, but he doesn't think we have much chance.'

'They're not the only ones,' Julie explained, nodding towards the weepy Dawn. 'There have been dozens of houses affected. Local councils were so greedy for the money that they gave out permissions as though they were sticks of candy and now it's all falling back on them.'

'Yes, but it's not falling back on the councils, is it. It's the poor house owners who are losing out,' said Zoe.

'They have prosecuted some of the mayors,' interjected Laura. 'Look at Marbella.'

'But nothing's been done to help the people whose homes are affected,' repeated Zoe. 'And there are plenty of other councils who've been up to the same tricks.'

Carla felt very sorry for this frail woman and her husband; they had gone after their dream and it had all crumbled around them. Arnie was a property developer. Could he have anything to do with this?

CHAPTER 17

Carla was looking forward to spending an evening in the company of Gerry and Chris; they were such a relaxed couple. She knew that for a few hours at least she would be able to unwind after the tension of the funeral, and it was nice to have someone on her side. They were the only friends, apart from Jenny, who had bothered to visit them after they moved to Spain. In the beginning that had been part of the problem; she had felt isolated and cut off from both friends and family. Her mother had a fear of flying and her father wouldn't visit without her. Her sister came out once, but hadn't enjoyed the heat and although she promised to come again in the winter, she never had. So that first year, Carla had flown back to the UK quite a few times to see them, but once she found some outlets for her business, she had been too busy. Now she wished she had kept up her old friendships and seen more of her father, who had died the previous year. She had missed their friendly faces at the funeral, but even her mother hadn't been able to attend; she couldn't drive. Her sister had moved to Canada and if it hadn't been for Jenny, Chris and Gerry, she would have felt completely abandoned. But it was this lack of family that bothered her most; she missed being part of a family unit. Maybe that was why she'd always wanted children of her own, but sadly it hadn't happened.

*

Carla sat by the pool watching Jenny swim elegantly up and down. She was pleased to have her there, at last she had someone she could confide in. She sighed. This was all wrong. She should be confiding in Harry, but recently whenever she wanted to talk to him about the things that were troubling her, he had walked away.

'Penny for them,' Jenny asked, pulling herself up onto the edge of the pool. Her hair was a slick, shiny cap, plastered against her head, and drops of water glistened on her arms.

'Nothing really, just thinking how nice it is to have you here for a bit.'

'Yes I have to admit I'm really enjoying a week out of the London traffic. Not that I don't love my job but it is nice to get away once in a while.' She rolled sideways and flopped back into the pool, disappearing under the water before resurfacing with a laugh to splash water over her friend. 'Come on lazy bones, the water's perfect.' She stretched her brown body and slid away on her back, her arms by her side, her feet kicking lazily.

Carla put down her book, removed her sunglasses then cautiously lowered herself into the pool. The water was cool and refreshing. She let herself float lazily by the steps for a few moments, allowing the water to caress her warm skin before striking out to join Jenny.

'So how did you get on with the lady golfers?'

'Okay. They're actually a really nice bunch.'

'Rich?'

'Mmmn. Some of them definitely.'

'Good. Did they like your designs?'

'Yes, I think so. They all took my cards and said they'd be in touch, so we'll see.'

'Well it's a start, anyway.'

'Yes, I think meeting Brian Red again may have been the turning point for me.' She turned towards the house. 'Come on Harry, come and join us,' she called, as he reappeared to refill his glass.

'No Darling, I'm busy. Can I get you anything? A glass of wine?'

Carla looked at Jenny, who shook her head. 'Not for now, maybe later.'

'Okay, enjoy yourselves,' he called and disappeared inside.

'Where was Harry today?' Jenny asked.

'To be honest, I'm not sure. He said he had to meet Arnie about something then I think he went to the club to play tennis.'

'He doesn't mind me being here does he? It's just that I've hardly seen him since I arrived.'

'No of course not. You know Harry is very fond of you. He's just got rather a lot on at the moment.'

'Everything is all right between you two isn't it?' Jenny asked.

'Of course it is.'

Carla turned onto her back and began to swim lazily away, her feet kicking up a tidal wave of her own. Jenny followed. 'Now come on Carla, you can't get away with that; I know you too well. Look, if you've got a problem, tell me. It can't hurt to talk it through, can it?'

Carla stopped. She had reached the shallow end and sat on one of the steps, letting the water lap around her waist. 'I suppose it's this baby thing. Harry just doesn't seem to understand how much it means to me. Now if I try to talk to him about it he loses his temper and storms out.'

'I suppose he thinks it's a challenge to his masculinity.'

'Maybe, but I think it's something more. He just refuses to talk about having babies.'

'Well he does have two children already, perhaps he doesn't want any more.'

'If that's the case why doesn't he say so? Why does he keep avoiding the subject? He says I'm always nagging him, but if he would only talk about it then I might understand.'

'You know men don't like talking about things that bother them.'

'A bit like ostriches, you mean, burying their heads in the sand?'

Jenny laughed. 'I suppose so. But are you sure that's all that's bothering you? I've noticed that whenever Harry mentions Arnie your mouth does that funny thing it always does when you're annoyed.'

'I'm not keen on Arnie I admit. What funny thing?' Jenny pursed her lips into a tight bunch. 'I don't do that.'

Her friend nodded her head. 'You do.'

'Anyway there's something strange about Arnie, I can't quite put my finger on it but something's not right. Harry says he's a legitimate businessman, but he seems a bit shady to me, and it worries me that Harry spends so much time with him.'

'What about his wife, do you like her?'

'She's all right, a bit quiet but pleasant enough. What can I say? If we were back in England she wouldn't be the sort of person I'd be hanging out with. She's not my type. We talk about the weather and her dog.'

'The weather, good God what's there to talk about? Sun today, more sun tomorrow. Doesn't she tell you what Arnie does?'

'No, apart from the fact that he owns a few clubs she doesn't seem to know much about her husband's business.'

'Don't you think you're being a bit paranoid about this? If Arnie's a club owner, he'll be making plenty of money anyway. Why should he necessarily be involved in anything illegal?'

'I don't know. I just get that feeling. You haven't met him yet. Wait until you meet him; you'll see what I mean.'

'When will that be?'

'Harry has arranged for us to go out to dinner tomorrow night with Arnie and his wife. Arnie's paying.'

'Good then I'll get to see what your bogey man is really like. Now come on, cheer up. Why don't you get us both a glass of wine while I plaster myself with some sun-cream?'

*

The restaurant was a bit too loud for Carla's taste but Jenny loved it. Their table was outside on the terrace; far below them was the coastal motorway and beyond that the lights of Benalmadena and the dark presence of the Mediterranean. A round yellow moon cast its rays on the sea, picking up the white-topped waves as they lapped on the shore. The air smelled of jasmine and *dama de la noche*.

'This is wonderful,' Jenny enthused. 'Look at that view.'

'It's even better by day,' Arnie said, obviously delighted by his guest's appreciation. 'Sit 'ere, then you can enjoy it even more.'

Jenny sat between Arnie and Harry while Carla and Arnie's wife, Dorothy, placed themselves opposite. Arnie wore a white jacket with a black silk shirt and tight black trousers. His hair was slicked down with some sweet smelling pomade, and on the rather stubby fingers of his right hand were two gold rings, one of which was set with an impressive diamond. A faint film of perspiration lay along his top lip, and from time to time he pulled out a large red handkerchief from his top pocket and mopped his face carefully.   He lifted his hand and snapped his fingers loudly. Immediately a waiter was by their side.

'Champagne, Adolfo and none of that cheap Cava crap, the real thing if you don't mind.' He beamed at his guests. 'I like to drink the best. What's the point of 'aving money if you don't 'ave the best, I say. That's right isn't it Dorothy?'

His wife smiled. She seemed an unostentatious woman. Tonight she was dressed in a dark blue dress and wore a double strand of gleaming pearls at her throat. Somehow Carla thought a blonde bimbo would have suited Arnie better, but she had to admit that he seemed very happy with his unassuming wife. Perhaps he saw enough bimbos in his clubs.

The waiter returned with the champagne, Dom Perignon no less, and Arnie nodded his approval. While it was being poured a second waiter handed out the menus. Carla's eyes as usual went straight to the prices but they weren't listed. It was like Harry's old joke, 'If you have to ask the price you can't afford it.' She hoped that Harry had got it right about Arnie paying.

'Great steak 'ere, best along the coast,' she heard him tell Jenny.

'Arnie always has the steak,' Dorothy chimed in. 'Prawn cocktail and steak. He never varies.'

As Carla looked through the elaborate menu she wondered why he bothered to come here; it was obviously not for the food. From the glitter of the women's jewels and the plethora of heavy gold Rolexes, the clientele appeared to consist of the wealthier members of the community. From time to time Arnie would raise his hand in greeting— a rather imperious wave she thought—and occasionally someone would respond and come over to their table to shake his hand. Arnie beamed his way through it all. She wondered what exactly it was that Arnie was mixed up in; he seemed very much at home among the rich and famous.

'So 'Arry, 'ave you told the little lady yet?'

Harry looked confused. He'd already finished two glasses of champagne and was now on his third.

'The job 'Arry, 'ave you told 'er about the job?'

'Oh yes,' he nodded. 'The job.' His speech was a little slurred, and she noticed that his eyes were taking on that all too familiar glazed look.

Arnie turned to Carla. 'So what do you think?'

'I think it sounds good. I'm sure Harry will do a great job,' she replied noncommittally.

She knew that Arnie was expecting some show of gratitude on her part but a streak of stubbornness in her wouldn't allow her to show it.

'Monday morning 'Arry, eight o'clock sharp. None of these funny Spanish hours, eight to five, a good old English working day.'

'Don't the Spanish mind working eight to five, especially in the summer?' Jenny asked.

'No idea. Don't employ any Spanish. Can't trust 'em further than I can throw 'em. All Brits in my clubs, well except for the girls; some of them are Scandinavian.' He winked at Harry. 'You know, long legs and blonde hair. The punters love 'em. Then we've got a few Rumanians and the Filipinos, very popular. But the rest are all Brits. Know where you are with them.'

'Do you speak Spanish?' Jenny asked.

'Yeah, enough to get by. Don't really need it in my line of work because everyone around 'ere speaks English. If they don't then they don't do business with me, simple as that.' He waved a hand towards the waiter who was returning with a further bottle of champagne. 'Even old Adolfo speaks English. 'As to, or 'e'd lose most of 'is customers. That's right Adolfo, isn't it?' The waiter smiled politely and replaced the empty bottle with a full one.

*

Carla had little to say in the car on the way home; she had elected to drive but was now beginning to feel sleepy. Jenny chattered happily at her side and she could hear Harry snoring heavily in the back seat.

'What did you think of Arnie?'

'Charming but a bit sleazy I'd say.'

'Exactly.'

'Doesn't mean he's into anything dodgy though.'

'Oh come on Jen. You've met him. I'm sure he's up to something.'

'He seems to think a lot of 'Arry.' She giggled.

'That's what worries me.'

'Ask Harry outright. See what he says.'

'I don't think there's much point. He just gets annoyed if I question him about it.'

'Like I said, maybe you're reading too much into this. All right, so Arnie is not very cultured and maybe a bit rough, but that doesn't make him a crook. I think you've been reading too many trashy novels.'

'So you think there's nothing in it?'

'Even if he's using his clubs as a front for something illegal it doesn't necessarily mean that Harry is involved. Just relax Carla. I've never known you to get so uptight over something. You do realise that being stressed is not going to help you conceive. And it seems to me that you're putting yourself under unnecessary stress over this Arnie business.'

Carla didn't reply but the significance of her friend's remarks didn't go unnoticed and she determined to heed her advice.

*

Later, once Harry had crashed out on the bed, Carla and Jenny took their drinks out onto the terrace.

'That was a lovely meal, thank you so much. I did enjoy myself,' Jenny said, relaxing back into the sun-lounger by the pool and sipping her wine.

'Good, I'm glad you liked it.'

'I really don't know what you've got against Arnie; he seems perfectly okay to me. Quite charming in a rough sort of way. There's something very sexy about powerful men, don't you think?'

Carla grimaced. 'So you like him?'

'Yes I suppose I do, he's certainly very entertaining. He's promised to take me to see one of his clubs before I go back.'

'Whatever for?'

'I just thought it would be fun. I've never been to a strip club before.'

Carla lay back in her chair and looked up at the sky. They'd switched off all the main lights in the garden so as not to attract any insects. The pale reflection of a yellow moon lit up the distant sea and cast a gentle light around them. Above her she could make out the constellations of thousands of stars. What was it about Arnie? Was she the only one who thought he was a crook? Even Jenny had been taken in by him.

'Just be careful of him, is all I have to say,' Carla said at last. 'There's more to that man than meets the eye.'

'I think you should get this baby business sorted out with Harry. I'm sure that's what's making you so neurotic.'

'Neurotic? I'm not neurotic. I just don't trust the man.'

'Maybe if you didn't have so many other things on your mind, you would be able to relax more. I must admit I've never known you so nervy before. You need to get this straightened out.'

'But how can I? Harry won't even discuss it, never mind go for any tests.'

'There must be another way of tackling it.'

'If you can think of one I'd be very grateful. It's getting so that I can't sleep at nights.'

'Well you know what they say, "If mountain won't go to Mohammed then Mohammed must go to the mountain."'

CHAPTER 18

They found a small bistro, serving French and Italian food, tucked in a narrow alley next to the Town Hall and hurried inside to escape the rain. The bowling had been tremendous fun and Carla felt relaxed and hungry; Chris and her son had won but not by as much as she feared.

The restaurant was only half full when they walked in, water dripping from their wet coats, but the steam rising from the damp clothes of the other customers gave the room a cosy, warm feel.

'God, I won't be able to have a smoke now,' moaned Gerry. A large 'No Smoking' sign hung just inside the entrance.

'Bit too wet for that, my love. Anyway, it's time you gave up.'

Geraldine ignored him and helped her two children struggle out of their wet anoraks. They chose a table near the window where they could watch the rain drumming on the pavements outside and ordered a bottle of Soave and two cokes.

'Okay, Carla what's all this business about the house?'

'I'm as surprised as you are Chris. Harry led me to believe that I could stay there as long as I wanted. I don't particularly want to keep the house. It was Harry's money that paid for it; if he wanted his children to have it that's fine by me. But I did think I'd be able to stay there for a few more years, at least until I'd decided what to do with my life. I'm not sure what I'm going to do now.'

'Do you have anywhere of your own?'

'No. I always intended to return to London if anything happened to Harry, but I hadn't actually planned for it. You don't, do you? You don't expect people to die.'

'What about money? Did he leave you anything at all?'

'Harry didn't have a lot of money left. Remember he hadn't really worked for twenty years. But I've got some savings and then there's Harry's life insurance. I'll be all right I expect.'

'Houses are expensive here now, you know.'

'Maybe I'll move into the country, up north or Scotland even.'

Gerry pulled a face. 'Come on Carla. You're a Londoner. Why move away from your friends?'

'To be quite honest Gerry, apart from you and Chris, and Jenny of course, I don't have many friends here anymore. What I'd really like to do is just stay where I am for at least a few more years. I had quite a good business in Spain until recently. I'd like to try to get it going again. I don't really fancy starting all over again in London.'

'What did Max have to say about them planning to sell the house against Harry's wishes?' Gerry asked. 'You said, he promised you could stay in it, didn't he?'

'He said that Harry's wishes had no legal standing. He said that once the beneficiaries have inherited the property it becomes legally theirs and it's up to them what they do with it,' Carla replied.

'I understand but there are other angles.' He paused then asked, 'Have you ever wondered if Tom and Sylvia are actually Harry's children?'

'What? Not his children? I don't understand.'

'Why didn't you and Harry have any children? I always thought you were keen to have a family,' Gerry interrupted.

'Never happened.'

'Did you have any tests?' Chris asked.

Carla felt a twinge of resentment at so many questions but she was intrigued with where it was leading. 'I did. They couldn't find any reason for me not to conceive.'

'And Harry?'

'Harry wouldn't go.'

Chris and Gerry looked at each other. 'It was the same with his first wife. They were married for years before Sylvia came along, and Harry wouldn't even discuss it with anyone.'

'But she became pregnant in the end.'

'Yes but neither of the children look like Harry.'

'Of course they do, well Tom at least.'

'No he doesn't Carla. Okay he's dark haired and thin, but that's all.'

'That doesn't mean anything. Lots of kids don't look like their parents.' She looked at Rupert and Nicola, younger versions of Chris and Gerry, hybrids of them both. Rupert's face in particular had a way of changing from his father's serious demeanour to the more mischievous look of his mother within moments. His genes were clearly obvious. Nicola on the other hand had the blond curls of her mother and Chris's pale, grey eyes but her face was all her own.

'No, there's more to it than that.'

'Well,' she paused, feeling herself blush at what she was about to say. 'Actually I do know that Harry had a problem.'

'You know?'

'Yes. I had his sperm tested.'

'I thought you said he wouldn't have any tests.'

'He wouldn't.'

'So?'

'Don't ask. Suffice to say I had it tested. I was fed up waiting for him to do something. It seemed to be so unfair.'

'And?'

'The results were inconclusive so the guy at the clinic suggested he have a blood test. That was easier; they test your blood for all sorts of reasons in Spain. Harry had been having a spate of headaches and so I took him to a private laboratory and had an analysis taken. Of course I didn't give him the full results.'

'Which were?'

'That he had Klinefelter's Syndrome.'

'Never heard of it.'

'It's something to do with having an extra chromosome; he had two XXs and one Y. It's not uncommon, about one in every five hundred men have it.'

'So why isn't it better known?'

'Apparently there are few outward symptoms so I imagine that many men never know they're suffering from it.'

'Until they want to have a child that is,' said Gerry.

'The only sure way to identify it is with a blood test.'

'Can't it be treated?'

'Some aspects can be helped with testosterone but the genetics can't be altered.'

'Did you say anything to Harry?'

'I tried but every time I brought up the question of babies he got angry and stormed out. He was drinking quite heavily by then,' she added. 'In the end I just resigned myself to not having any children. I had my work; I just immersed myself in that.'

'So there you are then,' Chris said, putting his knife and fork firmly down on the table as though to underline the decisiveness of his statement.

'But it's not actually proof unless you've still got the results,' said Gerry.

'Do you have the results?'

'No of course not, I destroyed them straight away. Harry would never have forgiven me if he'd known what I did.'

'Do you think he knew he had the condition?'

'I don't know but it could explain why he was always so resistant to have any tests done.'

Chris hesitated then said, 'He once told me, many years ago when we were both still single, that he thought he would never be able to have any kids. I didn't press him for any details; we were both a bit drunk at the time and I thought he was just being a little maudlin.' He paused and drank some of his wine. 'Never thought about it again until the other day at the funeral. You know how you start reminiscing on these occasions, well suddenly I remembered us standing on the bridge in Henley, pints of Brakespeare's best bitter in our hands and talking about the future. We'd just finished our finals and our lives stretched out before us like blank slates waiting to be written on. That's when he turned to me and said, I'm never going to get married Chris. I laughed at him but he was serious. Can't have children, so what's the point in getting married? I told him not to be so bloody stupid and to go and get us a couple of more pints.'

'So he did know there was something wrong.'

'Sounds like it.'

'And Barbara? She must have known.'

'Either that or got fed up waiting and got herself pregnant anyway.'

'Mum, can we go?'

'Soon Rupert.'

'So are you going to contest it?' Chris asked.

Carla didn't answer straight away; she scooped the last morsel of Bolognese sauce onto her spoon and popped it into her mouth. 'I don't know,' she said at last. 'It seems a bit mean dragging all this up now. Can't I do it some other way?'

'When do you see their solicitor?'

'Thursday.'

'You could get Max to speak to him and see if he can negotiate anything.'

'I suppose so, but I don't want to upset anyone. It looks as though Harry left them the house; it must mean something. Maybe he thought they were his kids after all.'

'Only Barbara can tell us that.'

'Chris we can't go to an old friend and ask her if her ex-husband was really the father of her children. It's too cruel,' interjected Gerry.

'It's all Carla's got to negotiate with,' he snapped. 'You could ask for a DNA test I suppose.'

'Oh Chris, that's awful.'

'Why is it awful? It would prove once and for all that they were his children.'

'No Chris.' Carla's voice was hard. 'No DNA test. I don't want to ruin their lives.'

'Well they don't seem to care about ruining yours, do they?'

'I just think I should go easy.'

'Dad ...'

'Okay Rupert, we'll pay the bill and go. All right?'

The boy's smile lit up the gloomy table and Carla took his hand and said, 'I'll buy some ice-cream at the amusement park, that'll be our pudding. What do you think?'

'Yeah. Well good.'

Carla's head was spinning. She had forgotten about the Klinefelter's Syndrome. At the time she'd been more upset that it meant she wouldn't become pregnant; she'd never even thought about the children Harry already had.

*

The woman in the *herboristeria* had recommended he take one or two grams a day for at least a month. She placed the bags on the kitchen table: white muesli, ipomea digitata, bala, mucuma pruriens and ashwagangha. None of the names were familiar to Carla but she was assured that if she mixed together any three of them in equal parts and gave it to him as stated she would soon be pregnant. It seemed a bit like witchcraft but she was desperate; she had to try something. She was thirty nine, soon to be forty; if she didn't do something soon it would be too late. She had been back to England for tests, but everyone said there was nothing wrong with her and they could find no reason why she couldn't conceive. If only Harry were more understanding, but all he would say was that if it was going to happen it would happen. She joined Fertility Friend and exchanged ideas with fellow sufferers on the internet. She bought books that told her how to take her temperature and gauge the best moment in the ovulation cycle to have sex; she gave up alcohol and insisted on having at least eight hours sleep a day. She avoided smoky environments and insisted that Harry do the same. She fed him food high in antioxidants, lots of fruit and vegetables; she gave him vitamins E and C to improve his fertility and zinc and folic acid to increase his sperm count. She read that selenium improved the swimming of the sperm and made him take that as well. She took them all and more herself, and each morning the tablets and powders were laid out on the breakfast table in little coloured rows alongside their organic muesli and goats' milk. She threw out his briefs and bought him boxer shorts; she insisted he eat less seafood in case it was contaminated with mercury, and she banned pesticides from the house. Harry went along with it all. Occasionally he grumbled when she wouldn't let him use the fly spray or when he was bitten by mosquitoes, and he insisted that her ban on seafood was going a bit too far, but generally he was happy to assist her as much as he could. The only thing he would not do was go to see a doctor.

'Not more potions?' he said one morning over breakfast.

'I just thought you might like to try them. The woman in the shop said that after taking them for a month there was a seventy-five per cent chance of becoming pregnant.'

'Why don't you take them?'

'Harry they're for you. They're herbs with special aphrodisiac properties.'

'I don't think that's the problem, Carla. Have I ever had any trouble making love?'

'No, I suppose not but I just thought they might help.'

'You know you are getting too wound up about this. I've told you before if it's going to happen it will. The more stressed you get about it the less likely it is to happen. And now you're starting to get me stressed. I don't want to feel that every time we make love I'm being measured and judged a failure if you don't conceive.'

'Oh Harry it's not like that. Honestly Darling I'm not blaming you.' But she was.

'Well it seems like it.'

'It's just that I do so want to have a baby and I'm frightened that if it doesn't happen soon it will never happen.'

'Well if it doesn't happen, it doesn't. We've still got each other or did you just marry me because you wanted a family?'

'Of course not. But I'm running out of options.'

'What about that acupuncture clinic you were going to go to?' He reached across the table and helped himself to a second slice of wholemeal bread and began to spread it with honey.

'I've an appointment for next Tuesday.'

'Maybe that will work.'

'But what if it's not me?'

'What do you mean?'

'What if there's something wrong with you?'

'There isn't. I've told you before, there's nothing wrong with me.'

'But couldn't you just go and have a check? Then we would know for sure.'

'We've been down this road before Carla, I'm not going. There's no way I'm going to one of those clinics to sit in a cubicle and wank into a plastic tube. Forget it.'

'You don't have to go to the clinic, I'm sure you could do it at home.'

'Leave it Carla. I said no. I'm not doing it. Have you forgotten that I have two children already? There is nothing wrong with me.' He got up and pushed his uneaten breakfast to one side.

'You haven't drunk your green tea.'

'To tell the truth I'm fed up of green tea and organic yoghurt. I'm going to Antonio's to have a decent breakfast, a bacon and tomato baguette and a very strong cup of coffee.'

They didn't mention the subject again, but Carla noticed that when Harry came back later that morning he went into the kitchen and drank the potion she'd prepared for him.

'Jenny telephoned while you were out,' she told him.

'Your agent?'

'Yes. She's coming out at the end of the week. You don't mind do you?'

'No not at all; it'll be good for you to see her again.'

'Yes, I haven't seen her since I went back for Dad's funeral.'

'I've got some business to see to today Darling, so I probably won't be back for lunch,' he said, heading for the bedroom. A few minutes later he came back wearing a light linen jacket, dark trousers and a white shirt.

'You look smart.'

'Arnie wants me to meet some of his associates; there could be some work for me.'

'What sort of work Harry? Lighting?'

'I'll let you know when I've spoken to them. See you later.' He kissed her on the cheek and whispered, 'Don't worry so much. If you're going to conceive it will happen and if not, then we've still got each other.' She hadn't missed the faint whiff of alcohol on his breath but she didn't say anything.

Jenny was coming specifically to take back some outfits she had ordered for a new client. They were almost finished but she still had the lining to put in one of the skirts and buttons to sew on the jacket so she decided to get on with it while Harry was out. She pulled out her machine and began to work; her concentration fixed on the task in hand and Harry pushed to the back of her mind.

CHAPTER 19

Ian Routh's offices were located in a tall Edwardian building on the Old Bath Road; she had no trouble finding them. 'I have an appointment with Mr Routh,' she told his secretary, an Indian girl, wearing a pale blue sari.
'Please take a seat. He'll only be a moment,' the girl said.

Carla sat facing the window. The offices were modern, with sleek, smooth lines to the furniture and pastel shades on the walls. For some reason she felt it resembled more a dentist's waiting room that a solicitor's office; it lacked the weighty sobriety of dark oak furniture and overflowing bookcases.

An aluminium and glass door opened and Ian Routh emerged. 'Mrs Wilkinson, I'm sorry to have kept you waiting.' He stood back to allow her enter. 'I'm glad you were able to come. It's so much easier to speak about these things face to face than on the telephone, don't you think?' Carla nodded and was about to reply but the solicitor continued, 'Please do sit down.' He indicated an uncomfortable looking chrome and black leather chair and took his place opposite her, behind a large ebony desk on which lay a leather blotter and a single sheet of paper. 'I had intended to write to you but my client said it was better to wait and tell you in person.'

'Your client? Sylvia you mean?'

'Yes. Sylvia and Tom, they are joint owners of the house now.'

'May I know why they have decided to sell the house against their father's wishes?' she asked.

'That's a purely private matter. I'm afraid; you would have to speak to Sylvia or Tom about their reasons. Suffice to say that they wish to sell it as soon as possible and want me to make arrangements for you to vacate the house.'

'What if I refuse?'

The solicitor looked up and for the first time she had his undivided attention. 'It could get expensive, you know legal fees etc.'

'Expensive for whom? Not for me.'

'It is after all their house. Why would you refuse? You have been living there since your husband died, that's a year now. I think my clients have been very fair in waiting so long.'

'Fair? Harry never gave me a copy of his will. I didn't even know he'd made one. He'd talked about leaving the house to the children, but said I'd be able to live in it as long as I wanted. Doesn't it mention that in his will?'

Ian Routh looked down at the paper on his desk. 'Yes, it does say that, but it's a request not a stipulation. The children inherit the house, and you are allowed to live there until they wish to dispose of it. I'm sorry, but now they want to sell it. I'm sure you understand. A house in Spain is no good to them.'

'My husband didn't want my life disrupted any more than was necessary. I am surprised that his children will not honour his wishes.'

He looked down at the blotter and adjusted its position slightly, then changed his mind and moved it back to its original place. 'I understand that you're upset about this, Mrs. Wilkinson, but as I said my clients have personal reasons for wanting to sell the property and these reasons outweigh any filial sentiment.'

They were going round in circles. 'I will need to speak to my solicitor before I give you an answer,' she said eventually.

He picked up his pen and unscrewed the cap. 'Fine. May I ask the name of your solicitor?' he asked, poised to write it down.

'Of course.' She handed him Max's business card.

'Ah yes, I am acquainted with Mr Atherton. I'll get in touch with him.'

'Is that all?' she asked

'Just one other thing Mrs Wilkinson, I wondered if you had a copy of your husband's death certificate with you?'

'Yes I do actually but it's back at the hotel. Why?'

'The family would like to know exactly how Mr Wilkinson died. They heard first of all that he had drowned, then something about some heart complaint. I'm sure you must understand how distressing it is for them not to know the exact details of his demise.'

'Yes I can understand, Mr Routh. It was as the coroner said on the death certificate, accidental death by drowning. Harry fell into the swimming pool and drowned. It's possible he had a heart attack, but we'll never know. I'm sorry I cannot give you any more information; I was out when it happened.'

She saw him look at the piece of paper and frown. 'So you cannot shed any light on how the accident occurred?'

'No I'm sorry. Maybe if his family had kept in closer touch with him they would have a better understanding of Harry's life and his death. Perhaps you could tell them that.'

The solicitor didn't reply but stood up, making it clear that their conversation was over. He offered his hand politely and said, 'I look forward to hearing from your solicitor, Mrs Wilkinson. And maybe, if it's not too much trouble, you could send me a copy of the death certificate. Oh, and of course the deeds to the house. You do have them with you, I suppose?'

She stared at him. The deeds? She'd never even seen them. Harry dealt with all that sort of thing. 'The *escritura*, you mean?'

'If that's what they're called, yes. Obviously we need that in order to sell the house. Do you have it?'

'Not with me. I expect it's at home among Harry's papers. I'll ask his solicitor about it, when I see him.'

She was beginning to feel faint. So many questions about how he died. And now wanting the deeds to her house. She took his limp hand and shook it briefly. What was going on? Did they think she had murdered him?

As she walked back to her car, she thought back to when Harry had told her that he'd like to leave something in his will for the children. It had seemed so inconsequential at the time; both of them were young and death seemed as remote as the stars. They had never spoken of it again. Life was good; they were happy together and she was beginning to build a new life for herself with the man she loved.

*

It was late when Harry returned, flushed and smiling, whether from the many drinks he had obviously had or from the job that Arnie had given him, she wasn't sure. He'd been working at least a couple of days a week for Arnie for the last few months but still there was no mention of anything permanent. As far as she could make out Harry's job was as a general factotum, or run-around as he liked to call it. She knew he still held out hopes of getting his old business off the ground but she had doubts that it would ever happen; he had let too much time pass.

'So how did it go?' she asked looking up from her hemming.

'Fine. Pretty good in fact.'

'So, tell me. What sort of job has he offered you?'

'Let me just get a beer and I'll tell you all about it. Do you want one?'

'No, not for me, thanks.'

After a few minutes he returned to the terrace with a bottle of cold beer in his hand.

'Well?'

'Arnie's bought a new club in Benalmadena; he wants me to install the lighting.'

'Is that all? I thought it was going to be something more long term.'

Harry frowned at her. 'What do you mean, is that all? It's pretty damned good. There were lots of guys after the contract and he's given it to me.'

'When I suggested you go back to work as an electrician you said it was too much of a come down,' she reminded him.

'This is different, this isn't fixing someone's fuse or redoing some dodgy wiring. This needs special skills. You'll see, this is the start I've been waiting for.'

She couldn't see the difference between putting in a new lighting system in a club and wiring up someone's kitchen; as far as she knew the skills were the same. Still it was good to see her husband so animated for once,' so she bit her tongue and asked instead, 'What sort of club is it?'

'An adult entertainment club I think they call it these days.' She saw a smirk pass across his face.

'You mean a strip club?'

'Well, partly, but he's hoping to put on musical entertainment as well, you know, local groups. That's why the lighting is so important. He wants it to be classy.'

'And when that's done?'

'He says he'll need a maintenance man for the place if I'm interested.'

Carla didn't reply. Harry moved close to her, putting his hand on her shoulder. 'Look I know it's not much but it's a start isn't it?'

'I suppose so. Harry I just wish you would decide what it is you're doing with your life, with our lives. We've been here for four years now and you still haven't got a proper job; it's as though you're in a state of limbo.'

'I don't know what you want Carla. I've been trying to get back on my feet ever since we arrived. It's not easy you know, but this could be the opening I've been waiting for.'

'You really think so?'

'It's a hell of a lot better than working behind the bar in Krazy Kats.'

'It was really nice of Brian to give you a job.'

'So you like the idea of your husband washing glasses for your aging pop star friends, do you? Not good enough for anything else, I suppose.'

'That's not true, Harry. I was only trying to help.'

'Well don't. I can handle my own life, thank you.' He slammed the empty beer bottle down on the table.

'Don't get angry, Harry. It's just that I think we're both too young to retire; we need something worthwhile to do.'

'You've got your sewing so that should keep you busy.'

He went into the kitchen for another beer.

'Harry you don't understand. You're not listening to me. We're living a fantasy life. It's not real. We have no children. You have no proper job. When you're not running around after Arnie, all you do is play tennis and drink with your friends. It's like being on holiday 365 days of the year.'

'So what's wrong with that? Honestly Carla, I sometimes think there's no pleasing you. What's happened to you? You used to be such a fun-loving girl.'

'Maybe I've grown up.'

'My God. Like I say, there's no pleasing some people.'

She bent her head over her sewing so he couldn't see the tears of disappointment shining in her eyes. 'At least you've got some work at this new club. When do you start?' she asked.

'Oh not for weeks yet; he's got to sort out the lease first.'

She felt the old frustration return. There was no point reminding Harry that this was not the first job that Arnie had promised him and so far nothing had actually materialised. She wondered how many more years they would be able to manage on the proceeds from the sale of his business. Well at least she was making good money from her 'sewing' as Harry liked to term it.

This was not what she had expected when she had given up her life in London. By now she thought they would be settled and Harry would have started a new business. She thought they would have a baby or at least that she would be pregnant. She thought that they would have broken away from Arnie's influence and made new friends. None of that had happened. True her new life had begun, her business was growing steadily, she had made a number of new friends and she was beginning to enjoy living in Spain, but Harry on the other hand appeared to be distracted, easily swayed by the indolent life around him, and dependent on Arnie for far more than was necessary. Worse still, he was totally blind to the fact that their relationship was fraying under the strain of his ever increasing drinking.

*

She had been up at least two hours and still there was no sign of Harry getting out of bed. When she wandered into the bedroom to tell him it was ten o'clock, he just grunted and pulled the sheets over his head. 'I've got to go out Harry. I'm seeing Julie at ten-thirty,' she informed him. He grunted something in reply and turned over. 'I'll put the dog in the garden. Don't forget to let her in if she barks.'

'Mmn.'

'I'll be back at lunchtime,' she added. There was no reply from the huddled figure in the bed so she went to the window and pulled back the curtains. The room had a strong smell of stale alcohol and sweat, so she opened the windows as far as she could. So what if the noise from their neighbour's lawnmower woke him; it was time he was up anyway. It angered her to see him wasting his life lying in bed like a pubescent teenager. 'Bye then,' she said but received no answer.

The first Wednesday in the month was when Julie held a coffee morning. Usually about ten women turned up, some were friends from the golf club, others whom she had met over the years. They were sitting in the garden when Carla arrived, under the shade of a thick wisteria that twisted its way along and over the stone pergola like a blue cloud. Heavy heads of blossom hung down, inverted bells, infusing the air with their fragrance. Julie's dogs lay stretched out on the lawn, one either side of the group, like ornamental lions. They lifted their heads lazily, as she approached but didn't move. The chatter of the women's voices drifted across to her, their animation evident by the rising cadence.

There was a brief pause as Julie called, 'Over here Carla, we're in the garden.' She indicated an empty chair next to her. 'So, how're things?'

'Fine.' Carla helped herself to a coffee and sat back to listen to the conversation.

'Problems at the golf club,' Julie whispered. 'The captain, ex-army, wants to stop women playing on Sundays.'

Carla raised her eyebrows. 'Can he do that?'

'No, of course not. Just because that's what they did at his old club in Cheltenham, he thinks he can do it here,' said Laura. The other women joined in, each with their own opinion on the matter. Carla decided not to comment; she really didn't know much about golf and was not that interested.

'How's the puppy coming on?' asked Julie.

'She's lovely, I'm so fond of her but she gets into all sorts of pickles. Do you know what I caught her doing the other day?'

She proceeded to give Julie and the others a graphic description of Jess's antics the previous morning and soon had them all laughing.

Carla hung back when the others left; she wanted a few minutes alone with Julie. She helped herself to some coffee while she waited. It was cold but she drank it anyway.

'Hi, you still here?'

'Yes, have you got a minute to spare?'

'Of course, Brian won't be back until half past two at the earliest. What's wrong?'

'Nothing really, I suppose, I just wanted someone to talk to.

'Harry?'

Carla nodded, she felt a wave of self pity wash over her. 'It's just the same old thing.'

'Babies?'

'Yes. It's so frustrating. I just can't persuade him to go to see a doctor. He says he wants us to have children but he won't do anything to help.'

'I thought he was being very co-operative?'

'I suppose he is, in a way, but he denies that the problem is with him and he cites his own children as an example.'

'He has a point.'

'I asked him if he missed them, his own kids. You see I thought that maybe that was the problem.'

'How do you mean?'

'Maybe he feels that he's abandoned them and because of that he doesn't want to have any more.'

'What did he say? Do you think he might be feeling guilty?'

'Not much, as always. He never talks to me about his children, or his life before I met him. But I think you might be right; maybe he does feel guilty.'

'How old is Harry?'

'He'll be fifty next year.'

'Perhaps he thinks he's too old to start again. Remember he's been through that once, the nappies, sleepless nights, the whole rigmarole.'

'If that's the case, why doesn't he say so? Why is he being so secretive about it?'

'He probably doesn't want to hurt you. So what did he say about missing his kids?'

'That's what so strange; I thought he'd fly into one of his moods but he didn't. He just looked at me and said: "What do you think?" I thought he was going to cry.'

'So he does miss them.'

'Yes, but he won't go and see them. He says maybe when they're older and can understand. I find it all a bit weird.'

'Is he all right in himself?'

'Harry?'

'Yes.'

'I don't know. He's definitely drinking too much and he seems depressed. He still wasn't up when I left.'

'Why don't you get him to see a doctor; he could prescribe something for him. Valium or something.'

'There's no way Harry will go and see a doctor. I just don't know what to do, Julie.'

Her friend leaned across and put her arm around her. 'There's not a lot more you can do. Don't worry, things'll turn out all right in the end, I'm sure, Carla. You know maybe it's because you're letting yourself get so wound up about it all, that you can't conceive. Why don't you and Harry go away for a holiday? Somewhere completely different, away from all his drinking mates, just the two of you.'

Carla smiled. 'That sounds nice. I might suggest it to him.' She picked up her bag.

'You don't have to go, you know. Stay and have some lunch.'

'No, I told Harry I wouldn't be long, and anyway I've left Jess in the garden. I'd like to get home while I've still got some lawn left.'

As she walked back to her car, she thought about Julie's suggestion. A holiday sounded a good idea, but she had a feeling that it wouldn't be enough. If she wanted to have any children she had to get to the root of Harry's reluctance.

CHAPTER 20

It was a long climb to the top of Coombe Hill and Barbara found that she had to stop more than once to catch her breath. Katy bounded on ahead, stopping to investigate the roots of trees, poking her pointed snout deep into the undergrowth, sniffing and snorting until, convinced that there was no more to learn, she would spring away to continue her search in another spot. From time to time she would turn and check that her mistress was still there before resuming the hunt for the elusive rabbits. Her routine was always the same but it still made Barbara smile; she would tear through the undergrowth as fast as her small legs could carry her and if she spotted a rabbit she would let out a shrill yip yip and set chase. Every so often the small brown dog would make a four footed leap into the air in an attempt to check the rabbit's position, her tail stuck out behind her like a golden standard. Invariably the rabbit went one way and Katy the other, but the dog's enthusiasm was undiminished.

'Katy, come,' she called.

She sat down on a bench near the Monument and looked out across the vast expanse of the Vale of Aylesbury, to her left the long, snaking ridge of the Chilterns spread westwards, their slopes covered with beech and spruce. It was a bright, clear morning with that touch of dampness in the air that was common early in the day. Grey clouds were scudding across the sky casting their fleeting shadows on the grass. She breathed deeply, letting the cold air fill her lungs and exhaled slowly, watching the smoky cloud of her breath hang in the still air for a moment, before it floated away. The fresh air revived her; up here she could always think clearly. Katy nuzzled her nose against her hand and settled down to wait.

For weeks Barbara had dreaded going to the funeral but now that it was over she was glad she'd gone. Carla was not the monster she had imagined, just another sad woman trying hard to keep her life together. She was beautiful even now, but she was not happy; that hard, calm exterior had not fooled Barbara. Carla had her share of problems too. She wondered if she'd wanted to have any children. Had Harry deceived her over that too?

Barbara had been very upset when Sylvia had told her that Carla was bringing Harry's ashes back to England; she'd shut herself in her bedroom and cried silently into her pillow. She didn't want to be reminded of the past. She had put all that behind her and was not ready to pull it out from the recesses of her mind and dust down the cobwebs. Her life had changed since then. She was no longer the meek, loving housewife that Harry had deserted. How strange life was; if Harry hadn't met Carla, Barbara would never have found out that she had a talent for business. She would still be baking apple pies on Sundays and growing her own vegetables. It made her feel uncomfortable to know that she was now rich but she knew she would never be so wealthy that she would forget how she used to sit pouring over her cheque stubs and adding and re-adding her accounts in the hope that more money would materialise, how she used to unpick Sylvia's jumpers so that she could re-knit the wool into a sweater for Tom, how she would wear laddered tights as long as the ladders remained out of sight above her knee, how she would make a pound of mince stretch into enough meals for two days. She would always be grateful to Ian and Doug for helping her to get her business started, but she knew that in the end its success had come down to her, to her tenacity and determination. It had been hard work at first but once the orders had started flooding in, there was no turning back. It had taken many years but now here she was with time on her hands; she walked Katy each morning after breakfast, she had her weekly appointment at the hairdresser's, she played bridge with three other ladies on Wednesday afternoons and there was her book club, the first Tuesday in every month. She was a lady of leisure, but if she were honest she would admit that none of it compared to the excitement of starting her own company.

*

Barbara chopped the green tomatoes and pushed them to the side then she started on the shallots. This was the part she liked least of all because try as she might to prevent it, her eyes always watered, nevertheless the rhythmic tap of the knife on the chopping board was relaxing and she soon had them finished, chopped and diced into small, purple veined pieces. She lifted some chopped apples out of the water where she had left them to stop them turning brown and put them in a large pressure cooker then she added the shallots, tomatoes and a small amount of water. She screwed down the lid of the pressure cooker and left it to cook while she went to check that her son was doing his homework.

'What's that?' she asked. Her son was sitting on the floor, surrounded by open magazines and books.

'It's some project work for school.'

'It looks interesting, what's it about?'

'It's on the Amazon rain forests,' he replied. 'I'm looking for frogs. My group are doing amphibians.'

'Really.' She smiled proudly at her son, he seemed to be doing so well at school these days. He'd taken the eleven plus the previous year and was luckier than Sylvia; he had a place at the local Grammar School. She wondered if he still missed Harry; he never mentioned him. He'd stopped wearing the Chelsea scarf that had become his comforter for so long after his father left, but it was never far from his side.

It had been Mary's idea that she should make the chutneys. Last year, not having the money to buy her friends Christmas gifts, she'd made them all some chutney. It had been very successful and Mary had suggested that she should bottle it and sell it at the Farmers' Market. She'd started with a straightforward apple chutney then began to experiment with whatever was in season; she made rhubarb chutney, green tomato chutney, tomato and marrow chutney, an orange chutney which everyone said was delicious with roast duck and even red and green pepper chutney. Now she not only sold it at the Saturday market but supplied the local butcher.

'Mum, Mary's here,' called Sylvia from the hall.

'Okay just coming.'

She switched off the timer and went into the hall to greet her friend. Mary quite often popped in for a cup of tea and a chat in the evenings; she said it was to check that Barbara was all right but somehow Barbara felt it had more to do with getting out of the house for a bit.

'Hi.'

'Hello there. Everything okay? I just thought I'd pop in on my way to the shops.'

'Everything's fine, Mary. Like a cup of tea?'

'Lovely. My something smells good. Don't tell me, let me guess. Apple?'

'Nearly, green tomato, but there's apple in it.' She led the way into the kitchen. 'Look why don't you make the tea while I finish off here?'

'Okay.'

Barbara unscrewed the top of the pressure cooker and ladled the contents into a large bowl, mixed in the spices and some vinegar then returned the mixture to the pressure cooker and switched it on again.

'Can I help?'

'No there's not much to do now; you should have come earlier when I was doing the peeling and chopping.'

'Sorry, had to wait for Bill to get home. Another late night, he seems to be working all the hours there are these days.' Barbara didn't reply but thought back to the days when Harry used to tell her how busy he was at work.

'So how's it going?' Mary nodded towards the empty chutney jars that Barbara was stacking in the oven.

'Really well. I'm having trouble keeping up with the demand. The man from Blackstone's Farm Shop wants two dozen apple and a dozen rhubarb.'

'That's good. What about the farm shop over at Cookham Dean, won't they take any?'

'Yes, he's already had some of the tomato chutney and he says it's very popular. He wanted to know if I made jam as well.'

'That's a great idea. People love home-made jam. It reminds them of their childhood and the good old days, but everyone's too busy to make it for themselves.'

'You mean when it was a treat to have bread and jam for supper? Anyway, hang on a minute, when am I going to get time to make jam as well as chutney? I still have to go to work you know.'

'Why don't you approach one of the supermarkets to see if they want to stock it? With a big order from Tesco's you could give up your job and do this full time.'

'I don't think so. That's a big step Mary. I'm not ready for it. I'd have to expand the production and then there would be Health and Safety checks. There would be VAT and I'd have to register as a company and pay tax. Oh God, I wouldn't know where to start.' She took the mug of tea from Mary and sat down. 'It would be moving up to an entirely different level.'

'It's something you could think about,' Mary suggested.

'Maybe in the future.' The truth was that she was doing very well with the chutneys. Sylvia had come up with a name for them and Tom had designed a label which he had printed out from the computer. They had agreed on 'Windmill Hill Chutneys' after the local energy company had installed a new prototype windmill right behind them on the top of the hill. Mary's idea was very tempting but she didn't think she could cope with the extra work; she was cooking every evening as it was.

*

By nine o'clock Tom was bathed and in bed and Sylvia was finishing her homework. She had been at her school for two years now and was doing very well, but whenever Barbara tried to talk to her about her school work Sylvia refused to discuss it. She'd become very independent since she had changed schools. Barbara decided she would watch the news whilst she ironed their clothes for the next day then retire to bed early and read the copy of 'Setting up a Small Business' that she had bought that afternoon in the newsagents.

She set up the ironing board in front of the television and switched on the 9 o'clock news, Nelson Mandela had become South Africa's first black president, Turkish soldiers had overrun the Kurdish capital and captured a number of militants, the Secretary of State had agreed to changes in the boundaries of Buckinghamshire, Berkshire and Surrey, while some footballer, whose name she didn't catch, was being sold to Manchester United for an undisclosed sum. She smoothed Sylvia's blouse onto the ironing board and carefully pressed the collar.

She could hear Sylvia talking to one of her friends on the upstairs extension. Sylvia, don't be too long. Our telephone bill was high enough last month,' she warned.

'Okay Mum.' She heard her daughter mutter something to her friend and hang up. Almost immediately it rang again. It was Ian.

'Hi Ian, how are you?'

'Fine, you?'

'Just about to go to bed with a cup of tea and a good book.'

'Isn't it a bit early for bed?'

'Yes but so what? I've bottled forty-two jars of chutney tonight, read through Tom's project work and done the ironing. I think I deserve an early night.'

'I was thinking of calling round to see you.'

'Oh Ian that would be nice but not tonight. What about tomorrow?'

'Yes, tomorrow's fine. I've got some news for you.'

'Good or bad?'

'Good of course; if it were bad I'd write to you.'

'Is it about Harry?'

'No, nothing to do with Harry. It's a business proposition.' She closed her book and sat up.

'What sort of proposition?'

'I'd sooner wait and tell you tomorrow.'

'Oh no you don't, you've got me interested now.'

'Very well. This friend of mine wants to invest some money; he's been looking at a number of small businesses and so I told him about your chutney.'

'And he's interested in investing in my chutney?'

'Well he's interested enough to want to talk to you. No promises mind you. He's a canny Scot and he only invests in things that he thinks have a future.'

'I don't know what to say.'

'How about saying yes?'

'Okay it can't hurt to talk to him, but I'm sure it won't come to much. Does he know I operate out of my kitchen?'

'Yes, that doesn't matter apparently. All that can be changed. It's the product he's interested in. If it sells and if it sells at a profit.'

'Okay then Ian, you set up a meeting and we'll take it from there.'

'And tomorrow? Can I still come round?'

'Yes why not. Come and have some supper with us. Say seven o'clock.'

'Fine, I'll be there.' This was incredible. Somebody was actually interested in her chutney. She couldn't believe it.

*

Douglas McGregor had suggested they meet at the Bull's Head for lunch. She knew the pub but had never had occasion to visit it; it lay on the road between Marlow and Henley, and The Bull's Head had been there, in one form or other nestled into the hillside, for almost two hundred years. Its exterior had changed very little, but since it had been taken over by a large food chain, the interior was quite different. The rather antiseptic smell of cheap cleaning fluid assailed her nose as she entered, and the low beams and stone flagged floor were not enough to detract from the accumulation of plastic signs and cheap bric-a-brac that littered the bar and window sills. Numerous small lamps in red glass shades cast a dull light from the tables, deepening the red velour of the chairs, and a series of framed prints of riverside scenes decorated the freshly painted walls. Everything had the mass-produced look of economy, and the glossy, laminated menus offered a limited selection of standard dishes that matched well with the decor, everything with French fries and trimmings, and the beer was all pre-cooled lager. She hoped there was at least a decent wine on the menu.

'Hello, you must be Barbara,' a soft Scottish voice said. A man in his mid-forties, with cropped, sandy hair sat at the bar smiling at her. He held out his hand.

'Yes. And you are Douglas McGregor, I take it,' she replied. 'Pleased to meet you.'

'What will you have to drink?'

She hesitated. 'A dry sherry would be nice, thank you.' She couldn't go wrong with sherry.

'Have you been here before?' he asked.

'No, have you?'

'Actually no, but I hear that you can get a good steak. I thought it would be convenient for you.'

'Yes, it's very convenient. I only live about ten minutes away.'

The barman placed their drinks on the counter and waited patiently while Douglas counted the money into his hand. Barbara sipped her sherry, it was cold and very dry.

'So,' he said, taking a sip of his whisky. 'Ian tells me that you're looking for a backer.'

'Well I'm not exactly looking,' she answered. 'Everyone keeps telling me I should expand the business but to do that I need money and I don't have any. To be quite honest it's more his idea than mine.' She explained how she had started making the chutney just as a way of supplementing her income and suddenly found that it was very popular. 'I can't keep up with the demand operating the way I do, part-time. I really need to take it on full time and employ someone to help me, but I can't do that without some security. I have two kids to bring up.'

'Do you have any accounts?'

'Oh yes I keep an account of everything I spend and earn. It doesn't amount to that much so I don't declare it. I suppose I ought to but I haven't got round to it yet.'

'Do you have them with you?'

'What here? No I didn't realise you would want to see them today.'

'No of course not. Tell me about the chutney.'

He listened intently as she told him of her recipes and how she was planning to start making jams as well. She explained her distribution method and how although she realised it was probably not very cost-effective to drive all the way to Goring Heath with only twelve jars of chutney, at least it was a regular weekly order.

'Okay, Barbara I like the sound of your business. I think I'd like to taste this chutney of yours and have a look around your premises.'

'That's the problem; I don't have any premises, everything is done from home. But you're welcome to come and see what I do.'

'Yes I'd like that and maybe I could take a look at your accounts at the same time.'

'I've drawn up a business plan,' she said rather shyly.

'Have you now. I'd like to see that too. Would next Wednesday be all right?'

'That would be fine as long as it's after six o'clock. I work at the Health Centre until four; a friend's covering for me today,' she added.

'Okay, six o'clock it is. Do you have a business card?' Barbara handed him one of the business cards that Tom had designed and printed for her from his computer. 'Windmill Hill Chutneys, nice name.'

'My son chose it.'

'Right, that's our business over for today. How about we have something to eat now?' He led the way into the dining room and sat down at a table near the window. 'Nice town Marlow,' he said. 'I've always fancied a little place here myself. Have you lived here long?'

He was very easy to talk to and she found herself telling him about the house and how she'd thought of selling it after Harry left but now was glad she still had it. It turned out that he too was divorced; his wife had left him for an American singer and taken their two children to California to live.

'That must be hard. Do you miss your children?'

'Yes I do but what can I do about it. The last thing I want is for them to be in the middle of a tug-of-war between me and Jill. It's better this way. They are with their mother and I get to see them from time to time. I usually go over in their summer holidays and the three of us go away somewhere for a week or two. It's not ideal but at least they get the chance to start a new life, make new friends and have some stability in their lives. I really couldn't bear to see them being uprooted every other week to come and live with me. Anyway California is a long way away. I certainly don't want to move there and Jill was never going to stay in England. The singer is quite a decent chap; he likes the kids and he and Jill are going to get married soon. You probably think I'm mad, but I like to think of my children having a stable home life even if I am excluded from it.'

'I couldn't do that.'

'You're their mother, that's different.'

'But is it? Why should it mean more to be a mother than a father?'

'Children need their mother.'

She thought of Harry and his seeming lack of interest in Tom and Sylvia. Was it self-interest or self-sacrifice? She couldn't be sure now.

'Dessert madam?' The waiter stood at her elbow with the dessert menu.

'No, not for me thank you. Just coffee.'

*

Barbara closed the door behind him and leaned her back against it, her heart racing with excitement. He'd inspected

281

her kitchen, sampled a couple of her chutneys and looked at her accounts. Everything seemed to satisfy him, even her rudimentary business plan. He'd left with a big smile on his face, a copy of both the accounts and the business plan under his arm and a bag of assorted chutneys, promising to be in touch within the week. She still couldn't believe it.

'What did he say Mum?'

'Is he going to give you the money?'

'Did he like it?'

Both children had followed her into the hall and were standing there eager for the news. Her heart was still racing with excitement as she smiled at them, this could make a difference to all their lives. 'Yes and yes. He thinks it's a great idea and he's going to send his accountant over to discuss the details with me. It will mean renting some premises in Wycombe, somewhere on the trading estate I expect, and buying new equipment. I'll have to advertise for staff and ...' She broke off and hugged them. 'This is going to be great. You'll see.'

'Will we be rich Mum?' Tom asked.

'I don't know about rich but we'll be able to buy that new computer you keep on about.'

'And a holiday? Can I go to Italy with the school now?'

'Yes Sylvia, you can.'

'What about your job?'

'I will have to hand in my notice; I won't be able to manage both. I've told Doug it will take a month or so to get up to full production and he's quite happy with that. Sylvia go and put the kettle on while I ring Mary and tell her the news.'

'What about Ian? Aren't you going to tell Ian?'

'He's coming round later, I'll tell him then.'

*

Barbara knew it was Ian as soon as she heard the door bell ring. 'Well?' he asked immediately.

She'd considered pretending that the deal had fallen through but when she saw his eager face she couldn't restrain her smile. 'Yes he's going to invest in my chutney.'

'Good, so this won't go to waste then,' he said producing a bottle of Veuve Clicquot from behind his back.

'Absolutely not,' she replied putting her arms around his neck and kissing him. She saw him blush with pleasure. 'Come on let's open it and I can tell you all about the meeting.'

'So what is his proposal?'

'He's suggesting an investment of about a hundred thousand pounds, depending on what the accountant finds when he looks at my books.'

'Wow, he must like your chutney,' Ian said pouring the champagne into the flute that she held out to him.

'He says I should contact this new whole-food supermarket chain that has just opened in the south of England. As my chutneys and jams contain no preservatives and my raw ingredients are all organic he thinks they will be very interested.'

'Tesco's are doing an organic range now. Perhaps you should speak to them too.'

'This champagne is lovely,' she said, savouring the flavour in her mouth before she swallowed it.

'Only what you deserve.' He put his arm around her and pulled her closer to him. 'So what's your first move?'

'Well I shall go into work tomorrow as usual and tell them I'm leaving. I've got some holiday owed to me so I will probably only have to work about ten days' notice. Hopefully that will long enough for them to find a replacement.'

'So you're sure about this then? What if his accountant advises him against the investment? Wouldn't it be better to wait until you've got the money?'

'No, he won't. He may suggest some changes, but Doug has all but agreed that he will back me. Sending in the accountant is just standard procedure.'

'Are you sure? Maybe you should hang on a bit before handing in your notice.'

'Ian, this was your idea in the first place. Why are you being so negative?' She stood up and moved to the chair facing him. The idea slipped into her mind that he might be jealous.

'I'm not being negative Barbara. I'm just trying to be sensible. You were so pleased to get that job at the Health

Centre, I just think you should wait a little before giving it up.'

'I told you, I discussed all that with Doug. He thinks I should get started on this as soon as possible.'

Ian sipped his champagne. He looked uncomfortable. 'Did he give you any idea when the money would be available?'

'Not exactly. His accountant is coming to see me next Friday so I expect I'll hear from him the following week. In the meantime I have a lot to do. When I telephoned Mary, she told me about a place that would be ideal for the factory; it's on the outskirts of High Wycombe, on the road to Lane End. It will take me no time at all to get there. I'm going over to see the agents tomorrow.'

'Barbara this is not like you; you're usually so cautious. Now here you are giving up your job and renting a factory before you even have any money in the bank to cover it.'

Spontaneity was not Ian's forte, she should have realised that he would want her to move more slowly on this, but it was too late, she had made her decision. 'Maybe I've been too cautious all my life, maybe now is the time to take a chance. Being cautious hasn't actually done me a lot of good in the past, has it?' She held out her glass so that he could refill it and continued, 'I didn't want to expand my business if you remember, it was you and Mary that encouraged it. But now that I've taken the first step, I'm keen to go on. It's time I did something with my life; time I took a chance. After all what's to lose? I can always mortgage the house if everything goes pear-shaped.' Ian nodded his agreement, albeit, she thought, rather reluctantly. 'So tell me about Doug. How come you two are friends?'

'We used to play squash together.'

'What at Handy Cross?'

'No, this was before they opened the sports centre. We had a mutual friend and he had access to the squash courts in a nearby public school. None of the pupils used the courts in the evenings so he would take a group of his friends over to play. That's how I met Doug and his wife Jill, they both used to play there.'

'What was she like, his wife?'

'Small, dark, good squash player, I don't remember much else. She became pregnant and then I didn't see her again.'

'So you never went to their house?'

'No. Why the interest?'

'No reason really. He mentioned he was divorced but he didn't say much about his family.'

'He never talks about his family, never did. He's not an easy man to get to know. We've known each other for almost twenty years but I couldn't say we were really friends. We just meet up from time to time for a drink. He usually gives me a ring when he's in the area.' Barbara thought Ian looked a bit irritated, not his usual relaxed self.

'He's a nice bloke, and a hell of a business man, but you need to watch him, Barbara,' he added.

'Watch him?'

'He's well, a bit of a ladies' man,' he explained, avoiding her eyes as he spoke.

So he was jealous, she tried not to smile. 'I'll remember that' she said. 'By the way, have you eaten?'

'A salad at lunchtime, that's all.'

'I've made some Bolognese. Would you like some?'

'That would be nice, I'm ravenous.'

'Bring the bottle, we'll finish it while I heat it up.' She led the way into the kitchen. Upstairs she could hear the children arguing about something. She switched on the radio, a pianist was skilfully building the crescendo to Rachmaninov's Second Piano Concerto. The music flowed through her and for the second time that evening she felt as though her life was about to change for the better.

CHAPTER 21

Carla was beginning to wonder if she was wrong about Arnie. Maybe he wasn't the one who had destroyed their life. She had to face the possibility that she and Harry had done it to themselves. Something had been bothering her husband for a long time and she had never been able to discover what it was; she hadn't even tried. Had she been too wrapped up in trying to make a new life for herself in Spain to remember that that's what Harry had been trying to do as well, but unsuccessfully? After all Arnie liked a drink, but he kept it under control. Why had she always blamed him for Harry's shortcomings? Had she been jealous of the fact that he saw more of her husband than she did? Where had she gone wrong? When had she stopped loving him? And why hadn't she done more to help him?

*

Julie had invited her round for coffee and a swim, but Tuesday was a busy day at the market and she didn't want to forego it, so she agreed to call in for a drink on her way home.

'Sorry I'm a bit late,' she said as Julie led her through to the garden. 'I didn't get away from the market until one.'

'Starting to pick up Spanish habits, I see,' Julie commented with a smile. 'It doesn't take long to lose that sense of English punctuality when you're out here, does it?'

Zoe and Dawn were already sitting in the shade drinking white wine. 'Hi there,' Zoe said, getting up and giving her a kiss.

Dawn smiled up at her, she still looked a bit depressed. Carla wondered if there had been any developments with her house but was reluctant to ask in case it upset her. She need not have worried, hardly had she sat down when Zoe began filling them in on what was happening.

'Dawn and Peter are going back to England next month,' Zoe told them. 'They can't afford to stay here any longer.'

'That's a shame. No news about the house then?' Carla asked.

'No, it's stalemate. They won't even return the taxes and licence fees that we've already paid them,' Dawn replied.

'But that wouldn't make much difference anyway,' Zoe told her sister. 'That's peanuts compared with the money you've spent on building the house.'

'It would help; we're absolutely broke.'

'What about the developers? What do they say about it?' asked Carla.

'Costa Build? They couldn't care less; they've made their money building the house. What happens next is our problem.'

Costa Build, Carla had heard that name before somewhere. 'Costa Build, are they a Spanish company?'

'No, English. We first got in touch with them back in London. We saw their ad in the Sunday Times. They brought us out here on one of those flights where everything is paid for if you end up buying a property from them. They seemed such a solid company. Peter really checked them out.'

'They probably are, after all they haven't lost anything have they,' retorted her sister.

'Only their reputation,' Julie added.

'So where will you go?' asked Carla.

'My brother-in-law's got a big house in Somerset, we'll go and live with him for a bit until we decide what to do. Peter says it's pointless staying here any longer; we'll leave it to our solicitor to sort out for us.'

'A Spanish solicitor?'

'Yes, he's very nice and speaks excellent English.'

'But he's not very effective, is he,' interrupted her sister.

'He explained that it takes years for things to go through the Spanish courts.' She looked as though she was going to cry again. 'We can't afford to keep renting somewhere; we'll just have to try to sort it out from home,' she continued.

'Peter'll fly back when it's necessary,' added Zoe.

'Not the sort of retirement you'd planned,' Julie murmured.

'No, not at all.' Dawn sniffed and blew her nose.

'Any more wine?' Julie asked, lifting up the bottle of Rueda. The women murmured their assent.

'Carla, while you're here I want you to give me some advice on what to wear to the Golf Club Ball,' Zoe said.

'Yes, good idea,' added Julie. 'You can help me too. It's next month and it's quite a posh affair.'

'I'd be delighted to.'

'Maybe you'd like to come. I can get tickets for you and your husband if you like. You can be on our table.'

'I don't know, I'm rather busy at the moment.'

'Yes, but you'll get the chance to meet some more women; they're not a bad bunch you know.'

'I'm sure they're very nice,' Carla replied. 'I'll have to speak to Harry and see if he's got anything planned.' She would love to go; it would be an excellent way to meet prospective clients and anyway she would enjoy an evening in the company of Julie and Brian, but there was Harry to consider. She knew what would happen if they both went; by the time they were due to set off he would be at best inebriated and at worst drunk. He would spend the entire evening making inane comments and gazing around him glassy-eyed. No, she couldn't face it, not in front of her new friends. 'Give me the date and I'll ring you,' she said at last.

*

Harry was watching a re-run of an old film on Sky television when she got back. He lay on the sofa, his shirt undone and a glass of beer in his hand.

'Hi, have you eaten?' she asked.

'Not really.'

'Shall I make us some pasta or do you want to wait for dinner?'

'Cook some pasta if you like but I'm not really hungry. I thought you were having lunch at that Red woman's house,' he added.

'No, it was supposed to be coffee but by the time I arrived they were onto the wine.'

She moved around the room, automatically picking up empty beer cans and emptying the ash tray. 'She wants me to make her something for the Golf Club Ball.'

'Urgh.'

'I've got a brilliant idea for a jacket for her, I found this pale green suede in Antequera last week. It'll be ideal with...' Her voice tailed off, it was obvious he was not listening. She sat down in the armchair next to him. 'Is everything alright Harry? You seem very down these days.'

'I would be if you stopped nagging me,' he said.

'Look, if it's about having a baby...'

'Not that old thing again. When will you give it a rest Carla? I've told you, if it happens all well and good.'

'I was just going to say that if you're unhappy about it then we'll give up the idea.'

'Look Carla, I'm not unhappy. I'm not depressed. I'm just tired; I had a late night last night and a lot to drink. Okay? It's as simple as that.'

'Maybe you should cut back a bit on the booze,' she suggested, timidly.

'So now it's the booze.' He held up the empty beer can. 'What harm can a few beers do? Isn't it enough to have me on this damned diet without cutting back on my beer ration?'

'I wasn't thinking of that; I was just thinking of you.'

Harry let out a snort of contempt and swung his legs off the sofa. 'I don't see you cutting back on the white wine,' he sneered. 'All right if I open a bottle of Rioja to go with the pasta, Mein Herr? Or have you locked it all away?'

'I'll get the lunch on,' she said.

Ten minutes later he came into the kitchen carrying two glasses of wine. 'I'm sorry Carla, I don't know what gets into me sometimes.' He placed the glasses down and put his arms around her. 'You know I love you, don't you?' he whispered in her ear.

She continued to chop the garlic as finely as she could. 'So what is it? You have to admit you haven't been yourself lately.'

'I know. It's just...'

'What? The fact that you've got no job? Or is it us?'

'No, Darling it's not us. Okay Arnie's not come up with a job yet but I'm sure he will. He's got lots of irons in the fire; he's planning to open an office in the Algarve.'

'Portugal?'

'That's right.'

'But you're not planning on moving to Portugal, I hope?'

'Of course not, he's already got a couple of guys lined up for that. I may have to run over there from time to time, but that's all.' Carla breathed a sigh of relief; the last thing she wanted was to move to another country just as she was beginning to make progress with her business. 'Don't worry, he won't let us down.'

She suddenly thought about Dawn and Costa Build. 'Is one of his companies Costa Build?'

'Yes, that's right, a development company. Buys up land in the country and then sells it with planning permission. Most of the time they do the build as well, but to the buyer's specification. That way the buyer gets the house he wants, in the spot he wants. It's been doing very well.' She tossed the garlic into the pan and stirred it around. 'Why the interest?'

'I met this woman at Julie's. She and her husband bought some land through Costa Build and built a house but now it seems that they have to pull it down because it's in an area where there aren't supposed to be any houses.'

'That's odd. Is it National Park or something?'

'I don't know. I just know that the Andalusian government are declaring a lot of houses in the area illegal. It's somewhere to the east of Málaga.'

'Yes, that's where Arnie bought a lot of land but I haven't heard anything about the houses there being illegal. Are you sure you've got it right?'

'Pretty sure. I just wondered if Arnie was mixed up in it.'

Harry pulled away from her. 'You've really got it in for Arnie, haven't you. It's not his fault if the regional government change the laws. I know for a fact that all his properties have planning permission from the local Town Halls.'

'But how does he get it?'

'How do I know? The usual way I suppose,' he replied then added, 'Look Carla, sometimes things get done differently here, especially in the countryside. These local mayors are like little lords; they have control over everything that goes on in their towns and villages. If you can get them on your side you've got it made.'

'All right, it just seemed a bit strange that's all.'

Harry drank the last of his wine and poured some more into his glass. 'Why can't you get it into your head that Arnie's a legitimate businessman and not a crook. If you don't believe me, ask him yourself next time you see him.'

Carla didn't reply, instead she tipped a tin of tomatoes into the pan and gave it a quick stir. 'Julie wants us to go to the Golf Club Ball,' she said.

'Mmnn.'

'Would you like to go?'

'If you want to.'

'So shall I ask her to get us tickets?'

'Whatever you like. I don't mind.'

'I'll wait until I know the date,' she added.

'Just as you like.' He refilled his glass and sauntered out onto the terrace.

The water had started to boil, so she added the pasta and turned down the heat. 'It'll be about ten minutes,' she called.

'Okay'

*

The following day Carla drove across to Julie's straight after breakfast. Her friend was just about to go out.

'Hi Carla, you're early, we haven't had our walk yet. Do you want to come?'

'Why not; I could do with some exercise.'

'Did you speak to Harry about the Ball?'

'Yes, he doesn't mind. What's the date?'

'15th November, it's a Friday.'

This was the point when Carla could make up some previous engagement and avoid going to the Ball without offending her friend. She hesitated. No, she would accept and try to make sure that Harry was at least sober before they arrived at the Golf Club. 'That's fine.'

'Maybe when we get home you can stay for a bit and talk about what I'm going to wear?' Julie suggested.

'Yes, I've already had some ideas, I'll sketch them out for you later.'

Julie beamed at her. 'I knew you'd come up with something.' She hugged her. 'I'm so glad that you bumped into Brian that day.'

'Yes, so am I,' replied Carla.

It was true, Julie was becoming more than a good client, she was fast becoming Carla's closest friend.

*

On the way home, Carla stopped at the newsagents and bought a newspaper. She had left Julie routing through her wardrobe for some silvery-green sandals that were lost somewhere amongst the myriad of footwear that filled the lower reaches of that extensive storage area. As she pulled into the drive she noticed that Harry's car was still in the garage, so she parked alongside and went into the house through the side door. She could hear Harry talking on the telephone.

'Okay, I'll go over and see them before lunch. What about the money? Right. He knows I'm coming to collect it, does he? Well then there's no problem. Yes, I'll ring you when I get back and let you know what he says. No, I won't mention the football ground unless he brings it up.' Harry put the receiver down.

'Who was that?' Carla asked.

'Arnie, he wants me to do a job for him.'

'What sort of job?'

'It's nothing much, just delivering something.' She said nothing but she was sure he was hiding something from her. She watched as he picked up his wallet and car keys. 'I won't be long, a couple of hours at the most.' He kissed her lightly on the cheek. 'Had a nice morning?' he asked as an afterthought.

She nodded. 'Will you be back for lunch?'

'Not sure, I should be. Why don't we eat tonight, just to be on the safe side?'

'Okay. I'll cook some fish.'

She waited until he had gone then she sat down and opened the paper. The headline that had attracted her attention was blazoned across the front page:

"Local mayor arrested on fraud and corruption charges."

She began to read:

"The mayor of Beniche, in the Axarquia region of Málaga, Don Adolfo Rodriguez Garres, was arrested yesterday morning, accused of receiving bribes from a number of property developers in return for illegal building permissions. At ten o'clock over a dozen police arrived to shut down the Town Hall and search the premises. A number of other civil servants have also been detained and the police have stated that they will be questioning some local businessmen later this week. At present no-one else

has been named but it is thought that at least one well-known UK based property company is involved."

Beniche, that was where Dawn's house was, she was sure. She picked up the telephone and dialled Julie's number.

'Hi, Julie, it's Carla. Have you seen the Sur?'

'Yes, I'm just reading it.'

'Isn't that where Dawn's house is?'

'Yes. It sounds good news; maybe they'll get the whole mess sorted out now.'

'I hope so.'

'They've bought their tickets you know; they leave on Saturday.'

'So soon. I feel so sorry for them.'

'Yes and especially when you think that those people have made a lot of money out of this and now couldn't care less about the mess they leave behind.'

'Do you think they're talking about Costa Build?'

'It doesn't say, but it could be.'

'Julie, don't say anything to Dawn, but I think Harry's friend Arnie might be mixed up in this somehow.'

'What?'

'Harry told me that it's one of Arnie's companies.'

'That doesn't mean to say that Harry's involved,' Julie reassured her. 'He can't be responsible for what his friends do. Anyway that company was going years before you came out to Spain; I remember Brian looked at them once but decided against them.'

'Very wise.'

'Yes, well Brian may look like a bit of an idiot at times but he's got his head screwed on okay. Not many people can pull the wool over Brian's eyes.'

'Don't say anything to anyone, will you?' Carla pleaded.

'Of course not. Look Carla I've got to go, there's a meeting of the Book Club this morning. I'll ring you tomorrow.'

'Have a good time.' Carla hung up the receiver. Her stomach was churning. She wished she had tackled Harry about it before he went out, now she would have to wait until his return. She went into her workroom and pulled out her sewing machine; as usual the best distraction was work.

*

It was after three when Harry returned. For once he was sober. He kissed her briefly and went straight to his office.

'I've just got a couple of calls to make,' he told her. 'I won't be long.'

'Arnie?' she asked but he didn't reply.

She decided she would ask him as soon as he finished. It was as good a time as any and she would try not to sound too accusing. If he became defensive she wouldn't learn anything. 'Everything all right?' she asked when he reappeared.

'Fine,' he said, helping himself to a cold beer.

'Did you speak to Arnie?' He looked at her and shrugged. 'What does that mean?'

'He's busy.'

'Have you seen the paper?' she asked and passed him the newspaper.

'So?'

'Are they talking about Costa Build?'

'Look Carla, this has nothing to do with us.'

'Are you sure Harry? Has Arnie got you involved in something illegal?' The words were out before she could stop them, but instead of being angry Harry just looked weary.

'I swear to you Carla, I haven't broken the law and for that matter neither has Arnie. All he did was offer some incentives in return for guaranteed planning permission. It's done all the time. No Town Hall will give a developer a licence unless they donate a percentage of the land to the community. The place I went to today is going to get a new football pitch. Sometimes it's a public park. If it's a big development then it can be something like a local library or a community hall. It's their way of making sure the developers give something back to the community, so that everybody benefits.'

'But what about the bribes?'

'Now I don't know anything about that. I know I haven't received anything except what Arnie tosses my way for being his run-around.' He sounded bitter and for a moment Carla felt sorry for him.

'But will the people whose houses are due to be pulled down get any compensation?' she asked.

'I've no idea. As I said I'm just the messenger boy.' He drank the last of the beer and threw the can in the bin. 'Look Carla, I don't know how deep Arnie has got himself in this but I'm pretty sure they won't be able to pin anything on him. It's the corruption in the Town Halls they want to stamp out. Besides, all Arnie did was pay the taxes and licence fees that were asked of him. What happened to that money afterwards is hardly his fault, is it?' He put the paper down on the table and turned the television on. There was nothing else to say. In a way she felt relieved that Harry was not as involved as she thought, but another part of her was angry that he didn't seem to be bothered by what was happening to people like Dawn and Peter.

CHAPTER 22

Barbara drove slowly through the village. It was a dreadful day, the rain had not stopped since early morning. It fell steadily on the grey slate roofs, filling up the drainpipes and emptying out into the street, it trickled down the window panes, shut tight, closed to the outside world, it gathered on the sills and dripped into the cottage gardens, soaking the rows of dahlias and roses, it blew up the hill, past the village shop, with its red Victorian post box set deep into the wall, it lashed at a last minute shopper, flattening her hair into wet, lank streaks, pulling at her raincoat and running down her wet stockings onto her sodden shoes. It dripped down the glowing Virginia Creeper that screened Spring Cottage, where Harry had once lived, making its way leaf by ruddy leaf until it disappeared into the dark earth, newly turned and weeded. The doors to the Yew Tree pub were closed, but the rain battered against its porch, running down the flints embedded deep in the old walls. It fell on the grave stones in the church yard, it ran down the gables and washed the stained glass windows clean, it revived the wilting flowers in their plastic holders and seeped into the holy ground.

This was the church where they had been married, where both children had been christened and now, where Harry was buried. She pulled up outside the church and got out, pulling up the hood on her raincoat. She'd brought some flowers to put on his grave, even though she knew there were dozens of wreaths already there. She just wanted a few moments alone to pay her respects to the man she'd loved for twenty years.

It had rained on the day of their wedding too. She remembered the white umbrella Phoebe had produced for her, in a rare show of affection. Her simple white wedding gown had been splattered with mud and the photographs had to be taken later, when the rain had ceased. Neither Barbara nor Harry had been bothered by the weather; they were too much in love to let a little rain spoil their happiness. But that was then. Now she had a new husband and a new life. She hadn't chosen to make the change. It had been Harry's decision. He had replaced her with a new love.

*

Although it had been Ian who had initially encouraged her to expand her small business, it was Doug who soon became the driving force. Barbara had liked him from the moment they met; he was someone she could talk to openly and easily. He listened to her ideas and threw in a few of his own. In no time she had leased the small factory that she had found in High Wycombe and invested in new machinery, she had hired some staff and begun production. Doug used his contacts to help her widen her market, and provided help and guidance all the way. He was not what she had expected in a silent partner, and although he left all the decision making to her, she could not deny his influence. The company began to flourish and within a year she had outlets for chutneys, jams and sauces in a number of large supermarkets. She purchased a van, hired a driver and continued supplying the small retailers who had been so instrumental in getting her business started; the farmers' markets and farm shops were not forgotten.

At first her relationship with Doug was strictly confined to business then one evening it changed. They were in Watford, having spent the day looking over a bottling plant that Doug thought was more cost effective than their existing supplier, and had returned to their hotel for dinner.

When they arrived at the hotel it was obvious that a private party was being held at one end of the dining room.

'Do we need to book a table, do you think?' she asked him.

'No, I wouldn't think so, but I'll ask if you like. What about a drink first?'

'Yes that would be nice.' She paused then added, 'Actually I'm not really hungry. I'm too tired to eat after walking all over that factory. I can't believe how many metal staircases we climbed today. That warehouse was enormous. Have you ever seen so many bottles and jars in your life?'

'It was impressive I agree. I have to admit I'm a bit pooped too. How about we order room service and eat in my room? Then we don't need to get dressed up and all that. Also it might be a bit quieter.' He nodded towards the table at the end where a young man was inciting the group to sing 'Happy Birthday' to a woman in a scarlet dress.

'That sounds much better. Order something simple for me will you, an omelette would be good. I just need to freshen up a bit then I'll be along.'

'It's Room 221.'

'Next door to mine,' she said, holding up her key card. 'See you in a bit then.'

She set off in the direction of her room, her heart beating with excitement. Nothing had ever been said between them but she knew that something was about to happen. Whenever they were together the air tingled with excitement, she felt her pulse quicken when he sat next to her and if their hands touched it was like electricity running up her arm. Sometimes she caught him looking at her in a certain way and felt herself blush but she never said anything. She knew he was single; he had told her about his divorce the night they met, but since then he had never mentioned his wife and family. It was as though they no longer existed for him. He never asked her about her life outside the business, and although she told him about Tom and Sylvia and he listened politely, she knew he was not really interested. Was that all about to change?

She stepped into the shower and stood for a few minutes just letting the water cascade down her back. She began to feel apprehensive; it was a long time since she had slept with a man. Harry had been her one and only lover. She stepped out of the shower and looked at herself in the mirror; she would be fifty next year and it was beginning to show. Her waist had thickened and her breasts were starting to sag. She pushed her shoulders back and pulled in her stomach. Barbara had never worried much about her appearance before, it had not seemed that important. Until now. Still her legs were firm and shapely and she knew her golden-auburn hair was striking. Maybe she was reading too much into Doug's invitation to eat in his room; they would probably have a drink and talk about work and that would be that. Nevertheless after she had changed into some jeans that were tight enough to hold in her wayward stomach and put on a clean t-shirt, she splashed herself all over with her favourite perfume. Then she applied a modicum of make-up to an already glowing complexion and combed her hair loosely over her shoulders.

By the time she knocked on his door she had trouble keeping herself from trembling.

'Hi, come in. Everything all right? You look a bit worried.'

'No, everything's fine.'

'Good. I ordered some Chablis, hope that's okay for you?'

'Perfect. Just what I need' She sat down in a rather deep armchair and instantly regretted it. 'I think I'd prefer to sit on the sofa if you don't mind,' she said. 'I'll be asleep in two minutes if I sit in that chair.'

She sat down next to him and before she knew what was happening they were in each others' arms. His mouth pressed against hers, gently forcing her lips open and she found herself responding to his caresses with a passion equal to his own. It had been so long since she had experienced such sexual pleasure that she couldn't hold herself back. Once, not long after Harry had left her she had thought that she could never let another man touch her, yet here she was, in complete abandonment and enjoying it. Doug was both a vigorous and considerate lover, and she responded accordingly.

A knock on the door told them that their meal had arrived. She dashed into the bathroom, leaving Doug to hurriedly re-dress and let the waiter enter with their supper. She looked at herself in the mirror; she looked different. A smile continued to play around her lips and there was a glow emanating from her body. Suddenly Barbara realised what it was; she looked happy. She was happy. She had moved on; for most of her life she had been in love with Harry, but now she could live without him. She took a towel from the rack and wrapped it around her body. 'Has he gone?' she asked, peering round the bathroom door.

'Yes, come and eat your omelette before it gets cold.'

He had set the tray on a small table and poured out some wine. She hoped he would suggest that she stayed the night with him but when they finished the food and drank the last of the wine he began to talk about an early start the next morning.

'We're due at Carter's at nine,' he reminded her. 'I think we'll have to be away by eight-thirty at the latest. Let's meet for breakfast at eight.'

'Fine,' she replied, trying to keep her disappointment to herself. 'Remind me, why are we going there?'

'I just thought we'd drop in as we're in the area. I met the owner when I was playing at Berkhamstead Golf Club last month. It won't take long, an hour at the most to look at the proofs and then we can be on our way home.'

'I'm not sure I really want to change the labelling,' she said. 'I rather like the slightly amateurish look of our labels. I think it gives the product a home-made look.'

'That's up to you but we've told him we'd have a look at what they've come up with.'

'As long as it doesn't take all day.'

'No, it won't. Anyway I have to be back in Edinburgh tonight.'

'I think I'll turn in,' she suggested, standing up and collecting her clothes from where they had been scattered.

She was beginning to feel embarrassed, standing there in nothing but his towel and hesitated, her hand on the door handle, hoping he would tell her to stay, but instead he looked at his watch and said, 'Good idea, it's almost midnight.' He followed her to the door and kissed her lightly on the lips. 'It's a good job you haven't far to go,' he said with a smile and kissed her again. 'It's been a lovely evening, Barbara.'

'Yes, hasn't it,' she replied as casually as she could manage.

And that was that. No romantic nonsense, no 'when can we see each other again?' His attitude to her was unchanged. Barbara knew that this was best; no strings attached, no romantic involvement, just good friends, but somehow she couldn't stop her heart singing, and she knew she wanted more from this man.

CHAPTER 23

When she got back to the hotel Carla checked with reception but there was no word from Jenny. She went up to her room and took out the death certificate and laid it on the bedside table. She would ask the hotel receptionist to fax a copy to Ian Routh. A business card slipped out of her document folder and fell on the floor. She bent down and picked it up. It was Arnie's: Arnold Good, Entrepreneur and Businessman. A pretty vague description for a pretty shady character she thought. There was a UK telephone number printed in the bottom right hand corner. With only a moment's hesitation she picked up the bedside telephone and dialled it. It was time she spoke to Arnie and asked him about Harry's involvement in his business. The sing-song voice of a young woman answered.

'May I speak to Mr Good please?' Carla asked.

'Mr Arnold Good or Mr Trevor Good?' the voice continued.

'Arnold.'

'Who shall I say is calling?'

'Carla Wilkinson.'

'Just putting you through.'

Carla heard Arnie's nasal voice on the other end of the line, 'Carla, what a surprise. I thought you'd be back in the sunshine by now.'

'No, I've a few loose ends to tie up first.'

'So what can I do for you?'

'I wanted to talk to you about Harry.'

'Sure, fire away.'

'I'd sooner come round to see you. I'm not sure that what I have to say is best said over the 'phone.' She could tell he was surprised by the ensuing silence.

'Okay. Do you want to come here to my office or shall we meet for a drink?'

'Maybe a drink would be best.'

'Right. I've got to be in Bristol tomorrow evening, 'How about I drop in to your 'otel on the way? It's the 'Oliday Inn, isn't it? I go right by it.'

'That would be fine. What time could you get here?'

There was a short pause then he said, 'About five. That suit you?'

'I'll wait for you in the hotel bar at five.'

'See you then Carla.' She could almost see the smirk on his face. Well it had to be done; she was determined to get all the skeletons out of the cupboard while she was here, then she could close the doors and move on.

*

Arnie was surprisingly punctual. Carla had just selected a table in a quiet corner and ordered herself a gin and tonic when he arrived. He was immaculately dressed in a dark blue suit and he wore what appeared to be an old school tie, which she was sure was not his own. He could almost have passed for a regular business man if it had not been for the tattoo on his neck which his shirt collar failed to conceal, the flashy gold rings that he always wore and the ostentatious gold Rolex that hung below his cuff. She wondered if he wore a gold medallion hiding beneath his blue striped shirt as well.

'Well I never expected this,' he said, a broad smile revealing a set of sparkling new teeth and a flash of gold. 'A date with the elusive Carla.'

New dental work, so that was what was different about him. No doubt he felt it made him look younger but his sallow skin still fell in folds around his neck, and the bags beneath his eyes were heavier than ever.

'Can I order you a drink?' she asked.

'Just a coffee. Don't want any run-ins with the Old Bill now do I?'

She ordered his coffee and sat down again, opposite him.

'Come on Carla. What's this all about? Want to get to know me a bit better now that you're footloose and fancy free?' He leered at her with his new teeth.

She sipped her gin and tonic before replying, 'Look Arnie, we've known each other a long time. I know we've never been close friends but you and Harry seemed to get on well together.'

'Yeah. 'Arry was a good mate. I'll miss him.'

She refrained from reminding him that he hadn't been to see Harry for almost three years before he died, and continued, 'I'm not trying to pry into your affairs but I need to know what sort of work Harry was doing for you.'

'Just odds and sods, helping out really. I felt sorry for 'im, giving up his business in England and that.'

'What kind of odds and sods?' she pressed. 'How much was he involved in Costa Build?'

He ran his hand over his bald head and sighed. 'Jesus Carla, I can't remember now. Hardly at all. He was just a runaround, nothing more. Why's it so important?'

'Was it anything illegal?'

'Hey, now look 'ere Carla, I'm a respectable businessman. All my clubs are legit. What d'you think I am, a crook?'

'I didn't say that but I want to know if Harry was mixed up in anything. He changed so much after we moved to Spain, I couldn't understand it,' she added sadly.

'Maybe you never really knew 'im. It was the booze that changed 'im, a sight too fond of the River Ouse, was your old man.'

'So those nights he was out with you he wasn't doing anything illegal?'

'No. If 'e was into anything, 'e wasn't doing it for me.' Carla put her glass on the table and leaned back, looking Arnie straight in the eye. Could she believe this man? 'Look I know what you're thinking but I can tell you 'e wasn't into anything.' He dropped his voice and leaned closer to her. 'Okay Carla, I'm completely legit now but I admit in those days I did 'ave a few shady deals going. 'Arry wanted none of it. He could have made a lot of money at one time but 'e wouldn't get involved. I'm not saying 'e wasn't tempted but in the end 'e chickened out, said you'd never forgive 'im if you found out.'

'What sort of shady deals?' she asked. 'Drugs? Prostitution?'

'Nah, nothing like that. Who d'you think I am, Reggie Kray? Nah, just a few shady property deals. You know the kind of thing, slipping a few quid to some dodgy councillors, greasing the wheels, so to speak. Everyone was up to it in those days. Nobody got hurt and a lot of people got rich.'

She thought instantly of Dawn and Peter. 'That's where you're wrong. Plenty of people have lost their life savings and ended up homeless through your shady dealings, and those of people like you.'

'It's not my fault if a few dodgy councillors reneged on their deals. I bought the land fair and square. I was just doing what all the other developers were doing. I can't 'elp it if I made myself a bit of money on the way.'

'But not Harry.'

'No, as I said, 'Arry didn't want to know. He said 'e was in enough shit with you as it was and didn't intend to make it worse.' Arnie finished his coffee and stood up. 'Look Carla, if that's all, I've got to get going. Christ I thought you'd got me here to tell me something important, not to grill me about my business ethics.'

'It's important to me,' she replied.

'Yeah, well it was all a long time ago. Put it behind you Carla and get on with your life, that's my advice.' He paused, then said, 'If you've ever wondered why he turned to the booze, you should ask that ex-wife of his. She shafted him, good and proper.' He glanced at her empty glass. 'Here let me buy you another glass of Mother's ruin,' he offered.

She looked up at him and shook her head. 'No thanks, but thank you for coming anyway.'

'Yeah, well see you Carla, maybe we could grab a meal together when you get back to Spain.'

'I don't think so Arnie.'

'Suit yourself. Now I really must get going.' He reached down to kiss her cheek but she forestalled him by extending her hand. He took it, but instead of shaking it, raised it to his lips. She snatched it away again and Arnie laughed. 'Still the same old Carla, eh. I told 'Arry you were too stuck up for the likes of us. Thanks for the coffee, doll.'

She watched him walk out of the bar and once he'd gone she called the waiter across and ordered herself another gin and tonic. 'A double please,' she said, 'with lots of ice.'

What had Arnie meant about Barbara? What had happened between them that Harry hadn't told her?

'There was a call for you, Mrs Wilkinson, from your solicitor. Could you telephone this number please, as soon as possible,' said the barman, handing her a folded note with her gin and tonic.

'Thank you.' It was Max's telephone number. 'What time did he ring?'

'Just after five o'clock.'

Carla looked at her watch; it was ten past six. It was too late now; she'd ring him in the morning. Right now she wanted to be alone to think about what Arnie had told her. Maybe she'd been mistaken about his influence on Harry. Had her husband been using Arnie as an excuse for not facing up to his responsibilities?

*

Much to her surprise Harry was quite keen to go to the Golf Club Ball. She hadn't needed to remind him; over breakfast he said, 'I think I'll wear my DJ tonight, if I can still get into it, that is. Is it clean?'

'I would think so; I sent it to the cleaners after we went to Cynthia's wedding last year. It's still in its plastic.'

'Good. Arnie and Dorothy'll be there,' he added.

'I didn't know they played golf.'

'They don't, the Captain asked Arnie to sponsor one of the prizes. He has to be there to present it to the winner.'

'Oh, does that mean we will have to sit with them? Only Julie and Brian have put us down on their table.'

'No, you don't have to sit with Arnie. He'll be on the top table, with the Captain.'

He seemed annoyed so she said, 'They'll be plenty of opportunity to talk to them, I'm sure.'

'Now why would you want to talk to my mate Arnie? You usually go out of your way to avoid him.'

She was tempted to argue with him but she wanted him in a good mood tonight and wasn't going to give him any excuse to go off on a drinking binge. 'I'll go and check on your suit. Which shirt do you want to wear?'

'Any of the white ones. You choose.'

She picked up the dirty plates and dropped them into the sink on her way to the bedroom. She had already chosen her dress for the evening, a low-backed, slinky number in electric blue.

*

Harry was ready before her, and was sitting on the terrace with a gin and tonic in his hand when she came down that evening.

'Wow, you look gorgeous,' he said, giving a low wolf whistle of appreciation.

'Thank you, you don't look so bad yourself.'

His DJ fitted him perfectly; he had the build and posture to carry a suit with elegance. He was still a handsome man, although she couldn't ignore the puffy, dark bags under his eyes.

'Ready?'

'Yes, I'll just get my bag and we can leave.' He swallowed the rest of the gin and tonic and got up. She looked at him. 'Don't worry, it was mostly tonic,' he said. 'I promised you I'd behave myself in front of your precious friends, didn't I?'

She slipped her arm through his and smiled at him. If only he could keep his word.

*

Julie and Brian were already there when they arrived at the Golf Club; she could see their silver Mercedes parked outside. The clubhouse was a very grand building, with marble floors, stone pillars and wood panelling. The broad stairway curved its way up to the first floor, past walls lined with wooden boards stencilled in gold lettering with the names of all the previous competition winners. Carla noticed Laura's name on one of the boards as the winner of the Bamber Cup in 1987 and Muriel's name appeared three times in succession in the seventies. At the top of the stairs was a rogue's gallery of all the Club Captains, past and present. Muriel's ruddy face beamed down at her from 1991. The room allocated for the evening's event would have afforded the guests a magnificent view of the golf course if it had been earlier in the day, as it was, all Carla could see was a floodlit putting green and the silhouettes of a number of tall trees. The tables, each large enough to seat ten people, were decorated with white linen tablecloths, fresh flowers and candles. Despite it being November the room had a fresh Spring-like atmosphere.

'Over here, Carla,' Julie called, waving to her. She knew most of the people there; besides Julie and Brian there were Dawn and Peter, Laura and her boyfriend, whom she introduced as Robbie, and Zoe and her husband Rick. Carla greeted and kissed them all, introducing Harry to those he hadn't met before and settling down eventually between Brian and Peter.

'I thought you were back to England,' she said, turning to Peter.

'We are, this is just a flying visit to sort out a few things with the solicitor. Zoe suggested we come along to the Ball as we were here anyway.'

'So you won't be in Spain for Christmas?'

'No, we fly back on Sunday. I expect we'll go to Dawn's brother's, so there'll be some semblance of normality, at least,' he said sadly. 'Anyway, let's not talk about that. I want to enjoy the evening.'

And enjoy the evening they did until it came to the prize giving. They had just finished the dessert, a fruity concoction, covered in meringue and cream, and were placing their orders for after-dinner drinks, when the

Captain stood up. He took hold of the microphone, tapped it a few times, muttered something then, happy that everything was working correctly, said, 'Ladies and gentlemen, members and invited guests, welcome to the Golf Club Annual Ball. As you know this is a tradition started over twenty years ago by the then captain, Sir Thomas Brown. Since then...'

Carla's attention began to wander, she didn't know any of the people he was talking about. She sipped her wine and stole a glance across at Harry. He certainly seemed to be in a good humour this evening; he was warming a large glass of brandy between his hands, whilst he chatted animatedly to Laura. He caught her looking at him and smiled.

'I hope you have all enjoyed your meal,' the Captain continued. 'How about giving a round of applause for the staff, to show our appreciation?' One or two men grunted their approval and they all clapped their appreciation for the prawn cocktail and roast beef. 'Now, before we begin the prize giving I would just like to say a word of thanks to our generous sponsors.' A wave of his hand acknowledged the guests sitting at his table, one or two smiled and nodded. She noticed Arnie smirking. 'The Bamber Cup, donated by Evelyn and Martin Shaw.' There was a ripple of polite clapping. 'The Ridley Bowl, donated by Ace Golf Tours.' More clapping. 'The Wellington Shield, a new competition this year, given by Eddie Standing of Standing Electrics.' Mr Standing stood and made a slight bow to the audience.

'And last, but by no means least, the Dorothy Good Plate donated by her husband Arnold Good, of Costa Build.'

Arnie was beaming his appreciation at the Captain when an inebriated Dawn leapt to her feet and, before anyone could stop her, shouted, 'Costa Build? More like Costa Cheat. You're a crook, Arnold Good. A dirty crook! What about the people you've swindled out of their life savings? What about them? You can go poncing about all you want, sponsoring competitions, toadying up to the committee. You'll never get membership in this club no matter how many silver plates you buy. Do you know why? Because you're a swindler. We've lost everything because of you, our home, our savings, even our health. You should be locked up.' She would have continued if Peter had not got up and pulled her gently away. Carla could hear her crying as he hurried her out into the hall. Everyone but Arnie looked stunned; she saw him turn to his wife, mutter something, then laugh. He seemed to think it was a big joke.

At last the silence was broken by the Captain saying, 'Well, ladies and gentlemen, I'm very sorry about that outburst. Let's get on with the prize giving, shall we? Right, the winner of this year's Bamber Cup is Angela Stokes.'

A plump, young woman made her way to the front to receive her prize, amid enthusiastic applause.

'She's a great golfer,' Brian whispered.

'And popular by the sound of it,' Carla replied. People seemed to have forgotten the disturbance and the prize giving continued without any further interruptions.

'What did Dawn mean about Arnie wanting membership?' she asked Brian.

'It's almost impossible to get membership of the Club these days,' he replied. 'It's not a question of money, really, there just aren't any vacancies. It's dead men's shoes only.'

'So Arnie is keen to be a member of the golf club?' she asked.

'He's been on the waiting list for two years now. I heard that they were considering giving him membership next year, but I doubt if it'll happen now.'

'Because of what Dawn said?'

'Yes, they're really picky about who they let join.'

'They let you in,' she said with a laugh.

'Yes, but that was years ago. They were desperate for the money then. Anyway, don't be so cheeky.'

'Why doesn't he join one of the other clubs? There are plenty about.' She knew there were dozens of golf courses along this stretch of the coast.

'Ah, but none as prestigious as this one.'

'So it's a question of snobbery?'

'In a way. Some of our members never even bother to play; they just like the membership so that they can bring their posh friends here for lunch and show off. Which is okay, it leaves the course freer for those who do want to play.'

'Like Julie and Laura?'

'Exactly. Although I shouldn't complain about Julie's golf; at least while she's playing golf she's not spending money.' He laughed again and drank some more of his wine. The band had begun playing and people were moving towards the dance floor. 'Fancy a dance?' he asked.

'Yes, good idea.' She glanced at Harry; Laura was leading him resolutely towards the dance floor.

CHAPTER 24

Barbara thought about Ian. Why is he so obsessed with how Harry died? Surely he didn't believe that Carla had done anything to hurt him? Or was this just another sign of the jealousy he struggled to control. Maybe he realised that she could never love anyone the way she'd loved Harry, but that was nothing to be jealous about. Harry had been her first love and her only one, until he had left her. She knew Ian had been jealous of Doug, even though he never said anything; she could understand that. Even she didn't know how she felt about the two of them. It was ridiculous; Ian had nothing to be jealous of now. Her brief romance with Doug, if it could be called that, had been about nothing more than sex. That wasn't enough for her and she'd soon realised that. It was Ian she'd married.

*

One evening Mary came round to see her, when she was in the kitchen ironing. Tom had gone to the cinema with his mates and Sylvia had gone back to university, only Katy, their new Cocker spaniel was there to keep her company. The dog lay curled up in her basket, paws in the air, offering her fat, pink stomach to anyone who wanted to tickle her.

'She's a sweetie,' Mary said, plonking herself down in the only comfortable chair in the kitchen.

'Yes, she is rather lovely. But it's the usual story, the kids went on and on about getting a dog and now that we have one they're never here to look after it.'

'So who takes her out?'

'Me, mostly. I only take her along the footpath. I just don't have the time to go any further.'

'What about Tom?'

'Oh, he says he will, but usually he can hardly find the time to get himself ready, never mind walk the dog.'

'Sylvia?'

'She's better, when she's here, but she only comes home at weekends and not always then.'

'She's enjoying life at uni then?'

'Very much, she's a different girl since she went there.'

'And what about you? How's your love life?' Mary asked. Barbara blushed and continued to iron Tom's shirt. 'Where's Ian these days? I haven't heard you talk about him much lately,' her friend continued, obviously intrigued by Barbara's silence.

'Oh Ian's all right. He comes round a couple of times a week for a meal or a drink.'

'Haven't you two set a date yet?'

'Don't be silly Mary.'

'What's silly about it? He's potty about you.'

'I'm too busy to think about getting married right now, anyway I prefer to be single.'

'Too busy mooning over that Scotch fellow, you mean.'

'Scots, Scotch is a drink.'

'Scots, Scotch, you know who I'm talking about.'

'I suppose you mean Doug?' As she said his name she felt her face redden.

'Yes, I can see it in your eyes. Where do you think that's going to get you? He's a confirmed bachelor, you told me yourself.'

'He's divorced actually.'

'Divorced, single, it's all the same. He likes his life as it is. Can you see him complicating his life with kids and dogs? Of course not. It's one night stands for him.'

'So? That suits me. Why would I want to tie myself down to a man again, anyway? It's better like this; we see each other when he's in the area and we have a good time.'

'Don't give me that old twaddle. I know you Barbara, you need romance, a husband, someone to love and cherish you, all the old-fashioned things. Don't throw your life away on someone who doesn't care about you.'

'He does care about me; Doug is my friend.'

'Yes, I know he is but he'll never be anything more than a friend. Ask yourself is that enough for you?' Barbara pulled a pair of Tom's jeans out of the laundry basket and spread them out on the ironing board. 'What does he think of Tom and Sylvia? Has he ever suggested you go out as a family? Where was he over the Christmas holiday? Off skiing with his mates. Is that the sort of man you want?' Mary continued.

'We have an arrangement.'

'Yes you arrange to be there at his beck and call. Let me ask you this, do you ever telephone him and suggest a night out?'

'No of course not.'

'Why "of course not"? That's what friends do.'

'Mary you're just being ridiculous. We're both quite happy with the way things are.'

'Fine, if that's true. But don't forget you aren't getting any younger. Don't waste too many years on him, especially when there's Ian waiting in the wings.'

'Ian's been a good friend to us, you know that.'

'Does he know about you and Doug sleeping together?'

'Nobody does, only you.'

Mary grimaced and shook her head.

'Dangerous game Babs, two men: one for sex and one for companionship. I would never have thought you had it in you.' She giggled and went to the refrigerator to help herself to a glass of wine.

Barbara folded the jeans neatly and hung them over the back of the chair. 'Oh that'll do for tonight. I'm fed up of ironing. Pour me one while you're there will you.'

The two friends took their drinks out into the garden and sat on the low wall that separated the patio from the vegetable garden. The damp evening air was filled with the scent of thyme and rosemary and the last rays of the sun were just visible on the horizon.

'This is new, isn't it?' Mary asked.

'The wall? Yes, Ian finished it last weekend. He thought it would stop the mud slipping down on to the patio each time it rained.'

'I didn't realise he was such a handyman.'

'He's not really but he enjoys having a go. He says it makes a change from sitting behind a desk all day.'

'Looks very professional.'

'Yes, it's not bad, is it. Mind you it took him ages, he's so particular about everything he does. Tom helped him; he carried the bricks and helped to mix the cement.'

'I think they did very well. You could do a lot worse than Ian, you know.'

*

After Mary left, Barbara could not get her words out of her head. Her friend understood her very well. True she loved Doug's company and the sex, when it happened, and that was not very often, was great, but she knew something was missing from her life. For the first few years she had been so busy bringing up the children and running her business that her arrangement with Doug suited her very well but now she needed something more. The children were growing up, soon they would leave and she would be on her own. She would like to have a more stable relationship with Doug but she could not see it ever happening. From the beginning she had tried to be casual about their relationship but it was not in her nature, she wanted more from him. Nowadays, perhaps because of her bad experience with Harry, she found herself wondering where he was and what he was doing when he was not with her, worse than that she began to wonder who he was with. She was not naturally a jealous woman, in fact, in the past, she had often been accused of being too trusting, but now she found herself inventing reasons for telephoning him and fabricating questions that would tell her more about his movements.

She poured herself the last of the wine from the bottle and returned to her seat on the wall. The house was silent. The sun had disappeared and the evening had turned gloomy, black clouds scudded across a purple sky to reveal glimpses of the pale moon starting its nightly climb. She watched a pair of kingfishers fly low across the river. In the distance she could hear an owl calling to its mate. That was what life was really about, having a mate, a companion, a husband, a partner. Call it what you may it was someone to share your life with, someone to love and someone to love you. She wanted a man who would share her concerns for her children, who would be there through the bad times as well as the good, someone like Harry. It was the first time she had thought about him in a long time. Once, long ago, she had believed she had the perfect marriage with Harry but she'd been wrong. She'd thought that if she could not have Harry then she could be satisfied with friendship and casual sex, but again she was wrong. What did she want? As she watched two swans glide slowly past, dark silhouettes in the dusk, she knew she could not answer that. But she also knew that it was time to stop making a fool of herself over Doug.

CHAPTER 25

Now Barbara was both retired and wealthy, but, as she had said to Ian that morning over breakfast, what was the point of having all that money if she couldn't do what she wanted with it. And what she wanted to do was give it to her children, she knew Sylvia needed money for Linda's school but she refused to accept it from her. Barbara loved her granddaughter; it made her sad to think of the little girl struggling with her reading. Neither Tom nor Sylvia had had any problems learning to read. She remembered Sylvia pretending to read her mother's books when she was barely two, sitting in the armchair studiously trying to decipher the squiggles from a book, which, more often than not, she held upside down. As soon as she was able to, she devoured all the books Barbara bought her: fairy tales, fables, adventure stories, animal tales, anything and everything. Tom on the other hand loved to have stories read to him, sitting wide eyed listening to his mother at bedtime but, although less enthusiastic than his older sister, even he had no trouble unscrambling the hieroglyphics in order to make sense of their meaning. Poor Linda, how sad it was that this important skill was eluding her. Barbara thought back to her own solitary childhood; she would have been lost without her books. They were her greatest companions. She had kept them all and the bookshelves of her house were weighed down with them, from the tattered copies of Enid Blyton and C S Lewis to Dickens and Tolstoy. Sometimes when she sat alone she imagined the hundreds of different worlds trapped between the dusty pages, the myriads of characters caught up in their own private lives and she knew she couldn't throw away a single one. She sighed as she thought of Sylvia; sometimes her daughter could be so stubborn.

It was one day at the beginning of September, when Barbara was collecting Linda from school that she realised that Sylvia had been making plans.

'Nana you will have to collect me from my new school next year. I hope you know how to get there.'

'New school? What new school sweetheart? I thought you liked your school.'

'I do, Nana but Mummy says I have to go to a new school. It's a much better school. If I go to the new school I'll soon be able to read like Sally.' Sally was Linda's best friend.

'That sounds nice, dear.'

'Do you know how to get there Nana?' The little girl crumpled her forehead in anxiety.

'I'm sure your Mummy will tell me. We'll ask her where it is when she gets home shall we?'

'What time will Mummy get home?'

'I suppose that will depend on what time her course finishes.'

'I might be in bed.'

'You might.'

'Will the little hand be on the seven when I go to bed?'

'Yes that's right Darling, seven o'clock is your bedtime.'

'Why is Mummy on a course, Nana?'

'Because your Mummy is a teacher and all teachers have to do courses so that they can learn new things to teach their pupils.'

Linda laughed at the idea of her mother being in school. 'Just like me,' she said.

'Yes, just like you.'

*

Barbara had just finished bathing Linda when Richard arrived home. 'Hi Barbara, sorry I'm late, we had problems with some local farmers. They've been storing their silage badly and it's been leaking into the aquifers.'

'That's okay Richard. Linda's in bed. She's had her tea and her bath. You're just in time to read her a story.'

'Great, I'll go straight up. Are you staying for supper?' he added.

'No, thanks, I must get back. Ian will be waiting for me.'

'Thanks again.'

He kissed her cheek and went up the stairs two at a time to see his daughter. Barbara could hear him calling to her; 'Hi Lindy Lou, it's Daddy.'

There was something about Richard that reminded her of Harry; she had thought that the first time Sylvia had brought him home to meet her. 'Ask Sylvia to give me a ring will you,' she called up the stairs after him.

'Will do.'

She'd had to struggle to bring up her children; she didn't want Sylvia to do the same.

*

Barbara didn't hear from Doug until about three weeks after Mary's visit. Then one evening he rang, 'Hi there Barbara, it's Doug. I've had an idea. Have you thought of producing picnic size condiments? You could do a range of relishes in plastic sachets. I'm sure they'd go down a bomb.'

'Sounds interesting.'

'I've been looking at the cost of packaging and there's a company in Slough that could do it for a reasonable price. I thought we might take a run over there on Thursday if you're not busy. There's a really smart hotel nearby, "The Black Swan." We could make a day of it, lunch, the works.'

'Yes, okay. I'm not busy. That would be fine.'

'Pick you up around ten.'

'Right, see you on Thursday.'

As she replaced the receiver she realised how fast her heart was beating; the sound of his voice had set her adrenalin racing again. Each time he called she was sucked back into a pattern that had been created by him to suit his needs, yet it suited her too. Or did it? She recalled Mary's words; it was true, she wasn't getting any younger. And then there was Ian; she was very fond of Ian but he didn't excite her in the way Doug did. She knew he wanted to marry her; he had hinted on many occasions that they would make a fine couple. She tried to imagine being married to him. It would be a comfortable life, safe and secure. She was certain that Ian would make a loving, caring husband. So what was holding her back? He'd been a loyal friend for years, the children adored him and he loved her; she knew that. She realised that Doug had never told her he loved her, not once in all the years they had been sleeping together. Tears came into her eyes; this was not what she wanted. She had been so happy before Harry had left her; her life had seemed perfect. She had two wonderful children, a beautiful home and a husband that loved her, or so she thought. She would not have changed a thing. But change there had been and for the sake of the children she had assumed a new role: that of breadwinner. She was not unhappy. She had moved on, past Harry, past the deceit, past the betrayal. Again she remembered Mary's words, how well her friend knew her. There was an emptiness in Barbara's life that Doug, for all his charm could not assuage. Yes she had changed, circumstances had seen to that, but deep inside she was still the same person. She needed to love and be loved in return. She needed the warmth of companionship. Sylvia was at university now and only came home when she'd run out of money or needed more clean clothes. Tom, if he got the results he wanted, would be going to university the following year. That would leave Barbara on her own. The thought of coming back to an empty house, night after night was not an attractive one. It was not a future she was looking forward to.

*

She was trying to make sense of a printout of the monthly accounts that Rachel, her able accountant had left on her desk, when her telephone rang.

'Mrs Wilkinson, it's Mr Routh for you on line one.'

'Thanks, Joyce.'

'Ian, this is a surprise.' He hardly ever telephoned her at the factory.

'Hello Barbara, sorry to telephone you at work. I know Wednesday's a busy day for you. Someone has just given me two tickets for the Mill at Sonning for tomorrow evening. I thought if you weren't busy we could go.'

'That sounds great, I'd love to, but I've arranged to see Doug. We're going to visit a packaging company. Maybe another time.'

She could hear the disappointment in his voice, as he said. 'It's not until eight o'clock. Won't you be finished by then?'

'I'm not sure. I'd hate you to be waiting about for me.'

'Okay. Another time,' he said and hung up.

She'd upset him and now she felt guilty. Did he know why it took them all day and evening to visit a packaging company? Did he know that Doug and she were sleeping together? For a few minutes she sat staring at the telephone wondering whether to ring him back and say she could make it after all.

'Excuse me Barbara, have you finished with the accounts?'

'Yes, Rachel, they look fine. I see the profit's down slightly this month.' Her eye always went straight to the bottom line.

'The cost of the new delivery van is in there. I did suggest we lease it,' Rachel explained.

'No, I prefer it like that.'

'So they're okay then?'

'Fine.'

'By the way, Bert asked me to remind you that you're due at a production meeting at eleven.'

'I'm just on my way.' She handed her the accounts. Maybe she should think about ending her relationship with Doug, but what could she say without it sounding like an ultimatum? That was the last thing she wanted. Well she hadn't time to think about it now. She picked up her white coat and hat and made for the processing room.

*

That evening Ian picked her up from work. 'I thought we'd have some supper on the way home. You did say Tom was out tonight?'

'Yes, he's playing football with some friends. A pub supper sounds good. I've had such a busy day, I didn't get time to have any lunch, so I'm starving.'

'I thought we'd go to that little place by the river, that you like so much,' he said, smiling at her. He seemed to have forgiven her for putting work before an evening at the theatre.

They ordered two glasses of wine and the house special; it was tasty and filling. Just what she needed to round off the day.

They didn't talk much. She realised that this was what she enjoyed about being with Ian; it was easy. She felt totally relaxed in his company. If she didn't want to talk there was no uncomfortable silence and if she wanted to disagree about something she could do so without worrying that he'd be upset. There was no need to impress him, or pretend to be something more than she was; she never needed to feel that she had to compete when she was with Ian. He accepted her just as she was.

'It's such a lovely evening, I thought we could have a short walk by the river,' he said, after paying the bill.

'I'd like that. I'm still rather full after that enormous meal.'

'You did have two helpings of Summer Pudding,' he laughed.

'What about you and that huge plate of Death by Chocolate.'

'What a way to go.'

'Yes, I think maybe a walk will do us both good.'

The air was soft and warm, there was almost no breeze and even the slight chill from the river was not enough to make her put her jacket around her shoulders. They walked along arm-in-arm, not speaking. The path was becoming narrow and she stumbled on a half-hidden tree root.

'I think we should turn back,' he said, pulling her towards him to steady her.

'It's such a lovely night; I could stay here forever,' she said.

They turned back towards the bridge. She could see the water eddying around its pillars, a silver stream that twisted and turned and vanished into the darkness. A heron flew low over the water, a black silhouette against the beams of light that danced on the water in a kaleidoscope of colours.

Ian stopped. 'Barbara,' he said, his voice deep and serious. 'You know how fond I am of you and the children.' She squeezed his arm in reply. 'I know we've talked about this before but I have to ask you again.' He hesitated. 'I can't sleep for thinking about you, Barbara. I've never felt like this about anyone before. I love you.'

She looked at him in surprise. She knew he was fond of her but she'd never thought he felt so strongly. The thought of Ian, whose life was always so well organised and under control, lying in bed unable to sleep because of her, was a revelation.

'You know you'd make me very happy if you would marry me,' he continued. 'I know I'm not a young man. I'll be sixty in a couple of years, but I'm still very fit. I know I could make you happy.'

'You do make me happy,' she replied. 'I enjoy your company immensely, Ian.' She should have guessed this was coming. Ian had been even quieter than usual all evening. She'd known there was something on his mind, but not this.

'It's ten years since the divorce,' he continued.

'Nine.'

'Okay, nine years. Don't you think it's time to move on?'

'I have moved on Ian. I just haven't wanted to get married again.' He didn't reply but she knew he was disappointed. She squeezed his arm again. 'Let me think about it,' she said at last.

'So you'll consider it?'

'Of course I will. I'm very fond of you Ian, and I think you'd make a wonderful husband.'

'But?'

'It's a big step.'

'We don't have to get married if you don't want to. We can live together. I could sell my flat and move in with you or we could both sell up and buy something completely different. I just want you in my life, Barbara.'

'I promise you I will think seriously about it and we'll talk about it again at the weekend.'

*

When he dropped her off at home, she didn't ask him in, making a feeble excuse about having to be up early the next morning, but she did let him kiss her goodnight and she felt his passion as he held her close to him.

Once his car had turned out of the drive and the darkness descended once again, she picked up the telephone and rang Mary.

'Hi, I hope it's not too late?'

'No, we're just watching the end of a film and I've seen it before anyway. What is it? Is something the matter?'

'I just needed someone to talk to.'

'Okay, hang on, I'll take the phone out into the hall.' She could hear the television and Bill's voice asking who it was then Mary was back on the line   'That's better, I can hear what you're saying now. So what's happened?'

'It's Ian. He's asked me to marry him.'

'So, what's new? He's asked you dozens of times.'

'Yes, but he says he loves me. He wants me in his life. He even suggested we live together.'

'My, he's got it bad. I never thought Mr Prim and Proper would consider living in sin.'

'He's not that prim and proper; it's just the way solicitors are.'

'So, what did you say?'

'I said I'd think about it.'

'What's to think about? He's not bad looking. He's got plenty of money. He gets on well with the kids and he loves you. Go for it, girl.'

'But I don't love him, at least not the way I loved Harry. I don't even fancy him the way I fancy Doug.'

'Barbara, you were seventeen when you met Harry; you're not the same person any more. You're not still in love with him, are you?'

'No, of course not.'

'And Doug, well you know that's lust pure and simple. It won't last forever.'

Barbara giggled. 'I know, but it's nice while it does.'

'Be serious. This could be your last chance. Doug is never going to ask you to marry him.'

'To be honest, I don't think I would want to anyway,' she replied, thinking that she'd always be wondering where he was and with whom.

'And Ian isn't going to wait around forever. I'm surprised he's waited this long; he must really have the hots for you.'

Thinking of Ian having the hots for anyone made both women laugh. 'Well he did get a bit passionate tonight,' Barbara added.

'Don't you feel anything for him?' Mary asked.

'Of course I do. I told you, I'm very fond of him.'

'Do you know what I think? This affair of yours with Doug is clouding the issue; you can't see your true feelings for Ian because you feel guilty about cheating on him.'

'How can I be cheating on him? I haven't promised him anything. We're just friends.'

'You're using him, Barbara. And you're leading him on. He's there whenever you call, he knows your family and friends, he eats with you at least twice a week, sometimes more, he is like a father to your children and the only thing you won't allow him is access to your bed. Sometimes I wonder why he stands for it. You want both men, one for sex and one to take care of you. But you can't have it that way forever.' Barbara was silent. Mary had never spoken to her like this before. Her words stung. Before she could reply, Mary continued, 'I think you're right, you do have to think about it. You should think long and hard because if you don't, you'll lose a man who truly loves you and you'll probably be thrown over by Doug as soon he finds someone younger that he fancies.' Barbara didn't know what to say. 'I'm sorry, but I can't stand by and watch you throwing away your chance of a happy marriage. Just because Harry turned out to be a sod, doesn't mean every man will be the same. Why don't you give Ian a chance.'

'I don't know,' Barbara began.

'Look I'd better go, the film sounds as though it's finished. Bill will want to go to bed.'

Barbara put down the telephone and went into the kitchen. There was a lot of sense in what Mary had said. Emotionally she was a mess. Harry's betrayal had left her suspicious and wary of all men. That was why she liked the relationship with Doug; it was sex, nothing more. She couldn't blame him. He had never promised her anything, not love, not loyalty, not even friendship. They were business colleagues who enjoyed having sex together, that was all. She smiled sadly, it could just as easily have been golf, or tennis. It was a physical activity from which they both derived a lot of pleasure. Maybe Mary was right; it was time to move on.

*

The packaging factory was on a small trading estate, in a low, brick building tucked behind the cooling towers. A rather attractive, but dour, middle-aged man greeted them in the reception area. He handed them white coats and caps and once they were suitably dressed, led them through into the wrapping room.

'Sorry about this,' he said, indicating the protective clothing. 'But we wrap a lot of foodstuffs and the hygiene people are pretty strict. This is the Christmas pack for a local confectionary company.'

Chocolate covered slabs were being fed between mechanical arms that steadied them, lined them up and guided them into the stainless steel wrapping machine that formed a sheath around each bar and heat sealed it into place. Barbara recognised the name on the products as they emerged fully clothed in their bright, shiny wrappers; they were Tom's favourites. She watched the colourful stream of chocolate bars continue along the conveyor belt towards a line of anonymous women packers, all identically dressed in white coats and with their hair caught up in hairnets. They paused for a moment to watch the women's nimble hands stack the bars into the festive Christmas boxes before their guide led them into a second room where a complicated network of machines was taking a thick red liquid from a large, stainless steel drum and injecting it into small sachets before heat sealing them closed.

'Tomato ketchup,' he explained. 'This would be the sort of process we would use to package your relishes, slightly larger sachets of course and clear plastic so that the contents could be clearly seen. If you come with me into the office I'll show you the ideas I have for the packaging.'

They followed him into a tiny, crowded office situated at the rear of the reception area. His desk was piled high with papers and the floor was littered with cardboard boxes. Before she could sit down he had to remove a stack of trade magazines from the only available chair. 'Sorry about the mess, we're in the process of moving offices.' Barbara perched herself on the edge of the chair and listened while he expounded on his ideas. She could see that Doug was not really interested and she herself felt less than enthusiastic. When they had looked at the last of the designs and he had given her a copy of the projected costs they thanked him for his time, informed him that they would consider his ideas and be in touch by the end of the week. They waited until they were both seated in Doug's new Jaguar before either one spoke.

'I'm not sure it's what I want to do,' she said at last, as they drove out of the car-park. 'I think I'd sooner wait until one of the supermarkets actually asks me to provide a picnic-size version than invest money in something we may find difficult to sell.'

'You're probably right; it's quite a commitment. Have you looked at his figures?'

'It's not that, I just don't want to diversify too much. It seems too risky.'

'Fine. Anyway if you are ever asked for picnic-size relishes now you know where to go.'

'So we'll leave it for now?' she asked.

'If that's what you want, yes.'

She took a deep breath, it was now or never. 'Doug, there's something I want to say.' She could feel her stomach churning and her hands had become hot and clammy; she hated any confrontation. Even as a child she had always been the peacemaker, the one who sought a solution for any arguments, who would agree to differ rather than meet a conflict head on. She took a tissue from her handbag and wiped her hands slowly.

'Yes?'

'Look, I don't want to spoil our working relationship and I especially don't want to spoil our friendship, but...' She hesitated.

'But?' He kept his eyes on the road ahead but she could see the hint of a smile working away at the corners of his mouth.

'I really value our friendship, Doug and you've been so good to me, investing money in my business, giving me advice. I really appreciate all that you've done.'

'But?'

'It's about the hotel.'

'It's supposed to be excellent. There was a write-up in the Times about it only last week, highly recommended. I thought you'd like it. But it doesn't matter we can always cancel and go somewhere else instead. Whatever you want.'

'No, no, it's not that. I'm sure the hotel is wonderful. Look Doug, this relationship isn't working, well not for me at any rate. I'm too old for casual sex. I'm sorry, but I'd like us to return to how we were before, just colleagues. No more nights together.'

He turned and looked at her and for a brief moment she thought she saw a more vulnerable version of the man she knew, then it vanished and the old confident exterior dropped back into place. 'Okay Barbara, just as you like. It was only sex after all. I thought you enjoyed it as much as I did.'

'I did, I do, it's just not enough for me. I thought I could cope with it but I can't. I like sex but there has to be more.'

'Don't apologise Barbara, you want the complete package and you know I can't give it to you. It's that simple.'

'But we can continue to be friends?'

'Of course.'

'And your investment? I could always borrow the money from the bank to pay you back; I'm sure they will look on me much more favourably now.'

'No way, I want to reap some profit from this business of yours. No, you're quite right; we should never have mixed business and pleasure. We'll go back to as we were. Think no more about it.' Was it her imagination or was he less confident than his words suggested. They drove in an easy silence for a bit then he said, 'I suppose you don't object to having lunch with me?'

'Of course not.'

'The table's booked at The Black Swan, so we might as well go there. I'll cancel the room when we arrive.'

'Fine.'

'So why the change of heart?' he asked at last.

'Ian's asked me to marry him,' she blurted out before she could stop herself.

'Congratulations.'

'I haven't accepted yet.'

He turned and looked at her. 'But I thought that was what you wanted?'

'It is.'

'So, what's stopping you?' There was no way she could tell him. 'Is it because of us?'

'I suppose so.'

'Oh Barbara, don't be silly. I'm very fond of you, you must know that, but marriage. No way. I tried that and it was a disaster. If you want marriage and roses round the door I'm not for you. You know what I'm like.'

'I never had any expectations,' she said.

'Look, Ian will never hear about our liaison from me, I promise you. I may not want to settle down with my women, but I never tell tales on them.'

With a jolt, she realised that she had not been the only woman in Doug's life; there was a plurality in his statement that told it all. How could she have thought that he would stay faithful to her all this time? What a fool she was.

'Doug, look do you mind, but I really don't feel like lunch today.'

'If that's what you want. It's a pity though, they do a wonderful Beef Wellington.'

He turned the car round at the next roundabout and drove her home.

CHAPTER 26

Sylvia telephoned her the following evening.

'Hi Mum, thanks for picking Linda up.'

'No problem, she's real pleasure to be with.'

'Isn't she and she's such a sweetie. Do you know what she said to me this morning? Had I learnt something new yesterday, to teach my class? She thought it was such a hoot that I had been to "school" for the day.'

'She's growing up fast.'

'Too fast.'

'She says she's going to a new school.'

Barbara could hear the hesitation in Sylvia's voice before she answered, 'Yes I'm thinking of getting her into Piper's Park. You do know she's dyslexic?'

'No, I didn't. I know you said she had problems with her reading but I didn't realise it was dyslexia.'

'Well it is and I, we, both think that she needs special help.'

'Is it a private school?'

'Yes.'

'Expensive?'

'Sort of.'

'You know I can help with the fees. I'd like to. Just let me know how much they are and I'll write you a cheque.'

'No thanks Mum, there's no need. We can manage.'

'Are you sure?'

'Positive.'

'Well if you need anything, please ask; I have the money and I'd like to help. She is my granddaughter after all.'

'Yes, thanks Mum but we'll be all right. We'll have plenty of money once Dad's house is sold.'

'So you're going ahead with it then? But what about Carla?'

'What about her? It's our house now. Why should she continue to live there rent free?'

'Oh Sylvia, you need to think about this. You're throwing her out of her home.'

'Why do you care after all she's done to you, to us?'

'But Sylvia that was all a long time ago. You can't do this to her.'

'I can and I am going to.'

'What does Tom say about it?'

'Tom knows we need the money.'

'But Sylvia…'

'No "buts" Mum, it's going to happen. Look I've got to go. I'll talk to you later. Thanks again for looking after Linda.'

Immediately Barbara rang her son. Of course Tom was very noncommittal when she spoke to him, as she knew he would be. She couldn't remember a single time when he'd spoken out against his sister; it wasn't going to happen now. Of her two children it was Tom that she worried about most; Sylvia had a hard shell that protected her from the world but Tom was a softer, gentler person. Besides which Sylvia had Richard to help her. They made a very good couple sharing similar interests and opinions about the world and of course they had Linda. They were a family. Tom was on his own, a loner, introverted, quiet, thoughtful and caring, as far as she knew there had never been a girlfriend until Charlotte. When he brought Charlotte over to have Sunday lunch with them and she saw how much he was in love with this girl she knew he would make a good husband and father, she just hoped that Charlotte felt the same way about him.

'But why do you have to sell the house?' she asked him.

'We need the money,' was his answer.

'But you know that your father wanted her to continue living in it; it's her home after all.'

'I know, that's why we didn't do it straight away, but he's been dead a year now. Anyway it will probably take ages to sell.'

'That's not the point Tom, you're throwing her out of her home. I thought you liked Carla?'

'She's okay. She'll find somewhere else. I'm sure Dad didn't leave her without anything to fall back on.'

'I've told Sylvia I can help with the money but she won't take it.'

'No she wants to do it her own way; you know how she is Mum.'

'But what about you? What do you want money for?'

'We all need money Mum, you should know that.'

'Look if it's for a new car or something I can help you, you only have to ask.'

'I'm moving up to Edinburgh after Christmas.'

She felt as if a door had opened and a cold wind had entered the room. 'To Edinburgh?' Her voice sounded faint. 'To live?'

'Mum are you still there? Did you hear me?'

'Yes Tom.'

'It's the job; they're closing the London branch and we're all moving to Edinburgh. Those that want to go of course. It makes sense, there're no big projects in the London area at the moment. All our new developments are in the north. The Edinburgh office has been going from strength to strength for years now.'

'Sounds as though you're pleased?'

'Oh yes, it's a good opportunity; we've got the contract for the new Festival building.'

'Will you be working on that?'

'Yes, in a minor way but yes. It'll be great experience for me.'

'What about Charlotte?'

'Mmn, that I don't know.'

'What do you mean, you don't know? Will she be going with you?'

'She has her own job, Mum. I don't know what she'll do.'

'I thought you two were going to move in together.'

'We talked about it but I don't know what will happen now. Anyway if we sell the house it'll give me enough money to buy a place in Edinburgh,' he continued.

Suddenly she was no longer so worried about Carla's imminent eviction, Tom's news had wiped everything else from her head. 'Well this is a bit of a shock,' she managed to say, at last.

'Don't take on Mum, it's not as though I'm going to Australia is it. I'll be back to see you, and I'm sure you'll be up to see me from time to time.'

'I hope it will be worth the upheaval,' was all she said.

'Better a move than no work,' he said. 'Anyway I might only be there a couple of years. Nobody stays still in my line of work for long, you have to go where the interesting projects are if you want to get on.'

She had always known this but so far Tom had been lucky, and for the past eight or nine years had been involved in the building of various new developments that had sprung up alongside the M1.

'Don't worry Mum. I'll let you know when it's all going to happen. I won't just disappear, or send you a letter telling you I've already gone. I'm not like Dad.'

*

The big change in her life had come when 'Country Products' had decided to buy out her company the year before. Doug as usual had been the one to tell her about their plans; he had invited their Managing Director, Christopher Little to visit her premises and arranged for Barbara to meet him. He was a young man, who had not held the position of CEO for long, but he seemed to know what he wanted. She thought he'd looked impressed with what he saw and, as they made their way back to her office, he explained to her that her relishes and jams were exactly what 'Country Products' needed to supplement their already popular range of organic produce. Then he had left and, for almost two months, she'd heard nothing from him, until one morning she received a telephone call inviting her to their head office in Newcastle. She flew up there the next day and, after listening to his proposal, promised to consider it carefully. Although she'd found his offer very tempting there was a sinking feeling in her stomach as they talked about balance sheets, cash flow statements, margins, implementation dates; she felt she was about to lose a member of her family, as indeed she was. 'Windmill Hill Chutneys and Jams had increased in size over the years; its turnover had grown and the numbers of employees had tripled but, despite that, she had always managed to retain a hands-on approach to the company. She knew all the staff by name; they were all local people that she had recruited personally. She knew about their families, how many children they had, where they lived and why they had come to work for her and she felt a responsibility for them all. Ian had often laughed at her attitude; he said she was better suited to the 19th century than the 21st, that she would want to build them workers' cottages next. So when she returned from Newcastle although the first things she did were discuss the offer with Doug and Ian, then seek professional advice from her accountants, she would not accept the seventeen million pounds that Country Products wanted to give her, until she had called a meeting of all her staff and assured them that their jobs were safe, at least for the next twelve months. She had been unable to persuade Christopher Little to commit himself to any further guarantees. So once again her life had changed; now, not only was she married, she was a woman of leisure and wealthy as well.

CHAPTER 27

Straight after breakfast Carla went back to her room and telephoned Max.

'Hi there, thanks for calling back.'

'Sorry I didn't ring last night. I didn't get your message until very late,' she lied.

'No matter, Chris has been on to me about this problem of yours with Harry's kids. As I told you last week I'm not sure we can make a case to stop them selling the house but we could put pressure on them.'

'Blackmail you mean?'

He laughed. 'Not exactly, in case you didn't realise it, blackmail is against the law.'

'What then?'

'Well,' he hesitated then said, 'Look maybe it would be easier to go over it in my office. Can you come over this morning? I've just had someone cancel their 11.30 appointment.'

'Yes, no problem, but you'll have to tell me where it is.'

She noted down the directions and hung up. It would only take about twenty minutes to get there. She looked at her reflection in the mirror, a tired face stared back at her. The strain of the last few days had pulled at the corners of her mouth and a permanent crease had appeared between her carefully shaped eyebrows. She touched her hair; it felt lank and slightly greasy. There was no way she could go to see Max looking like this. It was just nine o'clock; she could hear the newscaster reading through the day's headlines: yet more speculation about the new coalition. Plenty of time to get herself ready she decided, stripping off her clothes and heading for the shower.

*

At precisely eleven-thirty she was standing in Max's reception room, her blonde hair glossy, her make-up immaculate and wearing a honey, beige suit that she had bought the day before.

'Please take a seat Mrs Wilkinson. Mr Atherton will only be a moment,' the receptionist informed her.

Max Atherton was probably a few years older than Carla but he had retained the vitality of his youth: his tall, well built frame and muscular shoulders were evidence of regular work-outs at the gym, his blond hair had turned grey with the years but it was cut short in line with the fashion and gave him a boyish look. No longer the stereotypical Englishman, he looked more like a pop star. When she had spoken to him on the telephone, the previous week, she'd been surprised and flattered that he remembered her. Now as he opened the door from his office she saw his eyes light up at the sight of her.

'Carla, right on time. Come in please.'

He ushered her into his office and directed her to an armchair by the window. Everything was new; the building had been recently completed and as he explained they had only been in these premises a couple of months. He had chosen them because he wanted to be out of the town with its one-way system and crowded streets. Here he could think clearly, he said, pointing to the magnificent view. She followed his gaze to the river, far below them, glinting in the sunshine as it slowly drifted to the sea.

'It's lovely,' she agreed. 'You made a good choice.'

'Right now, down to business. You'll have to go through this in detail I'm afraid as Chris has only given me a sketchy idea of what you have in mind.'

'I'm not sure I've got anything in mind, Max. I'll tell you what I told Chris and Gerry and then you can see if it's useful or not.'

She repeated her suspicions about Harry's virility and her subsequent actions then sat back to see the solicitor's reactions. She felt embarrassed at having to admit what she had done and feared that he might disapprove; after all he had been Harry's friend as well as his solicitor.

'That's interesting but how do you explain his children? This condition, Klinefield's Syndrome?'

'Klinefelter's Syndrome.'

'Could it have begun later in life, after his children were born?'

'No, I'm pretty sure it's something you're born with. I think he's always been impotent.'

'But have you any proof, the results of the test for example?'

'No, nothing. There didn't seem any point in keeping them, at the time. After all it was only to satisfy my own curiosity. Remember I was desperate. And I didn't want Harry to come across them.'

'Yes, I can see that. The question is what do you want me to do with this information?'

'That's the problem, I don't know. I'm angry that Sylvia is doing this to me and especially in such a high handed manner. If she'd talked to me about it, I'm sure we could have come to some arrangement but to just go ahead and put the house on the market without telling me...' She stopped.

'As we discussed the other day you have nothing in writing that allows you to continue living in the house. She and her brother are now the legal owners of their father's house. Actually it's a pity that Harry decided to make an English will because under Spanish law you would have at least received half the house. As it is you have no legal claims on it at all.'

'As I said before Max, I was happy that Harry left them the house but I thought that I would be able to stay there as long as I wanted.' She realised now that she had been rather naive in that belief.

'So do you want me to use this new information to stop the sale? We'd have to get DNA tests done and even then I'm not sure it would work. I'll have to go over the exact wording of the will. Does it say that he left the house to his children or to Tom and Sylvia by name? If they are specifically named then it doesn't matter if they are not his biological children; they will still inherit and we will be no further forward. Unless you want me to blackmail them, that is?' He laughed.

'No of course not. Oh Max, I just don't know what I want.'

'Look leave it with me for now. I'll get out the will and check the wording. I'm pretty sure we would have inserted their full names but there again Harry had only just remarried, he may have wanted us to leave it open enough to cover any subsequent offspring.'

'Oh, I don't think so.'

'Leave it with me anyway. In the meantime I'll try to get hold of a copy of the deeds to the house. We will need those whatever happens. Do you know which solicitor handled it?'

'No, I'm afraid not. Harry never discussed those sort of things with me. But I know who might know, Arnold Good. He's an old friend of Harry's and he's here in England now; he came for the funeral. Would you like his number?'

'Excellent idea.'

'So what will you do about the children?' she asked.

'Nothing without speaking to you first; this is a very delicate matter. But Carla you need to go away and decide exactly what it is you want to do with this knowledge. Tom and Sylvia firmly believe that Harry was their father. Now he is dead and they only have their mother. What does this information say about her? Even if it cannot be proved it could destroy their relationship with her. It could ruin their lives.'

'I've thought about all this. That's why I came to you for help.' She could hear the quaver in her voice.

'Okay Carla, calm down. I'll look into it and let you know my opinion. In the meantime I think it's best to keep these suspicions to ourselves. We don't want Sylvia suing you for libel.' Again he laughed and added, 'Don't worry Carla. I'll telephone you in a couple of days.'

'Thanks Max.'

'In the meantime do as I say, think hard about what you're about to do, and I'll get in touch with Mr Good.' She nodded her agreement. 'I'm sorry to keep our meeting so short but I've got a client at twelve o'clock. Maybe next time we could meet for a drink rather than have you come here?' he suggested.

'Yes, that would be nice.' She stood up and extended her hand towards him but he came round from behind his desk and bent forward to kiss her cheek. He smelled of after shave and coffee and the slight rasp from the stubble on his chin sent a tingle down her spine. Yes, a drink with Max would be nice.

CHAPTER 28

Teddy was waiting for her by the gate as she walked up the hill towards his cottage. He was definitely looking his age she thought; it was reflected in his movements and the stoop of his back. He no longer walked with the spring of a younger man, muscles supple and yielding; now his back seemed stiff and tired, his legs straight, his joints painful. His step was cautious and his eyes viewed the world with trepidation. Harry's death had aged him, she felt sure.

'Carla Darling, I was so pleased to get your call. Come in, do.'

The path leading to the cottage was scattered with hawthorn berries, their burst orange skins staining the paving stones. Either side, banks of Michaelmas daisies and lavender bushes flanked their way. 'This is very pretty Teddy.'

'You should see it in the Spring, when the lilac is flowering and the bulbs are out. It's a delight. Alan looks after it you know; I don't have the energy any more. But he's got green fingers, only has to look at a plant and it blushes and bursts into flower. Has that effect on men too.' He laughed and held the door open for her.

'Is he here?'

'Alan? No he's at work. Someone has to bring in the money you know.' He stood his walking stick in the corner and led the way to the kitchen. 'So when are you off back to sunny Spain?'

'Ah well, not sure. Originally I planned to go this week but so much has come up that I will have to stay a bit longer.'

'So much being Sylvia's little surprise, I suppose.'

'Yes I have to admit it was quite a shock.' She looked at him. 'Did you know about the sale, Teddy?'

'No, not until the funeral, my dear.'

'You usually know everything that's going on.'

'That was then my dear, not these days. I don't go out so much anymore.'

'Would you have told me if you'd known?'

He smiled at her. 'Of course Darling. But as it turned out you knew before I did. Here have a pre-lunch sherry.' He handed her a glass of Tio Pepe. 'I've cooked us a casserole of Welsh lamb for lunch. I thought it would be just the thing for a cold day.'

'Mmn nice.'

'Come and sit down my dear, lunch will be at least an hour yet. Now you said you had something you wanted to talk to me about.'

Carla settled herself in an armchair in front of the fire, it was old and misshapen but extremely comfortable. It was so obviously Teddy's and probably had once belonged to his grandparents. A lace antimacassar hung across the back.

'It's about Harry.'

'Yes?'

'Do you know if Harry ever had anything wrong with him?'

'An illness you mean?'

'Not really, more like a genetic problem.'

'What had you in mind?'

Carla felt awkward, how was she going to put this. 'Did he ever talk to you about problems having children?'

'I remember that he and Barbara waited a long time before Sylvia and Tom came along.'

'But did he talk to you about it?'

'Not that I remember. Why?'

'Did Barbara talk to you about it?'

'Now why would Barbara talk to me about her problems with Harry?'

'Because everyone tells you their problems. You know they do. I tell you my problems. I even telephoned you from Spain to tell you about Harry's drinking.'

He laughed and said, 'You flatter me. You make me sound like the wise old uncle that everyone in the family turns to.'

'It's true. I just can't believe that neither Harry nor Barbara spoke to you about it.'

'Well if people do tell me their problems it is because they know I won't repeat them.' He tapped his nose with his forefinger and winked at her. It was true, she knew he had told no-one about Harry being an alcoholic.

'Teddy, Harry's dead now. Surely you could tell me.'

He sipped his sherry slowly, looking at her over the rim of his glass. His eyes were twinkling. 'What exactly do you want to know Carla?'

'Was Harry impotent?'

'Yes.'

She took a deep breath. 'How long have you known?'

'Since we were boys.'

'Did he know?'

'Of course he did.'

'And Phoebe?'

'Of course, she was his mother after all.'

'So all the family knew?'

'Only Mother and me.'

'But?'

'Tom and Sylvia? It's a long story and not a very nice one. Are you sure you want to hear it?' She finished her sherry and put the glass down on the table. 'Here let me get you another,' Teddy offered.

Carla didn't reply. She stared into the fire letting the flickering flames mesmerise her. The sherry had sent a warm glow through her body and she felt herself relaxing back further and further into the chair. Did she really want to continue this conversation? Did she want to know where it would lead?

'Barbara is a good woman, and I am very fond of her you know. If my persuasions had been otherwise she is just the sort of woman I would have liked to marry. She was a good wife to Harry and has been a wonderful mother to her children. It was a shame; she never asked for much, all she ever wanted from Harry was a family. He knew that when he married her. But Harry never told her he was impotent, neither before they were married nor after. I told him it was wrong to deceive her like that but he took no notice; he was in love. Maybe he thought his love would be enough for her but anyone with half a brain could see that Barbara was meant to be a mother; she craved motherhood. I think he tried to convince himself that the doctors were wrong, that he would be able to make her pregnant after all, but it didn't happen.

She went for test after test but they could find nothing wrong with her, so the doctors told her to be patient. She became thin and anxious. She gave up her job and tried to relax but still didn't conceive. She pleaded with Harry to go for tests; she suggested IVF but he refused. Then she told him about ICSI.'

'ICSI? What's that?' Carla was beginning to feel some empathy with Barbara; she knew exactly how she'd felt.

'Something to do with injecting the sperm directly into the egg. But that was not the answer and Harry knew it. He wouldn't go for the tests because he already knew the outcome but he wouldn't admit it. I tried talking to him again about it but he just told me to mind my own business.' He sighed. 'We nearly came to blows over that; it took a long while before Harry would talk to me again. Anyway Barbara's thirtieth birthday came and went and still she was not pregnant. In the end she came to me; she was desperate she said. She was frightened that if she left it much later she would be too old to conceive. I asked her why they hadn't considered adopting a baby but she said they had already talked about that and Harry had refused. He said he couldn't bring up a child not knowing who its real parents were. Poor Barbara, she was in such a state that, in the end, I agreed to help her.'

'You helped her?' Carla couldn't believe her ears.

'What else could I do?'

'You had an affair with Barbara?'

'Of course not. Not my thing at all, my dear; I thought you knew that.'

'So what did you do?'

'It was in the summer of 1979. Harry was in Scotland working at the Edinburgh Festival; he was away almost a month I remember. Barbara had come up to Nottingham to give me some ideas on furnishing the house, and it was when she was there that she sprung it on me. I had no idea what she was going to propose. It came as a complete shock I have to admit.' He laughed quietly. 'We were in the middle of painting the ceiling of the lounge a terracotta red, when she suggested it. I nearly fell off the ladder, I was so surprised.'

'But you went along with it?'

He nodded. 'More sherry?'

'I think I may need it.' She waited while he refilled their glasses and then asked, 'So what did she want you to do?'

'She knew I had a friend in the fertility clinic in Nottingham, a chap called Andrew. We had been quite close in the days before I met Alan. Anyway she wanted me to ask him to help her get pregnant.'

'But how? Didn't she need some sperm?'

'Hang on old girl, I'm getting there. It's not easy you know.' He drank his sherry down in one gulp then continued,   'She said it should be quite easy because she knew there was nothing wrong with her, all she needed was to become impregnated with someone's sperm.'

'Didn't she care who the donor was?'

'At first I thought she wanted an anonymous donor but then she dropped her bombshell.'

'She wanted Harry's sperm?'

'No, she knew that would be too difficult to do without his knowledge and I knew that it wouldn't work anyway. To be honest I was worried that she was going to ask me to get Andrew to steal some sperm from the sperm bank but she had already made her plan.'

Carla looked at him expectantly. 'Well?'

'She wanted me to be the donor. She thought because I was his brother any baby that we had would still have a family likeness. She wanted Harry to believe he was the father.'

'But she knew you were homosexual?'

'Of course she did, that's why she asked me. She said as there was no woman in my life it wouldn't matter. She wasn't taking anything away from anyone.'

'But Alan?'

'Alan doesn't know about any of this. What he doesn't know can't hurt him, I say.'

'But if it's genetic, weren't you likely to have it as well?'

'No, I knew I was clear. Mother had us both tested when we were fairly young. For some reason it had passed me by. Ironic isn't it.'

'So what happened?'

'Barbara had all the dates of her ovulation charted so we knew when it had to be done. She caught the train to Nottingham and I met her at the station then we went straight to see Andrew. He was surprisingly sympathetic actually, and said there would be no problem. As the following day was a Saturday he would do it then. So I booked Barbara into a hotel for the night and I went home. She could have stayed with me; we had plenty of room, but I didn't want Alan asking any awkward questions. The fewer people who knew about it the better. It was all pretty easy really. I picked her up from the hotel and we drove to

Andrew's house; he had everything ready for us. Then when it was done I took her back to the hotel. She insisted on staying in bed most of the day, just in case, and then I drove us both home that evening.'

'And then Sylvia came along?'

'Yes, nine months later there was Sylvia. She was such a beautiful baby, just like her mother.'

'And Harry? Didn't he suspect anything? Wasn't he surprised?'

'He never said anything to anyone. He must have known that he wasn't the father; he knew it was impossible.'

'Maybe he thought that he was; I read that there is an outside chance that men suffering from it can produce healthy sperm.'

'It's possible. But as he had never spoken to anyone about his condition before, he couldn't start then.'

'But to you, didn't he say anything to you?'

'No, as I said we weren't talking at that time. However I have to admit he surprised me; he was quite the proud father. He idolised the child, and for a while he and Barbara seemed sublimely happy.'

'And Tom?'

'At first I thought Barbara would be content with the one child but people kept asking her when she and Harry were going to have another one. I could see it was beginning to bother her. In the end she asked me if I would do it just one more time.'

'And you agreed.'

'Yes, but it was more difficult this time. Harry had stopped working for the Edinburgh Festival by then and although he still went away, it was for shorter periods. Eventually one of his trips coincided with her ovulation dates; he had to go to Wales for a rock concert and was away for five days so we had plenty of time. However Andrew had left Nottingham by then so we couldn't ask him to help, but luckily Barbara knew a local midwife who would help her.'

'So along came Tom?'

'Not straight away. He was a difficult little bugger; it took three attempts for her to conceive.'

'And how did you feel about it all?'

'I was delighted. I knew I could never tell anyone but that didn't stop me enjoying the children. I knew I was their father and it gave me great pride to see them. Anyway as far as anyone else was concerned I was their uncle and Tom's godfather, so I was free to indulge them as much as I wanted and nobody would think it strange. Perfect really, all the pleasures of fatherhood without the responsibilities.'

'And still Harry said nothing?'

'What could he say? He genuinely believed they were his children.'

'What about Phoebe? Did she know what was going on?'

'Goodness me, no. She did express some surprise when she heard that Barbara was pregnant but put it down to Harry's doctor making a poor diagnosis in the first place. She has never had a lot of faith in doctors. No she has always believed that Tom and Sylvia were Harry's children.'

'How ironic. All these years she's been desperate for you to get married and have children of your own and there they were, under her nose, all this time.' She paused. 'Was that what you argued about when you came to Spain?'

'Yes, I'm afraid it was. After all those years of keeping it secret, it all came tumbling out that night. We were getting on so well that I must have let down my guard and out it came. He was so angry; I'd never seen him like that before. He called me every name under the sun. Said he never wanted to see me or my children again. We were dead to him. I tried to reason with him, but it was no use. I told him that the only people who knew were me and Barbara, but it made no difference. I said that as far as the children were concerned he was their father; they knew nothing about it. He wasn't having it and if you hadn't been there he'd have thrown me out of the house then and there.'

'I know he was very upset, but he wouldn't tell me why,' said Carla. 'It changed him, you know. From that night, his drinking increased. I wish he'd told me. I wish he'd explained why he was so unhappy and angry. But he wouldn't. Why did he have to keep it all to himself?'

'That's how he was. Funny old world isn't it. Now don't you go telling anybody about this old girl. Mum's the word, all right?'

'Of course, Teddy.' She sipped some more sherry while Teddy disappeared into the kitchen to attend to the lunch. She had come here hoping to find out the truth about Harry's children and now she had it. But what could she do with it? It was exactly as Chris had guessed but she couldn't tell him that. This information gave her power over Barbara and her children but did she want to use it? She knew she couldn't destroy their lives like that. If one day Barbara chose to tell them the truth that was up to her, but Carla wasn't going to interfere. Max would have to find another way to save her home.

'Lunch is ready old girl.'

'On my way, Teddy.'

*

She was not quite sure exactly when it was that she woke up to the fact that the situation was out of control. For a long time now Harry had been two different people; at first there had only been glimpses of the monster, the Mr Hyde to his Dr Jekyll, and the former had been quickly obliterated by the love and kindness of the other, but gradually as the years passed this monster began to take over their evenings, then their afternoons and finally their entire days until only occasional glimpses of her original lover remained. The monster changed his appearance, turning him from an athletic man, fond of swimming and tennis, who would walk along the beach for miles before coming home and demanding eggs and bacon for breakfast, into an underweight, nervous creature with rheumy eyes. He refused to eat regular meals and snacked on chocolate bars and sweets, and when she tried to coax him with food he turned on her and accused her of behaving like his mother. He sat all day long watching the television with glazed eyes and drinking beer. At first she naively believed it was just beer he was drinking, until she began to find the empty vodka bottles tucked at the bottom of the rubbish bin, pushed behind a stack of spare tiles in the garage, hidden amongst the towels in the second bathroom, wedged behind the dog's old kennel. So now she started each day with a house search. It had become a game of wits between them; the more intensively she searched for his hidden cache, the more imaginative he became at hiding it.

She turned on the coffee machine and sat down in the kitchen to wait for it to brew. Julie had suggested they drive into Puerto Banus and have a look at the sales but she didn't have much enthusiasm for shopping. The truth was that she had little enthusiasm for anything these days. Her life seemed to be in ruins. One by one their friends had stopped coming to their house, people no longer telephoned to invite them for dinner or a hand of bridge; Harry's tennis club subscription lapsed and was not renewed. Even Arnie no longer called. Carla should have felt pleased that the man she despised, who had been controlling their lives for so long, now had no interest in them, but instead she felt angry. Even Arnie, with his illicit dealings, didn't want to be seen in Harry's company. As for the rest of their friends and neighbours, their absence gave her nothing but relief. She had come to dread sitting at a neighbour's dining table watching Harry gently swaying in his seat as he fixed his host with a glazed look. Occasionally someone would try to bring him into the conversation, and if they were lucky they would receive an incoherent reply before Harry lapsed into his customary silence. If they were unlucky, Harry would misconstrue their remarks as a personal attack, and a violent row would ensue. She had begun to invent excuses for not accepting invitations, and bit by bit people gave up inviting them. They dropped off the social map. Only Julie and Laura continued to ring her, and invite her to join them for coffee or to go to the book club, but even they never invited Harry.

A flashing green light told her that the coffee was ready so she poured herself a cup and took it out onto the terrace. Occasionally Harry ventured out on his own, to spend time in a little bar in the village, where he sat watching Spanish television without comprehension and drinking sweet strong coffee laced with brandy. She knew the locals called him '*Harry el borracho*,' 'Harry the drunk,' behind his back and occasionally the owner, Antonio Manuel would telephone Carla to ask her to come and take Harry home.

The crash of something falling in the kitchen told her that Harry was up. She didn't move; whatever it was she would clear it up later. The coffee was bitter so she stirred a little more sugar into it and sipped it slowly. There was no hurry; there was little to do. She felt lethargic without the demands of work to fulfil her but there had been no alternative; she couldn't look after the house, keep an eye on Harry and run her business adequately. She had given up her market stall last winter when Harry had fallen down the stairs, breaking his arm and splitting his head open. Since that accident he had come to rely on her more and more. Even today she was not sure whether she should leave him to go to Puerto Banus with Julie, anything could happen while she was out. One thing she was sure of, was that as soon as she left the house he would get down to some serious drinking.

Her husband wandered out onto the terrace; he was wearing boxer shorts and flip flops. In the bright morning sunlight he looked like a scarecrow, unshaven, his hair dishevelled, his bloated stomach barely supported by his scrawny buttocks and spindly legs. He was a man starving to death.

'Carla,' he said by way of greeting and sat down opposite her. 'I thought I'd sit and have breakfast with you on the terrace.' Even his voice had changed. She was filled with sadness as she looked at him.

'Did you sleep okay?' she asked.

'Not really. That bed's bloody uncomfortable.' She had insisted that he move into the spare room; she could no longer bear to lie beside the stranger that he'd become.

'Do you want anything to eat?'

'No, I've got a coffee.' He pulled out a cigarette and tried to light it. His hand was shaking so much that she thought she would have to do it for him, but at last he managed it and sat back puffing contentedly.

'What was the noise?' she asked. He looked at her through sad, yellow stained eyes. 'The crash in the kitchen,' she continued.

'Oh, that was just a mug. I dropped it.' He sipped his coffee then asked slyly, 'You going out this morning?'

'Maybe. Julie wants me to go to the sales with her but I don't know whether I've got time.'

'You should go. Buy yourself something nice.'

'What will you do?'

'I'll watch a bit of telly, I think. Don't feel too good this morning. Must be that fish you made me eat last night; I felt there was something wrong with it at the time,' he replied.

'You hardly touched it,' she retorted. 'It was more likely the two bottles of Rioja you knocked off with it.'

'Look Carla, things are going to change, I promise you. I'll stop drinking if that's what you want.'

'But when Harry? You've been saying that for a long time now.' Try as she might, she couldn't feel any sympathy for him. All she could think about was whether there was any brandy in his coffee cup. Harry put down his cup and came across and put his arms around her. He stank of alcohol, not just the brandy that had laced his coffee, but the sweet smell of alcohol that leaked through his pores and soaked his clothes. She felt sick and pushed him away. He looked at her like a dog that had been beaten, and sat down again.

Suddenly Carla felt angry; she couldn't play this game any longer. She leapt up, spilling the remains of her coffee and shouted at him, 'You're a pile of shit Harry, and you're never going to change. Every day you promise to make an effort but you never do. Why won't you go to the doctor? Why won't you let me take you to Alcoholics Anonymous? Our lives are drifting away while you sit there in your booze-sodden world.' There were tears running down his ravaged face now, but instead of the tears softening her heart they enraged her further.

'I think I'll go and lie down,' he said.

'Yes, do that, why don't you.'

'I'm not well,' he added in a last attempt at enlisting her sympathy.

'Then let me take you down to see Doctor Garcia.' she retorted.

Instantly his face hardened. 'No. Leave me alone.'

She watched him walk back inside, his gait unsteady, his head bent. Once she was alone she began to do her rounds.

Her first find was a half-finished bottle of vodka behind the cleaning fluids under the sink, then she checked the guest bathroom where a bottle of brandy was stashed amongst the towels. The rest of her round turned up a number of empty beer cans and an empty bottle of Smirnov in the garage. She tipped the vodka and the brandy down the sink and then put all the empties in a black plastic sack with the rest of the household rubbish. Her anger was replaced with a feeling of hopelessness; what could she do? Where did he get it from? She never bought it for him, either someone was bringing it to the house when she was out or he was getting it at Antonio's. It was amazing how devious he could be.

A vibration in her pocket told her that her mobile was ringing, she flicked it open. 'Julie?'

'Hi, just wanted to see if you're coming? Laura's up for it too. I thought we'd make a morning of it and have lunch in the port. My treat.'

'I don't know, Julie. I don't really feel much like it.'

'Of course you do. It's just what you need, a bit of retail therapy. Get away from the house and that husband of yours for a bit.'

A snore from the bedroom told her that Harry was sleeping. She looked at her watch, it was almost eleven. She could spend a couple of hours looking round the shops and get back before he woke.

'Okay, but I'll skip lunch.'

'I'll pick you up in ten minutes then.'

'Okay.'

'Chow.'

Carla looked at Harry sprawled across the bed. His mouth hung open and a little dribble of saliva ran down his chin. She bent over and wiped it away, gently. Was it wise to leave him?

CHAPTER 29

Max was already waiting for her in the Bull and Butcher, with a half-drunk pint of bitter in front of him.

'I'm not late, am I?' Carla asked.

'No, not at all. I came early; I wanted to read through your deeds.'

'Oh good. You got a copy then?'

'Yes your friend Arnold was most helpful. He sent me a copy of the original and the English translation. Very interesting.'

She bit back the desire to say that Arnold was no friend of hers, and said instead, 'I'll get myself a drink and then you can tell me what you found.'

'No, sit down. I'll get it. What would you like?'

'A glass of dry white wine, would be fine.'

'Any one in particular?'

'Whatever they have.'

While Max went to the bar, Carla looked across at the pile of papers which he'd obviously been studying while waiting for her. She was tempted to have a quick look at them, but decided against it.

'Here you are. I got you a large glass; I think you're going to need it when I tell you what I've found out.'

'Oh dear. That sounds ominous.' She tasted the wine; it was nice and fresh, Italian maybe. 'Well you'd better tell me. Don't keep me in suspense.'

'Let me ask you a question first. What's your relationship with Arnold Good?'

'My relationship? I don't have one. I can't abide the man. He was Harry's friend; it was because of him that we went to Spain in the first place. I admit he was very helpful when we first arrived; let us stay in one of his houses and introduced Harry to various people. But I always thought there was something underhand about him; you know, lots of dodgy deals going on. And he was too fond of Harry's company. I felt we weren't able to do anything without Arnie being involved.'

'What did Harry think of him?'

'Harry thought he was great. Wouldn't hear a word against him. Why all these questions about Arnie?'

'Well, I'm amazed that you didn't know, but a few years ago, Harry got into some financial difficulties and Arnold helped him out.'

'I didn't know that. What sort of difficulties?'

'I don't have many details, something to do with a company called Costa Build. Did you know he had some shares in it?' She shook her head, feeling bewildered. 'Anyway he went to Arnold for help.'

'Typical. He couldn't brush his teeth without checking with Arnie first,' she snapped. What new revelation was this going to be? What else had Harry been hiding from her?

'When did you say Harry bought the house?'

'Oh, I'm not sure of the year. It was about three years after we arrived in Spain, so that must have been in 1993 or '94.'

'And it was only in Harry's name?'

'Yes, he used the money from his business to pay for it. Come on Max, what's this all about?'

'Well in 2003, Harry sold the house to your friend Arnold.'

'I've told you, he's no friend of mine.' Suddenly Max's words sank in. 'What are you saying? He sold our house to Arnie? He never told me, and Arnie certainly never said anything. Why would he do that?'

'Well, I've found something else about your friend, Arnie; he's being sued over illegal house sales. It could be serious for him.'

'And Harry?'

'It seems your husband was implicated and had to pay some enormous fine. Apparently he got his friend to agree to let you both stay on in the house. Arnold only wanted it as an investment; he had no intention of living in it.'

Carla took another drink of her wine. Now it had a bitter taste. She put down the glass and stared at the solicitor. 'I can't believe this. Are you sure? Arnie's not an honest man I know. Is this some scam of his?'

'It's quite legal, I can assure you. Have a look at the deeds yourself. Here's the original *escritura* and here's the translation. The owner of your house is definitely Arnold Good.'

'But I've been living there all this time. Even after Harry died. Why didn't Arnie tell me it wasn't my house? Why didn't he tell me to leave?'

'I don't know. You'd have to ask him. Perhaps it was a way of getting Harry to keep quiet about his dealings with Costa Build. However I do know Arnold's quite willing to let you continue as before. His plans haven't changed; it's a long-term investment for him and he says he's unlikely to sell it until house prices improve.'

'I'm sorry Max, I'm having trouble getting my head around this. So there is no house for Harry's children to inherit?'

'Exactly. Whether they're his biological children or not doesn't come into it now; there is no inheritance.'

'Sylvia is going to be disappointed,' she said.

'What about you? Will you stay on in the house? After all that is what you wanted.'

'Do you know Max, I don't think I will. I have had enough of Harry's lies. I think I just want to put it all behind me and move on. I certainly don't want to accept Arnie's charity.'

'So as far as you're concerned, the subject is closed, then?'

'Yes.'

'Very well, I'll write to Ian and tell him the news.'

'Yes, please.'

'And no need to mention the doubts you had about his clients' paternity, then?'

Carla shook her head. 'No. Don't say anything about that. Why upset them all unnecessarily?'

'Just as you want.'

*

It was late when she arrived back at the hotel, but she knew Jenny would be awake; she was a night owl, often not going to bed until two or three in the morning. Carla had been thinking through the events of the last few weeks, and the news about the house meant that her life was going to have to change whether she wanted it to or not. She hadn't intended to leave Spain but now it looked as though it might be the most sensible alternative. She had friends there, she knew, but over the last few years she'd gradually had less and less to do with them. Her business was barely ticking over. Now it appeared that the house wasn't hers. It was time to make a complete break with Spain and return home. She had rebuilt her business once before; she could do it again. This time she would restart in London. She took out her mobile and dialled Jenny's number.

'Hi, Jenny, it's Carla.'

'Hi. This is late for you. Been out on the town? Or can't sleep?'

'I had dinner with Max.'

'And?'

And nothing. We had a very pleasant evening.'

'So why are you ringing me?'

'When are you down this way again, Jenny?'

'Sometime next week, I think. Why? What's going on?'

'I've decided to move back to London. Fancy being my agent again?'

'Wow, that's a surprise. I thought you'd turned your back on wet and windy England for good.'

'No, all in all, I think I'll be better off here. So what do you say?' She could explain it all to her once she had it clear in her own head.

'Great, I'd love to take you on again. Look, I was just about to go to bed, how about if I ring you back in the morning?'

'Okay, fine.'

'Oh and Carla.'

'Yes?'

'It's the best news I've had in a while.'

CHAPTER 30

Carla lay on the bed looking at the ceiling. Her head ached from the gin she'd drunk when she got back to the hotel, and she felt unbelievably sad. Had she been too wrapped up in her own ambitions to realise that Harry had needed her support? She'd loved him, she argued; she had done everything she could to help him. But was it true? She'd found his drinking embarrassing, and she was glad when people had stopped coming to see them. She blamed Harry for changing into someone she didn't know but did she do anything to help him? She didn't even try to find out why he was drinking so much. The slightest smell of alcohol on his breath threw her into a rage and she would push him away; she wanted nothing to do with him when he was like that. No wonder he didn't confide in her. She grew to detest his drinking and because of that began to detest him. It had been her choice to move him out of their matrimonial bed and leave him to fight his affliction alone. She had spied on him, stolen his hidden cache of bottles and poured them down the sink, berated him every time he helped himself to a beer from the refrigerator and worst of all despised him. Tears of shame filled her eyes and slowly trickled down her cheeks. He had needed her compassion but she had been unable to give it to him. He had been weak but so had she; she hadn't been strong enough to help him and in her frustration she had turned against him when he most needed her.

*

She looked at his body spread-eagled in the swimming pool. He floated face down, his arms spread out in a cross, his long grey hair drifting like the tendrils of some water plant.   She could not move, mesmerised by what had happened. For the first time in many a year he seemed relaxed, at peace with the world. Carla saw the wasted legs and the thin arms and felt a tremendous sadness. What had happened to the man she had married? Who was this pathetic creature dying in her pool?

The sound of the telephone awakened her from her trance and she walked slowly into the lounge to answer it.

'Hi Carla, it's Jenny. Just thought I'd ring and wish Harry a happy birthday. Is he there? Can I speak to him?'

'Oh hello Jenny.' She turned and looked towards the pool.

'No, I'm sorry, something's... Harry's dead.'

'My God, what happened?'

'He drowned.'

'Drowned? When?'

'I'm sorry Jenny. I have to go. I must phone the police.'

'Of course. Look, I'll teleph...' Carla replaced the receiver and sat down on the sofa. There was so much to do, so much to think about but somehow she couldn't organise her thoughts. She closed her eyes but she could still see his body floating there. After a few moments she picked up the receiver again and dialled 112.

'*Que servicio, policía, ambulancia o bomberos?*' the operator asked.

'*Policía,*' she replied, her voice barely audible.

'*Policía?*'

'*Si.*'

'*Dirección?*'

Automatically she went through the details of her address and telephone number. Almost immediately she was put through to the police department. Carla explained as briefly as she could how she had come back from shopping and discovered her husband floating in the pool.

*

She watched, uncomprehending, as the paramedics pulled his body out of the swimming pool and turned it over. They tilted his head backwards allowing his mouth to drop open. The younger of the paramedics placed a protective sheath around the mouth, pinched Harry's nose between his thumb and forefinger and began to blow air into his lungs, rhythmically twisting his head in order to suck in clean air and then blowing, sucking and blowing, once, twice. Then he stopped and placed the heels of his hands on Harry's breastbone and pumped steadily, counting to himself in Spanish, *uno, dos, tres* until he reached thirty. He repeated this ten, twenty times; she was not sure exactly, but still Harry didn't respond. He was dead. She could have told him that. She watched the older man place his hand on the young paramedic's shoulder and shake his head. They lifted Harry's body onto a stretcher, covered him with a black, plastic body-bag and started to close it.

'*Momento*,' she said.

They stepped back to allow her to approach the body, to bend down and kiss his cold cheek. She looked at his wasted body with its old man's limbs and the huge mound of his swollen stomach, and searched in vain beneath that yellow ravaged skin for some trace of the man he'd once been. She felt no anger now, only sorrow. Then she stroked his hair gently and murmured, 'Goodbye Harry, my love. Goodbye.'

She stepped back and allowed the paramedics to close his black shroud around him and carry him away. She felt numb. Harry was dead.

*

Later that day two policemen came to the house. Carla was still sitting where the paramedics had left her; she felt unable to move. She knew there were many things she needed to do, but somehow she had neither the strength nor the will to do them.

'I'm sorry to disturb you,' the older of the two policemen said, following her into the living room. 'We won't take up much of your time. I am Sargento Jimenez and this is my colleague Guardia Duran.'

'We just want to ask you a few questions,' the other policeman said.

They waited until they were all seated and then began. 'Were you in the house when your husband drowned?' asked Sargento Jimenez.

'No, I'd gone shopping with a friend,' she replied, pointing to the pile of carrier bags that were still spread out on the table where she had left them when she'd got home.

'To the sales? My wife is a sucker for the sales,' said Guardia Duran. His superior glared at him.

'So can you tell me what happened?' he asked.

'I was a bit later than I'd promised,' she said. 'When I got home I saw that the doors to the terrace were wide open so I assumed Harry was outside. I called him and when there was no answer I went out to see where he was.'

'And that's when you saw him in the swimming pool?'

'Yes.'

'Was your husband suffering from ill health?' he asked.

Carla hesitated, even now her loyalty to her husband made her want to protect him from their criticism.

'He hasn't been well for some time,' she said. 'Depressed and drinking rather a lot.'

The younger man scribbled something in his notebook. 'Had he been drinking this morning?'

'I don't know, but I rather suspect so.'

'The paramedics found a broken bottle of whiskey by the pool,' the senior policeman added. He looked straight at her. 'Would you say that your husband was an alcoholic?' She nodded. 'According to the paramedics he had a cut on his forehead, consistent with striking his head on the edge of the pool. Has he fallen before?'

'Yes, a couple of times,' she said with a sigh. 'My husband has been rather unsteady on his feet lately.' What an understatement she thought.

'Where are you from Señora Wilkinson?'

'England,' she said. 'We're English.'

The young Guardia closed his notebook and muttered something under his breath. She had the feeling that he'd seen this all before.

'I think it's safe to say that your husband's death was an accident. It appears that he fell while under the influence of alcohol, struck his head on the side of the pool, slipped into the water and drowned. A dreadful tragedy of course, but an accident. If you don't mind, Señora, I would like you to come down to the morgue sometime this evening to make a formal identification of the body and sign some papers. Then you will be able to dispose of his remains as you wish.'

'Very well.'

'Do you have anyone who could come round and stay with you?' he asked, his tone softening a little.

'I'll ring my friend,' she said.

The two policemen stood up. 'Thank you for your help, Señora Wilkinson. We're sorry for your loss.'

She waited until they had left then sat down and telephoned Julie. And still she couldn't cry. When she had realised that Harry was dead her first emotion hadn't been grief but an overwhelming sense of relief. Now she felt guilty. How could she feel like that? Why was her heart so hard? It wasn't that she hadn't loved her husband; she'd loved him from the moment they met. But the man she loved had died long ago; she'd already mourned him many times over. That still figure, lying on the wet tiles, with his bloated, red face and swollen stomach, was not him. That was the monster he had turned into bit by bit, day by day, drink by drink.

CHAPTER 31

The stonemason had promised to get the headstone completed within ten days and had kept to his word. This was Carla's last day, she had booked a flight to Málaga for that evening. The village was deserted, no sign of life behind the closed windows and nobody wandering down the high street, she noticed a couple of cars parked in the Yew Tree car-park but otherwise the place seemed empty. She parked her car outside Teddy's house and walked across to the church; she had promised to call in on him for lunch before she left. She carried a green, metal vase with a pronged base, a bottle of water and a bunch of chrysanthemums, a flower she hoped would resist the elements at this time of the year better than most. Today the church looked a drab and dismal place under the grey, gloomy sky and as she opened the lych gate its noisy creaking cut through the stillness of the churchyard and caused a robin in a nearby holly tree to take flight. She carefully closed the gate behind her and took the cobbled path through the churchyard and round the back of the church to where Harry's ashes had been buried. She saw the familiar elm tree ahead of her, with the Wilkinson family's gravestones at its foot but then stopped in dismay. Someone was already there, she felt the disappointment rise up into her throat like bile. She had wanted to spend these last few minutes alone with him. Now it was not possible. A woman was kneeling by the grave. She stood up and straightened her coat; it was Barbara. Carla hesitated for a moment then putting her disappointment to one side walked resolutely towards her.

'Hello Barbara.'

Barbara turned round slowly, a slightly bewildered look on her tear stained face. Carla could see the dark smudges under her eyes and trailing black lines across her cheeks.

'Hello Carla.'

'Sorry if I've disturbed you. I just wanted to bring up some flowers before I left.'

'You're leaving?'

'Yes, my flight's tomorrow morning.'

'So soon.'

'Yes I have a lot of things to sort out in my life now.'

'I suppose you have.' She gestured towards the headstone. 'It's very nice. I wondered what you would put on it.'

Carla looked down. The stonemason had done an excellent job, the blue black granite gleamed in the watery sunlight, its smooth surface a perfect looking glass for the troubled sky. The inscription was simple:

Harvey Wilkinson

1945-2009

Much loved

'I'm pleased you approve. Are those yours?' she asked pointing to the roses.

'Yes. They won't last I don't suppose.' Barbara sat down on the bench and watched as Carla pushed the metal vase into the hard earth, filled it with water and carefully inserted the deep russet chrysanthemums one by one. 'What a lovely colour.' Carla looked up. 'The flowers, they're just the colour of my daughter's hair, well when she was a little girl that is. It's more mousey now but you'd never know; she dyes it. But it's not the same, not that wonderful, warm flame colour it used to be.' Carla said nothing, the mention of Sylvia unsettled her. Barbara took out a damp tissue from her coat pocket and wiped her eyes. 'Sorry, it all came as an incredible shock you know.' She sniffed and put the tissue back in her pocket. Carla was unsure whether she was referring to Harry's death or their affair.

'Yes, it was for all of us,' she said, picking up the empty water bottle and sitting back. 'You probably think I'm a very hard woman. I wanted to cry at his funeral but I couldn't. The tears just wouldn't come. You must have thought that was a bit odd, his widow standing there, dry-eyed.' Barbara didn't reply, so she continued, 'I was very nervous you know. I suppose it was seeing all his family there and knowing that they hated me for taking him away from them.'

'Nobody hates you, Carla.'

'I loved him you know.' She pulled out a handkerchief and wiped her eyes. 'But I had already cried all my tears. You see as far as I was concerned Harry died a long time ago, long before he fell into the swimming pool. By the time I brought his ashes back to England my mourning was over. I had watched the man I loved destroy himself bit by bit for the last three years.' Barbara sat silently looking at the gravestone. Carla looked at her and asked quietly, 'Did you know that he drank?'

Barbara looked puzzled for a moment then replied, 'Well Harry always liked a drink, but nothing excessive. I suppose he was occasionally over the limit when we drove home from a party but then we all did it in those days.'

'My Harry was like that too at first. But then after we moved to Spain things began to change. Maybe it was boredom, maybe guilt. I don't know the reason; he never spoke of reasons. We lived a hectic social life that revolved around meeting for cocktails, going to dinner parties, drinks at the tennis club, eating out and, of course, central to it all was the booze. Some people can cope with that kind of social scene and manage their alcohol intake, but not Harry. At first it didn't seem to be anything out of the ordinary but then when he grew morose and angry, even violent sometimes, I knew something was wrong.'

'Did he hit you?' Barbara interrupted. 'I would never have called Harry a violent man, never.'

'No, Harry wasn't violent, but this monster that he turned into was. Luckily for me by the time he started to become aggressive he was no longer the fit, strong man he used to be. Apart from breaking a few plates and glasses he wasn't able to do much harm.'

She stopped and the two women sat in silence for a while. She could hear a blackbird singing nearby and in the distance the sound of someone mowing their lawn.

'It had happened slowly, at first I never noticed anything different although now I have to admit that the signs were always there. As I said, our life in Spain was very sociable; it was drinks at six, either on the patio with friends or at a neighbour's house, then there was always wine with the meal: a bottle of cold, fresh white wine with lunch and usually a bottle of Rioja at dinner.' She paused. 'I knew we were drinking too much but it was hard to stop because everyone else was doing it. In the early days there was hardly a night when we were not entertaining or being entertained. If I asked for a soft drink, people regarded me strangely and asked if I was pregnant or slimming. I began to limit myself to a couple of glasses of wine a day and became very adept at avoiding any top-ups. Harry on the other hand had an endless capacity. He enjoyed a couple of beers with his friends after a game of tennis; he boasted that he made the best gin and tonics on the coast and he could talk at length about the best wine vintages and the merits of a good Rioja. He became expansive when explaining the characteristics to look for in a decent sherry and knew all there was to know about vintage port. I never noticed that his consumption was rising until it was too late.'

'He always liked a drink,' Barbara repeated.

'Yes, but I should have realised where it was leading when he started drinking brandy; at first he would have one after dinner, to help his digestion he said, then one winter when the weather was unusually cold he began to have one with his morning coffee. This soon became a habit that he couldn't give up.'

'Didn't he get any help? AA or something? Do they have Alcoholics Anonymous in Spain?'

'Oh yes, but Harry wasn't interested. He wouldn't acknowledge that he had a problem. Even when I pulled out all the empty vodka bottles that he had carefully hidden away and lined them up on the breakfast bar he denied that they were his. He just walked out, straight down to Antonio's bar.'

'What about the doctor?'

'Alcoholics are not a rarity in Spain, especially along the Costa del Sol and especially amongst the ex-pat community. I talked to our local doctor about it but all he would say was that it was up to Harry. Nobody could help Harry but himself.'

'I can't believe it. We didn't know any of this.'

'Why would you? Harry was very careful when Teddy came over; he didn't want anyone back here to find out. But Teddy knew.'

'Teddy?'

'He was the only one I could turn to, the only one I could talk to about him.'

'He never said anything to me.'

'Well he wouldn't. Like me I suppose, he felt a bit ashamed of Harry's drinking. It's funny, isn't it, you can't help feeling that you are partly to blame. I know it's not logical but somehow you think it's your fault.' She paused for a minute, thinking back to the days when she'd gone to great lengths to avoid her friends in case anyone asked after Harry. 'You'd be surprised how good I became at inventing excuses, the lies would come tripping off my tongue like honey.' She laughed bitterly. 'It was like living a double life. Now looking back I can see I should have just been open about it: talked to his friends, got people to help us. Instead we were both in denial.'

'It must have been hard.' Barbara's voice was almost a whisper.

'So you see,' Carla continued. 'That's why I find it hard to grieve now. I feel I should, but it just seems too late.'

'You shouldn't blame yourself.'

Carla continued, her voice growing softer and softer, 'I didn't need to go out that day you know. I could have been there with Harry. I got up at eight as usual that morning.

Harry was sleeping at last; he never slept well. I would often hear him wandering around at three in the morning, talking to himself or watching old movies,. He couldn't rest.' She dabbed her eyes with a handkerchief. 'We didn't sleep in the same room any more. Sometimes I felt guilty about throwing him out of our bed, but the smell of stale alcohol and sweat was more than I could bear. It was sad to see him relegated to that small space, bare of personal effects, not even the picture of Sylvia on her wedding day.' She looked at Barbara and smiled. 'You wouldn't believe how pleased he'd been when Teddy arrived with it.' Barbara smiled sadly. 'When he got up that morning, he came out onto the terrace and said he wanted to talk to me; he wanted me to listen to him and believe him because he was going to change. But I didn't believe him. I couldn't. I'd heard it all before. I went out shopping instead. As usual as soon as I was away from him I softened; I began to think that maybe things could change. By the time I returned home I was calmer and I'd decided that at least I would give him the opportunity to talk about our future. Maybe I would even be able to persuade him to go to AA.

There was no sound from the house when I opened the door. I called Harry's name but there was no reply; he was not in the lounge but the French windows were open so I stepped out onto the terrace. That's when I saw him.

He was floating there, so peaceful. I don't know how long he'd been there, one minute, two minutes, ten minutes.

I stood for ages just looking at him. It was all so unreal. I suppose I should have jumped in and pulled him out but I didn't. I didn't even think about it. I just kept looking at him, thinking now it's finally over; now he's free.' She stopped and in the silence she could hear the blackbird again.

'Didn't you try to resuscitate him?' The sound of Barbara's voice brought her back to the present. Carla shook her head. 'So then what happened?'

'The telephone rang. I think it was Jenny. I don't really remember. Then I seemed to wake up and realised I had better telephone the police.'

'Do you, do you think it could have been suicide?' Barbara asked, her voice trembling slightly.

'I don't know. It's possible but I don't really think so. The doctor thinks it was a heart attack but I think he just tripped and was probably too drunk to save himself.'

'How awful. Poor Harry. Did they do a post mortem?'

'No, the police couldn't be bothered. For them it was just another case of a drunken foreigner suffering a tragic accident. They were very nice, quite considerate really, but after the doctor examined the body and said that Harry had obviously been drinking rather heavily, they weren't interested. The doctor made out the death certificate with cause of death as "heart attack leading to accidental drowning", signed it and that was that.'

'Is that why you left it for a year before you brought his ashes back?'

'I suppose so. I felt in a state of limbo, unable to grieve and unable to move forward. Maybe I also felt guilty that I hadn't done more for him.'

'And now?'

'Now I'll have to get on with my life. After all I have no family to worry about; we were never lucky enough to have any children.' She saw Barbara look away. 'Teddy told me about your children,' she said.

'The children?'

'His children,' Carla continued. 'That was very clever of you.' She could see Barbara look at her to see if she was being sarcastic.

'Why did he tell you? That's not like Teddy at all,' Barbara said.

'I asked him. I knew Harry was impotent; I'd had some tests done without him knowing.' She saw the horror in Barbara's eyes. 'I know, I'm not proud of what I did but I was desperate to know why I couldn't conceive and Harry wouldn't discuss it with me.   It turned out he had Klinefelter's Syndrome; it's a genetic condition that leaves most men impotent.'

'But Teddy?'

'Apparently Teddy didn't have it.'

'Did he know about it?'

'Yes, he and his mother knew, and Harry of course.'

'And nobody told me. Why didn't Harry tell me? Or his mother? We could have worked something out if I'd known,' said Barbara.

'But then you wouldn't have Tom and Sylvia, would you.'

'So many lies. You think you know someone,' Barbara continued. 'But you don't. I don't think we ever know anyone, not really know them. I thought I knew Harry. We had been together for such a long time, since we were teenagers, but I didn't really know him at all.'

'If it's any consolation he kept his secret hidden from me as well.'

'Are you going to tell them?'

'Tom and Sylvia? No of course not, what good would that do?'

'But the house? Would you like me to talk to Sylvia about the house? I could ask her to delay the sale for a couple of years. At least until you know what your plans are.'

Carla looked at Barbara in surprise, the simple look of concern on her face made it obvious that her offer was sincere.

'Ian hasn't told you yet?'

'What?' Barbara asked, a look of puzzlement spreading across her face.

'It didn't belong to Harry. It belongs to Arnie. Harry put the house up as collateral for some scheme he was doing; he signed the deeds over to Arnie.'

'But the will? He left it to them.'

'When he made the will, the house was in his name. It was years later that he sold it to Arnie. I've seen the deeds.'

'And you didn't know?'

'No. I think Arnie planned to tell me, but he couldn't see the need for any rush.'

'So there's nothing for them to inherit then?'

'No. I hope Sylvia won't be too disappointed.'

'She'll manage. I can pay for Linda's new school; I wanted to anyway, but Sylvia was too stubborn to agree. Maybe now she'll reconsider it.'

'Arnie says I can stay on in the house if I want, but I'm leaving. I don't want his charity. Anyway I think it's time to move on. I'll go back and settle up my affairs then I'm moving back to England.'

'Back here?'

'Well I don't know about here, maybe back to London. Jenny has said I can stay with her until I get settled. I'm not old enough to give up yet. It's time I moved into stage three of my life.'

'Do you think Harry knew they were not his children?' Barbara asked.

'It's possible but if he did, he never said anything.' Why upset her by revealing that Teddy had told him their secret?

'Well I wish you luck, Carla.'

'Thank you and you too, Barbara.' She placed her hand on top of Barbara's and said, 'I'm sorry if we hurt you. I really am.' Barbara said nothing. 'I'd better be going. Teddy's promised to cook me his special "chicken a la mode", whatever that is,' Carla added. Both women stood up, facing each other. 'Good luck Barbara.'

'Thanks. Have a good life Carla.'

Carla brushed the grass from her skirt, looked briefly at the grave with its fresh flowers then turned and walked away. She didn't look back but she knew Barbara hadn't moved. The rain had started again; she could hear its soft drumming on the umbrella.

THE END

Thank you for taking the time to read LOVING HARRY. If you enjoyed it, please consider telling your friends or posting a short review. Word of mouth is an author's best friend and much appreciated.

Thank you, Joan Fallon